Fifty Caliber Endorsements to Die For!

I can think of no other human being on Earth capable of mixing raw patriotism and humor with an unbridled knowledge of the mechanisms and machinery necessary to create the perfect co~~cktail of zombie apocalypse action.~~
George Hill writes as he is, incredibly kn
intense. I have known George for a long
of why I will call on George when the ou

~~~~ers

Nationally Syndicated Talk Radio Host-Armed American Radio
Concealed Carry Magazine Columnist and Author

George Hill has long been known as a talented blogger and journalist. Now his first novel, *Uprising USA*, shows readers he has a bright future in dramatic fiction as well. George's vivid writing takes readers on a fast-paced journey through a zombie apocalypse with enough detail to make you feel like a part of the human resistance. The narration is heavy with technical details that will entertain savvy readers, without bogging down the action. More than just an empty page-turner, *Uprising USA* revolves around important themes of family, responsibility, government, politics and freedom. At the same time, readers get a glimpse into the life and philosophy of George Hill, a man affectionately known to his friends as the "Mad Ogre." This is a good read for anyone, but particularly for freedom-loving Americans and fellow gun enthusiasts!

– Duane Diaker –
Gun Writer and Journalist

This is what you want to be a part of when the Zed outbreak begins. Every page erupts with relentless action as the story's vibrant characters fight for much more than their own survival. As I read, I felt like I was there, like I had my own place in this story and I could almost smell the smoke, the rot, the sweat, and the tyranny. *Uprising USA* is what zombie fans have been missing and it's chock-full of special delights that any gun lover will appreciate. 100% pure win!

– Daniel Shaw –
Host of Gunfighter Cast
US Marine Infantryman
Weapons and Tactics Instructor

Move over, *Zombieland*! The Mad Ogre has arrived with the ultimate post-zombie-apocalyptic gore and gun fest. Funny, demented, and right on target – like the author – *Uprising USA* is the latest and greatest addition to the zombie apocalypse canon. Read it now or face the wrath of Mad Ogre!

– Marcus Wynne –
Author of Warrior in the Shadows & Brother in Arms

UPRISING

USA

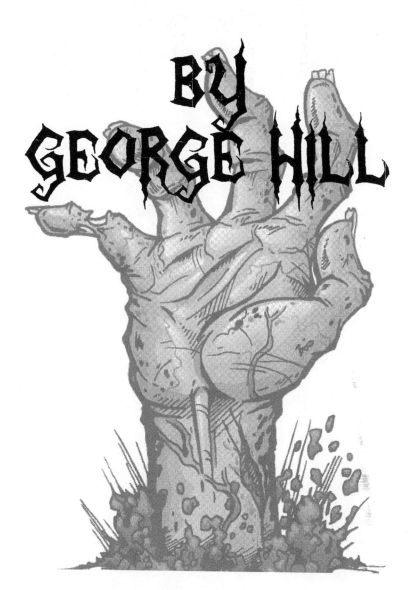

Published by White Feather Press. (www.whitefeatherpress.com)

ISBN 978-1-61808-015-8

Printed in the United States of America

Cover design created by Ron Bell of AdVision Design Group (www.advisiondesigngroup.com)

White Feather Press

Reaffirming Faith in God, Family, and Country!

Dedication

To my beloved bride, for always backing me up.

Special thanks to the members of WeTheArmed.com.

ONE

How it all Began

It **was a perfectly normal day** when my brother Zack and I were cruising along Highway 191 heading south into Vernal. We didn't say much, just looked out at the desert scenery as we rolled passed. I had the truck radio set to the normal station, AM920, the Uintah Basin's only Talk Radio station. I can't help it, I'm a news addict. Even if most of the news pisses me off.

This was Friday afternoon. A news report came on about a flight into Salt Lake City from California where a passenger on the plane went nuts and started to bite people. Sixteen people were bitten before the person was finally restrained. One person lost a finger, the Air Marshal. *Why do people wait until they get on a plane or go to Wal-Mart before they go nuts?* I shrugged it off. Maybe planes and Wal-Mart are what make people go nuts.

Zack was the first to call it. "Sounds like she turned into a zombie."

"You mean it sounds like the next Samuel L Jackson flying movie," I quipped.

"I'm tired of these mother-freaking zombies on this mother-freaking plane!"

We both had a laugh as we passed Steinaker Reservoir, but it got me thinking. Something about the news report made me uncomfortable. The passenger was a mother of three, and she had just got off a connecting flight from China to California. Shortly after the flight to SLC, she had complained about not feeling well, and soon fell asleep. It was after she woke up she started moaning and biting people. People said her eyes were weird. Nothing specific, just weird. That was unsettling to me for some reason.

I know zombies are the invention of Hollywood, but I like zombie movies... all of them. The classics with the slow methodical zombies and the new British import fast zombies. I think zombies are like bacon. You know how bacon makes everything better? Zombies make every movie or book better. Even *Pride and Prejudice*. I wouldn't call myself a zombie expert, I'm more of an enthusiast. So with my vast knowledge of zombie-lore, I can tell you, this news report had the classic zombie outbreak signature.

When we got back to Ogre Ranch, the news had further reports of people getting sick and then acting different. Some people were virtually catatonic, while others seemed enraged and violent. All of these people were on that plane. The reporter didn't say it, but I would bet good money that these were the first people the lady chewed on. One of them was the Air Marshal.

I pulled up *WeTheArmed.com* on my laptop. Many of my friends are members of the WTA forum, and I quickly found that this flight was already a subject of discussion. Some of the members had already observed that this sounded much like a zombie apocalypse scenario, especially since a similar thing happened on the flight from China. A reporter from Fox News had suggested that this was a form of rabies. One of the WTA members from Arizona who was following the story from multiple sources found that the Air Marshal was not on the flight from China, but boarded the plane in LA. This would not have given rabies enough time to cause any outward symptoms. Several members joked about activating their zombie plans. Several of the Utah members joked that their zombie plan was to come to Ogre Ranch. I laughed about it, but had an uneasy feeling when I shut down the laptop for the night.

I didn't sleep well that first night. My wife said that I seemed troubled and even while asleep I tossed and turned in the bed. I don't remember what I dreamed about, but I was glad to get up with the sun. Everyone else in the house sleeps in later than I do. It's not that I'm a morning person, because I hate morning people. I just have a long drive into town, and I've got to get ready for it. One can't be late to work.

When I got in the truck, the AM920 came on but the signal was poor as usual. I've only got one other station set on the radio, and that's for the Classic Rock station, FM92.5. I hit the button and was gratified to hear AC/DC in crystal-clear quality. Because the rock station doesn't play news very often, I didn't listen to any news reports.

At work, the day started out perfectly normal. I had my customary breakfast burrito and Rock Star Juice and walked through the back door. I was the first one in for the day. Getting the gun store ready to open for business is pretty straight forward. Run the vac, take out the trash, clean the glass counters. This morning I had some freight that didn't get put away from the day before. This can happen if we get busy with customers. I had some reloading components that needed to be stocked and a couple handguns. I was somewhat busy and it took me a while to realize that no one else had come in at first. It was after I wiped down the glass counter a second time when a couple coworkers finally made it in. Thirty minutes late was unusual, but I've been late before myself, so I'm not going to throw stones.

"Mornin, fellas." I said.

They were standing by the computer. "Guess you didn't hear the news." Troy said.

"No, what news?"

"Check it out." Boyd turned the flat screen monitor around. Parts of Salt Lake were in flames and riots. "What?" The news was the same all over California and other cities that had connecting flights from that flight from China.

A live video feed overlooking I-15 showed a lot of cars in a pile-up on the freeway. Some people were running. The image was grainy, but you could see that one person had a gun and turned around and shot the guy chasing him. The guy fell, then got back up and kept running at the shooter.

"Good hell."

"Guys, I gotta go." Roy said. He had gone pale as he turned and left.

"What's wrong with him?" I asked.

"His wife is in Salt Lake." Troy said.

"Oh shit. Serious?"

Troy just nodded. "Yeah. This is going to be an interesting day."

"I think I'm going to buy some ammo." I said and turned to the ammo racks. The employee discount isn't that great, but it helps when buying ammo in bulk. We had six cases of 5.56mm and I took all of them. Along with several cases of .40, a case of 9mm, and every double aught buck and slug in the store. Then I started thinking about what I really needed. I knew I was going to tap out the credit card, so I might as well go all the way. I grabbed cases of ammunition for everything I had. We didn't have any military MREs in the store. The outdoor community had better food packs, and I grabbed most of those, using a big shipping box to pile them all in.

"Your wife is going to kill you." Troy said.

"She loves me and wants me to be happy." I spent more than my wife would normally have approved of for a whole calendar year, but I think she would be okay with this. I got it all loaded up into my truck and covered it up. As I finished locking the truck up, I noticed the traffic in town. To be more specific, the lack of traffic. Only a few people were out.

When I got back to the counter, the phone rang. Troy picked it up. "Guns, this is Troy. Yeah, he's here. Hold on." Troy held the phone out. It was Zack.

"What's up, bro?"

Zack's voice was tight. "Remember that whole zombie uprising thing we talked about last night?"

"Yeah, I saw the news. I just got a shit load of ammo and supplies. Something tells me that we're going to need it."

I looked over, Troy was making his own pile. It looked like he was a little pissed that I had snagged all the same 7MM Rem Mag that he likes. Boyd was already piling up .44 Mag ammo and reloading stuff.

"Good, because we are going to need it right now. I just got off the phone with Sarah." Zack explained.

Sarah was our cousin who lived in Saratoga Springs with her husband and three kids. "How are they?"

"They're scared. They said they have real zombies running around."

I looked over that the computer screen, the live feed was back up. It wasn't pretty. "Yeah, so I see. I'm looking at traffic cameras and things are pretty horrific."

"Sarah said she watched the guy across the street eat his son's legs."

"Damn!" It took me a second to let that sink in. This is really happening. We had to get Sarah and her family out of there and back to safety, if any place can be made safe. "Are they holed up good and tight?"

"Yeah, but they only have enough to hold out for a couple days."

"Tell Sarah to fill the bathtub up with water, just in case."

"She already did that."

"Good girl. Pack up some stuff and get it ready to load up. We're going to be heading out fast."

"Roger that." Zack said and hung up the phone.

I got a couple other phone calls before I could get out of the store, and it turned out that so did Zack. Our friends out on the Wasatch were fighting a defensive battle. It wasn't even lunch time when all the land lines from outside of the local area stopped working. Cell phones still worked fine for now. It was no surprise to see a lot of people gathering out in front of the store.

People were scared. Word had it that the Mayor was trying to organize enough people for a city defense. The idea was to gather everyone together in one place and guard that. *A stupid idea*, I thought. Some guys, knowing my background, asked if this was a good idea.

"Why are you coming to me?" I asked.

"You're the State Rep. There is no contact with the Governor or the Lt. Gov, or our State Senator. The Mayor is... well, he's just the Mayor of Vernal and this is bigger than that."

"Well, we have the County Sheriff." I said. A couple faces back in the crowd, I saw the Sheriff. He looked me right in the eyes. "What should we do, George? What do you think of the Mayor's plan?"

"It's short sighted. We don't need to gather everyone at Western Park. In fact, that sounds really stupid." A lot of people nodded. I went into my command mode. "Vernal is one thing – but the whole Uintah Basin is what we need to protect. We're pretty defensible because of the geography, and we have resources we want to keep because we'll need them. Cattle, crops, oil tanks at the wells. This might be a long-haul situation, so we have to think long term. First thing we have to do is lock the basin down. We should put up barricades and road blocks to keep control of the whole area. The only people we let come in are people that are residents of the area or those that are personally vouched for by residents. This is important. We keep out anyone looking like they are sick or bitten, no matter who they are. They stay out. We have cell phones still, if they fail we can use short wave radios. If we have to we can use runners on motorcycles. Keep a bunch of well armed guys at each barricade. Enough to stop a problem."

I circled key points on a map. "County line between Wasatch and Duchesne County... good choke point, good place to put up a barricade. Raven Ridge by Dinosaur. Indian Canyon, here. Manilla and Dutch John... we want to keep Flaming Gorge. This point here at the White River crossing." I was getting nods, everyone was getting this.

"Who's in the National Guard unit here?" A few hands went up and I looked to them. "You guys need to get your stuff together and get to these check points Riki Tiki. Everyone needs to be armed. Citizens will back you up. You guys are all under the direction of the County Sheriff for now, since higher authority from the State Guard is unavailable." I got some nods and no grumbling as people understood the situation.

"Maybe ten guys at the small points of defense, twenty guys on the highways. Give these guys some big guns. Put some Fifties up covering the barricades and keep those guys hidden. This is their overwatch. We'll need more people able to respond if they need help... when they need help. Everyone will need to be rotated every 12 hours. I'll let the Sheriff set the schedule. We probably don't have much time because people are panicking. Get on the horn, we need to get people to these barricades real fast. Let people leave, but if they want to come back through – they have to be locals and they have to be clean, got it? Okay, things need to move fast. We gotta get the basin secured ASAP."

The guys nodded and everyone split up. Troy had come outside and was listening to everything. "So you're the boss now?"

"No, I'm just the State Rep. I have no authority."

"Yeah, didn't look like it." Troy said.

"Looks like I'm running into Salt Lake. Need anything?" Troy shook his head, "I'm not the one that needs anything. You need something though."

"Oh yeah?" I said, "what's that?"

"Some good luck. Say a prayer."

"I'll do that. Make sure the store doesn't get looted." I said and jumped into my truck. I drove back to Ogre Ranch. When I got home, my boys were standing on the front porch. My oldest had a shotgun, a Remington 870. I knew he could run it, because I taught him to fight with it. He had on his pouch of shells. My other boys had their rifles, scoped .223's and .22-250's and Ruger 10/22's.

My wife came out as I shut the engine off and jumped out. She had her short 870 slung over her shoulder. She didn't look happy. Zack had my tactical gear ready to go and my favorite long guns. I had my Rock River M4 in my truck, but he knew I'd want Lilith, my sniper rifle, and my tactical shotgun, just in case. We were loaded for bears, lots of zombie bears. I only hoped this would be enough.

"I don't want you to go," my bride pleaded.

I was unloading the food and ammunition while the boys took it into the house. "I have to go. Sarah is family and we have friends out there that might still need our help."

"I know. You have to. But I still don't want you to go."

I kissed my wife and hugged all six of my boys one by one and gave them their marching orders. One of my younger boys was angry that I wouldn't take him.

"Son, I love you too much to argue about this. Your job is to help stand watch over our house." He had his little Mossberg .410 pump and a pouch full of shells on his belt.

"I need all of you here where I know you guys are safe. I couldn't go if I didn't think you could be safe. I'm trusting you. Can I trust you?" He nodded and put a firm set in his jaw.

"Good. That's my boy."

I kissed my wife again. "I'll come home. I promise."

As Zack and I pulled away from Ogre Ranch, I was not happy. Leaving my family behind was tough, but pulling our other family members out of the fire in Salt Lake was important. I knew my wife was strong, and my boys were smart. They would be fine for a while and I knew I'd be back soon. Maybe a couple of days. I hoped.

Zack's Point of View (POV)

I had been sitting in the truck watching my brother George say goodbye to his family. The whole fatherhood thing was something I just didn't get and probably never would. There were whole sections of what people called "normal life" that I simply had no experience with.

What was happening now was far from normal, yet it felt perfectly comfortable. I was nervous, excited, and worried, but I felt in my place. In all honesty I felt a little too eager. All my life I had failed at everything. My lovely time in Iraq taught me that if there was one thing I was actually good at, it was fighting. When Abu Garhaib was attacked by over a hundred insurgents, I had felt more alive than at any other time in my life.

This felt the same way. Normally I lived in a dazed, half-dream world, but now my senses were burning clear and bright.

George was packing his favorite gear and so was I. I had my trusty AK, Elizabeta, and my PSL for longer range work. The quick-attach pistol belt held my AK mags on my thighs, a dump pouch for empty mags on my side, and my Beretta Storm in 9mm on my other thigh.

When we finally pulled out of the driveway heading out of Lapoint, a bit of relief washed over me. The sooner we got there, the better. For all the excited anticipation, I was also worried about my family. I had been friends with my cousin since I could remember, and if there was a chance to save them, we had to try. George knew a score of other people that also lived near Salt Lake and the more survivors with guns they could get, the better their chances were.

We had a full tank of gas and we didn't bother making any stops for the usual tradition of snacks for long drives. This was going to be a long drive, like the wait to see a doctor or take that test you've been dreading. We didn't say anything for a long time. We both knew what the stakes were. I took off my black "taco" cowboy hat and put it on the dash.

As we drove through Roosevelt we came to a roadblock that was being set up to stop people from entering from Salt Lake's direction. George pulled up to the men there.

"We're going to be able to come back this way, right?" George asked. "As long as you know somebody that can verify who you are or you got proof that you live here."

"Good. You guys might want to consider moving this roadblock further down the road. Put it up at the border of Duchesne County and Wasatch County, where the canyons start. Put a roadblock there and no one's getting through. You can seal off the whole basin area from that direction."

"Didn't think of that," the man said. "Guess that's where them Army trucks went."

"Don't think about it... do it. Get everyone moving over there ASAP. They are going to need help."

George then drove past and didn't look back.

"At least their heart's in the right place," I said in my usual half-joking way.

"Good intentions won't help you survive." George said as he looked at me sideways. "When it comes to survival, good intentions don't count. Zombies won't care about your ethics." He shook his head and got quiet. A few minutes later he spoke again. "Let's see if there's any news on."

He turned the radio on. The local rock station was still playing and I was tempted to ask him to leave it there. I could use some good AC-DC right then, but he switched it to the news channel. Usually it was talk radio, but now it was just local news. The man on the radio was speaking of reports of chaos in all the major cities. As usual the government was doing nothing useful. The Democrats were blaming the Republicans and the Republicans were blaming the Democrats and nothing was actually being done. They'd probably vote to raise their salaries and then go into hiding. They were saying that DC was in total chaos, and the talking heads that ruled the place were all scattered in different directions. Screw them. The less they did the better for everyone.

"Typical," I muttered.

"At the least the President is safe," George said.

"Thank goodness for that." My voice was filled with sarcasm that made George grin.

He switched it back to the rock station while I tried to call people. The first person I called was my twin brother, Josh. He was a cop back in Richmond, VA.

He answered. "Yo, what's up fool? Having a zombie party over there? Is it in season for zeds?" He asked as soon as he picked up.

"Oh, yeah. Me and George are going out hunting right now. We're heading to Salt Lake to pick up Sarah and Kevin and hopefully a few other people. We haven't seen anything yet, but what's it like there?"

"Freaking crazy man. I got the padres, Uncle Musket, Cappello, Hardgrave and Ugwu here as well. We're going to Ft. Picket right now."

"Nice! Do you think the two inept security guards were able to hold off the infected?" I asked.

Josh's reply was too quick. "I hope not. I don't want to have to sign a bunch of forms to check out a vehicle."

"What are you looking to get?"

"The Marines have a bunch of LAVs there. Also, MREs, guns and ammo."

"Pick up a SAW for me, would ya?"

"Sure thing."

"We're almost there. Gotta go. Cappello says 'hi'."

"Tell him that I still want his FS2000."

"He knows. Our plan is to convoy out to Utah. Tell you more later. Peace out."

"Adios fool."

I hung up, thankful that my twin was alright. Sounded like he had a good plan going. He had a great group there including some old Army buddies.

The news kept reporting the same thing, chaos in major cities, debate if the infection came from China or Africa and what the government should do about it. One talking head said to wait somewhere safe until the government solved the problem. They would be waiting there an awfully long time.

"Is this the end of the world?" I asked George, not intending to have asked out loud.

"No." He shook his head slowly. "I don't think so. I think it's just going to be really crappy for a while."

"Good." I nodded. George was usually right, so I liked his answer.

"Good?"

"Yeah, my life's pretty lousy right now, so if the whole world went to crap then I'd be on equal terms with it. This zombie apocalypse could be the best thing to happen to me."

George gave me a raised eyebrow. "You worry me sometimes."

"No need to worry. I'm not about to go universal soldier on you and start

14

collecting ears or anything."

We drove on for another hour while listening to the news.

"What's that?" George asked.

I looked up from my thoughts and saw a car on the side of the road. It looked like it had swerved off the side road, ran out into the field and into a shallow ditch.

We stopped and got out, guns at the ready. George had his pistol, and I covered him with my AK. When we got up to the car we saw someone moving around in it. It was hard to see inside as the windows were fogged up. Suddenly, a bloody hand clawed at the windshield. The shock of it made me jump. George's only response was to snap his gun up, leveled on the window. We moved closer and looked in, carefully. There was a woman inside and she looked sick. Her skin was pale, her eyes milky and her mouth hung open and limp. She was struggling to get at us, but she was still locked in with her seat belt and it didn't look like she knew how to open doors anymore.

"Zombie," I said. "Shame. She looked like she was pretty hot."

We could here her moaning as she pawed at the glass. George raised his pistol again to shoot the poor woman.

"Hold on." I raised my hand to stop him. "It's hot as balls out here. Her windows are closed and she ain't going anywhere. Her brain will cook soon enough. Might as well save the ammo. George lowered his weapon and just looked at the zombie. So did I. We noticed the bite mark on her arm. Deep teeth marks, some torn tissues, and blackened veins of infection branching out from it.

It was my first time face to face with one of the infected. The worst part was the eyes. There was no spark of humanity left in them. The woman's soul was long gone and only biological, bestial instinct was left. This wasn't a person anymore.

"Your right." George said. "We are going to need the bullets. But I don't like this. If we come back this way, and she's still here..." George didn't finish the sentence. "Hold on a second. I think I know her. Hey, this is Shelly. She works at a computer shop in Vernal. She was a complete bitch. I feel better about leaving her all the sudden."

We stood there for a minute longer, looking at what used to be Shelly. Then we shrugged and turned our backs to her, got in the truck and kept going.

I couldn't help but wonder what Shelly's story was. Did she wake up to what she thought was going to be a normal morning? It looked like she was smart enough to flee, but unlucky to have been bitten. She had tried and failed. And why did George feel okay about letting someone he recognized be slow roasted in a locked car? And here I thought I could be cold. We started the downward descent from the mountains and into Heber City.

Ogre's POV

*W*hen we passed the Point of Entry truck scales entering Heber City we saw the problems. I pulled over to the side of the road and grabbed my binos. I could see a lot of smoke. Some cars were burning. It was hard to tell but it looked like a couple could have been police cars. We'd find out as we got closer. People were running, people or zombies. I couldn't tell, everyone was covered in blood, wounds, and filth.

"Alright... looks like this is going to get busy." I put in my Surefire Ear Plugs and hit the gas.

"Let's do this," Zack said has he rocked a mag into his AK-47. We continued forward and soon we were passing cars and trucks that were stopped in the road. Some were off on the shoulder, and some in the middle of the road, just abandoned. One of the burning cars was State Police, the other was a Wasatch County Sheriff's car. We couldn't see any law enforcement officers around. I slowed the truck down but we were still rolling at a good pace.

The people I had seen earlier were a little further ahead, some were running around, others were just standing there, arms hanging limp at their sides, heads hanging down.

"Check this out!" Zack pointed off to the right. A guy on a motorcycle was trying to ride past people, but the people who were standing in the way started grabbing at him, pulling at him. We couldn't hear anything, but it looked like the guy was screaming as he was pulled from his bike. It was too late for us to do anything about it, so we pressed on.

As we approached the first intersection we noticed that some of the people started running at our truck. From the blood and torn clothing and the look of insane rage, I didn't think they wanted a ride. "Here we go!"

I got on the gas as Zack leaned out the window with his AK. He fired three rounds and dropped one of the zombies. I took the corner heading to Provo Canyon, and as I turned Zack ripped off almost a full magazine. There were a lot of zombies in the street. Some fell, while some continued running as they were hit. I stood on the gas peddle, and the engine roared as loud as the AK. Zack was looking back to the intersection as I saw a couple zombies come out ahead at a full-tilt run. I didn't have time to get my shotgun up, so I drew my Glock 23. One hit the front fender and the other grabbed for me through the window. I let him have it, and the grabbing hands fell away as I drove on. Up ahead there were cars blocking the road completely. Looks like they had a pile-up.

As I took the truck off the road into a field to go past we could see some of the zombies pulling at bodies on the ground. They were tearing at the flesh like wild animals. If there was any doubt about these people being real and actual zombies, all doubt was removed.

On the other side of the highway was the Heber Airport. It was small, but they had hangers full of aircraft, many of which could be ready to fly given a few minutes preparation.

"Look at those airplanes." Zack pointed. Several aircraft looked like they were ready for take off.

"Yeah, but look over there," I pointed to the hangers. A large group of zombies were milling around. "I don't think they would let us borrow one of their planes."

Zack shrugged his shoulders, "yeah, but it would save time and we could get a rental when we landed."

"You don't like my truck?"

"I think it's attracting Zombies."

My truck was loud. It didn't have mufflers or emission controls or anything keeping it politically correct or low profile. "Naw, I think they are attracted to the movement." I was just being difficult, because I knew he was right. Sound would attract them as well as movement. I wondered if smell would do it too.

The zombies were running at us from every direction now. I aimed the truck back to the road and crashed onto the highway. I had to swerve around a couple stopped vehicles, but we were quickly back up to speed.

The airport did give me a good idea. I could fly a small plane. Having owned my own ultralight, and flying several other small aircraft, I had a good sense of ability. If I had to, we could borrow a plane as long as it was daylight. I had always been into aviation. I even went to flight school, but I didn't have a license. I couldn't afford to continue the flight hours required to finish the process. I wasn't sure I wanted to test myself right now.

We got to Deer Creek and the stopped cars were making the road more crowded. Another road block of cars made us stop. "Can we push through?" Zack asked.

I looked at the vehicles in the road, one was a blue Toyota Avalon with nothing behind it. I nosed up to it and started to push. It didn't want to roll.

"I think it's got the parking brake on."

There were no zombies visible from the truck so we both got out. I pulled my 870 Police out and put it into "Contact Ready". Zack jumped up into the back of the truck to get a better look at the area as I approached the Avalon. I could hear moaning from somewhere but I couldn't tell where it was coming from. The Toyota was empty. The driver had probably thought he was going to come back to the car because it was locked tight. I looked back up at Zack standing in the bed of the truck, "Hey, you got a key?" I backed up away from the car.

"Yup."

He aimed at the driver's side window and fired a round. The window shattered perfectly. I reached in and opened the door. It took me a second to find the parking break and release it. With my head still in the Toyota, I noticed a zombie on the other side of the car looking in at me. It was a young woman, probably late teens. Her eyes were dead, milky white and unblinking. She was missing an ear and some skin from her cheek. She let out a moan that was answered by another moan from behind the other cars in the pile up. I backed up, slowly, bringing the big Remington up. Another zombie came into view from behind the stopped traffic. This one looked like a big construction worker. I took aim at the girl zombie. She started to move, coming around the Avalon quickly.

Zack was aiming at a third zombie that was crawling up over the mess of cars. I fired the 870 Police into the girl zombie, instantly racking another shell into the chamber. She fell back missing most of her head. Zack's rifle bucked three times, sending a zombie to the ground. That was two zombies down. The one that was left got to the Toyota and started around it, looking right at me. I took careful aim and slapped the trigger. The zombie's head exploded. I listened to the echo of the shotgun blast and for any more moaning. I heard none. It seemed that this was the last of them here at this point, so we got back into the truck and pushed the Toyota again. This time it rolled easily.

We had a similar problem again some miles later at the Deer Creek Dam. The road used to go across the dam, but had been rerouted some years ago. The new road dropped down to the left, going in front of it. Here the traffic was almost impassable with blocking cars and wandering undead.

We stopped the truck a couple hundred yards away and went on foot to the dam. We had a great position at the center of the dam, and I checked out the situation through the scope of "Lilith" my .308 Savage Rifle. Several zombies were milling around. "Okay, I'm on multiple targets." Zack observed through the Swarovski EL binos and called the target. "On scope... near target, green shirt, missing an arm."

"On target. Sending." Lilith bucked and I worked the bolt quickly to get the next round ready.

"Hit. He's down. Next target, huge fat zombie in blue."

"Got it. Sending."

"Hit. You took his off jaw, but he's still up. Give him another one."

"On the way." I pulled the trigger again.

"Boom! Headshot." Zack said. There was almost delight to his voice. He was having fun.

"Reloading." I had chambered the fourth round and wanted to reload while I had a round ready, just in case. I really wished Savage had made 10-round mags for the Model 10FCP. The little magazine popped out into my hand, and I started to push new rounds into it with my thumb.

When the Zombies found where the gunfire was coming from they started moving in mass toward us, some stopping at edge of the road, others going over the barrier and falling into the Provo Canyon. Only one ran around the roadway onto the dam. Zack dumped him with a couple shots from his AK, then he turned to the zombies on the road below us. It became a free fire zone.

The downside to the engagement was that I went through two boxes of Hornady TAP ammunition in about five minutes. The upside was that all visible zeds were neutralized. With the fun over, it was time to get back to work. It took a while to move enough vehicles out of the way to thread the truck through.

The worst part was dealing with the bodies. Not all of the dead got back up. These were not zombies we had dropped. These were human bodies. Women, children... still strapped into the seatbelts or half dragged out through broken windows. The kids were the worst. One little girl, you could tell she was cute, had the whole upper half of her head ripped open and an arm torn off. The driver, mom, had been bitten earlier and turned while driving. I had taken her down with Lilith while she was still holding the arm. Scenes like this were hard to take and I wanted to puke. *Was this what the whole world was like now? Madness and blood?* I shook off that line of thinking.

We were about to get rolling again now that the road was cleared enough. I saw something. "Hold on a second."

"What's up?" Zack was sitting back in the truck seat, topping off an AK mag from a box of ammo beside him on the seat.

"I gotta do something." I jumped back out of the truck. I know it was a waste of time and effort, but I've always wanted to do something.

A red Toyota Prius that Zack had pushed off the road was too tempting. I hated these smug little cars, as if owning one made you morally superior. They were overly expensive, complicated, and less efficient than a diesel Rabbit. As I walked to it, I pulled out my ZT knife and flicked it open. I'd been itching to do this.

I went under the car and used the knife to punch some holes in the gas tank. Some fuel leaked out, but not a lot. I stood up and used the knife to rip out a large swatch of fabric off the seat. A nice big section.

Zack tilted his head to the side trying to figure this out. He called out, "What are you doing?"

"Molotov Car-Tail." I quipped as I opened the fill cap. Air went in, allowing the fuel to pour out of the holes in the gas tank faster. I soaked the seat cloth in the fuel and lit it... then tossed it into the back seat of the Prius. By the time I had walked back to the truck the Prius was burning nicely.

"Was that really necessary?"

"Absolutely! I had to do it. If the world gets back to normal, I'd rather have it with less Priuses. Let's roll."

Zack put on his trademark gold-framed Elvis sunglasses and his black "taco hat". "Let's hit it."

The road turned into a nice divided highway and we picked up speed. Going downhill into Happy Valley was an easy ride since it was almost completely clear of any stopped vehicles. The lanes going out of Happy Valley were another story altogether. It was completely gridlocked. Driving past we saw a few zombies who were either milling around aimlessly or were busy noshing on severed body parts.

"Damn it." I grumbled.

"What's up?"

I stopped the truck in a wide area where we were away from any visible zeds. "This is going to get really ugly up ahead. I think we're going to have to hoof it soon.

I can always tell when Zack means it, because he never cusses.

"We'll go as far as we can, then we'll have to leave the truck. Unless we are really lucky."

"Damn it! I've got too much ammo to carry."

"We'll have to find more... not a problem. But we gotta get ready to beat feet."

We had a couple packs, and stuffed them full of ammo and MREs. We would have to leave stuff behind, and I didn't like that anymore than Zack did. One of the things I would have to leave was one of my two shotguns. *Hmm, my 870 Police or my Mossberg 930SPX?* I decided to take the Mossberg with me. It had a tactical light mounted on the front which might be helpful. What about killed me was the choice to leave Lilith. As much as I loved having a precision rifle with me, it was too big, heavy, and limited in the magazine department. It would have to stay. We put the packs and the guns we would take in the back of the truck, and everything else in the back seat so they could be locked up. "Ready?"

"Yup." Zack sounded less than enthusiastic.

We got moving again, and it wasn't very long before my hunch was proven correct. The highway's traffic directions rejoined and the fork between the road to Provo and the turn off to Orem was completely blocked. I pulled off and we jumped out of the truck. "We might be back." I said. I hoped we would be back. We grabbed our gear out of the truck bed and rucked up. Zack slung his PSL rifle across his back and slung his AK across his chest. I raised an eyebrow. "I'm not leaving my PSL." His face said that this wasn't something to argue about.

I took point as we moved forward on foot. I had my 930 SPX slung at the ready and my Glocks ready. My Glock 23 on my hip and the model 22 on my chest on the tactical vest. My Crusader Templar, an M4-type carbine, was dangling from the single-point sling. We were loaded heavy, but considering what was in front of us, we would need it.

We were soon threading our way through stopped cars, walking in a crouch. One car had a zombie trapped inside and it threw itself in vane against the window, smearing blood and puss. It was tempting to shoot it through the glass, but we wanted to keep a lower profile. We could hear moaning, but it was more random and not the urgent – "There's fresh meat" sort of moan. I held up my hand in the "Stop" signal and took a knee. Zack came up close and knelt down.

In a whisper, "In the bottom center pocket of my ruck I have a couple grey boxes."

Zack quickly pulled the boxes out. One was stamped ".45" and the other was ".33". I opened the smaller box and pulled out a cylinder. This was a .45 caliber suppressor prototype for Crusader Weaponry. Joe and I were going to show them off at SHOT Show, but it looked like SHOT was going to be postponed. My Glock 22 barrel had been replaced with a longer threaded barrel last month. I threaded the suppressor onto the barrel and put it back on the chest rig. The long can protruded through the end of the holster, but it carried just fine. The other can, I gave to Zack. "Put this on your AK. We built this for quick attachment without any tools or special mounts."

"When did you..."

"I was going to give this to you for Christmas. We've not even tested it yet. I hope it works."

"Christmas is a bit off."

"I could wait until December..."

"Ho ho ho!"

The can fit the AK perfectly. I wished I had a can for my Templar, but it wasn't finished before everything went to hell. I'd have to make do. The .45 can will work with a .40 caliber pistol, Crusader suppressors were meant to be multi-caliber and would still work just fine.

I started moving forward again, and we approached two zombies that were not going to be passable. We were about twenty five yards away when I stopped again and pulled out the suppressed Glock. I braced on the back of a Hyundai and took careful aim. The suppressor worked extremely well. The second zombie was completely unaware of fact the other one suddenly crumpled to the ground. A second shot cleared our path and we moved on. We could see that a lot of the traffic stopped on the road was due to collisions, and some were evidently from very high rates of speed. One overturned car was resting on top of another one. You could see a hand sticking out of the window of one of the cars but you couldn't tell which car the hand was actually coming out of.

As we neared the intersection Some of the cars appeared to have burned. Bodies were strung out, some charred, some chewed, many missing large parts. Zombies were all over the place. Some were hunched down eating off the dead like a pack of dogs. The smell of the dead was strong. Rotting meat stink smells sweet and sickening and made me want to gag. But the worse was the sound of tearing flesh and the zombies feasting.

It was at that moment Zack's cell phone rang.

Every zombie looked up and right at us. They moaned in unison and started coming at us. "Oh shit!" I shoved the Glock into the holster and unlimbered Templar. I didn't even have time to turn on the Eotech sight before I started firing.

The cell phone rang again. Zack pulled it out and answered it "Go for Zack."

I looked over at him, "What the hell dude?"

Zack just nodded and gave me that "Just a sec" look. I shrugged and blew a hole through the forehead of a zombie that looked like she was a BYU coed.

"Yo! This is Mike, are you guys okay?"

Zack shouted "It's Mike!"

I fired several rounds as fast as I could pull the trigger and dumped a few more zeds. "Tell Mike to meet us someplace. We can come get him."

"He says he has the EOD building at Hill locked down."

"Ask him..." I fired another burst and knocked down two more zombies, "if he can move south."

"He'll see what he can do."

I managed to turn on my Eotech and suddenly was able to make accurate hits.

"Try to make it to," more firing and then all the sudden I had an idea.

"Wait! Tell him to keep Hill open as much as possible. We'll meet him there!" I did a speed reload and fired again. "We'll need a ride for some people... about a dozen maybe. See what he can scrounge up."

"Here, you talk to him." Zack handed me the phone and pulled up his AK and started firing.

"Hey, Mike. Good to hear from you."

"You guys sound busy."

"Just having some fun. We're just getting into Orem right now. I had to ditch my truck so we are on foot."

"Just grab something else when you can. I picked up a new Land Rover before I came to work."

"Nice..."

"Then I fired my boss."

"I thought you liked him."

"Well, he wanted to eat me. I'm pretty sure that's some form of harassment."

"You'll have to file some paperwork on that."

"Yeah, I'll do that right after I find my Reflective Safety Belt."

Zack's rate of fire was increasing. "Hey Mike, look man... I am not sure how long it's going to take to make it up there, but we'll meet you there. Find something that can get us home."

"Roger, that."

The line went dead. I pulled my Templar back up and started picking off zombies. We could see a large number of zombies coming from Provo. We had worked our way near the underpass when I decided I didn't want to use more rounds than necessary, so I started shooting gas tanks and spilling fuel.

"More Car-Tails?"

"I think so. It worked so well on the Prius."

It didn't take long before gasoline was everywhere. Some of the Provo zombies broke into a run. Zack dropped them with his suppressed AK as I pulled out my zippo. The gas was running free and spilled over a wide area, soaking the entire road under the overpass. "Let's back it up." We moved away before I lit the gas off.

It started burning nicely, blocking the underpass with flame and smoke. Most of the Provo zombies stopped at the flames and started moaning. A few of them, however, tried running through the fire, which resulted in flaming zombies running right at us. Zack lowered the muzzle of his AK a bit and calmly shot them through the pelvis. They fell into the flame. "Let'm burn."

I shrugged. That was fine with me.

We started moving uphill and could see a huge number of zeds. There were a couple hundred at least coming down the hill. We backed down the hill and moved towards a bridge crossing the water that flowed from the Provo Canyon along the highway, ducking low as we went. We crossed the bridge and snuck around the gas station just above the highway. Above that was a residential neighborhood. It was safer going through there than it was trying to take on the hundreds of zeds who seemed to be attracted either to the fire and smoke or the moans from the Provo zombies.

We skirted the first group of Orem zombies cleanly and entered the residential slow and quiet. We moved from house to house, and avoided passing in front of windows as much as possible. We could tell that some houses still had actual people in them. We could hear people talking, some arguing, some crying... some moaning. As we passed by, we saw faces looking out of windows at us. Some, human faces, painted with fear. Some watched and others pulled their curtains shut as if dangling cloth would protect them. Other windows had faces of the dead pressed against the glass. Lifeless eyes followed us. I ignored them. Zack didn't seem to care. We moved on.

Some houses had cars in the driveway. Unfortunately they were locked. Zack tried the door on a mini-van and the door opened. "No, I'm not taking a mini-van. Besides, we don't have the keys to start it."

It would have been nice if someone had left the keys in a car... even a mini-van. I don't know how to hotwire a car. Guys do it in the movies all the time. But I'm not that guy.

We kept moving, crossing one block into another. This block had more damage, and broken glass was prevalent. "Look at this." I whispered just loud enough. Zack came over and looked. "Five five six cases." Spent brass was scattered around the sidewalk and across the grass. Bullet impacts marred the side of a house, shattered the windows and tracked across to the open door. There were a couple spent cases from a pistol, looked like a 9mm. Something black and shiny laid in the grass, and I bent down to pick it up. It was a Hi-Point magazine. Near the magazine blood covered the grass. We walked further and we found the pistol. It was jammed with a stove pipe. "But Hi Points are so reliable!" Zack quipped sarcastically.

At the end of the street we changed directions to the left and headed back to the main road that would eventually lead us to the I-15 on-ramp. There was a grocery store on the main road here. The parking lot was full of cars and we could see people or zombies milling around, moaning. Since they were moaning and acting strange, we guessed they were all zombies. Swinging wide and avoiding them, we came to house with a chain-link fenced yard. In it a small boy was kneeling over what was the family dog. The boy looked up at us. He had blond hair and milky white eyes. The zombie boy looked at us, regarded us for a moment, then went back to eating the dog. I pulled out my suppressed Glock and put a single round through the top of the blond head. The boy instantly went slack, falling on top of the dog. Zack just shrugged it off and kept walking but I was horrified. The boy was probably five or six, and the dog was a full grown Labrador... a dog that probably loved that little boy. After staring into the yard and thinking of my own family for a few moments, I finally turned and followed Zack.

We stopped looking into the houses as we passed, it was starting to get late and time was running short. Picking up the pace, we soon found ourselves in a jog. The street was mostly clear of the walking dead, but not bodies. Signs of violence were all around us, and the further we went the thicker it became. This all happened last night. Two days ago, this was a peaceful town. People coming and going, concerned with their smart phones and TV shows. None of that mattered now. We could hear distant screams, gunshots, and mayhem was all around. A few blocks ahead a big 4x4 truck roared out from a side street and turned west, heading away from us. I ducked behind a car. Zack came up behind me and ducked down as well. "What's up?" Zack whispered.

"Just a hunch. Give me your PSL." Zack's PSL was like a long-scoped AK-47 chambered for 7.62x54R, the Russian equivalent of a .308. I took the rifle and while leaning over the trunk, aimed the rifle through the busted-out windows and down the street where the truck came from. I flicked the safety off with my finger and got on the trigger, ready to fire. With a quick look at the BDC turret, I set it for the range and watched through the scope. A moment later a pack of six zombies came sprinting around the corner after the truck. I held on the second chevron in the scope's reticle.

"Sending."

The PSL bucked and as soon as I got it back on the targets, I picked another one and let fly another round. Four zombies remained. I fired again and again. Two zombies left. One stopped and turned back to us. It was filled with rage and looked like it was about to scream until I realized it had no lower jaw. I took careful aim on this one and squeezed the trigger. The PSL bucked once more as the bullet launched from the barrel at high velocity, climbed about an inch over the bore axis and started to drift down in its shallow ballistic arc. The bullet smashed through the front of the zombie's skull, through the nasal cavity, through the medulla oblongata, and exited out the back of the skull pulling blood, bone fragments, brain and spinal tissues with it. The zombie stood there for a few seconds unmoving before gravity exerted its inevitable effect, and the zombie fell straight backwards like a tree. I had to grin as Zack said "Nice shooting."

Through the scope, I looked for the last zombie but couldn't find it. I stood back up.

"Nice rifle," I said as I handed it back to my brother, who quickly changed mags to a fresh one.

We picked up the pace again to a nice jog crossing block after block of what used to be Orem, Utah. But nothing seemed as recognizable as it once was. Our gear wasn't too heavy right now, and it seemed to be getting continually lighter as we expended ammunition. This would become a concern, but I'd worry about that later.

"There we go!" I pointed up ahead. A used car lot. As we approached we looked at the cars. Mostly imports, sports cars and small sport utility rigs built off car platforms. Zack eyed the BMW 5 series. It was black with tinted windows. "Yeah, any other day, bro... but not a good choice right now."

I pointed instead to the Chevy Avalanche. "That's our ride." Zack nodded. It was black too, so I didn't think he would mind. I dropped the Templar on its single-point sling and unlimbered my 930SPX. "Let me find the keys."

Zack jumped up into the back of the truck and stood watch as I approached the small office building. Broken glass was an indicator that something had happened here, but no one else seemed to be around. I quietly opened the door which was unlocked. Slowly, slicing the pie through the little office, I lit up the dark corners with the Surefire light attached to the barrel. There on the wall was a lock box. Inside it were all the keys to the vehicles on the lot. As luck would have it, the box was locked. I was tempted to just shoot it but, I would risk damaging the keys I needed inside. The box was sturdy, prying it would be difficult.

I like big knives. My Ka-Bar Becker is a large bowie-like knife which I had attached to the belt on my tactical vest. Using this, I was easily able to pry the entire box off the wall. It had only been attached with a couple screws through wood paneling. I brought the box outside. Zack looked at me with a slight tilt to the taco hat. With a heave I threw the box as high as I could into the air. When it crashed to the ground again, the lock popped open. "That was easy."

The Avalanche keys were easy to pick out, and soon we were sitting inside on nice, black, leather seats. "This is a nice truck!" Zack said. I ran my hands over the dash and controls. I had to agree, it was nice.

"Sure beats your twenty-year-old clunker," Zack opined.

"Hey, I like my old truck." I said.

"I like this one."

"I'll get my old truck back."

"Sure, after you get used to this one, you're going to go back and get that old POS?"

"Hell yeah, I'm going to get back my old truck. It's got Lilith in it for one. And I like the engine."

I fired up the Avalanche's engine. It was smooth and quiet. I have to admit it was nice as hell. "See, this one doesn't sound right."

"Uh huh."

I pulled out into the street and headed west. We soon came to State Street and we rolled slowly through the intersection, weaving between stopped traffic and around an overturned Orem City Police car.

"You want a Dew?" Zack pointed to the gas station. It had lights on and the door was open.

After the long jog and the hot day, that sounded really good. "I could kill for something cold to drink." I meant that too.

We pulled in and stopped at the pumps. We could see some zombies milling around off in the distance, but if we played quiet like, maybe we wouldn't attract them here. "Let's go soft here." I pulled out my suppressed Glock.

Inside I could see movement, but couldn't see what it was. Zack checked the suppressor on his AK and nodded. We crouched as we approached the door and I went in with my gun up and ready. We could hear noises coming from behind the counter. Wet noises. I looked over and saw the clerk eating the nose off the body of a police officer. The clerk was a younger lady, probably a teenager. She looked up and her milky eye, like a dead fish looked into mine. Blood poured from her lips as she started to moan.

Started to, but the sound an empty .40 caliber case bouncing off the tile was louder. I looked at the faceless cop and felt very sad for the guy. He was probably a good cop and didn't want to shoot the girl when she was acting strange. His gun was still in its holster. It was a Glock as well. I went around the counter and checked. It was a model 22 in .40 caliber. I pulled the magazine out of the gun and took all four of the cop's spares. The Tazer was interesting. On a whim I took that too. I pulled the cop's radio and turned it on, scanning channels. There was some chatter on one, two cops talking about coordinating a defenses around the police station and that a group of people had locked themselves in the SCERA theater.

Zack didn't even look over at the counter, instead he went straight for his addiction. He opened the cooler, grabbed the first Mountain Dew within reach and started chugging. I looked at the till and considered cash, but figured cash was the least of my worries in the foreseeable future. I looked over to Zack just in time to see the flying tackle. Zack's awareness was fully engulfed in the Dew, head back, drinking deep. He hadn't seen the zed running at him from the side. The impact was jarring and knocked the Elvis shades and the tactical taco hat right off his head. Both Zack and the zombie smashed into the Plexiglas window, and bounced off to the floor. The zombie, latched onto Zack like a leech, quickly moved on top of him. My brother was stunned, but still in the fight, and managed to keep the zombie away from his face and neck. The zombie threw it's head back and let out a shriek.

Thunder filled the small store.

The zombie fell limp on top of Zack without a head as I lowered the 12-gauge autoloader and pushed another shell into the magazine. I came around the counter and walked over to my brother. "Are you okay? Get a bite on you?"

Zack checked himself, his arms, his hands. "No, I'm good."

I helped Zack up to his feet then walked over to the cooler and grabbed an orange Gatorade. I chugged down a third of it then filled it back up with a Red Bull. This is my Gator-Bull, my favorite thirst quenching, energizing beverage. "Ah, man... I really needed that." I grabbed a couple more Gatorades and a couple packs of Red Bull and took them to the counter.

Zack looked down at his shirt. It was covered in zombie gore. The Chevron station had a small rack of t-shirts. He pulled his tactical vest off, then his bloody shirt and started to clean off his vest with some Wet-Wipes. The shirt he tossed over the counter on top of the clerk and cop pile.

This particular Chevron also had a Gandolfo's sandwich shop attached. While no one seemed to object, I made sure I washed my hands carefully and I started making some sandwiches. Gandolfo's has great roast beef.

"What kinda of cheese, bro?"

Zack was looking at his new t-shirt options. "Do they have Pepper Jack?"

"Yup."

"Do they have Swiss?"

"Yeah."

"Pepperjack."

I finished the sandwiches, a couple to eat and a couple for the packs. Zack somehow managed to find a black AC/DC t-shirt in his size and pulled it on. It's always best to wear a t-shirt promoting something metal under tactical gear.

As we stood there in the Chevron eating our sandwiches, and sipping on our drinks, another truck pulled in, a big Ford. A tall, dark-haired guy climbed out of one side. He was dressed in normal business casual save for the tactical rig on his thigh. He looked into the store carefully. I waved at him and held up the Gator-Bull. He smiled and waved back to the truck, a tall, lanky teenager climbed out wearing a wide-brimmed cowboy hat. He had on a tactical thigh rig as well.

These guys looked familiar, and all the sudden I recognized them. I went outside, "Marshall Dodge and his boy John Wayne! How are you guys doing?"

"Ogre? That you?"

"Hey guys." Zack had followed me out, munching on his sandwich.

"What are you guys up too?" I asked.

"We've got our homestead secure and came out for some supplies. You?"

"Oh, we came out to pick some folks up, do a little shopping ourselves. The coolers are still cold. You guys should grab some drinks and make some sandwiches. It would be a shame for the food to go to waste."

"That sounds good to us."

We talked for a while. Marshall had paid a visit to Van Wag's just down the street and was going to stop for some gas. Marshal's boy figured out how to activate the pumps and him and Zack put some gas into the trucks. The freeway on and off ramps at the Lehi exit were total gridlock according to Marshal. "That's exactly where I needed to go, get through Lehi."

"Not going to happen. There's just too much there."

I looked up when Zack started firing his suppressed AK-47. Evidently a few zombies noticed them out there pumping gas. Thankfully, because of the can on the muzzle, this wouldn't attract more.

"There are thousands of zekes all around. You best find another way."

I nodded. "Nice rig you got there."

"Like it? I just picked it up this morning. I got really good financing terms on it."

"Sweet."

I packed up a bunch of the deli meat and cheese and some of the bread they had and I shoved it into our packs. Marshal and I shook hands, wished each other luck, and we went our separate ways. They had family to attend to, and we had family to extract.

We rolled down the hill towards Utah Lake. Getting on I-15 here would be impossible. Overturned and burning cars would have normally made things very difficult to get through, but the area was wide and flat. Getting on the freeway would lead us to Lehi and into a hornets nest. Suddenly, a zombie sprinted out in front of us. I didn't even lift off the gas.

Thump thump!

Zack looked over at me, "Does that count to the total score?"

"Sure it does."

"If we can't go through Lehi, how are we going to get to Saratoga Springs?"

I looked out of the truck across the lake. Saratoga Springs was visible on the other side of the water. Suddenly, I remembered something. "There used to be a boat dock down by Geneva Steel. Maybe there's a boat we can grab. A canoe, anything that floats."

"Can't go around it – go across it? That's the plan?"

"That's what I was thinking. Not much of a plan so far, but it beats going through Lehi from what Marshall was saying."

"You know of course, we're doing this all wrong." Zack suddenly announced.

"Yeah, I know. But I hate shopping malls."

Mike called again. Zack handed me the phone. "Larry has it all tied together up at his place, and they have the whole valley up there secured and locked tight. After you guys get here, I'm going to go up there and give them a hand."

"That's cool. He could probably use a good hand."

"Ben called."

"Oh, how's Norseman doing?"

"He's fine for now, but could use some help. He's getting low on supplies, but he has plenty of ammo. He said he's going to make his way to Cabela's."

"Okay, if you can, call him back and tell him to meet us there. We'll be there before dark."

"Roger that."

"Now for the good news."

"I can use that."

"Got you a ride lined up."

"Excellent!"

"So, we'll probably see you tomorrow then. I'm guessing about lunch time?"

"Probably. I don't think we can make it up there by tonight, and it's probably not a good idea to try to make it very far in the dark."

"Yeah, they mostly come out at night, mostly." Mike said, then the line went dead. I looked at the phone, then handed it back to Zack. The part that made me wonder was "We". Who was up there with Mike?

I drove to the Geneva Steel road and hung a right. I thought I remembered a boat dock up that way from back in my college days at BYU. I remembered as an ROTC "SPOT" we used the Utah Guard's boats and we put them in the water some place over this way. But that was so long ago I didn't even know if the place was still there. Geneva Steel wasn't. Parish Chemical wasn't.

But the little marina was. I pulled up wide in the parking lot and we jumped out of the truck, taking our gear with us. From the parking lot nearer to the water I could see a large houseboat parked on its trailer. We could see movement from inside and there was a lot of moaning. Soon other moans started all around us. Zack's AK was up and ready. I drew out my Glock 22 and made sure it was topped off. A few seconds later they came out. Zombies, attracted by the moaning started to gather. They milled around, aimless and lethargic. What was twenty zombies soon became a hundred and twenty.

Zack and I stayed low behind the cars in the parking lot. We crouched as we moved, making our way to the boats. Two items of gear were given to me some time ago by a buddy who was a police chief. I kept them, but never thought to use them until now. If we were to get to the boats we couldn't be seen.

We needed a distraction and concealment. These came in cans now.

The first grenade I pulled out was a standard flash bang. It was shaped like an oversized can of beans. I pulled the pin, careful to hold the spoon down, cocked my arm back, and threw it as hard as I could across to the other side of the parking lot. The flash bang bounced and tumbled under the parked houseboat. It went off with a thud, insuring all the zombies in the area looked that way. The second grenade I pulled out was smoke, white smoke. I tossed the grenade. As the grenade left my hand, the spoon released, flipping up and off the grenade with a "ping". It sailed through the air as the smoke started to release. A few seconds later white smoke started billowing out in a good volume. We waited for ten seconds. This was enough. Smoke obscured our view of the zombies, so it would obscure their view of us.

We ran to the ramp. A red truck was pulling a red trailer, which was still in the water. Floating off the trailer, but still attached was a bright, red fishing boat. It said "Ranger" on the side. A big Ranger Z21-I Bass Boat. That's our ride! We ran to the boat and climbed in. So far, the zombies didn't care about us. The keys were not in the boat and this boat had an ignition just like in a car.

I got out and started to sneak over to the truck. Zack laid low in the bow of the boat, AK at the ready. In the truck, the keys were hanging from the ignition. When I pulled them out, that's when the truck started to chime at me. Some door ajar warning or something. I looked at the keys and could see one had RANGER stamped on it. That's the key we needed!

The sound of the moaning is what gave me warning. I didn't run back to the boat, I sprinted. The instant I jumped to the boat, Zack opened up. Those zombies had been right on my heels. I fumbled for the key again and tried to get it into the ignition. I finally got it in and cranked the engine. Zombies came out of the smoke at a full tilt run. Zack opened up, firing fast, but still taking aimed shots. Zombies were dropping off left and right as I engaged the engine in reverse to pull away from the ramp. But the boat didn't go anywhere.

"Shoot the line!"

Zack turned back to look at me, "WHAT?" I pointed at the trailer, and he saw the cable going from the bow to the pully on the trailer. "Shoot it!"

Zack took a second to aim the shot and nailed it. The boat instantly began pulling away as the zombies reached the trailer. Zack and I both started firing. I unloaded a full magazine on the closest zombies as they strived to reach the boat, but they came no closer than the water's edge, so we stopped firing. A few minutes later we were in open water heading directly to Saratoga Springs.

Zach's POV

*T*he boat came up on the weed-covered shore. I had already forgotten what George had called it. A Ranger bass boat or something. Not like I paid attention to boats. They were show ponies for the rich that had nothing else to do. I slung my AK and took out my PSL. The AK was starting to run lower on ammo than I liked, so I figured I'd give it a break. Also, there were a lot of wide, open streets to give some advantage to the PSL's range, at least to a certain point. I wasn't exactly supremely confident of my abilities to hit anything at long range. I also wasn't confident that my ammo would hold out.

We made our way to the long, empty road that led to Sarah and Kevin's small neighborhood. Saratoga Springs wasn't exactly a thriving metropolis and it was pretty spread out, but even fifty of those ghouls was more trouble than I wanted to deal with. We stayed down low in the bushes and avoided walking out in the open.

It was a small walled community, but there weren't gates. It was filled with typical suburban houses with small front yards and large walled-in back yards. He had heard that it was the exact opposite during the 50's, that people did all the fun stuff like barbecues out in the front because they'd talk to their neighbors and knew the people in their neighborhood.

"How far is it?" George asked as we came to a street that led in.

"About four blocks."

"Damn."

Four blocks was a long way when there were zombies freaking everywhere. I also hated walking. Period. The worst ride was better than the best walk.

George turned on the red dot sight on his M4 and we started down the street, staying close to the houses. Most of the houses had closed doors, but enough had open doors or broken windows to let us know that not all was well here. The place looked like a riot had passed through.

Somewhere in the distance were gunshots, but they sounded so far off as to be in another city. One of the houses had a car through the front door and one of the houses was on fire.

Then a zombie stumbled out of one of the houses. It saw us and let out a long moan. George was quicker on the target than I was and shot it clean in the forehead creating a small hole, but splattering its brains on the wall behind it. The unsuppressed shot rang out and echoed off the houses. It was unbelievably loud, a stark contrast to the relatively quiet.

Suddenly, the sound of more moaning came from other houses and further down the street. More zombies came into view, coming from houses, back yards, garages and cars with open doors. They were like freaking prairie dogs coming out of holes in the ground.

I lined up my shot on the closest one using my iron sights and fired. I hit it square in the chest and blew a huge hole in it. It staggered back but stood up straight again. I aimed again and shot its head; it popped open like a watermelon and the zombie fell down and was still.

"Maybe if I played more first person shooters, I'd be more used to trying for head shots. Freaking center of mass my ass."

Then they started running towards us. We controlled our shots and took careful aim, firing as fast and as accurately as we could. Pop, pop, pop, pop. We took out the first small group of four that was nearby but there were more down the street.

"We have some coming up from behind," George said.

"They're closer. You deal with them and I'll get these guys up there."

"Got it."

I heard his M4 start firing away, and I controlled my breathing and tried to hold the PSL as steady as I could. Shooting from a bench had nothing to do with actual combat. My adrenaline was going, and I just couldn't be as calm like I would be on a firing range.

There were a lot of them and they were running right towards me. Fortunately they were a block away so that gave me a little time. I clicked the range on my scope, lined it up on the first zed and fired. The right half of its head blew open and it tripped on its own feet and fell over. There was something very satisfactory about seeing a shot connect.

I killed three more but by then, they were a lot closer. I switched to my iron sights and began firing a lot quicker. It was easier to acquire targets through irons. They were getting mighty close, and I was going to have to switch back to my AK, but then George came up beside me and started firing away. For a moment I thought his gun was full auto. I was amazed that my brother, while firing so fast, was making aimed shots. With every pull of the trigger, a zombie fell.

They were still getting closer, at least a dozen of them, so we started moving backward. This wasn't good, not good at all. We were falling back and they kept coming. Some of them looked just like people, but crazy. If it wasn't for the white eyes, I'd have thought they were just lunatics. There was a woman in a business suit with blood all over her face. She was screaming and running at me to kill me. I couldn't explain it, but I took it personally. I shot the bloody zombie-woman in the face.

I kept firing until I ran empty and the bolt locked back. I tore out my mag and locked in a fresh one. I emptied this mag also, but when I looked up from loading in a new mag, they were all dead. I had to admit, that so far, my PSL wasn't proving to be the best anti-zombie weapon. Give me a target with anatomy that mattered and I'll be good. Still, it was better than nothing.

"Any more?" I whispered.

"Assume there is." George snarled as he slapped home a fresh magazine from his vest without looking. We continued moving forward, keeping a careful eye on all the windows and doors. Then we got into range of Sarah's house.

The door was busted open and there were zombies milling about the door, as if waiting their turn to get in.

"Shit!" I yelled out.

"We're too late!" George said before letting out a stream of weapons-grade profanity. Those zombie bastards. We were too late and those mindless, ignorant ghouls got there first. I raised my PSL and fired. I hit a fat man in the head and he fell right over. Two of the zombies turned around and saw us. George fired his auto-loader shotgun and blew two zombies' heads into a red spray. I slung my PSL, swung out my AK and ran forward. They were packed together trying to get into the doorway and I fired away at head level until none of them were standing any more.

We got to the house and slammed against the wall. "You lead the way here. I've never been inside." George said.

I sliced the pie, careful to keep my AK pointed at anything I might see coming around the corner. There were more zombies inside and their frustrated moaning was like a loud stereo playing heavy metal. I fired quick aimed shots at almost point-blank range and put them all down.

I quickly looked up the staircase to see what they had been after and saw a bed being used as a barricade. Sarah and Kevin were there behind the bed using a baseball bat and crowbar to keep the zeds at bay.

"Zack!" Sarah said with wide, unbelieving eyes.

"Man am I glad to see you!" Kevin said.

"Zacky's here?" I heard their 10-year old daughter Alexia say.

"Is everyone alright?" George asked as he came in the house. He was watching the street, with his M4 up and ready.

"We're all fine! Just really tired. We've been doing this for an hour!" Sarah said.

"Don't be a pansy. We had them," Kevin said, clearly joking. If they had their sense of humor intact, then all was well.

"When we saw your door open, I thought the worst," I said.

"Okay, Sarah, Kevin, grab your keys. We're going to use your truck to get out of here. We have to go now before more show up," George said.

"Let me grab a few things," Sarah said.

"Go ahead, but hurry," George said.

They threw a few things into some bags and we ran out to the truck.

"George, I'm awfully low for my AK," I said as the three kids piled into the back of the truck with Sarah. Kevin jumped in the driver's seat.

"We'll load you up at Cabelas, make your shots count."

"There's not room in the truck for everyone. I'll jump in the back and provide some fire support," I said.

"Wait, I just thought of something. We're not far from Camp Williams. If we go to Cabelas, we'll need to grab everything we can. One truck won't be enough." George was thinking out loud.

"You want to raid Camp Williams?" I couldn't believe what George said.

"You drove a Humvee in Iraq. We grab a few hummers or whatever else we can find, then hit up Cabelas. Plenty of cargo space."

"A humvee would be a lot safer going through Salt Lake."

"Not one humvee, at least three and with trailers. We should raid supplies for home. That way we won't want to have to come back any time soon."

"I like it. Maybe I can find a SAW there." I didn't want to get my hopes up.

"Let's go!" Kevin shouted.

George took shotgun with his shotgun and I jumped in the back in case some zeds wanted to try the back door. I was exposed, but I could also fight back better.

I looked at Sarah and Kevin in the truck with their three goofy kids. The kids looked scared but they weren't panicking. I was just glad that they were alive. It seemed that it had taken days to get to them. At least his family was safe.

Kevin knew how to get to Camp Williams, and he knew the neighborhood. He pulled out of the driveway, almost slamming me into the cab. Then he peeled out, tires squealing. He made his way to the main road where all the traffic and stores were. There was no traffic but there were a lot of zombies.

TWO

Getting More Firepower!

Kevin found a lot of fun in ramming stray zombies with his truck. I was getting worried when I looked over at him and he was grinning like a Mad Hatter. But considering the last 24 hours, I couldn't blame him. Every so often I'd let loose out the window with a blast of 00 Buck from the Mossberg, when Kevin missed one to the right of the truck. In the back of the truck, I could hear Zack's AK pop off once in a while, picking off occasional zombies that decided to run after us. In the back seat, Sarah and the kids were resting. They had been through a lot of stress.

We turned right onto Redwood Road, passing construction and zombies who were walking together in a large group. The zombies started running after us. Zack used the iron sights on his PSL and took his time picking them off. He hit a fat zombie wearing a suit and tie low in the gut and it fell, sliding on its front. When it got back up, it was missing a large portion of its face, but it kept running. Zack fired again and the zombie lost the rest of its face, along with the back of its head. It fell and slid to a stop unmoving. As Kevin put distance on the zombies they started to drop away on their own, and soon they were just wandering around in the street, as if they had forgotten us. Zack started to top off his magazines.

As we approached Camp Williams, we noticed a distinct lack of zombies, but we didn't see anyone around either. We pulled into the main gate and rolled slowly through the base. Kevin asked "Where are we heading?"

"We want to get to the Motorpool, the north east part of the base."

Kevin headed that way. I thought I saw movement from the corner of my eye, but when I looked, I didn't see anything. At the Motorpool, Sarah and the kids stayed in the truck as Zack, Kevin, and I checked the area out. No zombies. No moaning.

There were a lot of military vehicles to choose from. The one thing about military vehicles that I like, you don't need keys. Zack grabbed a Humvee in desert camo with four doors and a sloping rear cover. On the bumper it had the numbers "625" stenciled on it. I knew that unit. I looked inside to see if there was anything familiar about it. Instead I saw one of the new Blue Force Trackers. I knew what it was, but didn't know anything about it, so I didn't touch it. "Kevin, this one is yours."

"Alright!" Sarah and the kids changed vehicles. Sarah didn't seem to be too bothered, but the kids were excited about the new ride. "Are you guys hungry?" I pulled my pack out of the back of Kevin's truck and opened it up. Footlong Gandolfo's Sandwiches and some Gatorades. I gave them all to the family. I kept the Red Bulls though. "You'll have to pick out the hot peppers."

Zack pulled up in another rig, this one was a green four-door with a pickup truck bed. "Dibbs". It also had 625 printed on it, with another Blue Force Tracker in it. I'll have to learn how to run them, some other time.

Zack sauntered off to pick out his rig.

I heard children's laughter from Kevin's Humvee and as I turned to it, I turned face first into the muzzle of an M4 held firmly in the hands of a soldier. "Who are you?" he yelled in my face.

"Whoa! Hey!" I slowly raised my hands. "I'm George Hill, Utah State Representative from..." He cut me off.

"Do you have authorization to take these vehicles?"

"I..."

"Who gave you Authorization?"

"Take it easy, Specialist. We're not stealing them. We'll turn them back in to the motor pool at the Vernal Armory. We're just borrowing them."

"Vernal?"

"Yeah, as I was saying, I'm the elected State Rep from Vernal."

The muzzle of the M4 lowered. "You look familiar." He dropped the M4 on its sling and stood up straight. "Where do I know you from?"

"I write on a blog..."

"You're the Ogre!"

"Yeah..."

"Man... Dude... I read your stuff all the time." He held out a fist. I knocked it with my own. "You can take them... whatever you want." He picked up the radio mic that was clipped to his web gear. "Stand down, gentlemen, the situation is cool." A squad's worth of soldiers came out from everywhere. Zack was being led by gun point back to us by a female soldier in a black beret. "It's cool, Speedy." The Specialist said.

Introductions went around, Specialist Meyers was the most senior enlisted. There was an officer on base, but he was a Doctor with the rank of Captain, who kept himself locked in his office. They were expecting more soldiers to show up, but no one else had come yet. The Guardsmen all had families to take care of first before they could break away and muster.

"Okay, Specialist Meyers. As a State Rep, I don't really have the authority to order anything other than a pizza, but I might make a suggestion. When you get enough people together, you guys need to start going out on patrols, killing zombies. The Utah Guard needs to take back Utah, one block, one street, at a time. Clear each house. Clear each shed. Clear each building. It's going to take time. Don't mess with people, and don't waste time in areas that the citizens have under control. You don't have time for that. Let them be, and move on. This isn't Martial Law. If you see people looting – it's not your problem. Find local police officers, they need to help clearing and searching, bodies will have to be taken someplace and burned. But the first thing that has to be done is reestablish chains of command. Are you guys in contact with Draper?"

"Zombies overran Draper... no one had a gun... they had no chance. No one is left."

"Damn. See... that's why I wanted everyone in uniform to wear a gun as part of the uniform. Make that SOP now. What about Tooele?"

"They got that place locked down tight. No one in or out. That's all I know. That's what the Captain said."

"Any news from the State? From the Capitol?" Meyers shook his head.

"Okay, standing suggestion then... as I said... Start clearing operations when you can. Help people when you can, but the mission is killing zombies." The soldiers seemed to have no problem with those orders.

"Where do we start?"

"Flip a coin," I shrugged. "I'd probably start working north first, clearing the residential areas."

"Roger that." Meyers said with a grin.

"We could use a hand hooking up some trailers... and... say... can I get a peek into an arms locker?"

Twenty minutes later we were ready to roll in a three-truck convoy, each rig with a trailer, fueled up and we had extra fuel cans ready to go. We could drive all the way to Vernal if we had to. But first, we had to check out the arms locker.

The Arms Locker

"You guys don't ever use these anymore?" I held up a LAW rocket. "That's ancient stuff. You can have them."

"Oh yeah!" I put the LAW back in the crate "Private Daniels, if you would take these and put them in my Humvee, I would appreciate it greatly."

"Yes, sir." Daniels grabbed the whole crate like it was nothing and packed it out. Did he just call me "sir"? I shrugged it off and grabbed an M204 and checked it out. Zack picked up a SAW.

"Big Medicine. I like this one. I'll trade you for this." He unslung the PSL off his shoulder and handed it to Meyers, who took it.

"Deal. I always wanted one of these," he said, admiring the rifle. Zack had packed an M249 SAW in Iraq, and he was good with them. I didn't really see anything really that I wanted, but snagged some fragmentation grenades.

Daniels had returned from packing the crates of LAW's out.

"Daniels, these grenades..." The PFC looked at the crate and shrugged. He packed it out to my Humvee as well.

Meyers was still admiring the PSL, "So what are you guys planning on doing?"

"We've got to meet up with some folks, work our way up to Hill Air Force Base to catch a ride back home to the Uintah Basin."

"You can't. Salt Lake City is crawling and from what I heard, Hill is a ghost town. No contact."

"We've got a friend up there. We've been in contact." I picked up an M4 and stripped it down. "He's got a ride secured," I said as I started swapping parts with my Rock River. I traded out the bolt carriers and lowers, but kept my upper, grip and stock. I tried the trigger and found it sucked compared to the Crusader trigger I gave up. Now, my M4 was really an M4. I picked up another M4 for Kevin and slung it.

"You guys have any NVGs?"

Meyers pointed.

I grabbed a few sets as Daniels came back in. "That ammo." I pointed to a stack of ammo cans. Daniels swore under his breath as he bent down to lift the heavy cans. "Hey, Daniels" He looked up. "Use that." I pointed to a hand-truck standing in the corner. He looked at it for a second before he realized he could have been using it all while. "The whole stack."

I have to admit, for an E-3, Daniels could swear like an accomplished E-7. I went outside and saw the sun would be setting soon. As I passed Kevin, I unslung the M4 and pushed it into his arms. "Check the Aimpoint and make sure it has working batteries." Kevin was dumbstuck, as if I had just handed him a winning lottery ticket. Put a set of NVGs in each Humvee, which were by now attached to trailers and gassed up. Daniels finished loading the ammo into the back seat of my Humvee, along with the other goodies. It seemed like we were taking a lot, but considering the massive quantities they had, it wasn't even a drop in the bucket. They wouldn't even miss the LAWs.

Zack fondled the SAW, doing function checks and getting it ready to rock and roll.

"You guys don't happen to have an M-60 do you?"

"Yeah." Meyers pointed to a locker.

I felt giddy. That was my favorite. I opened an old locker and in there was a couple M-60 machineguns standing up in there. I looked them both over and saw that they were slightly neglected. I stripped them both down and examined the parts, putting the best parts in one gun. Once it was assembled, I cradled it in my arms. The second M-60 I put back together and returned it to the locker.

I held out my hand. Meyers threw me a salute first, then gave me a shake.

"You're a State Rep so if there is no one left at the Capitol, I think that makes you Governor or something like that."

I about choked. "Yeah, let's hope there is someone else."

"I think if there was anyone left, we'd have heard from them. In the mean time, we'll just consider you the acting Governor of Utah."

I chuckled on my way out. Kevin was stretching, standing by his Humvee. I threw him his new M4. "Hey thanks."

I circled my finger in the air. "Saddle Up!"

We pulled out of Camp Willams and turned left, back the way we had come. We had to make it to Cabela's. Instead of heading to Lehi, we turned left again down a small road that went past the State Police training track and across a small bridge over the Jordan, and into Thanksgiving Point. From there, we drove through a fence, stopping long enough to cut the wires with my Leatherman. While we were stopped, Zack was up in the turret of his Humvee with his SAW. While I was cutting he let loose a couple long bursts and killed a few zombies about 400 yards away. I shook my head as I climbed back into my rig. Zack was just grinning from behind his sunglasses.

We soon pulled into the Cabela's parking lot. We didn't see any people, but I had a feeling there were some around. There were bodies of what had been zombies laying on the pavement. I could see the glitter of spent casings across the ground as well. I pulled in front of the door and the other two Humvees pulled in behind me. I looked inside the store through the windows. The doors were shut, and I couldn't see anything moving inside. I picked up the microphone hanging off the dash, keyed up the loudspeaker, and then thought better of making loud noises. I just got out of truck. I quickly looked at my M4 and my 930SPX and decided on the shotgun. I hate 5.56mm inside buildings.

As I approached the doors, I called out, not too loudly. "Ben! Hey Norseman! You here?"

From under a pile of camo I saw the barrel of a big rifle move. Up from the pile, popped the close-cropped head of the Norseman. "Ogre!" He opened the doors and I got a big Nordic Hug. "I saw those Humvees coming up, and I didn't know what to expect. I was looking for a Chevy, so I had to be ready."

Just past the camo pile there was a camo tarp. Ben threw the tarp off and there gleamed a big, shiny Gatling Gun, the one from the Gun Library. I laughed. "What if it wasn't me?"

"That would have been real interesting."

"I bet!"

Zack and Kevin came up and I made the formal introductions. "Is the building clear?"

"It is now." Ben held up his rifle. It was a gorgeous Winchester 1895 in .405 Winchester. I nodded my approval, very nice. Ben was decked out in the best clothes Cabela's had to offer with a nice hunting vest over the top. The cartridge loops on the vest sported large brass .405 Win cartridges where I think it was meant to hold shotgun shells. He looked ready to safari in Africa like a character from a Hemingway novel.

Kevin motioned to his rig and Sarah and the kids piled out, heading to the restrooms. I looked around. The sun was setting over the mountains. From this vantage point I could see lights on in the city as street lights came on. Some areas remained dark. "We should rest here for the night."

Kevin and Zack both nodded in agreement. Since the Humvees were loaded with stuff and we didn't want to lose them by someone else coming up and helping themselves, we decided to do a security rotation. We grabbed some good Motorola radios, with head sets, and set them up. All the adults had one, so we could all be in communication. Plenty of spare batteries were available, so we took all of them.

I don't know how you would spend the night in a store like Cabela's, but I was completely beat. When I woke up earlier that morning, the day was just a normal day for me. Now, here I was, slaying zombies all day, stealing trucks and stuff, and I just might even be the Governor of Utah for all I knew. I was tired to the bone. I probably could have slept on tile and have been just fine. But that's not what I did. I pulled out a big air mattress, filled it up with an electric pump, laid out a really nice sleeping bag, and found a soft, thick pillow that looked like a great big trout. Sarah followed suit and put the kids on air mattresses inside a tent that the store had on display. Kevin made some sandwiches from sliced elk meat. I opted for the wild boar Bratwurst. We ate our fill, drank some refreshing beverages, and next thing I knew, I was out like a light.

Ben kicked me awake at about 2:00AM. "We've got company. Zack's outside, in his Humvee turret, keeping low, but keeping ready on his SAW."

I keyed my radio, "What do you have, bro?"

Zack whispered into his radio, "I've got movement, lots of zeds on the road coming up here into the parking lot, and I can see lots more to the southeast away from us, but they are moving slow. Looks like a migration from Alpine."

"What are the zeds nearest us doing?"

"They are just wandering around, not really coming for us, but they are getting closer."

"So they don't know we're here."

"No, probably not. They are quiet... no moaning."

"Put down the SAW."

"I like my new SAW."

40

"It's loud. You'll attract more than you can kill."

"I don't know... I can kill quite a bit."

"I'm sure you can, but how many zombies are out there?"

"Good point. I better use the Hushed AK just in case."

"Don't fire unless you have to. Keep me posted."

"Roger."

If one of these zombies nearby lets out a moan, it could bring all the zombies from Alpine down on us. I looked over at Ben. "We might have a problem."

We only had two guns that were quiet enough. My Glock pistol and Zack's AK. Ben and I started shopping the gun counter. Cabela's doesn't have the selection that Basin has, but they do have some good guns. They did have a PS90, which I grabbed. Not for me, I don't really care for it, but the 50-round magazines and light recoil would be ideal for Sarah protecting her little ones.

Ben pointed out certain guns, but they were loud. How loud was too loud – we didn't know. "I've got an idea."

Behind the mountain, under the cafe... Archery! Ben looked at the bows and didn't seem too excited. "You are kidding right?"

"This will be fun," I said as I picked up a PSE Stinger compound and handed it to Ben. The Stinger was a simple bow that already had a sight and an arrow rest attached. Hopefully the guy that put it together took some time to at least get it lined up right. It looked okay. I grabbed another bow and tied on some string loops, quick and nasty, but it would hold. Releases, a good old Hurricane worked. I didn't have time to cut arrows and glue in the inserts, so we just grabbed all the arrows from the range. "Help me out here."

We unscrewed all the field tips and started screwing in broadheads of every make and model. We had a couple good bundles of arrows, and the empty packs or broadheads littered the floor.

We needed to get high up so we looked for a roof access. We found it in the upstairs corner of the store, through a door and up a ladder. We took our bows and arrows, and we were soon on the roof looking down over the group of zombies. It was very dark with no stars and no moon. Off in the distance we could see city lights and fires. I nocked an arrow and hooked up the re-lease. Ben did the same. "How far do you think it is?" I asked Ben.

Ben looked at it, "About 60 yards counting the angle."

I keyed the radio, "Zack, get ready. I'm going to try something."

"Where are you?"

"On the roof."

I pulled back on the bow and aimed with the bottom pin on the sight. The zombies were aimlessly wandering around, slack-armed, and heads hanging. I loosed the arrow and it flew fast, but lower than I wanted. It skipped off the pavement and sailed into the crowd, sinking deep into the pelvis of a woman zombie wearing hip hugger jeans and a t-shirt that said "I'm kind of a big deal". She looked down at the arrow and stopped walking. She just stood there. I adjusted the pin on the sight and nocked another arrow. I aimed at the same zombie. This arrow flew straight and true, right into her legs, sinking to the fletching. I made another adjustment and nocked another arrow. The female pin cushion looked around. This arrow sunk deep into her breast. "Almost there."

Ben had been watching and started making his adjustments off of a rough guess based on what I was doing. The Fem-ghoul looked up, right at me as I pulled back my next shot. Even in the low light, I could see the whites that used to be her eyes. I loosed the arrow as she started to open her mouth and fill her undead lungs with air so she could moan. The arrow sunk to the fletchings right through her eyebrow. The only sound she made was a thump as she fell forward on to her face.

"Nicely done, Ogre. My turn."

Over the radio I heard Zack whisper, "Are you guys shooting arrows?"

"Yeah, I just got one."

"Robin Hood, Zombie Killer."

Ben's bow bent back and I could hear him inhale deep and hold his breath. Then suddenly the arrow launched. I looked at the Zombies in time to catch a glimpse of the arrow sinking into the bald head of a zombie that looked like John Goodman, who fell like a puppet with cut strings. "Nice!"

It didn't take long before we were having some fun on the roof. After a while Ben had dropped the last zombie. We had three arrows left. Ben looked at his bow and regarded it with approval. "Not a bad bow."

"I think we're clear," Zack whispered through the radio. We left the bows and the remaining arrows on the roof and went back downstairs. Kevin was sitting in a camp chair surrounded by ammo cans and magazines for his M4. He was methodically loaded them up, putting them in a Cabela's brand messenger bag. He was loading up FMJ rounds from the green bulk cans. I went up the ammo section and pulled a bunch of Hornady ammo. 55 grain V-Max and 60-grain TAP FPD. I unfolded a chair and sat down next to Kevin. "How you doing, Kev?"

He didn't look up. "If you guys didn't come when you did..."

"You held up. You protected your family. You did good."

"Five minutes later it would have been too late, we'd be done."

"Yeah, it was close, but your kids are safe. Your wife is safe. We can't ask for more than that."

I started loading all the empty magazines in my ruck and topping off the mags in my vest. Sarah came out of the tent.

"Can I help?"

I slid the PS90 over to her. "Nope, but you can load up your own though. You're a big girl."

After showing her how to load the strange P90 magazine, and getting her more mags and more ammo, Zack came up. Ben had relieved him on watch. "Good idea."

Zack found another chair and soon we were all sitting there in silence with the only sound being brass cartridges clicking into magazines. I had not realized how much ammunition I had gone through. The worst part was that I didn't know how much more ammo I needed. Rifle mags, all filled with ballistic tipped ammo. Pistol magazines all filled with hollow points. I even grabbed a few more magazines and filled them too. That all being done I went and laid back down on my air mattress. I was instantly asleep again.

When I woke up, I called a head check. Ben was with the kids looking at the fish, lecturing on what they were, where they lived, and how to catch and eat them. Kevin and Sarah were shopping, both had carts full of stuff. Zack was pissed. He had paid a visit to the Gun Library. There was a space in the Gun Library with a take that said "FS-2000", but the related rifle wasn't there. He was back outside in the Humvee turret with his SAW. Everyone was okay.

After I cleaned up in the bathroom and changed clothes into fresh Cabela's gear, I felt a lot better. For breakfast I gnoshed on an elk sandwich and downed it with cold Mountain Dew. We started taking stuff out to the Humvees as the sun began to rise. I grabbed a lot of gear in a bunch of sizes for all my boys. Good coats, gloves and boots, MRE type meals made for civilians, and packs of batteries filled the back of my Humvee... along with, of course, more ammunition.

"Where are we going to head next?"

"Draper."

"I thought you had a rule about Draper. You don't go to Draper."

Suddenly the lights in the building went out, and we looked around in the dark. Life had suddenly become more complicated.

"We need to see about Steve. We've had no contact with him."

Zack pulled out his cell phone. "No Service."

I'd expected this would happen, so it was no surprise. But it was not very helpful. Alright.

Outside, Ben was trying to figure out how to mount the Gatling up on the turret of Zack's Humvee. He had brought cases of .45-70 ammunition, every can of powder the store had, and every primer. I looked over his haul. "Good thinking. What about case lube?"

Ben popped a cotter pin into the mount and patted the big, shiny Gatling. "I'm getting to it."

Ten minutes later the convoy pulled out of Cabela's having raided everything we could fit into the vehicles, including packs and sleeping bags and tents.

We didn't even think about getting on the freeway. I-15 was a huge mess, an overturned tractor-trailer blocked the on ramp anyways. We took the Frontage Road that went alongside the freeway, and just bypassed much of the problem. I was driving point, Kevin and Sarah in the second vehicle, and Zack drove Tail End Charlie, with Ben manning his .45-70 Blinged out Gatling gun. He was wearing Goggles and looking like he was having a good time of it.

I keyed the radio, "Ogre to Norseman."

"Go for Norseman."

"Does that thing even fire?"

Over the roar of the Humvee's engine and tire noise, I could hear the stuttering fire of full power .45-70 Government as Ben ripped into a stopped UTA bus on the freeway.

"Yup. She works perfectly, Governor." I could hear the grin in Ben's voice.

"Zack!"

I could hear laughing over the radio. I just shook my head and laughed too.

As we drove down the north slope of Point of the Mountain, I looked ahead at the situation. Draper was a dynamic, throbbing hell hole during the best of times. I wasn't looking forward to this place now.

We started passing stopped vehicles as we got closer. Suddenly I stood on the brakes and stopped the truck. The other Humvees pulled up into flanking positions as I jumped out. Up ahead a woman was running our way. She had blood on her, she was wearing jeans and a torn shirt that flew back with her long, black hair. Even from a distance I could see that she was not a zombie. I could see fear in her face, and I could see hunger in the faces of those that followed. I waved and yelled to her, "Come on! Come here! This way!" Her stride lengthened as she put on some speed, increasing the distance between her and her pursuers.

The zombies were yelling unintelligible, garbled sounds that were not any sort of language but communicated excitement. I considered the sounds as the woman streaked past me and dove through the driver's door. I immediately opened fire with my M4 as Zack unleashed his SAW. The noise was almost deafening. Ben's Gatling gun made sure it was. My rounds tore into zombie heads better than before thanks to the ballistic tipped ammunition. For the first time I flicked the selector lever all the way around and held the trigger down. The gun ran past what would have been a 3-round burst and continued for another 9 rounds before I let off. An M4A1 lower.... nice... full auto instead of the stupid 3-round burst. The gun stopped and I tilted my gun over. The bolt was locked back on an empty magazine. I flicked the gun over as I pressed the magazine release and the mag went flying. A fresh magazine slammed into the mag-well and I hit the ping pong paddle and exercised better trigger control.

Zack didn't bother with trigger control. He fired in long strings, cutting zombies down on the run. He only stopped long enough to reacquire more targets. For Zack's volume of fire, I have to admit he didn't waste rounds. Every round he fired went into a zed. Ben's Gatling however, was ridiculous. Each round penetrated one zombie through and through and into the zombies behind. I guessed his rounds were zipping through at least five or six zekes before they stopped. Ben was cranking the gun hard, letting it roar. Every once in a while, he'd stop and pull out a prefilled loader, and the gun would roar to life again. He was a machine, but he wasn't smiling about it. I picked off some zombies, but Ben and Zack mowed them down. When Zack ran dry, he called out "Reloading" and instantly popped open is loading tray cover and laid in a new belt and hooked on the carry pouch all in one movement. While he worked his gun, I let my M4 bark. It felt small in my hands compared to our machine guns. *I think I need more firepower.*

I emptied three magazines and suddenly it was quiet. I could still hear the echoes of the gunshots, but it was quiet, nonetheless. The zombies were gone. I looked into the truck. The woman with the long, dark hair was sobbing, curled up in a ball in the footwell of the passenger side. She was bleeding and crying in hysterics with shuddering sobs punctuated by screams. Hysterical woman... in my Humvee... with large breasts pushing out through the torn shirt. Nice ones. Both of them. I tilted my head and considered my possible courses of actions, trying to find one that didn't include my wife killing me when she found out.

I turned around and keyed the radio. "Ogre to Sarah... I need you over here. Right now, please."

Hysterical Hot Latino Woman

We stood around the idling Humvees, waiting for Sarah to get the hysterical woman calmed down.

After a while we found out her name was Rosa and she worked at the Cafe Rio in Draper. She had locked the doors and hidden in there over night and thought she could sneak away. She lived downtown in Salt Lake and thought she could catch a Light Rail or something. She was cut and scratched, but not bitten. Sarah was doing her best talking to her, but Rosa was a native Spanish speaker, and Sarah wasn't. I handed Sarah a t-shirt I had snagged from Cabela's. It was too small, but I thought it would look fine on her. I was right, it looked *great* on her. Sarah gave me a glare, but didn't say anything about the undersized shirt.

When Sarah got Rosa calmed down enough, she explained to her that Zack was a Spanish speaker and that she would be safe riding in Zack's truck. As Rosa slithered bustily out of the Humvee, she looked up at me with large, brown, doe-like eyes. "Gracias, Senior Ogrrre." I liked the way she rolled the "R", and after Sarah had wiped the blood off her face... good gracious this girl was gorgeous!

"You are welcome, Rosa." She pulled herself up to her full height of about four foot ten and walked with pride to Zack's rig. Before she opened the door to the front passenger seat, the radio buzzed. "I love you, bro." I had to laugh. Ben, who had been topping off his Gatling and his loaders looked up at Rosa and dropped a loader full of .45-70. She was an impressive figure. I was smiling when I noticed Sarah standing there, glaring at me.

She punched me in the shoulder. "Pig."

I laughed again and jumped into my Humvee.

"Kevin to Ogre."

"Go for Ogre."

"How am I in trouble for anything?"

"You're married." I answered as I pulled forward, rolling over crunching and squishing zombie bodies.

We snaked our way through Draper, past the intersection with the Cafe Rio's, pushing small hybrid cars out of the way as we went. Zombies were everywhere. Zack was up in the turret with his Hush-K while Ben drove. Any zombie that took too much notice of us or came too close, got riddled by 7.62x39 Hornady V-Max.

We pulled into Steve's apartment complex. Zack and I, with our less than loud weapons up, made our way between cars up to Steve's building. As we went, I looked for a familiar white car, but didn't see it. At the door, I knocked softly and waited. Then I knocked again, a little louder in the classic "Shave and a Haircut" pattern. Zombies wouldn't do that, so anyone inside would know zombies are not going door to door. No answer. I went around to a window that had the curtains pulled partially aside so I could see in. I saw nothing moving inside, and the apartment was tidy, with no signs of violence or horror inside.

Behind me I heard a moan and looked in time to see a raging zombie running at me at full tilt. He was on me in a blink. Zack had been back at the front door in case someone answered and probably didn't hear anything. The zombie slammed into me so hard I heard ribs crack, my knee twisted and popped and I bit my tongue. My Glock 22 went flying. The snarling zombie was all teeth, having no flesh anywhere around his mouth. His eyes were sunken and yellowish white. I grabbed his shirt and used my right hand to push him up, away from me. The zombie was unbelievably strong and it was all I could do to lock my elbow to keep the thing off me. The easiest weapon I had access to was my knife, a large Becker Combat Bowie from Ka-Bar. The zombie had no flesh on its finger tips either, and they frantically racked me, not so much like claws, but more like a Garden Weasel.

This was nothing even remotely human in this creature any more; it was a wild thrashing animal. Its teeth clicked as it struggled to bite me, but I managed to get the Becker out and I pumped it up into the zombie's chest. The blade was cutting wide gashes all the way through, coming out the thing's back, but to no effect. I had no leverage to get a different angle with the blade, so I had to make a risky move. This zombie had clawed my face, knocking my glasses off, and pissing me off. I let my right arm bend, letting the zombie drop onto my forearm and I was able to roll it off me enough for me to get a blow in with the big knife in my left hand.

I roared as I swung, putting everything I had into it. The zombie's head flew off its neck and landed on top of a bush, with its teeth still chattering, trying to bite me. "freaking zombie mother..." I was still swearing as I picked up my Glock 22 and stood up. Zack came running around the corner with his AK ready. I was bleeding, pissed off, and heavily armed. Becker in my left hand, Glock in my right, cussing at two hundred miles per hour. I shot the severed zombie head until the slide locked back. "Whoa, bro! Easy man. Slow your roll."

I looked over at my brother and stopped the flood of profanity. I started to breath again.

"Are you okay? Are you bitten?"

I had to think about that. "No. I'm not bitten. Shredded but no bites." I looked around for my glasses. They were busted in half. "For hell's sake." I bent down to pick them up and all of a sudden my whole chest felt like I was hit with napalm. "Aarrggh!" I fell to my hands and knees, "I think I have some broken ribs." I grabbed my ribcage but I couldn't feel anything but pain and M16 magazines. It hurt to breath.

Zack picked up the two halves of my glasses and helped me up. I was hobbling pretty good as my knee was swelling and I held my chest. Zack helped me back to the trucks. As we rounded the corner and came into view, everyone jumped out of the trucks, including the kids and Rosa. "Ogre!" I must have looked horrid. I pulled off my vest and threw it on my hood so I could breath better. It didn't help. "Yeah, I got some busted ribs"

"You're bleeding pretty bad." Sarah dug through the loot from Cabela's looking for one of the first aid kits. Rosa started spouting off rapid-fire Spanish. Zack answered. I made out the word "bitten" as he shook his head. "No, I'm not bitten, Rosa." She made the sign of the cross and said some more stuff in Spanish that I didn't understand. Sarah produced the first aid kit and started pressing my face with a pad of gauze.

"Man, I hate Draper."

Soon I had a wrap around my chest, and the bleeding from my face had stopped. The chest wrap was tight, and it felt better. I put my gear back on and retrieved my sunglasses from my pack. Prescriptions. As the world came back into clarity, Rosa said something in Spanish again. Zack laughed. "What?"

Rosa smiled, "I said you look better." She puffed out her magnificent chest, "More Macho. Strong!"

"I just got my ass kicked."

"You still look better." She insisted.

Sarah piped up, "I agree. You look better. We can see less of your face." Kevin laughed. I looked up at Ben who was back at his big gun and he just shrugged.

I dug out my favorite camo ball cap and pulled it down over my head. "We've got a long way to go. We should get moving."

We got back into the Humvees and got rolling again. Maybe I was pissed off. Okay, I know I was pissed, but I drove fast. We snaked our way up State Street deeper into the city as I swerved around cars and into zombies. My chest ached as I breathed. Looking behind me I saw I was putting distance on Kevin's rig and Zack was further yet. I slowed down and regained control of my hostility a little. Instead of driving fast, I stuck the barrel of my Mossberg out the wind and shot a zombie that was standing on top of a Volvo. It fell off the car and I almost dropped the gun. My ribs didn't like buckshot so much.

We drove passed some familiar territory when I pulled off to the left side of the road No one was around, no people, no zombies. It was quiet. Over the radio "Why are we stopping?" We were parked across the street from *Get Some Guns*, a class three dealer. A car had tried ramming its way into the store, and it rested crumpled up against the concrete barricades they put up just to prevent that sort of thing. Marks on the door told the story of people who tried to break their way in, but had failed.

I got out of the Humvee with something in my hand. "I need to grab some things," I answered into the radio. Kevin's rig pulled up behind mine, and Zack pulled up behind Kevin's. I was in a foul mood. "Should I knock first?" I didn't wait for an answer. I extended the LAW launch tube and leveled the rocket at the door. It had been a while since I fired one last, but I remembered exactly how to do it. The rocket slammed into the reinforced door and blasted it open. Get some guns.... great idea. I dropped the empty launch tube and grabbed my M4.

My knee was stiff and painful, but I limped across the street with a purpose. Inside, I saw there had been someone else inside the store. Its lower half was just behind the blown door, and the upper half was tossed over the counter. Milky eyes stared at me as it tried to pull itself up onto the counter to get me. I didn't have time for this. I pulled up my M4 and put a burst through its head. I've talked to guys at *Get Some* before, and they were nice enough fellows. But those guys were not here anymore. I looked around the store. Bushmaster ACR Enhanced Models. I keyed the radio "Anyone want an ACR?" I didn't wait for an answer. I grabbed one. There on the wall was an FS2000. I pulled it down and checked it out. I liked my M4 well enough, so I didn't really want anything. Zack came in slowly and I just held the FS out to him. "YES!" I knew he'd like it.

What I really wanted was in the back. Gemtech. AAC. Tactical Solutions. I grabbed all of them. Looking through the selection of suppressors, I found one that fitted my flashhider and I attached it to my M4. There was one for the SAW, a big one. I tossed that to Zack, "Here, use this." I didn't discriminate, really. I piled them all up into a Blackhawk pack and slung that over my shoulder and headed outside. At the Humvees I pulled out a couple cans for Kevin's M4 and for Sarah's PS-90. I threw the pack up to Ben who caught it with one hand. "Find something for your guns... I don't think there is one for your Big One."

Back inside Zack was fitting a can to the FS. "Oh Baby, I'm in love." I saw some movement out of the corner of my eye and I spun, bringing my M4 up to bear. Inside the firing range, a *Get Some* Employee stood there staring at us. He had the shirt, but his slack jaw, bite mark on his neck, and dead fish eyes told me he wasn't really there anymore. "Hey, you don't mind if we grab some guns, do you?"

The zombie just stood there. I picked up a Barrett 98 Bravo. It had a Nightforce Scope on it. I looked at the ammo racks and found plenty of .338 Lapua Magnum on hand. Nice! I grabbed it. I made a couple of trips, but ended up taking all the ammo too. Why do I need this gun? Well, I did have to leave my other long-range gun. As I was about ready to leave the store I looked over to the rental wall. "I think I love this little store." A pair of Uzi's hung on the wall. Not the micros, not the full-sized job, but a couple full auto "Mini-Uzi's". I slung my M4 across the back and picked up the Israeli submachine guns. And yes, they had magazines and suppressors. I loaded up a couple magazines and put them into firing condition. Holding up both Uzi's with a big grin on my face, Zack walked in. "Oh, no way, dude!"

"What? I love these things!"

"No, I can't let you go commando on me."

"Dude, these are classics."

"You want a headband too?"

"I've always loved Uzi's."

"Gonna go sleeveless?"

"They're cool."

"Grow a mullet and wear mirrored shades?"

"I'm not the one with a Camaro."

"That hurt. Don't you want that too?" Zack pointed in the case. Trijicon ACOGs. I went behind the counter and started acting very discerning. Picking and choosing and reading packages. "Which one do you want?" Zack asked.

"All of them." I scooped them all up at once. Back at the truck I pulled off my EoTech and threw on a 4-power with a green chevron reticle and a fiber optic for increased light. I took a minute to fire a few rounds at a parked car about a hundred yards away. I got it dialed in to my satisfaction. This was so much more accurate than my EoTech, and with the can on the muzzle. I was loving this. My anger was gone now. I was a happy ogre again.

Zach's POV

Meanwhile....
I waited outside of Cabela's in George's Humvee messing around on the Blue Force Tracker. With it, I could see every military vehicle that was logged on into the system. I checked in on the Camp Williams guys. I saw them driving around South Jordan. That was good, it meant they were still alive. Then I started looking further out. I checked what was happening at Ft. Sill, where I went to basic. There were still plenty of units moving around, including helicopters. Awesome. They had enough tanks and self propelled units there to run over any zombies. Also, the largest nearby city was pretty small. I checked other places too like Ft. Dix in New Jersey. I didn't see any movement. The east coast was dead. Same with the west coast. More people meant more zombies.

Later on I watched as George rained arrows down on nearby zombies. I never understood the whole bow thing, but their silence was proving pretty useful.

One good thing about this whole situation was that I didn't have to pay Cabela's prices anymore. I filled my Humvee up with every round of 7.62x39 that I could find. Hopefully I wouldn't be doing any more raids into Salt Lake Valley. I grabbed a few guns and enough ammo for them. It wasn't for me, but for people back in Vernal. The more people with guns the better.

Eventually Norseman came out and replaced me at guard duty. I went in and saw everyone having a magazine-loading party. The only AK mags they had there were TAPCO plastic ones. They were alright, but not my favorite. Still, a backpack full of mags was never a bad thing.

Then I looked over and saw George laying down on an air mattress.

"Where the heck did he get that?" I asked. They showed me the mattresses and I filled it up. If there was one thing I hated it was camping. Any bit of comfort or luxury I could find, I'd take it.

In the morning we were on the road again, heading towards Draper, a place neither me nor George really wanted to visit, even without the zombies.

Suddenly the convoy stopped. I angled my Humvee to get a view of what was going on. There was a screaming woman running away from a small crowd of zombies. Crap! I jumped out of the Humvee with my SAW and raised it. George was firing away with his newish M4. I waited for the girl who looked hot from a distance to get out of the way and then I held the trigger down. I felt the familiar, constant recoil of the SAW as it went full auto. The weight of it let it rock on full auto while staying very stable. I did short, controlled bursts like I learned from *Aliens* and aimed my shots. I watched as the zombies fell away like I was using a weedwacker. I forgot how much fun a SAW really was.

Once the zeds were dead, I waited while they got Sarah to go up and talk to the woman. I was a bit curious because the chick looked hot. I hoped it wasn't one of those girls that looked good from a distance, but up close were beasts.

I was a bit surprised when they sent the girl to my Humvee. As she walked up to my Humvee, I saw that she was indeed pretty. Her shirt was a bit tight, but I didn't mind.

"Hola," I said.

"Hola. Soy Rosa."

"Rosa? Mucho gusto. Soy Zach."

It turned out that she did speak English, but wasn't comfortable with it. We chatted on the way to *Get Some Guns*. I loved the selection that *Get Some* always had. It was my kind of gun store. It was full of class 3 stuff. I was still kicking myself for trading my PSL so when I went in, the first thing I was going to look for was a replacement.

However, when I went inside, after George blew the freaking door off, I saw him standing there holding an FS2000. It was like at the end of the long quest, my holy grail was before me. I took it and held it in my hands, savoring the feel of the thing. This should be ideal for shooting from a vehicle; it also just looked really cool, and that was what truly mattered. I wasn't going to survive the apocalypse looking like a dork. No, sir.

I quickly located the one PSL they had in the store and began loading all the cans of 7.62x54r in my trailer. Rosa was in the Humvee holding her cell phone out of the window trying to get a signal. I didn't try to correct her.

Back inside I loaded up a few more guns, a SCAR, a P90, a full auto Krink and two Skorpion pistols. The Skorpions I attached to my belt, in case I had to look like a total badass and wield both of them at the same time. The necessity might come up.

"Wait, you have issues with my Uzis, but you're sporting those?" George asked.

"Heck yes I am. These are so much cooler than Uzis."

"And far less effective. At least Uzis actually work."

"Don't be a hater."

"I'm not a hater."

"You're hating. That makes you a hater by definition."

"That would be someone that frequently is in the act of hating. I'm just hating this once."

"You're participating perfectly in the form of being a hater."

"Whatever. I'm going to find a bandana now."

"Don't forget your sleeveless jean jacket."

I thought about giving Rosa a gun, but she'd be far more dangerous to me than the zeds. Maybe once we get her back to Vernal we could take the time to properly train her.

Ogre's POV

*W*e piled our selves and stuff back into the convoy and headed north again. We turned off State in Murray and stopped on the side of a wide main road.

I didn't want to pull in as the Humvees are not the most stealthy, and with the trailers, I didn't want to get held up. Gundoc's house was just down the hill from us in a little cul-de-sac. Wanting to redeem myself from Draper, I told Zack to stay with the convoy. Everyone's guns were hushed up, so they could take care of a lot of business without attracting too much attention.

I worked my way down through the trees onto Joe's street. From there, I went along white picket fencing to Joe's driveway. I was almost there when a pair of zombies came out the front door of the house across the street. I put the green chevron on the nose of the first zombie. The sound was not that of a gunshot. There was a thump to it, the sound of the action cycling, the ejected brass, and the bullet's crack as it zipped out and smashed through the skull of the zombie. That was impressively quiet compared to a naked M4 muzzle. The next zombie's head exploded before I pulled the trigger. *What the?*

The radio crackled, "Got your back."

Zack was kneeling up on the main street with his hushed and ACOG'ed FS-2000. I approached the corner of Joe's drive way and sliced the pie as I worked my way around it. At the end of the driveway by his house, there was Joe. Standing there, arms limp at his sides. His head was down.

"Oh no..."

I didn't realize that I had said it out loud. Joe suddenly looked up, saw an armed man crouching at the end of his driveway. In a blink, Joe was gone. I caught a glimpse of a weapon in his hand as he darted for cover.

"Joe!" I called out. "Joe, it's, me... George! I'm coming in." I lowered my gun and stood up, walking slowly, letting my weapon hang on the single-point sling.

"George?"

"Yeah, bro. The Ogre is here!" Joe came out and threw me a hug.

"Man, am I glad you're here."

"Dude I saw you standing there and thought they'd infected you for a second!"

"Yeah, that." He pointed to the body, half on the driveway, half on the grass. "You shot my next door neighbor."

"I'm sorry."

"Don't be. I've wanted to do that for years."

"How's your family, Joe?"

"We're good. We're all safe."

"We came to get you just in case you weren't." I explained what we were up to, and what the plan was. Joe nodded, but they had other plans. Their truck was loaded up with gear and supplies, and they were going to go to Colorado to his wife's family's place in the mountains. Sounded good to me.

"You set on weapons?" He had one of our Crusader Broadswords. "Follow me." At the trucks Zack and Ben bumped knuckles with Joe. "Hey guys." I gave him an ACOG that was matched to .308 and an AAC suppressor for it. "Hold on." I pulled out a case of 150-grain Hornady Superformance ammo. "Here, you're going to need it, but I hope you won't need all of it. Oh, and stop by *Get Some Guns* on your way. I left the door open. You might want to pick up a few things."

Joe and I parted ways for the time being. I had a feeling that I would see him again soon. I was also getting the feeling that most of my friends on *WeTheArmed* were all going to be just fine, wherever they were. Ben would have been fine too, but who wants to battle zombies alone? It's more fun with friends.

We hit the road and made our way to the freeway and jumped on I-15 heading north to Salt Lake. The traffic going into the city was almost non-existent. It was easy to make our way and we were making good time. We stopped on a high overpass. This place was a pretzel of freeway on ramps and off ramps. I got out and looked at the freeway below us. This junction to I-80 could take us home, if the entire freeway in view wasn't completely jammed up. Zombies were milling around below us in thick numbers. Ben, Zack, Rosa, Sarah, Kevin, we all looked below us. "Look at all of them. I've never seen so many. I want to have a little fun with them."

I grabbed a heavy pack from the back of my rig and pulled it over to the edge. I rooted in the pack and pulled out a simple flare. I lit it and dropped it over the edge. We looked and saw zombies that had been milling around lethargically, suddenly become energized. They leapt to the flare looking for fresh meat.

I pulled something else out of my pack. It was round and heavy for its size. I pulled off the safety and pulled out the pin.

Zack looked at what I was doing and shook his head smiling.

"Fire in the hole," I said as I gave the fragmentation grenade a light toss. We ducked behind the concrete and heard a loud crack that reverberated the air. We looked back down. "Look at that. We made a clear spot."

More zombies flooded in replacing the ones that were gone, so we dropped more grenades, and soon it became a game. Zack cheated and let one cook off a couple seconds before he tossed it over. This one air burst and cleared a wide area of zombies.

The more zombies we blew up the more were attracted to the area. For every one we killed, a hundred came to take its place. A couple cars had ignited amidst the blasts. The smoke was rising up to our position, making seeing below difficult. It was time to get rolling again.

As we passed the turnoffs to down town, the traffic started getting thicker. This wouldn't do to get stuck in gridlock, so we took an exit, and went up an off ramp that was more open. Driving at high speed on the freeway into what was oncoming traffic was disconcerting, but we were actually making good time.

We passed Bountiful when we saw a Utah Highway Patrol car flip around and turn on its lights.

"We're getting pulled over." Zack said into the radio.

We, being good citizens, pulled over and stopped. I rolled down my window and looked at the trooper in the mirror. He got out of the car, hand on his weapon. He was walking strangely. He looked into Zack's rig and passed it. He was looking into Kevin's when I saw the blood on his arm. I opened my door and stepped out.

"Get back! Get back in your vehicle, sir!"

"Take it easy, son. You're hurt. You need help. Are you shot?"

"Get back in your vehicle, sir!"

This was strange. He's worried about me getting out of my Humvee, but didn't notice Ben and his Great Golden Gatling on top of the first one he looked at. He approached me with his hand gripping his pistol. "I said get back into... SIR!" I held my hands up and backed up towards my door.

"Okay, Trooper, I'll get back into my truck. It's cool." I didn't want to turn my back on him. As I stepped slowly back I noticed the ripped sleeve and that the trooper was sweating bullets. I keyed my radio, "Kev," I whispered, "get over here...we're going to take this trooper down. He's not well." The radio clicked twice.

"I said, SIR!" The trooper screamed. Kevin had quietly exited the truck, and with his M4, snuck up behind the trooper. As he closed in, I had to keep the trooper engaged.

"Did you get bit, Officer? Did someone bite you?"

The trooper's eyes rolled in his head and he staggered, but his hand was still on the butt of his pistol. "SIR!" He screamed again as he drew his pistol. The gun cleared the leather and he fired a shot into the ground in front of him. Kevin tackled the Trooper, coming in low, dropping his shoulder and catching the trooper behind the knees. I dove forward and grabbed the gun. The Trooper laid there on the ground, unmoving, but breathing heavily.

Kevin rolled the cop over and we looked at him. His eyes were rolled up in the back of his head. We looked at his arm. It was a bad bite. The teeth marks were deep, but certainly human – or post human – whatever you wanted to call it. Around the bites, the flesh was blackened and streaks of dark purple radiated from the bite up the arm. You could see discolored streaks going up the neck from the arm.

"He's turning."

Zack came up. "Is he okay?"

"No man. He got bit. Some time ago. He's turning into a zombie."

Zack pulled out his Beretta Storm and put a round through the Trooper's head. He didn't look up but what he said gave me chills. "If I was starting to turn, I'd want you to do that to me. I don't want to feel that change. If I don't do that myself – do it to me."

I could tell my brother was dead serious. He turned around and walked back to his rig. Kevin and I watched him, then we just looked at each other, then back at the Trooper. I bent down and read the name tag. "Leslie".

"I'm sorry, Leslie." I took the pistol and the magazines, but otherwise left him alone. I walked over to his cruiser and opened the door. The driver's side window was smashed. Broken glass was all over the interior. His car had been surrounded and attacked by the looks of the bloody handprints all over exterior. There was blood inside the car too, spent cases from Leslie's pistol, and empty shells from his shotgun were on the floorboards and some on the dash.

I picked up the radio and keyed the mic. "This is Utah State Representative George Hill, calling any station, over." I listened for a few seconds before an answer came back.

"This is Utah State Trooper John Douglas, go ahead Mr. Hill."

"We are on I-15 just north of the last Bountiful exit. We came across Trooper Leslie. He had been bitten by a zombie, looks like some time ago. Over."

The radio was quiet for a second. "He's dead now?"

"I'm afraid so." More silence was the only response. I asked "How many Troopers do we have available now?"

"Nine."

"Where are you guys?"

"All over. There are nine of us left now... in the whole state."

"Where are you right now?"

"I'm on State Street, just south of I-215. I'm here with a Salt Lake County Deputy."

"Roger that, John. Who's the highest-ranking Trooper that's left?"

"I think I am."

"John, I haven't been in any contact with any state official higher than myself. I'm not taking charge, but I'm making suggestions. I talked to some Guardsmen at Camp Williams last night and made some suggestions to them too. John, you and the other troopers are going to be under the Direction of the County Sheriffs until a Chain of Command is reestablished. If there is no Sheriff available, the highest ranking Deputy is in control in his County. You got that?"

"No, not really."

"The Sheriff is the highest ranking Law Enforcement Officer in his area of jurisdiction. He's an elected official and a Deputy represents the Sheriff. You troopers are law enforcement officers with no oversight at the moment.

Get it?"

He hesitated before answering. "Roger that."

"What are you guys doing right now?"

"Getting some more firepower."

I had to smile.

"Looks like someone was already here. They blew the door. They took a few things already, but most all the guns are still here. Looks like they took a couple rifles and a couple Uzi's. No accounting for taste."

I shook my head. Everyone is a critic. "Get what you need and get rolling. I would suggest clearing out a hospital, make sure we have EMS available. Not everyone that gets hurt becomes a zombie." I held my chest, which was aching pretty good.

"What are you doing?" The trooper asked.

"We're heading north to Hill Air Force Base. We have a ride to catch."

"Good luck."

"Keep your powder dry."

I went back to Zack's Humvee. Ben was scanning the area, keeping an eye on some zombies off in the distance. "Hey Zack, I was just thinking." Zack was playing with the Blue Force Tracker and explaining it to Rosa, who was riding shotgun with Zack's AK-47, wearing Zack's Taco Hat. She was still wearing the tight fitting camo t-shirt I had given her. She looked a lot better than when we first found her. Rosa had no family in Utah, no where else to go, so she had elected to stay with us. Zack was happy about that. He looked up, "Yeah?"

"Medical Supplies. We don't have any. If people are fleeing the cities and making it to the Uintah Basin, we're going to probably need more supplies. Even if they don't, we will eventually."

Zack just nodded. I motioned to the computer screen. "You got it up?"

"Yeah, I can see all three vehicles here. We can even send messages back and forth."

"That's pretty slick. So... anyways... I'm thinking we need to hit a hospital. There is a clinic ahead of us in Farmington, or there is a hospital back in Bountiful?"

"I'd rather go forward than back."

We headed north. The biggest thing in Farmington was the amusement park, "*Lagoon*". No one but the kids wanted to go to *Lagoon*. As we approached it, they got excited. Sarah's little girl got on the radio and pleaded her case for it. "I think *Lagoon* is closed right now, Sweetheart. Maybe we can all go when they open it again."

She made me promise, so I said okay. This is why I only had boys. I tried not to think about them and what was happening. I imagined that they were okay, with the boys reading some books and the wife burning cookies.

I followed my memory to get to the clinic. I remember a long time ago stopping in to visit an old girlfriend that worked there. Farmington, outside of *Lagoon* was a peaceful town hiding out between bigger cities. Unfortunately, a lot of people that lived here, worked in the cities, and after being infected, came home to infect everyone else. Signs of violence and horror were everywhere. We rolled slowly. Ben was riding high with his Gatling ready in Zack's rig. Sarah was driving the second Humvee and Kevin was up top with his suppressed M4. I didn't have a turret in my rig, which was a fact that I was regretting now. Maybe I could have had Rosa riding shotgun with me. Maybe I was safer this way. I wasn't afraid of Rosa, nothing would happen, I had no fantasy about that. I was afraid of my wife taking things out of context. I'd rather face a hundred zombies. Actually, I was pretty sure she was already mad at me because I didn't bring her.

I nosed my Humvee up against a stopped Volkswagon and pushed it out of the way. The VW rolled a little and bumped unto a mini-van. The mini-van had been apparently empty, but now all the sudden it was writhing inside. Children. White-Eyed little children clawed at the windows and the van rocked on its wheels. It looked like they had torn each other apart as they turned. There was an adult seatbelted into the front seat, but it was impossible to tell if it had been Mom or Dad driving. The children had eaten most all the flesh.

I rolled on.

I could hear Kevin's M4 open up and "Contact Left!" over the radio. I looked left, up a small tree-lined side street. Zombies, shoulder to shoulder, filled the street. They were lumbering toward our convoy. Farmington was suddenly a very bad idea. "Let's Roll! I answered into the radio. I glanced to the right and saw another pack of zombies coming our way. I hit the gas, and sped up as much as I dared. Stopped cars meant no real velocity and pulling trailers meant we could only maneuver so much. The zombies broke out into a staggering run, not the wild sprint we'd seen before. Evidently they didn't recognize the guys in the turrets as food... yet. They were only attracted to the motion and sounds and moaning from the little zombies in the mini-van. The streets had been clear of zombies just before and within moments of startling the kiddie-zeds, we had hundreds now. That was a fast response. Kevin and Ben were riding low, firing their hushed weapons as fast as they could. I cut the path through the debris, over the occasional body, around vehicles, and sometimes through fenced yards. The scores of zombies seemed to be getting closer as we went.

The rate of fire was impressive. Kevin had mastered the fast reload. He and Ben were holding them back, firing in every direction, but this rate was not sustainable.

Some zombies must have crossed a line because Ben dropped his rifle and grabbed the Big Gun. Whump! Whump! Whump! Whump! Whump! Whump! Whump! Whump! I could hear the Gatling come to life over my Humvee's engine and through my rolled up windows. I looked in the rear view mirror and caught a glimpse of Ben up there cranking the old Gatling. I could see Zombie heads exploding, bodies being blown to chunks.

I found an open road and turned onto it; this road had fewer vehicles on it and we were able to pick up speed. Soon we were pulling away from a flood of zombies that were pouring out of every side street and alley way. Kevin stopped shooting and radioed "I need to reload mags... getting low." We raced along 225, and I could see I-15 up ahead. We were able to speed up some more, and pretty soon all the shooting stopped.

This was too close. I could have gotten everyone killed. Great idea, good cause, but I didn't think it through. I wouldn't let that happen again. A raid on a hospital would have to wait for a better opportunity. I-15 was dangerous enough right now. We turned onto the on-ramp of I-15, and it was mostly clear.

My Blue Force Tracker suddenly lit up. Zack had said he put it into standby. There were indicators of our three vehicles, moving on the freeway, with an overhead map. That would have been handy earlier. A point appeared ahead of us marked "OBJ". An "Objective". A message appeared in a pop-up box. The BFT didn't have a mouse, so it must be a touch screen. I clicked it. There was only one word. "Rite Aid." I about slapped my own forehead. Why hit up a hospital or clinic, when a nice pharmacy would work just as well? Easier to get in and out. I tapped the screen again and a line appeared connecting me to the OBJ. It was marked ROUTE. I started to really like this gizmo and wished we had them when I was in. I touched the screen and dragged it down. Hill AFB we marked, as a unit designated "Mike" that was at Hill, and another unit marked "O.B.". O.B.? I didn't know what that was.

The route indicated a turn up ahead. Eyes back on the road, I could see the turn. There was an overturned car that was smoking, and a fire truck that was on its side. One of the best things about Utah was the wide roads. We only lifted off the gas as we went around the obstacles made of vehicles that were abandoned or crashed. The turn-off curved around a bend that made seeing ahead difficult. So when the woman stepped out in front of my Humvee, I only had enough time to recognize that she had her eyes clawed out, and her upper lip torn off. As she bounced off the hood, I glimpsed a nose ring. I was as relieved as I was startled, but I kept the Humvee on course. The zombie held on. Her head had left a dent in the hood, but she held on. She was snarling now.

"Guys, slow down. I've got to get something off my hood."

The other rigs backed off to give me some room as I rolled the window down. I took one of my Uzi's and held it out the window and sprayed a magazine full into the zombie. When the gun stopped firing, I slammed on the brakes and she went flying. As soon as she was off, I hit the gas again. My tires did what the bullet's didn't – destroy the brain. There was a small couple of bumps as I sped back up.

We made it almost to the Rite Aid pharmacy, but we couldn't get near it.

A multi-car pile-up that included a bus was blocking access. We would have to run in on foot. I wasn't looking forward to that.

"Top off your mags, Zack. We're going to have to stroll over there." I grabbed a couple extra mags that I had laying on the seat next to me.

"10-4. Give me a second."

"Ogre to Norse. Stay off the big gun until you don't have a choice."

"Roger that, Ogre. Gotcher back. And, uh... see if they have anything to drink. I'm getting sick of Mountain Dew."

I double-clicked my mic button to acknowledge. I looked back at Sarah and Kevin's rig. Kevin was up top already, keeping low in the turret, looking around. "Ogre to Kevin. How's it look?" I couldn't see anything from where I was.

"We've got a few zeds just behind the bus from you. Looks like they are having lunch. They're not paying attention to us. Another couple at the corner of the building, just standing there."

I looked around some more and didn't see anything else.

Zack radioed in. "I'm ready, bro. Let's do this."

Kevin chimed in, "Ogre's banged up and getting old. He's not moving like he used to. I can go." I could hear objections in the radio before Kevin's signal cut. Yeah, I'm not about to let him risk anything any more than he absolutely has to.

"I'm a better shot than you, Kevin. I don't have to outrun anything I can outshoot, but I appreciate the confidence boost."

"Ogre, I can make the run." Norse offered.

"You going to let Rosa run the Gatling?"

No reply.

Cross-dressing Zombies

*W*e both opened the doors to the humvees at the same time and stepped out. Zack was wearing his sunglasses but didn't have his tactical taco hat. Instead he was wearing a ball cap. I didn't want to take this as a bad luck omen or something, but I was suddenly less comfortable about this. I cinched the single-point sling up a little and flicked the safety off. I was locked and loaded and ready, but my knee was stiff and soar, giving me a pronounced limp as we moved quickly. My chest wasn't feeling any better either. I could grab some stuff for that and worry about it later. I've had worse.

We moved quickly to the bus and as I rounded the rear bumper I pressed the trigger and held it down. A stream of bullets cut down the feasting zombies. Zack's FS2000 barked several times as he was administering head shots. Brass made pleasant tinkling sounds as the empty cases hit the ground. I executed a tactical reload on the move as we headed to the building. Zack covered to the right side and to the rear as we moved, guns up, to the objective. The zombies by the building dropped easily with two well placed shots thanks to the ACOG's ability to allow greater precision.

We pushed our way into the pharmacy, shoving away a bin of discounted candy bars that had been shoved against the door. *There must be someone in here*, I thought as we moved past. We did a quick sweep of the store, but didn't see anyone, alive or dead.

"Grab a shopping cart."

Zack grabbed one as did I. We rolled them to the back of the store as that was where the actual pharmacy was located. As I passed the row of regular over the counter pain meds, vitamins, sleep aides, I raked my arm through them and dumped them into the cart. Zack did the same with the over the counter Cold and Flu and allergy meds. I like liquid Centrum; that's a good vitamin. I made sure I didn't miss those.

The door into the Doctor's Note area, was locked. As I put a burst of rounds through it, I had the thought that it was locked from the inside. That suspicion was confirmed when someone started screaming like they were being murdered, which, come to think of it, I'm sure they thought they were. I had to push this door hard as well, as there was a chair that had been propped up against the door to try to block it, but the chair slid. I lowered the M4 and brought up my Glock 22. I checked around one tall shelf, then another, when all the sudden I was struck in the head by a coffee mug. It rang as it bounced off my forehead. My eyes almost crossed as I pointed my gun at the figure that was picking up another cup. "STOP THAT!" I shouted. The cup sailed anyways and I moved enough that it struck my vest. Right over my cracked rib. It felt like I had just got shot. I think I had tears in my eyes from the pain, both head and chest, so I couldn't focus on who was throwing, but I wasn't about to take another coffee mug. I closed the distance with a lunge and used my elbow to land a blow that dropped the person to the ground. Zack rushed in behind me and stopped.

"Judas Priest, dude!"

"I know, just took a coffee mug to the brain." I was seeing spots. Zack went over to the person I had hit. I took my glasses off and wiped my eyes. I still didn't know what I had elbowed. When I put my shades back on, I saw the person crumpled to the ground had long hair and wore a floral print blouse and a skirt. Oh hell, I just hit a girl.

Zack suddenly jerked back, when the person looked up at me, I could recognize the depth of the voice as that not of a woman. "That monster hit me! I think he broke my nose! You saw that, he hit me!"

Jeff Harris. I recognized the voice and the face now. He used to be a dancer back in Vernal. I know this because he was my wife's dance partner, back when he acted somewhat male.

"Shut up, Jeff! You hit me first... twice."

"I thought you were going to rape me!"

"Your wishful thinking will get you nowhere."

"You're a brute."

"You've given me a headache before... but now... wow!"

Zack looked back and forth. "You know this guy?"

"Yup. I knew him when he was a guy. The cross dressing is new."

Jeff curled up into a ball and made weeping noises. I know some other guys that are homosexual, and they don't bother me in the least. But guys that act like helpless princesses get tedious.

Zack didn't say anything else. He just started to grab medications and toss them out of the pharmacy window into the carts.

"Jeff, go grab another cart. We'll need another."

"I'm bleeding over here, aren't you going to help me? You don't even care."

"I have a convoy of military trucks outside. Once we are done here, we're going to catch a ride back to Vernal, where there are no zombies. Now, you can stay here and cry about your boo-boo, or you can help, and save your own life. Wait a second. Are you crying?"

He was really crying. Oh hell!

As we about finished up looting all the pharmacy goodies, something dawned on me. *The other humvees were pretty full. Jeff was going to have to ride with me.* I let out a tired sigh.

We had five carts full of meds. I looked in the cooler, which had power, so everything was cold. No beer for Norse, but they did have orange juice. I grabbed him a couple big OJ's. Maybe we'd come across vodka. Norse would like that.

We started pushing the carts out the door and heading to the trucks. Zack and I both pushed two carts, as Jeff pushed his one. He was faster and practically ran with his cart to the Humvees.

The rattling of the shopping cart's wheels on the pavement made quite a racket. Heads started poking up in the bus, and some zombies started to make appearances. I was about tell Jeff to roll softly when a flying tackle took Jeff off his feet. Norse swung his M4 around, but the zombie was already on top of him. I didn't have an angle on the shot because right behind the zombie was the Humvees. Norse held his fire for the same reason. If he opened up, those rounds would have taken out Zack and I. I dropped the carts and started running as fast as I could limp, angling to the side to try to get a shot.

Jeff was screaming again as the Zombie tore at him. I was almost there when Jeff's screams were cut short by the zombie ripping out a chunk of his throat. When I had the shot, I took it. Four rounds of 55-grain V-Max opened up the zombie's head right then and there. Chunks of skull and brain tissue splattered all over. Jeff was clutching at his throat and kicking wildly. More Zombies came out at a dead run. Zack brought up his FS and started firing in one direction and Kevin and Ben opened up in others.

I went back to my carts and grabbed both with one hand. I dragged the carts along as I fired short bursts with the other hand.

"Come on guys!" Ben said through gritting teeth.

We were almost there as masses of zombies emerged, some loping along, others at full steam. We were instantly cut off from the Humvees. I dropped carts as did Zack and before we knew it, we were back-to-back firing and reloading. Kevin was being careful on conserving his ammo, but making accurate shots and dropping zeds left and right. Ben was doing the same with his M4. But the zombies were not looking at them; they were coming for Zack and I. Empty mags were starting to pile up, but we were managing to keep the zeds off of us at about a 10-foot distance. The more we killed, the more they came, but if they came within 10 feet, they got shot. Another empty magazine and I felt that I was on my last pouch. Zack ran dry first and drew his Beretta. I had the luxury of a couple extra mags, but at full auto, I burned through those quickly and then I was on my pistols, both Glocks in hand. When either of us said "Reloading" we spun around each other's backs to cover better. When Zack's pistol ran dry with no reloads, he pulled out his Cold Steel Recon Tanto and his AK-47 Bayonet.

Now the fight got personal.

When my last .40 cal rounds were expended, I let the Glock drop and pulled out my Becker Bowie and the smaller Becker Companion. A zombie grouched low, hissed at me and launched. I side-stepped the leap and let the big Becker come down across its neck as he went past. I swung again and make a cut across the eye of another one, deep enough to almost cut the top of the zed's head off.

Zack was targeting hands and arms. It's hard to grab with no hands. What he lacked in finesse, he made up for in anger and motivation. He was a dervish. Living in rural Utah and chopping wood every year, my pimp hand was strong and I was splitting heads like cord wood. I realized I was yelling in Gaelic, ancient curses. It was then I realized I was doing that at the same instant the zombies in front of me started exploding in chunks of blood and meat.

What the... ? I looked over to the trucks and I could see Norseman up on top with the Big Gun, cranking away like an engine. Some of his rounds were flying within mere inches of me. Zack was getting tired, his swings were slow. Kevin had run out of magazines and everyone in that rig was hurrying to reload magazines.

The shocker was when the door to the Humvee opened up. I saw the silencer on the end of the AK come around the door and above that was a black taco hat. Under the AK were two large breasts inside a tight camo shirt. She opened fire and zombies started dropping. The look on her face was that of a ferocious animal and not the pretty girl. We still fought with the blades but not for much longer. It was over as quickly as it had started. The zombies were laying still.

I was exhausted.

Rosa ran up to Zack chittering in Spanish and took him back to his Humvee. Norse and I got the carts and loaded the stuff into the Humvees. I still had room in my trailer, but we were doing pretty good. We were gearing up as I was drinking another Gator-Bull.

No one had noticed Jeff's corpse start to move again. He rolled one way, then another, and it looked like something pulled him up off the ground by strings. He didn't move like Jeff, who was a good dancer. He lurched, and jerked and came up behind me. Sensing the aroma of Channel No.5 or whatever smelly water he had worn, I spun around and punched straight through his forehead with the big Becker knife.

He dropped like a rock.

"Zack."

"Yeah."

"Don't tell my wife that I flatlined her old dance partner."

"Nope. I'm not telling her that. After all, you didn't flatline him. The zombies did that."

Good, I thought, because she would have been pissed.

"I will tell her though that you busted his nose, knocked him out and then after the zombies got him, you stabbed him through the brain to finish him."

"Come on. Let's go."

Zack started to laugh.

"That's not funny."

We were rolling again. Next stop, Hill Air Force Base.

Hill Air Force Base

I drove with my knee holding the steering wheel as I reloaded magazines. I had dumped all the contents from individual boxes of 5.56mm into a small bucket and dipped into that like it was movie popcorn. It was slow going but I needed to reload as there was no one in my rig to do it for me. My head hurt. My chest hurt. My arms hurt. My knees hurt. Everything hurt and this adventure was no longer fun. *What the hell was I doing?*

I looked in the rear view mirror. Following me were the other two Humvees. I could see faces in the second rig, a family that had survived hell. They were smiling. That sight instantly made me feel better. In the third rig, I could see my brother's gold rimmed sun glasses, and up top, shining like a beacon of destruction, a big brass Gatling.

The roar of the Humvee's cooling fan meant that listening to a stereo just wasn't going to happen. I-15 was not completely blocked. We snaked in between stopped cars, wrecked cars, and overturned and burned cars. The most common reason for the wrecked cars was the drivers who were turning into zombies while driving, which made crashing more likely to happen. As we rounded a Porsche, I glimpsed down to see that it had slid almost all the way under a Nissan Pathfinder during a collision. The Porsche was totaled, but the Nissan looked like you could get in and drive off the little sports car. The moral of that story is not to "Turn and Drive" I guess.

As we neared the Air Force Base, I turned to the Blue Force Tracker. Mike was clearly marked on the screen. Another mark was indicating another unit designated "O.B." This unit was sitting on the end of a long runway. It must be in an airplane. There was no one at the main gates, but the entry was blocked with abandoned trucks. We stopped just for a moment before we recognized a section of fence that was knocked down a hundred yards away. We rolled up to the curb and over the grass to the gap and entered.

Hill AFB is a large place, and navigating the base is something that can get the uninitiated lost even on a good day.

This wasn't a good day.

I don't understand how zombies light cars on fire so often, but there always seems to be a plethora of overturned and burning cars. It's like they are soccer fans or something. Okay, sure, I've lit up a few cars, but that was yesterday and I had no choice. I've not lit a car on fire all day! The Prius, that just felt good.

As our little convoy rolled around an overturned Osh-Kosh truck, I just had to wonder how that was even possible. That's a big truck. I caught movement between buildings. A glimpse of uniforms, that was probably another security team getting ready to ambush us when we stopped. Okay, let's just get this over with. I pulled my Humvee to a stop and waited for the soldiers to come out.

I didn't have to wait long. They came running at full tilt, but they didn't carry weapons. I saw blood covering the uniforms. As they came closer, I noticed their eyes looked like dead fish. *Oh great.* Within seconds they had my Humvee completely surrounded. They clawed at the windows, but couldn't get in. I let out a sigh and finished reloading my magazine and grabbed another empty one.

"Zack to Ogre."

"Go for Ogre."

"Why are we sitting here?"

"I'm reloading."

"Oh, well. Please, take your time then. I'd hate for more zombies to pile on us."

"Hey, you have a crew in your rig that can help reload your mags."

"You want Rosa to ride with you? She's entertaining."

"Sure, I... No." I wasn't sure where this was going. I pulled out an MRE bag and ripped open a pack of crackers and chased that down with some Gator-Bull. The zombies outside my window looked like they were hungry too, but I didn't feel like sharing. Once my last magazine was topped off, I tucked it into my pouch.

The moaning of all the zombies brought a massive number of undead into this area. My Humvee was completely surrounded with some zombies climbing on top. I put my rig into gear and started rolling forward. There was a lot of resistance as the Zombies seemed to want to push on the truck, but once I got over the first couple, it was much easier. I had the truck moving, through the zombies, who didn't catch the meaning of the fact that they were standing in front of a moving vehicle. It felt like I was driving over a rocky, dry riverbed, only bumpy and squishy at the same time. The popping sounds of bursting skulls made me cringe.

One zombie pulled himself up onto the hood. This was getting annoying as I now had a hard time seeing where I was going. He was also bleeding from large, open wounds. Thick, black blood was smearing over the vehicle as he thrashed about the hood. He got himself turned around and was now facing me, clawing at the window. I was tempted to shoot him through the glass, but I'd rather not ruin the window right now. I could see that the guy used to be an officer in the Air Force. I'm not sure what he did in the military, probably weather reporting. Either that or the guy was responsible for the distribution of reflective safety belts. Several of the more fashion conscious zombies were wearing them.

Then something happened. It sounded like a gunshot, then the front end of my Humvee dropped to the right. *What was that?* My tire had blown, and steering had become difficult. That's enough of this. I pushed the accelerator to the floor. The big engine roared in response, and the truck surged forward. The zombie on the hood was pulled off by other zombies as we moved through them. The Humvee wanted to pull to the right, but I was able to fight the wheel and keep it straight.

We came into a big, open area, dragging the mass of zombies with us. I sped up a little more and circled. Both rigs followed me.

"Ring around the zombies."

With the zombies no longer directly at my window I was able to roll it down. I used one of my Uzi's first and started thinning the numbers. The others did the same. Even Sarah was getting into it, firing her PS-90. I pulled out a grenade and tossed it into a thicker mass of zombies that had built up in the middle of the circle. The explosion sent pieces of post-people all over the place, some bits splattering my windows.

Zack's SAW did some impressive work too. He let the gun rock out with some long bursts of fire that mowed down zeds by the bushel. While Rosa drove, Zack was enjoying the turret time. Ben must have been in the back just taking it easy. After a while the zombies numbers were reduced to zero. Most of the zombies were in uniforms... none of them armed. They did have a lot of reflective safety belts, but those didn't seem to have helped much. I made a mental note to talk to someone about this.

The Blue Force Tracker had a route marked, and we started following it again. We drove to the EOD building first. I felt relieved when I saw the old T-62 Tank come into view. For some reason, about a dozen years ago, a T-62 showed up in front of the EOD building. What a tank had to do with EOD or the US Air Force was unclear to me. There was probably a story about it, but no one knew it.

My Humvee was getting hard to drive, and steering was difficult. As we approached the EOD building, I could see a couple guys standing outside. Mike was there, standing casually, with the butt of his Crusader Broadsword resting on his hip, sunglasses up on top of his head. Next to him was Tony, another EOD tech. He was decked out in full tactical gear and sunglasses like Mike was, but wore the addition of a cunning, orange knit hat. I pulled up to a stop, and the other trucks pulled into flanking positions.

"You guys sure took your sweet time getting here."

"I was having some trouble with my Humvee; it's not running right." I said as I climbed out of the truck.

Mike looked at the Humvee. "Well there's your problem."

I turned and looked. About five different zombie bodies were wedged up in the wheel wells, and I also had both front tires flat. I'm not sure how that happened, but I had to laugh.

"You look like hell, George. Not that you looked great before."

"Nonsense, I'm in my prime. You guys look like you stepped out of a Blackhawk Catalog – all clean and sharp looking."

"First general order – look cool."

We had some laughs and I got fist bumps from Mike and Tony.

"It's really good to see you guys. How have you been holding out?"

"Pretty good. We've got a little distance from the other buildings and we've been able to hold the zeds off from the roof. My Broadsword has been keeping them away, but they've not been bothering us for a while. I looked at Tony's rifle, a standard military SR-25 topped with a 1-4 scope. I nodded, "yeah, I can see guys have the hardware for it."

Mike motioned to Ben's Gatling. "Not as well as your crew." I looked up at the big gun, gleaming gold in the sunlight. It looked out of place on the top of a Humvee, but somehow it really fit.

Everyone in the trucks had climbed out. The kids were dancing, because they needed to use a facility. Mike motioned inside the building, "It's clear. Down the hall to the left." Sarah and Kevin took the kids in.

We talked about the adventures of getting here, the conversation with the State Police and the National Guard at Camp Williams. Mike explained that the guys they had left at Hill were able to keep certain areas secured, including the flight line and the supply buildings.

"So how many EOD guys are left?"

"You're looking at two of them. Andy is up on the roof."

I looked up. Andy was holding a Barrett .50 cal, looking down with a grin. He threw me some devil horns. From the distance I heard a racing engine. Mike nodded, "Here comes your travel agent."

I turned around and saw a big, tan four-wheel-drive rig coming our way. It was bigger than a Humvee with a long, wide hood that made a Humvee look like a snub-nose. "What in the world is that?"

"That's a M-ATV."

The big rig pulled up, and out jumped a familiar face. "Outbreak!" We had never met before, but porn-stash was recognizable.

"Hey Ogre! I thought that was you doing doughnuts in the parking lot. He paused, "you look terrible." Outbreak was in his flight suit with a vest over it, Beretta 92 in the chest rig, and an FN SCAR slung over his shoulder. "You look good too. Is that stash reg?"

He just laughed. "Mike says you want a lift home. I got you a ride. It's fueled and ready, just waiting for the Governor to get here."

I looked at my Humvee. "We've got a lot of supplies we need to take with us."

Outbreak looked at the Humvees, "It's cool, we'll just roll them on, and you can roll them off." He got on his radio, "Make room for some vehicles with trailers. The Governor has some freight."

I ignored the Governor part. "I need some new tires."

"We don't have time... you can just have the M-ATV."

"You are the best, man. The best." We started throwing my loot into the new vehicle. The trailer was easy to move and hook up the M-ATV since I had plenty of room in it left. We got the kids loaded back up. Outbreak showed me how to operate the M-ATV as we drove to the runway. We were directed to stop near a hanger. Outbreak explained that they were unloading some cargo out of a C-17 Globemaster to make room for our rigs.

"That's a big aircraft. Can it land in Vernal?"

Outbreak stopped and looked at me. "How long is the runway?"

"I don't know."

"Let me go find out."

Outbreak jogged off. We got out and stood around the vehicles. While I was admiring the M-ATV, I noticed a crate that caught my attention. I walked over to it and ran my fingers over it. A Mark 19. As I was looking at the crates, I noticed something else. "Oh yeah!" It was a motorcycle. It used to be a Kawasaki KLR-650 at one time, modified with an 8-gallon tank and a diesel engine. I walked over to it. There were about a dozen of the bikes. I jumped on the first one. It fired it up and I rode it around the hanger, as I pulled it back into the hanger I reeled it around and took it to my trailer.

"What are you doing?" Zack asked.

"I found something."

"Drop the tailgate on the trailer."

Zack shook his head and pulled the pins on the gate. "Don't know how you're going to load it"

I lifted the front wheel using some RPMs and ran it up into the trailer. Leaning forward and using more throttle, I hopped the rear wheel up and the bike was inside.

I was shutting the gate when Outbreak came back. "We can get the C-17 in, but getting it out would be a challenge."

"Option?"

"We fly Hercs."

"You have Hercs?"

Outbreak just grinned. As he grinned, four C-130 Hercules flew in low with their wheels down.

"We have Hercs."

"Let's load them up."

A black Chevy Suburban pulled up. The long truck had once been clean and shiny, but was now covered in streaks of blood and hand prints. Three armed men jumped out, hands were on their weapons, no smiles, "Mister Hill?" one of them demanded. Their dire attitude put me on guard. I put my hands on my hips, to look more casual, but to also get my hand closer to my Glock 23.

"You've been a hard man to catch up with. We've been trying to find you since we learned you were in Salt Lake."

"Who are you guys?"

"Sir, we are the remainder of the Governor's security detail."

"So how is he?"

"You seem fine, sir."

I got dizzy. "What?"

"The previous Governor was killed yesterday, along with most of his security."

"I'm sorry. So you guys survived."

"We were not at the Capitol. We were off duty. Zombies flooded through the building, killed the Governor, the Senate, and every member of the House that was there."

"Who's left?"

"You, sir."

"I wasn't there. I didn't know I was supposed to be."

"It was fortunate that you were not, sir. Be that as it may, the fact remains, you are the highest elected official still alive in the state of Utah. That makes you the Governor."

He looked at my weapons. "You are not a normal politician."

"I represent my district. I don't have to be a politician."

He raised an eyebrow.

"Governor Hill, your security detail is at your service."

Some time later, as the sun was about to set, four Hercs banked to the right and began their descent to the Vernal Airport.

THREE

Back in Vernal

The next morning I slept in late. I was seriously tired and I hurt...
everywhere. Getting up out of bed was just something I didn't
want to do, but my bladder told me different. *Okay, okay, I'm
getting up!*

I stumbled into the bathroom feeling like a zombie, and luckily no one
shot me as I went. The mirror, I looked in it, and I didn't like what was in
there. Half of my face was a mess from that Garden Weasel Zombie, my ribs
hurt like hell, and my knee was swollen and stiff. I took two extra-strength
Tylenol and four Ibuprofen. That should help in about 20 minutes. In the
meantime, the pain was just getting to be unbearable.

There was a tapping at the door. "Yeah?"

"It's just me."

I opened the door and let in my beloved bride. "You slept like a rock."

"I feel like I got hit by one."

"It was a coffee mug."

"Zack told you, huh." *Damn it, Zack!*

She kissed me. "You did what you had to do."

"That's right. I did. I didn't have a choice otherwise."

"Here, let me look at this." She started unwrapping my chest. A sudden
intake in breath told me she didn't like what she saw. "You need a doctor."

I turned and looked in the mirror at my left side. There was a mark that
was shaped just like a sprinkler head. I must have landed on it when that
zombie tackled me. There was also a sliver of bone jutting through the skin.
Wow, no wonder it hurt so bad.

"I'll go find one today. I need a shower first... and a shave."

I got my head wet and broke out the shaving gel. When I went to raise
my left arm up to apply the lather making foam, pain prevented me.

"Here, let me help."

She's never helped shave my head before. She's always been against it, preferring me to grow it out long again. I looked her in the eyes as she made use of the Mach 3 razor. If I ever run out of these suckers, I'll stop shaving altogether.

"There! Smooth and shiny."

Before I got into the shower, I brushed my teeth twice. I was starting to feel human again. In the shower, the hot water felt great until it ran across my side and down my shredded face, but I stayed in it, letting the water rinse away dried blood. After carefully blotting me dry with a towel, my bride got some fresh gauze and a pressure bandage for my side. She wrapped it carefully and then helped get me dressed. I still felt stiff and sore, but feeling clean was one hundred percent better.

The last two days had been a living nightmare that I had wished remained a bad dream. From the bedroom window, I looked outside. A huge desert tan-colored military vehicle was parked outside. I looked at it for a second before my brain processed that, *yes, indeed, that was the truck that replaced my Humvee.* It still had the trailer attached, as did the other two vehicles, the other two Humvees. I walked out on to the porch and looked down at the trucks. Zack was showing my eldest son the mechanics of the M-249 SAW.

"Glad to see you awake, boss." Ben grinned while looking through one of the Gatling gun's barrels. It was torn down and he was in the processing of cleaning it and lubricating it with Slipstream.

"What time is it?"

"Almost noon I guess."

I grunted as I sat back down into one of my porch chairs.

"I never told you thanks. You saved my ass."

Ben just grunted again. "You owe me a beer."

"I'll get you a case."

"Governor Hill, you are awake." The man speaking was wearing pretty much the same sort of outfit that I was: desert BDU's, and a dark shirt with long sleeves, but he was strapped with a tactical vest and a number of weapons, the primary of which was an M203.

"I'm sorry, I don't remember your name."

"It's Hudson. Matt Hudson."

I held out my hand for a shake. "Nice to meet you, Matt. Welcome to Ogre Ranch."

"Governor."

"My wife calls me George, my boys call me Dad, and my friends call me Ogre."

"I'll try to remember that, sir."

I could tell he was just as uncomfortable as I was.

"What's the plan for the day, sir."

"Well, I need to take the medical supplies we picked up over to the hospital and while I'm there, I need to see a doctor."

"You're injured?" He sounded genuinely concerned.

"Broken rib is sticking out of my side; it hurts pretty bad." Hudson picked up his radio and was about to bark some orders when I cut him off.

"We'll go in a few minutes. I'm starving, and I want to see my boys first."

"Sir."

"Ogre."

"Ogre, sir."

I shook my head and looked over to Ben, who just shrugged. My littlest son came out and climbed up on my lap. He told me stories about being a tiny robot and eating monsters for snacks. He pointed at Ben's Gatling, "Big Boom-Boom!"

Rosa came out a few minutes later with some breakfast tacos, eggs, bacon, salsa, and some beans wrapped in doubled up corn tortillas. "Thank you, Rosa. This looks wonderful."

She smiled and said something in Spanish. My wife came out with a can of Coke and leaned down to whisper in my ear. "I know it's your little fantasy to have a hot Latino house maid... but she isn't staying here... so enjoy it for now mister." The she smiled, kissed my forehead, and muttered something in Gaelic that didn't sound reassuring.

"Hey, Hudson."

"Yeah?"

"Did you guys eat breakfast?"

"Most important meal of the day, sir."

I nodded as I pulled a long drink from the ice-cold can of Vanilla Coke. Hudson was looking out across the valley. "You have a great view here."

"That's why we moved here. Million dollar view."

After I finished my breakfast and felt like the painkillers were working, it was time to get busy. I directed the unloading of the vehicles save for the medical supplies. Those of which, we kept some of what we needed. Basics, like the OTC pain meds, allergy, and other stuff. I slipped a bottle of little blue pills into my pocket. You never know.

The motorcycle I put into the shop, and the extra weapons and ammunition into the house. The grenades and LAW rockets went into a special hiding place. Sarah and Kevin were moving into the house behind Ogre Ranch. The previous owners had divorced. It was messy and since then the house has been empty. We had the key to take care of it, but I don't think that was a problem for anyone anymore, since the previous occupants were probably zombies by now.

There was a loud roar and everyone looked up. The C-130's were flying back to HAFB and as they passed overhead they waggled their wings for us. I waved back and quickly found that I should have used my left arm. "I think it's time to go get checked out." I pointed into the sky and made a circling motion. "Saddle up!"

I left Ben, Zack and the rest of my zombie-killing raiders at the ranch. They needed to rest up and just relax. The M-ATV didn't have a radio that I was used to working so, after fiddling with it to no luck, I turned it back off and just drove. Hudson had insisted on driving since I was injured. I hate not driving when I'm in a vehicle. It's just one of those things. I have a simple policy. "I drive." He relented.

The rig drove very well, smooth and fairly quick compared to the Humvees. The seats were even comfortable. Hudson rode shotgun while two more manned the back-seat doors. The last guy, Adams, rode up in the turret keeping the M-240 at ready. It's not an M-60, but I can deal with that. It came with the truck. Who am I to complain?

I thought about stopping in a couple places, but instead put off the inevitable. I drove to the hospital. Once there I asked for a certain Doc to come out. An orderly ran off to find him. Evidently phones were having some issues here.

The Doc was a great guy. I had helped his wife pick out guns for him for Christmas for the last 5 years, one of which was a Thompson. I love those Thompsons. He came out and took pause looking at the big tan-colored truck.

"Doc I have a trade for you."

He smiled, "Oh? What's that?"

"I need you to stitch me back up" I pointed to my side and pulled up my shirt. The pressure bandage and wrap were bled through.

"I see... but the hospital can't trade services." He spoke as he unwrapped my chest. He made the same look my wife did.

"I think you can this time." I said, as Hudson started unloading all the loot from the Rite Aid Pharmacy.

The Doc's eyes lit up. "I think we can work something out. Let's get you to X-ray."

After about two hours I was ready to go. I had been mended, injected with some good stuff, and given two bottles of stuff I had just dropped off which just happened to double the hospital's supplies.

Just as I was leaving the building and getting ready to climb into the M-ATV, all of the cities' power went out.

"Oh great."

I drove around a few blocks and checked things out. The power was just plain out, everywhere. Some of the gear that my personal body guards brought with them were satellite phones. We had one, there was one at Ogre Ranch, and we had one at HAFB and one was sent to Camp Williams. I called the ranch. "Hey, how's things going?"

One of my boys had answered and wasn't very chatty. "Fine."

"Did the power go out?"

"Yeah."

I rubbed the bridge of my nose. "So everything isn't fine."

"Everyone is okay."

He had a point. "Is your mother there?"

"Yeah."

"Can you take the phone to her?"

"Sure."

I heard foot steps, and then after a moment, "How's my Governor? Did you see a doctor?"

"Yeah, I'll be fine. They removed a piece of bone and stitched me up. I'll be good as new in a few weeks. But that's not why I called."

"If you called about the power, I paid the bill last week."

"For all of Vernal?"

"No, not so much."

"Looks like the power is out everywhere. I just wanted to make sure you guys were okay."

"We've got a handle on it."

I knew my wife was resourceful and smart and could take care of herself. But sometimes I still worried.

We pulled into the parking lot of *Basin* and I picked a spot that would allow an easy exit. One of my buddies, Yebache, was standing out front armed with his plum furnitured AK slung in front, wearing his tactical vest and his boonie hat. He was gawking at the M-ATV as we pulled in. I told my security detail that he was cool and I trusted him. As protocol, my security team jumped out first, checked the area out. Hudson approached Yebache and checked him out. "The Governor is here. You play it cool and keep your weapon on safe."

"The Governor?" David, aka Yebache, looked surprised again. "Why is the Governor here?"

"They sell guns here, right?"

"Yeah."

"He seems to like guns."

Then Hudson turned and nodded. I wasn't allowed, for security reasons, to get out until the area was secured. I could tell already and this was just the second time, that this was going to grow very old. I opened the door and jumped out. I was going light, as I was in the hospital, armed only with my Glocks, one on the hip and one on the vest.

"Hey David, how's it been since I left?"

David was stunned beyond words, then he caught up to speed. "So that was you with the C-130s last night?"

"Yeah, it was easier than driving all the way back."

"So where's the Governor?"

"I'm right here."

"What?"

I smiled and walked in. The store was dark inside. With the power out,

Basin Outfitters was a cave. I took off my sunglasses and put them up on top of my head. It looked like the store had been severely picked over. All the flashlights, batteries, camping gear and such supplies were gone. Niki was at the front counter. "Hey Niki, how are you doing?" I didn't even break stride as I walked back to the gun counter. The owner's son and Troy were there. A lot of guns were gone, as was all the ammo, every single box. "You guys have been busy." As I spoke, they both turned flashlight beams on me.

"George! I thought you went to Salt Lake."

"Been there and back."

"Bullshit."

My security detail flanked me at that moment. Hudson chimed in, "Governor Hill went through Orem, Lehi, and all the way up to Hill Air Force Base."

I could tell they were not believing any of this, as anything that happened outside of the Uintah Basin didn't really happen. "Any word from Kyle?"

"No, phones are still dead and now so is the power."

"I see that. Hey, uh... Troy, I'm going to have to take some time off. Can you make sure I get my vacation pay lined up?" I had to laugh.

Troy just shook his head.

"How was Salt Lake?"

"It was a mess. I only saw a few people who were still alive. I'm thinking most folks have locked themselves inside their homes."

"Did you get your cousins?"

"Yeah, we got there just in time. We went from there to Camp Williams and traded a truck for some Humvees."

They gave me that "we-don't-believe-you" look again.

"Let's step outside into the sunlight. There's no reason to stand around here in the dark."

We went back outside. Yebache snapped to something like attention.

"Governor."

If he saluted, I was going to sock him. He didn't. He was lucky. Mark and Troy just stared at my new truck. The M-ATV dominated the parking lot. It was this huge tan thing that should not be there.

"At Hill Air Force Base, my Humvee went down so I traded it for this M-ATV. It's new, the Army just got these things. They're pretty cool. Anyways, since I'm the Governor I've got to take care of some business." I made my saddle-up gesture and the security detail started climbing on board. "Hey, Dave! Come on. You're rolling with us. I need you more than they do. Hop on."

"Yes, sir." He smiled as he climbed into the big armored off roader. We pulled out of the parking lot without looking back.

"Let's head over to the power company and see what's up."

The sat-phone rang. Hudson answered it, speaking only one word. "Hudson." He was a man of few words.

74

"Sir, Camp Williams is on the line. They want to know where to meet to reestablish the state's leadership. The State Capitol is not secure."

I thought about it for a second.

"Western Park, here in Vernal. It's next to the National Guard Armory." Hudson passed it along and then hung up.

"We've got some Sheriffs and a couple City Managers coming out."

"How are they getting here?"

"Helicopters, mostly."

We pulled into the parking lot of the building the power company used as the local offices and everyone piled out and did the secure-the-perimeter routine. David had jumped out too, to see if the Mayor was indeed inside. He was. I got the nod and I jumped out.

I walked into the office and evidently my look startled the receptionist behind the counter. She screamed. "I don't have any money!" People came out of back offices and looked and ran back inside and locked the doors. A large fellow came running out with a little Walther P22 pistol. He was waving it around with his finger on the trigger, "Stop it! Stop it!"

Hudson didn't even blink before the guy was flattened on the ground and had the little pistol in control. "Please, don't point guns at the Governor of Utah."

I held up my hands, "Calm down everyone! What the hell is wrong with you people?"

David leaned over to me. "You look like a villain from an action movie." I looked at him and didn't know what to say. "I... uh..." I thought about it for a second. "I'm not wearing a suit." He just shrugged.

"The Governor?" The large fellow said with a tone of surprise. "I, I'm sorry! I thought..."

I walked over and held out my hand, "I know what you thought. It's okay, I'd have thought the same thing. I'd probably have shot first though, but I'm glad you didn't."

Hudson handed me the gun with the slide locked back on an empty magazine. "No bullets, sir."

"Really? No rounds in the gun?" I shook my head. "Never mind that. Look, I'm here about the power. We don't have any. That must mean the DG&T Power Plant has run out of coal and hasn't had a train load delivered." The man nodded, "That's right... er... sir."

"Sir? Come on... yesterday I was your State Rep. You know me. My wife taught your girls dancing." I took off my sunglasses. I could see the recognition now in his eyes. Then he asked, "How did you know about the coal train?"

"It's my job. You've got to know these things when you're the Governor."

Ah, the guy nodded. "Yes, the coal train delivers it, we burn it, that makes the steam that spins the turbines that generates the electricity. Without the coal, there is no steam."

"Yeah, I get that. So where do we get the coal?"

"From Price."

Price was a small city south of Vernal across some mountains. It was a hop; far enough to be a ways, but close enough to be almost local. A two-hour hop. The coal mine there was where I had myself purchased coal for burning through the winter. Unfortunately coal doesn't chop well, and I like chopping.

"If I get you a train full of coal, can we get the power back on?"

"Yes, sir, George."

"Okay, well then. We know what needs to be done."

We went over the Utah National Guard Armory; it was almost across the street. Soldiers were standing outside the building's entrance armed with M16 rifles. They had seen the M-ATV at the power office and had been curious. We jumped out all together and as I strode through the entrance, they had actually thrown salutes. Evidently the word had gotten around to these fellows. I guess the word of mysterious C-130's landing just up the street and military vehicles off loading and driving off into the night just might raise some questions.

The highest rank around was a Captain. Captain Oslo of the local engineering unit.

"Governor Hill, it's a pleasure, sir."

I shook my head, "Not really, Captain. Everything is chaos and we've got a lot of work to do. What's the status of our unit here?"

We sat down and looked at maps for about an hour. We were able to confirm that the last train to hit the power plant was a week ago with no sign of it since. So it was either still in Price or some place in between either full or empty. The Guardsmen were spread thin. There were only a few people left that were not assigned. "How are you guys communicating between the checkpoints?" The Captain explained that they had Humvees and MRAPs with Blue Force Trackers in them, and there was one vehicle near if not at, each check point. There had been some encounters, stray zombies or zombies in small groups. One car had a guy that had been bitten, a little Hyundai that had tried to run the checkpoint. A Stinger strip flattened the tires and brought the car to a stop. When they opened the car, the guy inside was turning from the bite on his neck and hands.

Wait! A guy in a Hyundai? "What color was it?"

"Hell if I know."

I really hoped it wasn't Kyle. "So they put him down."

"Yes, sir. They had to. He was turning."

"Yeah, I know how that goes. So we're short of people, but so far the checkpoints haven't had a lot of problems. That might change, but we'll need some guys to go find the train."

"How many?"

"That's hard to say. Probably at least six, but I'd rather have two fire teams."

"I can help." Yebache stepped up. He wasn't military trained, but he was good and better yet, he was smart on his feet. I looked at him and I could see he was up to it.

"Okay, David. This is your game. You're going to take the Guardsmen, find the train, make sure it's loaded, and get it back to the power plant."

"Captain, David is in Command of this mission." I could see him bristle with indignation. "You are in charge of coordinating and gathering every Guardsmen we have in the state. You have a bigger job to do than to worry about one train. I need the Utah Guard to help bring this situation back under control. We've got some at Camp Williams, some Air Force guys at Hill, and I don't know about all the other armories. What about Airport Number Two? We had Apaches there. I have no idea if they are still intact... or if they have any crews left. I need to know. Get in touch with Williams and see if we can't get people over there."

Captain Oslo nodded as he took in the big picture. He'd get on it.

"David, as soon Captain Oslo gets some men together, I want you to head out."

"You guys have a couple spare Humvees?"

Oslo said, "We have one and an MRAP we can send."

"Fantastic."

"Sir, what rank does he hold?"

That was a good question. "Treat him as a First Lieutenant, he's a Special Agent to the Governor. He's under your tactical command, but will report to me as needed."

I looked over to Captain Oslo. "He needs to swear his Oath."

Captain Oslo looked at Yebache, "Raise your right hand, son, and repeat after me."

After the Oath was sworn I shook hands with David. "Congratulations, Special Agent Yebache. You have your mission."

"Uh, wait... one thing."

"Yeah?"

"How do I drive a train?"

Meanwhile, back at the Ranch

We went back to Ogre Ranch, with the idea that we would have lunch. While the security detail munched on elk sandwiches and fried potatoes fresh off the grill, I whispered into my wife's ear. "I've got to go get my truck. Keep them fed. I'll be back by dinner time."

"Don't go alone."

"I want to ride that motorcycle. Besides, the ride in is pretty much clear. I can get in, get my truck, and drive back. I'll be back by dinner if not sooner. Promise."

"Oh, I know you'll make it back. But if you get hung up. What do I do with these guys?"

"Well, the security detail can sleep in rotations. There's the ranch hand room behind the shop. That's what it's for."

She gave me a hug and a good kiss, forgetting that I had some seriously sore ribs.

I waited until I got on Highway 40 before I really opened the bike up. I twisted the throttle hard, all the way to the stops. It didn't open up much. Apparently the Marines, when they contracted for these bikes, didn't request something called "Throttle Response". Power did come through, but there was a long delay before the engine decided to go ahead and agree with my request for speed. It got up to about ninety before it topped out. I have to admit that ninety on a motorcycle is usually fast enough, but there are stretches that I'd have liked a bit more juice. The upshot was that there were few places I had to slow down. The cities of Roosevelt and Duchesne were most of those places. Cities were a generous description. Towns are probably more apt a description. Speed traps are another.

I was soon past Starvation Reservoir, and the bike was chugging along perfectly. Traffic was nil. Highway Patrol were nowhere to be seen. Off the highway I could see Antelope and Mule Deer. It was good to note that they were not infected.

There was a checkpoint up ahead and I slowed to a stop. This was at the County Line at the mouth of a small canyon. A good natural choke point to take control of. Men with guns had been sitting around, some had been looking out for trouble, others napped under make-shift shelters. Some were in the little gas station. Across the highway was a couple cattle gates, not much security, but the heavy steel piping that made up the gates wasn't something one would want to try to ram through.

A big, bald, stern looking fellow walked up. "Hey fellas. You guys have any trouble?"

"It's been quiet since morning."

"What happened this morning?"

"A truck full of guys, armed, from Provo. They came up and demanded food. They pulled their guns on us. Big Daddy tore them a new one."

"Big Daddy?"

The guy, who used to work at Ponderosa Feed and Tackle before it shut down, pointed up on the rock face behind me. I didn't even have to look.

"A fifty?"

He nodded with a grin.

"I'll be coming back through in a couple hours. I'll be in a silver Chevy truck. I left it in town and I think I want it back."

"You went through a couple days ago, but I didn't see you come back."

"I came back a different way, but I plan on returning this way, this time."

"Cool."

They moved the gate for me and I rolled through. As I was passing through Strawberry, I spotted a small car that had driven off the road. I pulled over and got off the bike. As I approached I didn't see movement in the car. The windows looked like they were fogged up from moisture trapped inside. Seeing in was difficult, but I could make out something in the driver seat. Michelle, or the zombie Michelle, was still there. She looked desiccated. Her head was back and her jaw was hanging down. Her eyes were sunken, and wide open, nothing but white showing. She looked like the girl in the movie *"The Ring"*. The one that was found in the closet. She wasn't moving. I pulled my Glock 23 from my hip holster and used it to rap on the glass. The body jerked and shrugged and her head fell forward. One hand came up to the glass. Unbelievable. I took aim and put a 165-grain Winchester PDX1 hollow point through the side window and into the brain. The zombie jumped and went still. From the shattered glass, a powerful reek wafted out. "Oh man!" I covered my mouth and nose and backed away. The smell made me retch and gag and I almost threw up.

"Girl, you're looks finally fit your personality."

I got back on my bike and rode on.

As I turned left in Heber, I noticed it was a lot quieter. Zombies still wandered around, but none paid attention as I passed through. They milled around, no sign of anyone else alive here so they didn't bother moaning. Fifteen minutes later I pulled to a stop at my truck. It was right where I left it, windows and doors still intact. In the truck's bed, there was the tarp still covering ammo and MRE rations. Good. I looked back at the bike, then back at the truck. I didn't want to leave the bike, but the truck bed was too high for me to try to hop it in. *Come on, improvise.*

A couple of zombies shambled my way. As if they expected me to just stand there and let them come have a snack. My Glock 22, with the suppressor dropped them with a few shots each. Looking around, no more could be seen at the moment.

There! A contractor's truck. It had a ladder. I walked over and looked in the truck. The driver was there, an arm missing... looks like it was chewed off. I noticed something. The truck was dead, having creamed into the back of a Ford Taurus, and that's probably why the truck's steering wheel was bent into the dash and the driver's head caved in, but the radio was still on. Someone was talking. The person on the radio was talking nonsense stuff about martial law. It took me a minute to realize that this was an XM radio and the speaker was from St Paul. Or more accurately, from near St Paul. As interesting as that was, Minnesota wasn't my concern.

I used the ladder as a ramp and rode the bike up into the bed easily. I was about to toss the ladder but after a brief moment of consideration, I slid it into the truck's bed as well. About the time I finished tying the bike down, more zombies were arriving, which meant that it was time for me to go. I shot five or six more zeds before I jumped into the truck and cranked it back to life. I watched them run after me as I sped up, heading home again. I looked at my wristwatch.

"I'll be right on time."

We Clear the Road

It was the fifth day since the Uprising. The situation was grim. Across the nation the zombie infestation had wiped out all major metropolitan centers. I could go through the list of every city, but all the major ones were pretty much crawling with the dead. For Utah, the estimation was over 80% casualties state wide, the most being along the Wasatch Front. Utah got off easy. Logan, the Uintah Basin, Price, Ceder City, and Moab. These cities were able to keep the zombies down and out and were holding on. Lines of communication were established, and survivors from the cities were making their way to safe zones.

Rolling past Park City on I-80 I was saddened to see the damage that a fire had left behind. Without firefighters to suppress it, the fire had spread through the city and up the ski slopes. Most of the mountain was still smoldering while some buildings were still showing flames through broken windows. Part of me wondered how much of this fire had been set on purpose, since I doubted a wildfire could have jumped large parking lots. The other part of me set it to a lower priority and I turned back to the highway. The rig in front of me was a large tractor-trailer tow truck, with a massive push bar welded on front. The idea was that this rig was going be able to push stopped vehicles out of the way, or drag them out if they couldn't be pushed. It had already proven itself going through Heber City. It's code name was "Ram Rod" for radio communications. The driver thought it was cool, but he had evidently never seen that stupid comedy movie *Super Troopers*. I had to hide a snicker a few times when he called us.

Hudson had offered to snag everyone in the M-ATV a bottle of syrup. It was generous, but I declined. I'd rather drink a Gator-Bull – my Gatorade and Red Bull mix. Chugging a bottle of Maple just didn't sound all that great to me.

We had upgraded the M-ATV with a belt fed up top. An M-60 from the Utah National Guard. They were more than willing to lend it to me as they were all about the M-240's and 249's; they even laughed when I said I wanted it. They didn't know how to run The Hog like I did. First thing I did was give it a good cleaning and lubricated it heavily with Slipstream. It ran flawlessly.

Part of me wished Ben was up there with his Great Golden Gun, that old

.45-70 Gatling he snagged from Cabela's. Ben had taken my old full-sized Bronco early that morning and had headed north. He was intent on getting away from everything in Wyoming's Wind River mountain range. I can't say I blame him. These were very dangerous times. I was just amazed how fast he was able to throw a new oil pump in that old beast and get it running like it was brand new. Last view I had of him he was roaring up the highway with that big gun mounted in the back of the Bronco, peeking out the back window. I had a feeling that I would see him again. But not for a long time.

Rosa had latched on to Zack. More so, she had latched on to my youngest son and she loved playing with him. But whenever Zack was around, she was almost doe-eyed when looking at him. Zack was at first uncomfortable about this, but this morning, when he thought I wasn't looking, I saw a quick embrace between the two of them. Rosa had given Zack a quick kiss before putting his tactical taco hat on his head as he climbed into his Humvee. I liked Rosa. She was hot looking, but better yet, she was a great cook and took command of Ogre Ranch's kitchen. My wife was livid at first, but I nudged her and pointed out the look she gave Zack when he walked by. Ah... she said. She got it. Rosa was still able to make fresh tortillas from scratch with no power in the house. Hopefully she would teach my bride. A woman that can run a grill is just a fantastic thing.

Sarah and Kevin and their little family were doing just fine in The Back House we now called it. Their kids were great and played with my younger ones, and that was good to see. Kevin wanted to saddle up and roll with us, but I pretty much put the kabosh on that. No way. There was no need to risk it. He was here, safe with the family. I tasked him with keeping our home base zed-free in case some shamblers made their way in. Not like it was all that likely. Our checkpoints had been very effective, even if we pulled a few men off them.

Park City would have to wait. Investigations would one day find out, but right now...

My train of thought got derailed as I watched Ram Rod slam into some small cars, sending them off the freeway, and stray zombies flying. I guess the name was fitting. He had slowed down before the impact and of course I done the same, rolling about 25 miles per hour we passed by a couple bodies that had been riding motorcycles. Harley Davidson leathers, nice, big shiny motorcycles. I didn't think of it but all of a sudden in dawned on me what was wrong. I stopped the M-ATV and called for the other rigs to stop as well. Hudson pointed up and Jenkins from the back jumped up to man The Hog. I got out with my 930 SPX in hand and checked 360 around me before I moved over to the bodies.

"What's up?" Hudson was at my elbow and Zack was moving up as well with his suppressed AK-47 in hand.

"Look at this." I said, and pointed.

"A couple dead bikers." Hudson shrugged.

"No, what's wrong with them."

"They were on Harleys."

"No... well... yeah... but that's not what I'm talking about. Look again."

Hudson's prior life as a Law Enforcement Officer kicked in. "The blood is red."

Blood from zombies is dark and thick. Blood from a dead body that has been laying out dries dark as well. I knelt down and touched the back of my hand to the cheek of one of the bodies.

"Still warm." I pressed my fingers into the carotid artery and felt no pulse.

Hudson checked the other body. "I got a pulse here!"

He rolled the body over and ripped the leather jacket open. His chest was riddled with small holes. "Looks like .223 FMJ rounds... hit in the back, exited the chest." Hudson was checking breathing when the man opened his eyes. Blue eyes. The man was in his late 60's and he was very pale from the loss of blood. His breathing was very shallow. "White Dodge." he said it in a quiet whisper. Looking him in the eyes, I could see the lights go out. He died right there.

"White Dodge." I repeated.

"This must have happened pretty recently. There is a lot of blood, but with the wounds he caught... His laying face down slowed the bleeding. I'm guessing within a half hour at the very most."

Zack walked away, his head down, like he was in deep thought.

"I'm guessing these guys were riding along and a White Dodge came up behind them and opened fire."

Hudson looked at me and said one word. "Murder." I nodded. That's what this looked like.

There was a lot of things that could have happened, but considering these bikers were not zombies, and evidently not bitten, this looks like it was a homicide. Great. Arson, now Homicide. It's nice to know that the dark side of human nature survived along with the rest of us.

These guys were from Wyoming, Hudson pointed to the bike's plates. Big Harley's have storage compartments. Both bikes, these storage compartments and hard saddle bags were all still locked shut, so this wasn't a robbery. I pushed the bottom of the old dead guy's jacket aside. He had a revolver on his hip. I pulled it out and looked at it. A stainless S&W 686 Plus, a 7 shot .357 magnum. The man had a pocket full of speed loaders, all full. "He didn't get a shot off." I handed the rounds and the gun to Hudson.

"I'm not a Wheel Man," he protested.

"Fine... but this isn't something I'd just leave around. Throw it in the M-ATV."

I checked the other guy, and he had a Hi Point in an Uncle Mike's shoulder holster. I left it there.

"Casings." Zack called out as he bent down and picked one up. "Steel cased 556... Wolf."

I walked over and took the case. "So we know the shooter or shooters were in a White Dodge something, and they shoot Wolf." I muttered.

"In the backs." Zack finished.

"That should narrow it down." Hudson said, with obvious sarcasm.

I shrugged, "They are heading into Salt Lake. How many people are left alive that are driving white Dodges and shooting Wolf ammo?"

I looked at Hudson, "Get on the horn and see if we have anyone in the Summit County Sheriff's Department. We want to let them know about this."

Hudson nodded and went to the M-ATV.

"If there is anyone left that cares," Zack said.

"I care." I walked back to my rig.

This didn't sit well with me. Killing zombies is one thing. Drug Cartel thugs... no problem. But a couple old guys from Wyoming out on a ride? That's a problem. Once everyone was back on board we got rolling again. Ram Rod leading the way.

As we made our way west through Parley's Canyon on I-80 from Park City it was all down hill. The further we went, the more zombies we encountered. Ram Rod was pushing more vehicles out of our way. The driver was a friend of mine from Vernal named Willie. Headshot Willie. Willie was a good guy and a former Marine, and he was getting good at pushing abandoned vehicles. But the number of vehicles needing pushing was increasing. A large, jack-knifed semi-trailer was blocking most of the freeway. A normal truck could have slipped through a gap between the trailer and another big rig. However, our convoy rigs were just a little bit too wide. We stopped about a hundred yards away, giving Ram Rod plenty of room to work on his pushing and shoving. Some zombies were visible on the other side of the concrete dividers. From our position we could see a section of freeway that was a mile ahead because of the way the road bent and curved and came back up hill. I could see movement on the road. I pulled up my Leupold Mojave binos and got a closer look. It was a pickup truck, white, with some people in the back. It was a Dodge. "THERE!" I pointed and handed the binos to Hudson.

"Our white Dodge."

I got on the radio, "Ogre to Zack."

"Go for Zack."

"Are there any units on the BFT near the mouth of the canyon?"

"Let me look." A few seconds later he came back, "that's a negative. Closest unit, an NG Humvee is on State Street. Looks like it's in front of *Get Some Guns*."

"Roger that. Send out a BOLO for a white Dodge truck full of guys, they are on I-80 west bound into the valley."

"Sure thing... er... what's a 'Bolo'?"

"Be on the look out."

"Gotcha."

I few seconds later, I had a message pop up on my Blue Force Tracker.

"BOLO: White Dodge Truck, Armed and Dangerous Men. Use Caution and if possible, take into custody. On I-80, West Bound into SLC from Canyon. BOOG."

I guess that would do. Wait. "Zack, what's BOOG?"

"By order of the Governor."

I just shook my head, but everyone else had a laugh. I wanted to catch these guys. But first, we had to get through this blockade. Willie had turned Ram Rod backwards and was hooking up a tow chain to the trailer. Evidently pushing it didn't work. Zombies on the other side of the freeway were starting to gather at the barrier with a couple of them trying to climb over them. I called out over the radio "10 O'Clock."

The answer was streams of fire from the M-60 and Zack's M-249. A few quick bursts and those zeds were mowed down, but more were coming. The sound of the M-60 firing, its slower, more potent sounding shots felt very comfortable to me. Zack's M-249 was suppressed, which was a good thing, but the hypersonic bullets were still loud and the high cyclic rate made the SAW sound unique from any other weapon we had. I noticed those rounds were fired with accuracy that was less than optimal, more torso hits than head shots.

"Zack, who's on the Saw?"

There was a delay and I was about to ask again when Zack came back with an answer I wasn't expecting. "Kilo Hotel Hotel."

KHH... the initials of my eldest son. I tried not to freak out about this. I took a deep breath and held it for a moment before letting it out through my teeth. "You have anymore unauthorized personnel aboard?"

"That's a negative. Clearance was given by the Governor's wife this morning. I thought you knew."

I hung the Microphone back on my shoulder, not knowing what else I should say, but feeling it was best not to say anything. I was pissed. I looked over at Hudson, "You knew about that?"

Hudson turned pale, "Yes, sir, but we were told not to tell you."

"But you... You're kidding me."

From behind me, Larson chimed up, "She's scary, sir."

"I..." They were right... my wife was scary. I dropped the subject.

The M-ATV was a cool rig, but it was big, kinda slow compared to regular trucks, and while it didn't have a stereo, at least the AC was arctic blast cold. "Wish this thing had a stereo."

Larson spoke up again. "Thought you would never ask."

From behind me I heard the opening notes to a song from "*Disturbed*". The notes were hard and heavy.

"Drowning deep in my sea of loathing,
broken your servant I kneel...
Will you give it to me!"

We were headbanging as Ram Rod pulled the trailer wide, like a huge gate."

I put the M-ATV into gear and we ran through to the other side and took up an overwatch position. Zombies had been working their way up from a gap in the barrier, once used by Highway Patrol to turn between the traffic directions. Some of these zombies started running and even through the armored windows I could both feel and hear the loud moaning the rest of them were making. Like a tidal surge, zombies started coming over the barrier as well. Their numbers were in the hundreds. "Guns Up!" I yelled for someone to man the Hog and I glanced back to see Larson scramble up and pull the bolt back as he swung the big sixty around. He opened up with it immediately and through the windshield I could see tracers lancing out, into and through the oncoming rush.

"Ogre to all units. Let's roll!"

"Ram Rod to Ogre. My Tow Cable is still hooked up!"

"Roger that, Ram Rod. We'll cover for you!"

I could hear the high-pitched crack of 5.56mm being fired as Zack's M-249 opened up. The higher rate of fire really chewed the zombies down fast, but with less accurate shooting, Kilo was turning running zeds into crawling and dragging zeds. We could really have used that big golden Gatling right about now. Where was Ben?

I angled the M-ATV so I could open up my door and bring my 930SPX to bear. Hudson jumped out of the passenger side door and climbed up on the side. I was reloading a couple shells when a zed sprinted out of nowhere and leaped at me. He was within inches when The Gauge spoke its judgment. Buckshot ripped through its skull and torso, opening up the zombie like a ripe melon. It was dead in the air, but the corpse' impact slammed into me, taking my breath away and reigniting the pain that was my rib cage. I could see Kilo working the M-249 into a thick group, but from behind a zed was making a full-tilt sprint. If I didn't stop it, the zombie could be up on top of the Humvee and all over my son. I thumbed in a slugger round and aimed carefully. The Gauge rocked and I caught a glimpse of the 1-ounce chunk of lead arch out and slam into the zombie's upper torso. The impact ripped open the whole chest like a scene from *Terminator 2*, its head hanging sideways and upside down from the ruined and rotting chest. Disoriented, the zed continued to run, but curved away from the Humvee. I let it run.

"Ogre to Kilo – Watch your Six!"

Kilo looked around, saw the disfigured zombie, and cut it down before going back to the group coming over the barrier wall.

"Ram Rod is rolling." Willie called out and I could see black diesel exhaust belch out from the dual stacks.

"Ogre to Ram Rod. We need to really bust our way through, Willie. There is a white pickup truck we need to catch up to. He's going slow enough we can catch up if we don't have to stop again!"

"I like this truck, Ogre. I don't want to bust it up."

"I'll buy you a new one."

Willie's answer was more revs, and in a flash Ram Rod flew past us, smashing a Lexus out of the way like it was a matchbox. I gunned the M-ATV's engine and got behind him. Zack's rig was right on my bumper. Larson dropped back down into the truck, but I could still hear Kilo firing.

"Check fire, Kilo. We don't need to gun down anything we can drive away from."

The chase worked its way slowly down the canyon, and I had a feeling that we were closing in. I could see on the Blue Force Tracker that the unit that had been on State Street was moving along I-215 to the I-80 junction. If the white truck turned south, we might have him, or we could get lucky and catch up to it before it reached the junction.

We passed the East Canyon exit and I knew we were running out of time. Ram Rod was bashing things out of the way that the Dodge had to go around. "There it is!" Ram Rod called out on the radio. As I came around the bend and pulled wide of Ram Rod, I saw the truck. There were armed men in back that were watching us intently, and the truck seemed to speed up, knowing now that it was being pursued. It had a couple hundred yards on us. It took the South I-15 exit!

One of the guys in the back of the truck opened fired on Ram Rod, spraying the windshield. Ram Rod jerked to the left and hit the brakes.

"Jensen! Get on the Sixty!"

I pulled right, putting the big rig between me and the Dodge and when I came out from behind it, Jensen was up on the gun and ready. He opened up with a long burst that sent tracers into the rear end of the truck. One of the guys in the back dropped his rifle and slumped down before the others ducked. The truck went across the overpass and out of sight.

I looked at the BFT and could see the intercepting unit closing and then stop. *We got them!*

"Ogre to Ram Rod."

No answer.

"Ogre to Ram Rod. Come in, over."

Still no answer. I saw Zack's Humvee pull up next to the big rig and I stopped. Willie has some kids and I didn't want to have to tell them their Dad was hurt. Come on Willie.

"Looks like Willie is okay. Yeah, he's fine. Says his radio is shot."

That was a relief! I gunned the engine and went up the off ramp to the overpass. As the M-ATV came around the bend I could see the stopped Humvee. Off in the distance, the white dodge was pulling away at full speed over open freeway. There was no way I could catch up. This truck just wasn't fast enough.

I pulled up to the Humvee and stopped. I could see the driver through broken glass. "Grab the med-kit!" We jumped out and I ran to the Humvee's door and jerked it open. The driver was a pretty blond girl with a black circle pinned to her hat. An ROTC Cadet. A "Spot" as they are called. Cadets learning on the job to act like officers. There was blood on her shirt, spreading. Her name tag was "Jackson". I could see in her eyes, shear panic.

"Okay, Cadet Jackson – we got you."

I looked back out at the disappearing truck and swore I'd get those bastards.

"Come on now, Jackson, let's get you out of here."

Hudson was on the satellite phone. "We've got a chopper coming to pick her up!"

That was some good news. I pulled Cadet Jackson out of the truck and got her on the ground. She was small, thin framed, and light. I opened up the blouse and could see the wound just above her left breast. If the bullet had hit the aorta she would already be dead.

"What school are you going to, Jackson." She looked at me, confused, as if she didn't understand the question. "You're a Rotsy Cadet, right?" She nodded. I used a knife to split her t-shirt open. Her bra was white on one side, red on the other. The hole in her chest was small. I held direct pressure on the wound with one hand as I fumbled to open a pressure dressing.

"You're still a student?"

"Brigham."

"BYU, eh? I went to ROTC there. Good program."

Larson came up and helped with the dressing. I noticed bubbles coming up through the blood under my fingers. "Here, get that dressing on this, quick." Larson pressed the bandage against the wound as I pulled my hand away. "Let's take a look at her back. Roll her your direction."

If there was no hole coming out her back, that was bad, meaning more tissue damage internally and she probably wouldn't make it. If there was a hole, that could be better as the bullet wouldn't have fragmented and it could have passed through with less damage and she might make it.

Larson pulled her shoulder and hip while I gently lifted. There was blood. I used my knife to unzip the fabric of Jackson's shirt from bottom to the top of the neck. The exit wound was small, but it looked the right size to indicate a clear pass through without any fragmenting or tumbling. I reached for another pressure dressing. Zack had come up and had opened another one and had it ready.

"Thanks."

"Had to help. She's hot."

I had to admit that she would have been very hot if I was 20 years younger and single and she wasn't shot. I worked to get the pressure dressing on over another whole packet of Quik Clot. The bandage in place, we rolled her back down where her body weight, what there was of it, would help keep pressure on the exit wound, further helping to stop bleeding.

"I need some plastic... like an MRE pouch bag."

Larsen pulled out a big brown thin pouch. "This is for chest wounds. Self adhesive. Seals good."

I'd never used one before, so I nodded to him, indicating for him to do it. He opened it up and used it like a large Band-aid. The slight whistling sound stopped as soon as it was applied.

The sun was beating down on the wounded girl's face. We treated for shock and I had Zack holding up a jacket to block the sun from her face. Larsen pulled out a saline bag and started to push an IV. He looked up at me. "I was trained too."

He nodded as he slipped the needle into a vein. "That's why I let you take lead."

"How long until the helicopter gets here?"

"It took off from Williams... probably a little while longer yet."

I stood up and took the saline bag and held it up as I looked towards Williams. I could see a black dot in the sky. It was getting bigger, but not that quickly.

Zack jerked around. "Did you hear that?"

"What?"

"I think we have company."

"Get ready for contact! Guns Up!"

The belt feds swung out to cover the freeway in both directions. We could hear moaning, getting louder. They were getting closer. Movement on the over-pass. Hudson was on the M-60, but he was holding fire. The sixty was not suppressed and it made a lot of noise. It would beat back a bunch of zeds, but it would end up attracting more.

Larson finished the IV and stood up. He pulled his M4 off his shoulder and looked at the chopper. "Five minutes maybe less."

I handed the saline bag to Zack. "Here, we'll cover you until we can't." I ran back to the M-ATV and switched my shotgun for my Crusader M4. Willie got out of Ram Rod and climbed up on top with his rifle. Everyone braced for what was about to come.

The zeds were coming across the over-pass at a shambling jog. They some how knew we were here and we were on the menu. From the other direction, a smaller group was coming.

"I don't think we have five minutes."

"Let's throw the chick into a truck and let's roll!" Zack said through his gritted teeth.

"We can't move her. She's critical. We have to hold for the medivac. If we don't, she's dead." I went back to Cadet Jackson and knelt down beside her. She could hear everything we were saying and I could see panic in her eyes. She whispered so softly, I could barely hear, but I knew what she said.

"Don't leave me."

"I wont, sweetheart. We're going to put you on a helicopter. You are going to make it. You'll be just fine."

I looked up at the oncoming zombies, and started to have my doubts.

"Wait until they get closer."

"Don't give us that Whites of their Eyes thing."

I needed the humor. "I was going to say wait till you think you have a clean shot."

Larson pulled his rifle up and fired a single shot. A zombie fell.

"Smart ass!" I pulled my rifle up to my shoulder and centered a zed in my ACOG, putting the chevron right on its nose. The gun bucked slightly and the zed fell.

"I guess you were trained again."

"Nope. I'm just lucky."

The zeds in both directions broke into a run. Hudson and Kilo both opened up at the same time. Tracer fire lanced out in both directions, working back and forth, dropping zombies as they ran. Zombies fell, but others jumped over their... comrades... competitors. The ferocity of a charging zombie is disconcerting. Absolutely no humanity left in them. It was animal, primal, frantic and dark. They were driven by something other than hunger.

Larson opened up and so did I. We fired over and over.

"Reloading!" Larson called out and I spun around and fired a few rounds at the zeds coming in his direction. "Up!"

I spun back to my direction and fired. I realized that I had been holding my breath and concentrated on controlling my breathing as I picked my targets. My gun stopped firing. I flicked it to the side and looked down into chamber. It was empty. "Reloading!" I flicked the gun over the other side while I hit the mag release. The mag went flying, but my left hand was already bringing a new magazine up to the mag well. Larson spun and sent rounds to the group I was covering, dropped the three closest ones and spun back. I slapped the ping-pong paddle to close the bolt and I was back in the game. "Up!"

Kilo just held the SAW's trigger down, spraying rounds back and forth across the onrushing zombies. Zombies don't feel fear. They don't feel pain. So when the SAW savagely removes limbs from bodies, arms, legs, or opening up a torso like a rack of ribs; they may fall, but they keep coming. Suddenly the SAW went quiet. Kilo had run dry. He popped open the feed tray cover and reached for another belt. Looking at the zombies and not reaching the belt, Kilo instead drew out his 9mm S&W M&P pistol. Using a two-handed isosceles grip, Kilo made his shots count, aiming for the head.

"Zack, we're going to need some firepower here."

Zack looked down on the girl and decided not to give up on her. He knelt and put the saline bag in his left hand and pulled his FS-2000 up with his right. From the kneeling position, Zack opened up one handed. He worked the FN gun and pounded a steady rhythmic beat, making each shot as best he could.

"Reloading!" Larson again.

I looked over and could see his direction was getting thin so I didn't worry about firing in his direction. A particularly fast zed sprinted with unearthly speed for Kilo's Humvee. I sprinted as well. I could see Kilo drop a magazine and look up at the zed that was almost on top of him. He froze. My gun was up but there was no shot. I was empty too. The zed was almost there, so I put everything I had into legs and screamed as I launched myself. I could hear screaming from behind me as I flew through the air. The zed made its leap as well. Just before impact, I turned my head. We collided in mid air and I felt bones crunching... I could hear the crunching. My breath was knocked out of me even before we hit the ground. I was blinking spots as I spun off the zed and got to my feet. My Becker was in hand and got my bearings. This was difficult. I was dizzy and numb. The zombie I had tackled moved all wrong. I had broken its back but it was still alive. I stumbled over to it and dropped a knee into its spine as I plunged the big black knife into the back of the zed's skull. I could hear more zombies around us, and thought that we were about to be overrun.

Suddenly I could hear what sounded like a motorcycle rev its engine and I watched as a white-orange line reached out and obliterated everything it touched. Luckily it was only touching zombies. I looked up in time to get a face full of high velocity dust and debris.

The chopper was here.

The chopper was armed.

The guys in the chopper were very good shots.

The big bird slowly came to a hover near our stopped vehicles. Miniguns on both sides of the bird fired long bursts that rained brass down to the freeway. Soon, the bird stopped firing and lowered to the ground. Crew members leapt out and ran. Zack dropped the FS-2000 and lifted up the IV bag. The crew members lifted the girl and carried her to the chopper.

"Where are you taking her?"

"We've got the Primary Children's Hospital under control. There is an ER team ready."

"When you finish up with her, I want you on station over head. We have some hunting to do. The assholes that did this. We're going to find them."

The pilot nodded.

"Go, go!"

Soon the Blackhawk lifted up off the ground and it leaned over into forward flight. As quickly as it arrived, it was gone again.

We picked up our spent mags and took a moment to police the area.

"Larson, take the Humvee and follow us."

"Roger that."

We needed to find a more secure location to hole up and reload magazines and take a breather. I wasn't sure where that place might be, but I knew it wasn't here.

We saddled up and got rolling again. I took lead, since nothing needed to be smashed out of our way at the moment. We followed 215 and the whole time I hoped to catch up to that blasted white Dodge. We got into Murray when Hudson suggested the Golf Course on the other side of the freeway. We had no trouble getting on to the course even though we hadn't called ahead for a tee time. Ram Rod parked politely in the parking lot, and Willie jumped aboard our newest, slightly perforated Humvee. We drove into the center of the course and stopped by some trees. We were careful not to drive across the greens as that would have been rude. One day, people would play here again. Maybe.

After we cleared the area and found no zombies, we pulled out some MREs and started loading magazines again.

"This is a nice spot." I said to Hudson, holding up a Gator-Bull. "Good call." Hudson nodded and raised his bottle of Evian.

"Used to play here. Once a week. I met my wife over there by that sand trap." Hudson then looked down and was quiet for a second. "It's one of the worst courses I've ever played on, but it's familiar."

I drank deeply from the refreshing caffeinated beverage. I was sitting next to a tree and leaned back against it. The grass was cool and the shade, welcome. I closed my eyes.

"That was a good tackle on that zombie." Without looking, I knew the voice was Larson.

"I'm feeling it already. But I had to do it. I owed them." I said, pointing to the scratches on my face that were starting to heal. "Next time, you can do the flying tackle."

Larson chuckled and filled his mouth with an MRE version of a cracker with cheese on it. That reminded me of something.

"I'll wager anyone here, that they can't eat one of those packets of MRE crackers in two minutes, without a drink."

Hudson came over and sat down. "I've heard it's impossible."

Zack brought over a case of 5.56mm ammunition, "I heard a guy in Iraq tried it, and died from it."

"No," I shook my head, "It's not impossible, just improbable. And no one has died from the cracker unless they choked on it, which is probably entirely possible."

"Okay. I'll take up the challenge. What do I win if I do it?"
I looked down at my gear and I pulled out my cord wrapped BK13 knife.
"I'll wager you my little utility knife." Hudson nodded. "Okay... I'll play for that."

"Hold on now. Not so fast. What do you give up if you lose?"

"I'm not going to lose."

"Just for the record – should you lose – what bit of gear would you give up?"

Hudson checked out his gear. "This." He held up the compass that was hanging from his pocket. Dead serious, he said, "This compass was a gift to me from the Princess of Canada."

We laughed. "Okay, here's the deal. Once I say 'go' you have two minutes to eat the contents of one regulation MRE cracker pouch. You may not drink, you may not spit, you have to show your mouth is empty, and you can't act like a wood chipper and try to spray crumbs so you have less to eat."

"I got this."

"You want a drink of water before you start?"

Hudson shook his head. "Let's do this."

"Go."

Hudson ripped open an MRE packet and went to work. He broke chunks of cracker and started filling his mouth. He was confident. He was eating fast. But I wasn't worried. I knew from experience that a mouthful of cracker was going to work against him. He had two thirds of the cracker gone, but had a big mouthful he was working through.

"One minute."

Hudson responded by putting more cracker in his mouth and you could see him chewing for all he was worth.

"Minute-thirty".

All the sudden Hudson's eyes showed fear. His chewing slowed, taking more effort. The cracker was fighting back.

Zack and Larson were being encouraging. "Go, go, go!"

Willie was laughing like crazy.

Kilo was watching with a smile, but not saying anything.

"Time!"

Hudson spit out a solid wad of cracker and reached for his water bottle.

"That stuff sucked all the moisture from my head. My eyeballs feel dry!" Everyone had a good laugh as Hudson was drinking his water.

"And once again, the crackers win."

Hudson tossed me over the compass. I looked at, holding it up.

"The Princess of Canada is a cheap bitch, isn't she?" Everyone laughed and it was good that we could. If we couldn't laugh anymore, we would be in trouble.

I pulled some ammo over and dipped in. Eight magazines later I was topped back off and ready. I checked my pistol magazines and looked at the blade of my Becker. The blade was still razor sharp. I wiped it off with a cloth with a little oil on it. Gotta keep the edge ready.

"Got one over here." Kilo pointed off into the distance. There was a zombie shambling across the greens. It must have been in a sand trap or something because we hadn't seen it previously. Our laughter must have roused it.

"I got it." Larson said as he pulled up his rifle.

"No no. That's too easy." I handed him my suppressed Glock. "One shot".

"That's a hundred and fifty yards!"

"It's in range."

Larson took the gun and stood in a modified Weaver stance. The gun bucked with no indication as to where the bullet may have went.

"My turn." I said as I took the gun.

Larson snorted as I pulled the pistol up and took aim. "No chance in hell."

The gun bucked and the zombie's head snapped back. The zed fell without taking another step. I sat back down and pulled the magazine out of the pistol to top off the two spent rounds.

"How did you make that shot?" Larson was squinting at me.

"Just lucky I guess."

"Luck had nothing to do with it."

Zack came over. "Hey, on the other side of the freeway, there is that little strip mall right by the Fashion Place mall."

"You want to go the mall? You know malls and zombies are a bad mix."

"No, at the strip mall there's a Borders Books." He explained that he wanted to get some history books and that Kilo wanted some books too.

"Okay, but a couple conditions – you guys be really careful. You keep an eye out."

"Of course."

"Find me some Horus Heresy books that I've not read before."

"Cool."

"One more thing. If you get *The Zombie Survival Guide*, I'll have to kill you."

Zack laughed as he walked over to his Humvee and high fived Kilo. I wasn't too worried, because I could see their location on the BFT. But I was still worried. I'm a Dad and Kilo is my boy... Zack is blood... so I had a lot of family going on a run for books. That gave me reason enough to maintain a low-grade worry.

I tried to relax and went back to my tree. It looked like it needed more leaning on. I chewed on some sort of an energy bar called a "Hooaah-Oorah Bar". It wasn't that bad and before long I was asleep.

The radio crackled. "Whiskey Six to Ogre. Whiskey Six to the Ogre, Over." I opened my eyes and saw the sun was high overhead. Hudson, with a bottle of water in one hand, handed me the radio with the other. This was a handheld unit from the M-ATV.

"This is Ogre, go ahead Whiskey Six."

"This is Whiskey Six, I'm at Angles Ten flying from Papa Charley Hotel to I-15."

"Roger that, Whiskey Six. I want you to stay high and look for a white Dodge pickup truck."

There was a pause.

"There is a dealership on State Street."

"The one we are looking for is probably going to be the only one moving. There are at least six gunmen in the truck, maybe as many as eight. They are the reason you went to Papa Charley Hotel. We need to bill them for that trip."

"Roger that, Ogre. Whiskey Six, out."

With a helicopter at high altitude looking across the valley, a bright spot moving along the roads would normally be hard to find. The only bright spot might be easier.

I picked up the mess from my MRE and gathered up our things. Everyone helped and soon we were ready to roll again. "Let's get Willie to his big rig."

We moved to the parking lot and Willie got out of the Humvee.

"Willie, you did a great job. You opened a route just like we needed." I shook his hand. "I think things are going to get nasty. You should get back to your kids." Willie protested, but not too hard. I could tell he wanted to get back. I hired him to help us punch through and he did just that. I didn't hire him to go hunting in harm's way.

We said our goodbyes and Willie fired up Ram Rod and drove off. He would be able to make it all the way back home non-stop. If he kept rolling, he'd have no problem. If he did have a problem, Willie was resourceful and could handle it. I had no doubt about that.

We rolled to the I-15 junction and stopped. I looked at the BFT and I could see other units. Whiskey Six was over the center of the valley, looking like he was running a racetrack pattern searching. Two national guard trucks were on I-80 near the Airport. Another one was in Sugar House. The next closest unit was in Draper, looks like he was parked near the freeway, at the gas station. All we had to do was wait for Whiskey Six to spot our prey. I wasn't going to let them get away.

Shoot to Thrill

An hour later I was about to call it. Whiskey Six was about 5 minutes from Bingo fuel, with no sign of the white Dodge. Word came through that Cadet Jackson was out of surgery and was stable. The fear of that having passed turned into a cold anger and calling off the hunt was something I really didn't want to do.

The virtual silence of the valley was interrupted with the sound of thunder... an explosion. *Where did it come from?* It was distant, but it was large.

"Whisky Six to Ogre."

"Go for Ogre."

"Explosion observed. Moving in for a better look."

"Roger, where was it?"

"Stand by."

I looked over at Hudson. "It's north of us. Let's roll!" Hudson got on the Blue Force Tracker and sent a message to Zack's Humvee while I pulled onto I-15 heading north.

"Whisky Six to Ogre, looks like the explosion was on State Street just north of I-80. The Salt Lake County Government Center just blew up. Hold on. We've got movement. Trying to get an ID."

I hit the gas and we roared up the freeway at a maddeningly slow 65 miles per hour, which was about as fast as the M-ATV would push. Larson, in the second Humvee was not quite as fast and I was starting to pull away from him.

Then Whisky Six said those words I've been itching for. "Target located."

"Roger that, Whisky Six. Stay on station and track, over."

"Whisky Six, that's a negative. We are Bingo Fuel, RTB to William."

"Negative, Whisky Six, that's a negative. You stay on that target. When you have to set down, you can find a place and we'll get you fuel to that location. We will not lose this target. This is a priority."

There was a pause before Whisky Six responded. "Roger that, Ogre. Tracking target. Target is moving south. Over."

"Ogre to Zack."

"Go for Zack."

""You copying this?"

"10-4, we're rolling. We started heading north as soon as the call came. We are on 700 East, just passing 4500 South."

Zack was running parallel to us on the opposite side from State street from our location. We cruised on, closing in on our target. I could feel my adrenaline flowing. Larson's boom box started cranking out AC/DC's *"Shoot to Thrill"*. Matthew Richardson had been quiet, but his personality was starting to show. I looked back at him and he just grinned as he chambered a round in his M4. I looked over at Hudson and he just shrugged as he checked his weapons.

I looked in the rear-view mirror and Larson's Humvee was a distant spot.

"Ogre to Larson."

"Go for Larson, Ogre."

"We're going for a hard stop on the target. When you finally catch up, the situation may not play out peaceful like. Be careful approaching."

"Roger that, Governor. Be careful engaging."

I took the exit at 3300 South and started to make my cut over to State Street."

Whisky Six got back on the radio, "Whiskey Six to Ogre, target vehicle is moving slow. Looks like they are firing on zombies as they are moving. Wait! Check that. They are pulling into a car dealership. Men getting out. I think they are going for a vehicle change. They must be running low on gas too."

"Roger that, Whisky Six. Stay on target."

Hudson was watching the Blue Force Tracker. "Looks like Zulu is on 3300 and closing."

"Ogre to Zack, hang back a little, swing north on..." I looked at the map, "200 East. If this works, I am going to hit them in the grill and I want you to come in from the side."

These guys were playing right into my hands.

"Whisky Six to Ogre. Target Vehicle is now a Red Ford Truck, say again, Red Ford Truck, Over."

I said a quick prayer in my mind. Please, God, let these bastards be moving south. Please!

"Target Vehicle is on the move again."

Come on you bastards. Come to the Ogre!

"Moving south."

I could feel my teeth grind. Yeeesss!

"Roger that, Whiskey Six. Stand by."

I gunned the engine. State street coming up ahead fast. I let the M-ATV drift to the right, and let the weight of the rig shift off center to the right as I then made the left turn, applying all the power that it had.

"SWEET JEEZUS!" Hudson cried out as the big M-ATV slid in a four-wheel drift around the curve, barely missing a Volkswagon Golf that was on its side. The M-ATV's tires were screaming as I was fighting the steering wheel, but the rig tracked well and remained very stable. Up ahead there were some stopped vehicles in the road. A police car, a Volvo, and a Dodge Durango. Past that was a large, red Ford truck. The red Ford was the only vehicle moving.

I pulled to a stop and Hudson and I jumped out of the M-ATV. Richardson selected another song as he climbed up to the M-60. Metallica... "*I Disappear*". I smiled as I pushed in my Surefire earpro. The red Ford's engine revved up and I could see a guy hanging out the passenger side window with what looked like a stainless Mini-14.

"Okay, that's how you want to do this." As I extended the tube, the sights popped up. Hudson looked over at me as I shouldered the LAW. His eyes got big.

"This is how I do it."

At 100 yards the rocket streaked out and sunk into the grill of the Ford. For just a split second I thought perhaps the round was a dud but then the truck erupted. The front of the truck was peeled back, engine parts, fender parts, front wheels... all went flying out in different directions. The hood was thrown up into the windshield. As the truck's wheel-less front end hit the ground a guy from the back of the truck went flying over the cab directly at us, but landed and slid to a grisly stop a good fifty yards away.

Not everyone in the truck was killed. In fact, it seemed that the only casualty was the truck's engine, and Superman there. I was disappointed.

The doors of the truck flew open and armed men poured out. Each armed with rifles: a couple AK-47's and Mini-14's. One guy had an AR-15 and I put my sight on him. My M4 barked and I could see the guy with the AR-15 hunch up from the hits. I hit him in his right side. He tried to run for cover but stumbled. Another burst and the man hit the ground twitching.

Hudson fired several rounds, but I didn't see the results. Someone threw something at us, but it only landed half way. It exploded and I could hear shrapnel buzz through the air. A pipe bomb? Really? The guy who threw it went prone under a parked SUV, right under the middle of it. No cover at all. I put the chevron of my ACOG on the ground right in front of the guy and fired a single round. The bullet hit the ground and skipped off the pavement right into his face. He flopped over grabbing his face and didn't move again.

Vip! Vip! Vip!

Rounds zipped past my head. I fell backwards to get out of the incoming stream of fire.

"OGRE!" Hudson called out, but then saw I was okay. I rolled over into the Urban Prone position, keeping my knees tucked up behind the wheel of the police car. I saw some legs under the same SUV and fired at them. One of my rounds hit the foot and the owner fell down into my field of fire. I held the trigger down. The M-60 opened up and tore into the wrecked truck. A guy had stood up in the back of the truck and was instantly struck by four rounds of ball and a tracer. He fell out of the back of the Ford. A hostile with an AK returned fire at the sixty and I heard a distinctively wet slap sound and the sixty stopped firing.

From behind I heard a roaring engine. As I turned to look, I saw Hudson turning as well. That's when it happened. Hudson's head and neck were struck. I could see pink chunks of brain splatter out the exit wound as his head distorted. He was dead before he hit the ground.

Larson's Humvee pulled up and the door opened. Larson bailed out and dove for cover behind the Volvo as the Humvee rolled into the Dakota and stopped. "Hudson!" He screamed. "Hudson!"

"He's gone!" I yelled at Larson as I slapped another magazine into my M4. I rolled up and got my feet under me again, keeping my head down. The tires of the police car had become less than air-tight and the car settled down onto the wheels. I carefully looked through the windows of the police car. I could see some armed men taking cover behind another car, but I had no shot. I'd have to move. From the police car I could move to the left and work my way to the side of the street where there were more cars. The armed men were now looking off to the side.

Tracers zipped across the street and ripped into the cars, the truck and everything. It was 556 fire from an M-249. Zack had entered the fray! Tracers intersected through one of the gunmen, scraps of cloth and chunks of meat, bone and blood sprayed out and the man fell like a marionette with its strings cut. Mini-14's and AK's started firing, but the men were doing a lot less aiming now. I slid to the rear of the police car and switched shoulders with the M4. I came down on my left side and found I had a shot on the guys with the AK-47's. One was crouched down, sitting on his heels. He turned and saw me as I put a 55-grain V-Max through his nose. He crumpled instantly and I just held the trigger down again and let my rounds walk all over the next AK shooter.

I could hear occasional big thumps from the distance and saw what looked like rounds punching through the side of the Ford and through a gunman with a Mini-14. The Ruger rifle was thrown up in the air and before it hit the ground, the owner was struck once more. I didn't know who that was shooting, but that was some good work.

Larson made movement to where Hudson was laying, breaking cover from the Volvo without calling for some covering fire. I popped up to fire a volley when a gunman beat me to it. Tracers fired from a Mini-14 zipped past Larson as he ran, but not all of them. Larson was struck several times.

He screamed as he fell. That quickly, I felt very much alone. I knew there was at least one or two other gunmen left. They were keeping their heads down.

The M-249 stopped firing, and so did whatever that other gun was. They probably didn't have an angle on a target. I knew I didn't. I looked over at the Volvo and thought about moving to it or moving in the other direction to try to find an angle on the targets. Another pipe bomb arched into the air. I couldn't see quite where it came from, but from the trajectory, I had a good idea. The Caddy. They were behind the Caddy. But to get an angle, I'd have to cross a danger zone without covering fire. If I can't fire around the obstacle, maybe I could fire through it. The car looked like a CTS that had its front end crushed in a collision. I thought I saw two heads. I couldn't be sure. I fired into the car but my rounds were not penetrating through to the adversaries. A V-Max wasn't ideal for punching through metal.

A shadow passed over me. Large and wide. Whiskey Six came in low and angled sideways so the door gunner could get a line of sight. From where I was, I could hear a high-pitched electric whine as the mini-gun opened up. A long stream of continuous fire spewed out. Sparks were flying off the CTS, shattering glass sprayed out, the whole car was engulfed in flashes of flame, tracer fire, dust, and smoke. The big chopper curved its flight to the right, and I could see it setting down behind a Wendy's.

Everything got quiet.

I carefully got up, keeping my M4 up on my shoulder with the sight just below my field of vision. I moved up on the closest adversaries. Both were dead.

From behind Wendy's I could see Zack moving in a crouching walk with his AK up, just as I was moving. I could see he had another rifle over his shoulder. Wait. Was that a PSL? I brushed off the thought as I approached two more bodies. One of them I had shot in the foot. The other guy was holding his face but he was still alive. I pressed the hot muzzle of my suppressor into the guy's chest. He screamed and his hands went to grab my gun, but grabbed scorching metal instead.

"Don't you move!" He looked up at me. He had his cheek torn open and was bleeding from an eye. Torn up, but he would live.

Zack moved around the big red Ford and came back to where I was. "All clear, this guy's the only one left breathing."

"You guys have been having a fun day."

"It's the end of days, motherfucker!" The gunman spat.

I looked around, then back at him. "It's the end of yours... your friends too."

Fear came into the guy's eyes. He must have been maybe 21 years old. "Where did you come from? What were you guys doing?"

"Fuck you!"

I pressed the hot barrel of my weapon to the guy's throat. "Answer my question."

"Evanston.... Evanston! We were just having some fun!"

"Killing people is fun?"

"I... we were just shooting zombies, man. Just zombies."

"Two old guys on motorcycles. A soldier girl in uniform, driving a Humvee."

"They were zombies, man."

"They were people. Living people. Did you burn Park City?"

"What? Just fun, that's all."

A guy in a flight suit holding a Beretta M-9 came running up. He was wearing an Air Crewman's helmet. His pistol was held stiff armed, aimed into the ground.

I looked at Zack and nodded. He covered the kid on the ground while I pushed my rifle around behind my back and then grabbed the gunman's armed and twisted it, forcing the gunman over onto his stomach. In my tactical vest I had some zip-cuffs. I had threaded them through my vest's gunbelt. Very handy, especially here and now. I pulled one out and looped it around a wrist, then another one around the other wrist and through the first zip tie. I cinched them tight. I stood up, pulling the gunman to his feet. I pushed the kid to the crewman. "This guy is a prisoner, put him in the chopper and strap him in."

"We're out of gas, Governor. Bone dry. My engines cut out as soon as I set down."

Zombies from the surrounding area, attracted by the gunfire, started moving in. We had to go.

"How many people are on your bird?"

"There are four of us, the others are with the helicopter."

"Okay, we've got to go."

We could hear moaning. It was coming from all around us and I could see some zombies coming from the north. "You guys are set down behind the Wendy's, right?"

"Yeah, it was the closest secure spot we could find."

"Go get your crew ready to move out, I'll bring my truck around and pick you up."

I looked at Zack who was frowning deeply.

"I picked up a couple of survivors. Didn't expect to get into a tussle."

"Survivors?"

"Children."

"You got kids in your rig now?"

"Yeah, two of them."

"Okay, we're going to have to boot scoot out of here fast."

We walked over to Hudson and Larson, and I knelt down beside them. Hudson was unrecognizable. I didn't know what to say. I looked at Larson who's eyes were open and staring. "I'm sorry guys. We should have planned this better."

The prisoner started laughing, "You dumb fucks..."

I pulled my suppressed Glock and fired a round through the guy's knee. He fell to the ground screaming and I put a round through the other knee. He screamed again and I leapt up on top of him and covered his mouth. What I really wanted to do was slit his throat.

"Listen to me really good, jackass. You are cuffed and now you can't run, walk, or even crawl really fast. I'm going to leave you right here. Zombies are coming already. You scream again, and they are going to come faster. You stay quiet and try to crawl, maybe you can find a place to hide for a while. I don't care, but if I was you, I'd shut the hell up." The kid's eyes were wide with panic and pain. I stood up.

"Zack, get back to your rig. We're going to get back on the freeway. I'm going to head to Camp Williams. You guys should head back to Vernal.

Make sure my boy and these kids are safe."

Zack nodded and jogged back towards his Humvee. I picked up Hudson's and Larson's weapons and ammunition. Then as an afterthought I reached into my cargo pocket and pulled out the compass. I laid it on Hudson's chest.

"You are a good man, my friend. It was an honor to know you."

I looked around the battleground. Zombies were getting closer. I jogged back to my M-ATV and opened the door. I looked into the back seat. Richardson was sitting there, covered in blood from a high chest wound. He was still breathing! I climbed into the back seat and started cutting off his armor. His eyes opened up and he looked at me, with a half smile. "It's cool man. Don't worry about that."

"I can't lose you too! Hudson and Larson are gone!"

"I know. It's cool. They are with their families now. I'll be with mine too in just a bit."

"Families? I... I didn't know."

"They died the first morning of the uprising. We had nothing left."

"I'm sorry."

"It's cool..." Richardson's voice was as soft as breeze through tree leaves. "My family is waiting for..." His eyes unfocused and he let out a long slow exhale. He was gone too.

I climbed into the front seat and got behind the wheel. It was hard to drive with my eyes full of water, but I pulled around the Wendy's and I saw the Blackhawk in a big empty parking lot. I pulled up to it close and jumped out. "Help me out for a second."

We put Richardson in the Blackhawk and slid the doors shut. We'll be back. The Blackhawk crew climbed in and we pulled back out on to State Street. "I'll take you guys back to Camp Williams and we'll get you boys a fuel truck and an escort so you can recover the chopper."

Before we got out of line of sight, I stopped and looked back at the wounded gunman we left. Zombies had found him and had fallen on him. I couldn't hear his screams, but they would not have lasted long anyways. I saw what looked like the guy's leg get ripped off his body. He earned his reward. I got the M-ATV rolling again. The crew of Whiskey Six had a lot of questions, but I didn't feel like talking. After a few miles they stopped talking too. We drove the rest of the way back to Williams in silence.

Back at Camp Williams we got Whiskey Six a fuel truck and an escort to go refuel the Blackhawk and bring it, and the fuel truck back to base. With that taken care of, I pulled my M-ATV up to the fuel depot and started filling its tank. It took a while, as the rig has a huge tank giving it much greater capacity than one would have thought. Topped off, I loaded back up and thought about what I was going to do next. I checked the Blue Force Tracker and saw that Zack was well inside the Uintah Basin Secure Zone and was out of danger. He would have a clear drive the rest of the way home and all he had to worry about was stray mule deer.

Mule deer... wild life... the zoo. I didn't know anything about the zoo or what its condition was, but I could imagine a lot of animals in cages starving to death if they were not taken care of. The thought saddened me on what was already a depressing day. We had come into Salt Lake for a specific reason: to break the trail through so trucks could come in and harvest teams could begin transferring canned and dry goods from stores and warehouses back to Vernal. No sense in letting them age and rot... might as well put them to good use. Well, the mission was accomplished. I could return back to Vernal, but I didn't feel like going back just yet. I also didn't feel like talking to anyone. Sitting there in the M-ATV I felt tired. I opened up a pack of beef jerky and ripped off a big chunk.

There was a tapping at the armored door, and I looked down to see a specialist looking back up at me. I opened the door. "You alright, sir?"

"Yeah, I'm fine."

"You've been sitting there for half an hour."

Really? Felt like about a minute and a half. "Just thinking about things."

"You got anymore of that Jerky?" He asked with a bit of hesitation.

"Here." I handed him the rest of the pack. He seemed more than grateful. Maybe I did need to talk to people. Get a restoration of my humanity. I thought about people back home. My family, my wife, my boys. I should bring them home something they would enjoy. Zulu and Kilo made a shopping spree at a book store. Maybe that's not a bad idea.

I closed the door and the specialist took a few steps back while shoving a wad of beef jerky into his mouth. I pulled away from the pumps and decided to head back into "Happy Valley." I went down the hill from Camp Williams and crossed the Jordan into the Thanksgiving Point Gardens, staying on pathways until I hit the Highway again.

I had been here before, but things looked different this time through. Zombie corpses laid out. Smashed vehicles. This wasn't our work; this was someone else's work. I'd have to keep an eye out for survivors, and hopefully they would be less hostile than the one's from Evanston.

As I drove, I finished off a Gator-Bull and some interior pressure made a need apparent. I had to go. I could pull off the freeway and relieve myself, or I could find a place to stop, take a leak, wash my hands, civilized like. I didn't feel civilized. I pulled the truck over and stopped. Instead of getting out, I climbed up out of the turret ring and stood on top of the M-ATV. The M-60 was locked in place with a belt of ammo hanging out of it. I reached down and made sure it was on safe. I looked around and didn't see anything or anyone near by. I unbuttoned and let it out.

I was feeling better now, letting my stream wet I-15, careful not to wet my truck. That just wouldn't do. Up ahead off the freeway I could see the famous Lehi Roller Mills, made famous by that Kevin Bacon movie, "*Foot Loose*". I hated that movie, and as a result, the Roller Mills, and by default, Lehi. Lots of stopped cars on the road. A couple of them were still smoking. From standing up here, I had a pretty good view. I took it in as I finished and buttoned back up.

That's when I saw it. Movement. I jumped down into the M-ATV and rooted around for my glass. Leupold Mojaves. I climbed back up and stood on the truck again. The binos helped me out immensely. Wait. Was that a big green dump truck? Someone was rocking the zombie apocalypse with a dump truck. I shook my head and got back underway. I had considered giving chase and making contact, but that just probably wasn't a safe route to take... especially alone. That and I doubted I could catch even a dump truck. The M-ATV was a large heavy vehicle, but it actually handled very well. It just wasn't fast. I decided I'd hit the Barnes and Nobles in Orem. Grab some books and stuff for my boys; they would love that. I doubted Kilo got anything for them.

I pulled off the freeway and made my way through the back streets. No signs of life in any of the houses that I observed. No kids playing. No lawns being mowed. As I passed one house with a fence that had been knocked down, a dog came running out. I stopped the truck and was about to open the door, when I looked at the dog. Its eyes were completely bloodshot, not the zombiefied dead fish eyes, but something else. This was like the Rage Virus from *28 Days Later*. The dog was frantic, enraged, and biting at the truck. I noticed one of its ears had been torn off and part of its tail was gone. It had what looked like human bite marks on its back. *So the zombie plague can infect animals if bitten.* I climbed back up through the turret and pulled my pistol. The dog was jumping and growling and snapping. This was the most ferocious Corgi I had ever seen. I aimed carefully, not wanting to hit it in the head, and fired a shot. The dog was hit, but didn't yelp or whimper. It just fell back to the ground kicking a little then laid still.

I hit the timer on my watch and sat down on the turret ring. I was hungry. From my cargo pocket I pulled out the remainder of the MRE I had for lunch. I had the entree left and peanut butter to go with the cracker I had not eaten. The entree was beef stew. I used my knife to cut open a corner of the packet and started to squeeze stew out and into my mouth. You know... it wasn't that bad. I missed chicken a la king and the omelet. I didn't think they made those anymore. Classic stuff. I turned around and leaned up against the M-60 and pushed more stew. I closed my eyes and chewed, trying not to think of anything.

A strange wheezing sound came from below. I checked my timer. Four minutes. I looked over the edge and saw that the Corgi was standing up again. The Corgi looked disoriented and turned in circles. I pulled back and finished my stew, ate the peanut butter and crackers, taking more than two minutes to accomplish the task, and then I drank a long pull of Gator-Bull. Once satisfied, I leaned back over the edge. The Corgi was about ten feet from the truck, just standing there. "Hey, Puppy." I said, in a normal tone of voice. The dog turned and looked at me. It wheezed at me. I think this was a doggy version of a zombie moan. What surprised me the most was the eyes. There were dead fish eyes already, almost completely white in just a few minutes. That was very strange. I fired another round and this time put the bullet into the dog's brain. It fell down and didn't move. I looked at the timer. Twelve minutes and the dog was back on its feet in just 4. Interesting. I got back behind the wheel and drove to Barnes and Nobles.

FOUR

3 Hot, Heavily Armed Girls

The parking lot across the way was full of cars. University Mall was always crowded. Over here on this side, kitty-corner from the mall, the parking lot was mostly empty. I shut down the engine and carefully looked around. I didn't see anything moving. No cars. No people. No zombies. Not even a cloud in the sky. Everything was completely silent. A lone seagull glided into view. At first I took this as a good omen. Then I watched as it glided down to a corpse that was bloated right in front of the Burlington Coat Factory store. The gull landed on the body and started pecking at it.

A message popped up on the BFT. Whiskey Six was back in the air. The security escort was RTB. Just out of curiosity I messaged them. "If you have the chance, look into the Zoo." I also noted that Zulu and Kilo were about to arrive back home at the ranch, safe.

I don't even know what I'm doing here. But, since I'm here, why not pick up a few things? The store was dark inside, and I couldn't see very far in. This seemed like shotgun work to me. I grabbed my Mossy and my shell pouch and opened the M-ATV's door slowly and quietly.

The gull took wing and flew off, heading east. It was quiet. I kept the shotgun's buttstock up into my shoulder as I approached the door. Seeing nothing move inside, I pulled the door handle. It opened. I didn't think it was worth sneaking too much, since I'm sure anything inside would have noticed the giant military vehicle that pulled up in front of the large window panes. But still, if anyone was in here asleep or tucked into a book... You never know. Keeping my gun at a low ready, I stepped inside and let the door shut behind me.

"Hello."

Nothing.

"Anyone in here?"

Nothing at first. Then I heard some shuffling from deep inside the store. I slowly pushed the safety off and tightened the grip on the gun.

"One last chance... anything that doesn't speak might get wasted."

A small voice from the back of the store. "Don't hurt us."

It was too dark to see with my sunglasses on. I tilted them up onto the top of my head. That was somewhat better. I had more light to work with, but less clarity of vision. It was a trade off I had to make at this time.

"Are you a zombie?"

"No."

"Then I'm not going to hurt you. Why would I?"

"I don't know."

"Come out where I can see you."

"How do I know you wont hurt me?"

"Your gun is bigger than mine?"

The speaker had a soft, feminine voice. It might be a girl this time. I couldn't tell. Last one was... questionable. The figure that stepped out of the shadows was holding a large handgun in both hands, in a low ready. It was a revolver and even without lenses over my eyes I could tell a few things. First off, the gun was huge. Second, her thumb was over the hammer. Lastly, her trigger finger was along the frame of the gun, not on the trigger. I lowered the muzzle of the shotgun and flicked it on "safe".

"You said, 'us'. You are not here alone?"

"There are three of us." She said as other girls came up on both sides of me. Each one armed. One with a rifle and the other a shotgun, both in low ready positions. The girl that had been doing the speaking came closer and into more light. I lowered my sunglasses to see the details of her face, then I put them back up again.

"You look familiar. Do I know you?"

The girl came up to me and tilted her head to the side just slightly.

"George?"

"Jen?" It couldn't be. Jen was a student at the private school my wife taught at years and years ago. She was a gangly girl back then, but now... she'd filled out, had a figure, had some meat on her bones... athletic... strong. I could tell the strength because she gave me one hell of a hug. She wrapped both arms around my neck and squeezed me. "Easy there, girl. I've got broken ribs... hard time breathing here." She pulled back and had a huge grin on her face.

"It's good to see you! How is the family? How's my teacher?"

"Fine, fine," I said, refilling my lungs. "We're all good."

"Where are they?" She was bouncing on her heels.

"They are back home and doing well. I came here to pick some stuff up for my boys. You, how about you? What's going on?"

"We were held out here since yesterday. Supposed to meet some people here, but they never showed. We couldn't decide what to do, then you drove up in that tank and scared the hell out of us."

"Tank? It's just a big four by four. So... tell me..." I said, as I looked at Jen's friends. "Who are these ladies?"

"This is Joy." Joy was a pretty black-haired, blue-eyed girl with high cheek bones. She was tall and dressed like a biker. Black leathers, boots, a knife on her hip and the shotgun in her hands.

She smiled. A nice smile. She held out her hand. "Joy Ansfrida."

I took her hand and shook it. "George. I'm the acting Governor of Utah."

The other girl held out her hand, "April Peterson." April had a nice rifle, an FN SCAR. She was not as used to smiling, the lines in her face told me she didn't do it much before things went to hell. Now, from the looks of it, she might not ever again.

"Nice to meet you, April." I shook her hand as well. "Nice rifle."

April looked down at it. "It's okay."

Jen put her arms around my neck again. "This is so awesome, guys! George taught me how to shoot! I knew he'd be okay through all this, and if he was okay, his family is okay. Governor now? When did you run for that?"

"I didn't. I'm just the only official left that was elected to the State Legislature, so I'm the default guy until we have an election or find a survivor that was higher up on the food chain."

Jen was a sweet girl that spent some time with my family as she got her bearings again. She had a difficult youth... problems with guys. Young guys and old guys... all wanting to get to know her a bit too intimately. She always trusted me, I guess because I never tried to get into her pants.

"So what have you been doing, Jen?"

She explained that she had been working at a Lenscrafters.

"Wait, Lenscrafters? You said Lenscrafters?"

"Yeah, I..."

"Oh good. I need new glasses! All I have is these prescription sunglasses."

Jen laughed. "Sure thing, I can make you a new pair if we can get to my store."

"Where is that at?"

"Just off I-15 on 800 North."

"We can get there."

April went back into the store and found her backpack. "I'm ready to get out of here." She slung it over her shoulder and kept her rifle in hand. Joy didn't have anything other than her shotgun, but she looked ready for anything.

"So where are the guys you're waiting for?" I asked, not looking forward to the answer.

"They went to the mall, to get stuff." Joy sighed. "I told them to go across the street over there to Big Five, but they said they knew what they were doing."

"Who are these guys?" I asked again, not wanting to hear what I feared I would hear.

"They are just some guys we know. NOT boyfriends, but they think they are now."

"No, I mean, what did they do before all this crap happened. What did they do before life changed."

"Oh. Uh... " Joy seemed unsure. "I don't think they did anything other than drinking Keystone and playing like they are gangsters."

"What did they do to make money?"

"They got money from their parents."

"Money from mom and dad... yeah, that's straight outta Compton. OG style. So they went to the mall to get stuff. Okay. Did they have guns?"

"They had their 'Nines'." Jen answered. "I have this." She held up her S&W X-Frame revolver.

"Is that a .500?"

"Didn't you tell me to get the biggest gun I could handle?" She smiled sweetly.

"Yeah, I did say that... but this is a bit much."\

Jen's sweet smile changed into a wicked one. "It's okay, George... size doesn't matter... it's how you use it."

We had a laugh about that, but the reference made me a bit uncomfortable, coming from a girl that last time I saw was... very young. She wasn't so young anymore.

"How many rounds do you have for it?"

"I have a box."

"So you have 25 rounds. Five in the gun and 20 for reloads."

"Yeah, that's all I have left. We've run into some problems."

I looked over at Joy. "How much ammo do you have?"

She flicked her hair to the side and said, "Not enough."

I appreciated the sentiment. "Of course, not enough, but how much do you have left."

"I've got about 25 rounds myself, plus what's in my gun." Her shotgun was a Remington 870 HD model... five in the tube, plus one in the chamber I would assume.

April volunteered her status. "I've got two magazines left, and a full mag loaded." April was wearing hiking boots, jeans, and a long-sleeved t-shirt that had the Opsgear logo on it with the sleeves rolled up. I started to really like April. She had thick, long, auburn hair pulled back into a pony tail. She was in pretty good shape too. Athletic build, almost as tall as I was, and had some tats on her arms. Small, tight, Celtic knots around the wrists. She had green eyes. I was guessing she was Irish.

"Okay, first order of business. I'm going to do what I came here to do...

grab some books and stuff for my kids. Then we are going to get you guys some ammo and..." I looked over at Jen. "Some guns more suitable to the targets and the environment. Okay? Then we are going to find your gangster boyfriends."

"Do we have to?" April panned.

"Well, if they went into the mall and got themselves in trouble, they could still be alive in there."

I grabbed a couple Barnes and Nobles book bags and went up and down the aisles looking for books for my boys. Young adult books, sci-fi and fantasy, mysteries, suspense, and some picture books by Richard Scary for my littlest one. I filled both bags. I also grabbed a bunch of music CDs. All kinds of stuff... hard rock, Celtic, and a little country because I like some of that once in a while. The girls helped picking out books. Well, Jen and Joy did. April had grabbed some music and then spent some time looking out the windows, keeping watch. Once loaded up with goodies, we went out to the M-ATV and threw everything into the back.

"Shotgun!" April called it, but that's not where I wanted her.

"April, I want you up in the turret. Here are some goggles for when we're moving."

"Turret?" She looked up at the M-60.

"From up there, you can use your rifle. I'll teach you how to run The Hog later."

"Seriously? Are you for real?" I nodded. "Fantastic!"

"Jen and Joy... you guys can flip a coin for the shotgun seat."

"I'm the one with the shotgun."

Jen was looking in the back seat and saw the boom box. "I'll take the back seat."

April climbed in and stopped. "There's dried blood in here. A lot of blood."

"That was from my last turret gunner. We got into a firefight with some seriously screwed-up guys from Wyoming. He was one of my body guards."

April continued to climb into the M-ATV, and I have to admit the view from behind was distracting.

"What happened to the others?" Jen asked.

"They didn't make it either."

"Just you?"

"No, my brother Zack was there, and my oldest son was there. They are okay... probably home now. And I had a helicopter that helped out. It's a long story."

Jen put her hand on my chest, "Are you okay?"

"Physically? Pretty much... I'm banged up... broken ribs... but I'm fine."

"But what about emotionally?"

"I...uh... I'm fine."

Joy climbed into the front seat. "Can I use one of these?" She picked up my M4.

"No, not that one... that one is mine. You can use that one there. Give that other one to Jen."

"Oh, hey... April... Gunfire attracts zombies. So only shoot when you have to. Conserve ammo when you can."

"Got it."

Jen climbed into the back door. "Here, I'll trade you. Seven shots instead of five."

"That's cute... no thank you. I like my .500 Magnum."

I shrugged and climbed in. "Buckle up."

We hit State Street and as we passed through the intersection, heading north, we had about five zeds running after us. As we drove, some stopped chasing, others joined in. I sped up a little and after a few blocks they all gave up chasing.

We pulled into *Gunnies*, and I could see that the lights were off and the door was shut. "April, how does it look up there?"

"We've got some zombies coming up on us."

"How far?"

"150 yards."

"Can you get them?"

"Sure." She raised her rifle.

"Hold on. We want to take them quietly. Jen, pass up that M4."

April took the M4 and adjusted the stock in and shouldered the weapon. She fired a couple bursts and the zombies were down. "I like this!"

It was good shooting. I was impressed. I grabbed my shotgun again and opened my door. Since the front door was locked, opening it meant smashing it with a couple blasts of 12-gauge slugs through the locks. We quickly moved through the store, clearing it of zombies and we found none. *Gunnies* was a pretty good shop and they had what we needed. Plenty of ammunition for Jen's .500 Magnum which she had sworn to not give up, and a good supply of buckshot and slugs for our shotguns. 5.56mm ammunition was kind of thin, but enough for our needs. There were some more magazines for AR type rifles, and some pouches to carry them. I found a shotgun shell pouch with a belt for Joy, who strapped it on and filled the pouch with buckshot. TacStar had a Side Saddle for the 870 that I grabbed.

"Here, let me see your scattergun." I quickly attached the Side Saddle and put some slugs in it. "There you go."

Joy looked at her shotgun and grinned. "Nice!"

"Shotguns can run dry real quick. Let's find you a side arm." I introduced her to the Glock 22, which she didn't care for. Then to an M&P .40 which she liked. I found some spare mags, mag holders, and a holster. She attached that to the same belt as the shotgun shell pouch. She looked as ready as ever.

April had already found her side arm, the Glock 22 that Joy didn't like.

I'll take this one." Ammo carriers, holster and the full monty. April was set.

"Okay, Jen. Which one do you want?"

Jen picked up another .500 Magnum, but this one had the shorter 5 inch barrel. Galco made a chest carrier and a shoulder holster for the .500's and Jen strapped both on at the same time. The short gun under the left arm, the long one right below her breasts. The straps went around and between her breasts, magnifying them. She was an impressive sight to be sure. The bust outperformed the revolvers, if you know what I mean. I didn't know such a thing was made but she also had an ammo belt for .500, and Jen started filling that up with cartridges. The belt matched the cowboy style boots she had found. On the strong side of the pistol belt, she hung a large bowie knife.

"This is a good look for you, Jen."

She looked up at me with a smirk, "You like it?"

"You need a hat to go with the outfit for the full effect."

"You're right." She walked away to go look for hats.

"April, you should grab a knife too. A big one, like Jen's. Trust me, they come in handy."

I looked around and found a small display of Surefire Earpro. I grabbed a bunch of sets and handed them to the girls, explaining the use of them. These would come in very handy when we went through the Mall.

Finally, we were geared up and ready. Like before, we didn't raid all the stuff, but rather took only what we needed, which was a lot, but if other survivors came after us, they would still find plenty of guns and ammunition to take care of their needs.

Jen, wearing a brown tactical taco hat, came up to me, too close for my comfort. "You geared us up. Now let's get you taken care of." I swallowed hard and squirmed, not exactly taking her meaning. Then she tapped my sunglasses, and I breathed a sigh of relief.

Lenscrafters was not very far away, and we didn't have to break the door in to gain entrance. Jen had a key. I selected a pair of round-framed glasses. Simple, and easy for Jen to grind. Scratch resistant of course, and if possible – yes, it's possible, transitions lenses, thank you very much.

My prescription had changed. As I sat in the chair with my eyes into the Big Goggle Thing, Jen was just right there on the other side of them, looking through them. She was so close, I could taste her breath. She smelled of flowers and a recently chewed breath mint. I didn't know why Jen seemed out of breath or something, she was breathing heavy. I was less than comfortable.

True to the advertisements, I had my new glasses in about an hour. It took a few minutes to get used to the new lenses, but I was able to put my sunglasses away.

Zombies with Jewelry must Die

*I*t was starting to get late in the evening, and the sun was low in the sky as we headed back to the University Mall. Since it was getting late, or the moon was already up, or just because it was supper time, there seemed to be more zombies out and about. This wasn't a good sign.

"They mostly come out at night... mostly." I almost shuddered.

Before we got rolling again, I went over the operation of the M-60 with April. Feed tray cover, open bolt, laying a belt in, simple enough weapon, it's just something that has to be shown to someone. We would talk disassembly and cleaning later.

The M-ATV rolled over the curb and into the parking lot with no problem, hardly even a jolt. And with that, we were at the mall.

The one thing I have sworn I'd never do... was to go into the University Mall again. I circled the mall, looking into the windows, looking in through the doorways. Also, since I was going rather slow, and we picked up a large number of zeds following us, moaning, running, lurching, and unstopping. Most looked like they were customers from *Hot Topics,* so I couldn't quite tell if they were zombies or not, but figured we might as well shoot them anyway.

"April. Use the M-60 and mow these things down quick!"

April swung the M-60 around and cut loose. She fired an entire belt of ammo and cut down the whole lot of them. Because of the noise on this side of the mall, we continued around to the other side and pulled up to a stop right in front of the doors nearest to what used to be an arcade. Shotgun in hand, I climbed out and covered the door. I could see movement inside, down the hall and in a shop. There was movement visible through all the doors, but this was the least... our safest bet going in. And the M-60 firing may have pulled more zombies away from this door to the other side. I hoped.

The girls came up behind me. "Are we ready?"

"I'm always ready." Jen quipped.

April nodded. Joy looked nervous. "If you want, Joy, you can stay in the M-ATV. It's armored, nothing can get in it. You'd be safe there."

"No, I want to be with you guys."

"Okay, let's go."

I pushed the door in and we filed through. I pulled out my hushed Glock and pulled it into a high compressed position. I turned to the girls, wishing we had radios for everyone. In a whisper, "We need to stay low profile and quiet. Your M4's have suppressors on them, but they still make a racket, so fire sparingly. Jen, your big magnums are really loud, so don't unleash those unless you absolutely have to."

"No one has ever complained about my big magnums before."

Jen was starting to give me a headache.

We followed the wall, keeping low and moving quickly. It was starting to get dark outside, so there was no light that came through the skylights. The after hours interior lighting was spartan and dim with lots of shadows. This was good and bad. We made it to the intersection of the main hall without attracting zed attention. I sliced the pie around the corner and looked for any sign of human life. The mall was in surprisingly good shape. A few kiosks were knocked over, and there was a lot of blood on the floor, smeared around, and blood splattered on windows. A clean-up crew could have the mall ready to open in about a day of hard scrubbing. There was power to the mall, and a couple stores here and there had lights on inside. I could hear music, but not much else.

Looking to the right, I could see *Macey's*. That didn't strike me as a place some wanna be gangsters would want to go "Get Stuff". I chose to come through this door because right across the main hall, there used to be a knife shop. I thought perhaps the young thuglings would want some knives. Unfortunately that store was no longer there. I looked down the hall to the left and decided that this situation was completely FUBAR and we should probably bail back out.

Okay, if I was a thugling, what would I want here. Nothing says gangster in the middle of a zombie apocalypse like *Bling*. Jewelry Store. There was one down this hall on the right.

I moved out, and the girls followed. The zombies in the stores stayed in the stores. Mainly because these stores had closed doors and zombies couldn't read push or pull. Some stores had the metal gates pulled down or only up a few feet. I guessed the mall was just opening when the plague of infected hit them.

We passed a couple stores quickly when I saw a zombie notice us. It was in the main hall, directly in our path. The zombie stopped its random shuffling and started coming our way. I put the dot of my front sight post on the zombie's head and fired a single round. The bullet impacted the zed's face and blew the back of its head out. The sound of the shot was as loud as the brass that ejected and hit the tiled floor. It was loud compared to the relative quiet of the mall. The zombie fell backwards and we hurried passed. The jewelry shop that was closest wasn't very far away, but from my perspective it seemed like a mile. Another zombie came out from behind a kiosk. It was a female zombie wearing a tight dress. She may at one time have been pretty, but the fact that she had almost none of her face left, kind of ruined it for me. We ducked down behind one of the 756 cell phone kiosks within two hundred yards and we stayed quiet. The faceless female zed turned and shambled around. She was circling a sunglasses kiosk, because its one thing you can't have too many of, cell phones and sunglasses. She went around the kiosk and I made my move. I pulled my Becker Combat Bowie and rushed.

As the zombie came back around my Becker was already in full swing. The knife intersected her head right at eye level and the heavy blade passed through bone and brain. Dark blood splattered the sunglasses. This zombie fell straight down, not having time to react or to make a sound. I crouched and looked around. We were clear. I motioned for the girls to come up and we moved out to the jewelry store. Its gates were shut, save for one which was half open. We ducked under the gate and went in.

The zombie in the store was wearing a name tag. *Steve*. He was wearing a white shirt, half tucked into his black slacks and had on a yellow neck tie. His nose was bitten off, as was a chunk of flesh off his head. His hands were bloody, his sleeves were shredded and he looked like he had been dead a long time. Steve lurched forward. I pulled up my hushed Glock and fired twice, one round going through the zombie's throat and hitting the wall behind him. The other round went through one of his sunken eyes. Steve fell forward. I looked at Steve, his name tag had the name of another store. So he wasn't the guy that worked here. He came in here after he turned, probably after someone. I looked around the store. The glass display cases were smashed, and a lot of the jewelry was missing. On the floor were some brass casings for pistol rounds. I knelt down and picked one up. 9mm. Looks like there was a chance our boys were here. There were bullet holes in some of the framed posters, and one of the mirrors was shattered.

I pointed out the evidence. "Take a look at this. I think they could have been here. So 'stuff' was jewelry." I whispered. In a very quiet voice, "I like jewelry." Joy looked at the options in the cases that were still left. Some rings, some earrings, and a broach. Nothing really interested her and she didn't take anything.

"I think there is another jewelers down the hall. Lets check there." We moved single file, quick and low. We moved further down the hall, this time staying in the middle, keeping obstacles in front of us. I could see up ahead a group of zombies, probably twenty five to thirty of them. They were in front of the *Victoria's Secret* store. We would have to get past these zombies. It turned left into the next main hallway. Some zombies went into and out of the store, milling about but not leaving. They were interested in something in there. I looked to my left and saw a toy store. I looked back at the zeds. I had an idea.

We slunk into the toy store and found in the back, two zombies that were both pulling on something. It was an arm. We interrupted their tug of war with a quick application of violence. The arm was pink and relatively fresh. I didn't say anything to the girls, but I think April and Joy noticed.

I opened up a pack of batteries and the packaging to a radio-controlled car. I used tape to attach a noisy flashing toy on top of it. I tested the obnoxious combo and the car drove fine. Okay, let's do this. I turned on the noise-maker and its lights blinked frantically as it beeped, buzzed, and made alarm sounds. Instantly a number of the zombies turned. I drove the little car out of the store and down the hallway. The zombies were in rapture at the horrible little toy. They moaned and ran to it. I drove the car around their legs and grasping, reaching hands and all the way into *Nordstroms*. The zombies followed, eagerly, even pulling more zombies out of other stores. The car darted into Nordstroms and went under some racks of clothes where it continued to make a racket.

April whispered into my ear. "I can't believe that worked."

"I know." I looked back and Joy was shaking her head.

Jen just grinned, "That was pretty smart."

"Let's check this out." I made a low run into the *Victoria's Secret*. There was blood everywhere in here. Fresh wet blood. April, when she ran in, skidded across the blood, but stayed on her feet. Joy wasn't so lucky, she slipped and crashed into a rack of teddies. Not much sound, and we were lucky on that. Jen came in with more grace than I would have thought in cowboy boots. She slid past me on her back like she was on a bloody Slip and Slide. Something soft cushioned her abrupt stop. She picked herself up and looked. We all froze. It was a zombie, engrossed in pulling out the innards of some guy. The zombie was making wet ripping sounds with the body.

"Roger!" April said.

The zombie, having been knocked into and not caring, suddenly became alert at the sound of a voice. It spun around. Jen was within arms reach! Jen gritted her teeth as she pulled her bowie. The zed grabbed her boot and moved to bite Jen. I started raising my .40 when Jen's knife slashed out. The zombie stopped moving and then in slow motion, the head fell forward and rolled away. Jen jumped up. She was coated in smeared blood.

We all walked over to the body. "Roger." Joy confirmed. You couldn't tell from the absence of flesh from the neck up, but on one of its shoulders there was a tattoo that said "BEAST".

"I guess this leaves two guys left?"

April nodded. Joy turned around and looked out of the store, not because she was sick or squeamish, but because she was pissed. "Idiots!" She hissed.

I looked over at Jen. She had taken off her shoulder rigs. "What..." I was going to ask what she was doing. But I didn't have to ask. She was stripping. She peeled the bloody shirt off, and used the cloth to wipe off the leather straps of the shoulder holsters. Then she pulled off her bra. She was certainly endowed. When she smiled at me, I realized I was staring and spun around. "Not a good time, Jen."

"Maybe we'll have a chance later then... but right now, I want out of these bloody clothes."

I pinched the bridge of my nose. That headache came back all of a sudden. You've got to be kidding me. She must have been 24 or 25 now, but I remembered her as a 16-year-old troubled girl. I was looking out the door, gripping my shotgun as Jen swaggered past completely naked. She picked up some negligee and poured her self into it, then some thigh-high stockings. Then some tight jeans and a little jacket.

Oh come on. Seriously?

"We've got to move, Jen. Quit teasing the Governor." Joy hissed again.

"I'm just having some fun."

Joy looked at me. "In case you get any ideas. Jen is mine." Then she smirked as she looked me up and down, "If you want some of her, you have to have some of me too."

"I'm happily married. Seriously."

Joy smirked again, "Of course you are."

I walked past Joy and up to April. "Are they serious?"

April looked back at Joy and Jen. "I'm afraid so. They've been going out for a couple years. They were going to go get married in California or something."

"So how do you know them? Are you..."

"No, no... I just lived next door to them." April explained in a whisper. "I was going to school."

"Oh yeah? That's cool. For what?"

"Accounting and business. I want my CPA."

"You don't seem like the accountant type."

"You should read a book called *MHI*."

"I know the author."

"Really?"

"Yeah, maybe I'll introduce you one day."

"Is he still alive?"

"Are you kidding? *MHI* is practically autobiographical." I held up my hand, "just give me a moment to process that you've read *MHI*. I'm still in shock."

"You're in shock about that, but not about Jen and Joy?"

"No, that really didn't surprise me."

"No? Not with all that 'check out my tits stuff she was doing."

"Come on, she's a hot twenty-something and I'm a broken-old man."

April looked over at me, "You're not that bad."

"Thanks."

Jen finished changing and threw her shoulder rigs back on. "How do I look?" She asked me for the second time that day.

"Fine." I growled.

"Just fine?" She said, sounding indignant.

"Just fine... at least you're not naked anymore. What, you want to take the wrapping off the zombie's happy meal? Come on, we're wasting time."

"Okay, look over there," I pointed out to the girls. "That store sells jewelry and the gate is wide open. That's where we are going."

I looked to the right, down the hall to *Nordstroms*, where the zombies were milling around trying to locate the source of the noise. They were moaning and other zombies were gathering from other parts of the store. I so wanted to pitch a grenade in there. So I did. A smoke grenade, instead of a frag. Not as much fun, but it covered our movement from the *Nordstrom* zombies as we headed out. Not as quickly as last time, but quick enough to cover the distance.

We ducked into the store and found it had been emptied. The only thing glittering was a lot of brass cases on the ground and broken glass. The display cases were completely emptied. Across the hall was a watch shop with high-end wrist watches. I could see brass cases in there, and another body covered in red blood. I pointed it out to the girls.

"Looks like that's Jerome." Joy said. "He liked fancy watches."

"One left then."

"Mikey."

"Where do you think Mikey would have wanted to go?"

"He liked knives."

"Follow me," April said as she led the way out and down a few stores to disappear into another shop." This store was dark, but it was light enough to tell that the cases had been raided. There was brass on the ground, it made sounds as it got kicked around.

I kicked something heavier and bent down to pick it up. It was a pistol locked back on an empty casing. It was a nickle plated Bersa with pearl grips. It was a better pistol than I would have expected. I expected a Lorcin or Jennings. I ejected the magazine and found that it was empty. I set the gun down. "Okay, if Mikey came in here, ran out of ammo... what would he grab?"

There was a sword rack on the wall. Two slots were missing the items they were holding. "Japanese swords, of course."

I was about to turn and leave. Hmmm, a Spyderco Native with the Stainless handles. I've been wanting one of those for over a decade. I grabbed it. It clipped nicely to my vest.

"I saw that." April said.

"Oh?" I nodded at her belt. A new Benchmade knife was clipped to her waist. "Isn't that the one they made to ape the Cold Steel AK-47 knife?"

"Completely different design."

"Uh huh."

It was at that moment we looked down the hallway and noticed something. A zombie, a big zombie with long hair, goth fishnet gloves over his arms, black t-shirt, and Juggaloo face paint... and a bright blue cord wrapped handle sticking out of its chest.

"He could still be alive."

"I'm doubting it."

At least April was honest. Grim, but honest.

"Hey, listen."

Banging sounds. "Is that?" April asked.

"Someone banging on something, yes."

"Let's go. Guns up!"

We moved quickly down the hall where I dispatched the big goth with the sword growing out of his chest and back, and hung a right heading into the food court. The sounds of the banging was from somewhere in this area. We didn't know where. But what we did know was that we ran into a big pack of walking corpses.

"Light'em up!"

I opened fire with my Mossberg and the sound of thunder filled the food court. Jen pulled out her Magnums and let off a round with a gun in each hand. The noise was deafening, even with the EP3 Earpro in my ears. The rounds however, were potent. One round penetrated multiple zombies, causing massive amounts of damage, knocking some zombies down, splattering others.

Joy and April got their M4's rocking and rolling. We were soon back to back, the four of us, firing into the zombies that had us surrounded. I shucked shells in four at a time, fire four, reload four, keeping this up, if it got real harry, I still had three in the magazine. Each blast obliterated a head or shattered a rib cage or crushed a pelvis. Either way, if a zed was coming, a hit from the 12 gauge stopped it right there. Jen started shooting one gun at a time. Blasting several zombies in line, then reloading. Joy was rusty with her M4, but April ran her SCAR with great skill. We ran out of zombies before we ran out of bullets... this time. But most of the zombies were not dead, just mobility killed. Meaning they were alive, but dragging themselves or were otherwise limited in their ability to come at us. Joy pulled out her M&P and started popping them in their heads.

"Hold on, stop. Save your rounds."

April covered the hallway, occasionally firing off single shots, dropping any zombie that wanted to come to the food court. I went to one of the shops and pulled out a large pan of cooking oil. I splashed it across the still living/ undead and went and got another pan. I pulled and splashed five more pans of oil over the zombies.

"Jen, follow the sounds."

"Got it!"

The banging sounds had stopped while we were shooting, but now picked up again, frantically.

"It's Mikey!"

"He's still alive?!" April was shocked. He was hiding in a supply closet of a Japanese joint, but some how got himself locked in. We quickly pulled him out and got moving again.

"Let's get moving, back to the truck." I lit a table rag and tossed it to the cooking oil. The oil caught and started burning, filling the mall with smoke that smelled like egg rolls and corn dogs.

We ran out of the hall around the corner and out an exit. Jen and Joy pulling Mikey, April pulling Tail End Charlie. We were out in the night sky... out of the mall. Never again! I swore under my breath.

"I hate shopping malls." April muttered.

We headed across the parking lot, with the M-ATV in sight. We were almost there. Mikey fell and neither Jen nor Joy could catch his fall.

"Oh crap."

"What?"

I turned and looked, Jen was pointing at Mikey's leg. There was chunk of flesh missing from the back of Mikey's calf muscle. We could see it through his ripped pants. I opened up the Spyderco and cut the pant leg away from the wound. The wound was red, and the meat looked dry inside. Like meat left out too long. Around the wound, the flesh was blackened, rotten.

"Oh crap." I stood up and backed away.

Mikey convulsed on the ground. "Yaarrrbble..."

Suddenly there was a flash of light. Wham! Mikey flopped to the ground, his head splattered all over the pavement like a smashed melon. The street lights in the parking lot made the brain matter glisten.

"I never liked Mikey." Jen blew smoke from the muzzle of her .500 Magnum.

A Little R & R at Camp Williams

We drove north through Orem on State Street, navigating around stopped traffic. In the darkness of the night, I could see that some areas had power, while others were blacked out. While I drove, the girls were talking about their plans. They came to the conclusion that hanging out with me was safer than heading out on their own.

"Can we?" April asked.

"Can you what?"

"Come with you... for a while." She sounded sheepish, not like the April I was coming to know.

"You think I was just going to drop you off someplace? Sure. You girls can ride along."

This seemed to make them feel better and they relaxed. Jen put on some music, Pink Floyd, which was the perfect selection.

"Hey, is there any Red Bulls and Gatorade back there?"

"Just empties." Jen answered.

I'll have to fix that. Up ahead on the left was the same Chevron that Zack and I had stopped at that had the sandwich shop attached. It still had power. I slowed down and rolled passed it slowly. It looked clear of any threats. I circled the area and then pulled in. Joy jumped out with me. We went in and gathered up cold beverages and put them in the back of the M-

ATV. I poked my nose into the sandwich side of the gas station. Things at the counter had started to go off, so I didn't make any sandwiches from that stuff. However the cooler still contained the large chunks of roast beef and turkey that they sliced to make sandwiches with. There were some vegetables, three different cheeses, some condiments, and a huge pack of kaiser rolls. The rolls felt a little stale, but they were still edible. It all came with us.

"I'm starving!" Joy exclaimed as I started bagging everything.

"We'll eat when we get to Camp Williams and we can relax."

"Sounds almost too good to be true."

"It's true."

With our little shopping done we drove straight back to Williams, cutting through Thanksgiving Point and entering through the back gate. As I drove through the gate, the soldiers pulling guard duty saluted. I stopped the truck, returned the salute, not thinking about it until after I did it. Returning a salute was old hat, I guess. We made introductions and I shook their hands. The soldiers were happy about that, being treated like people instead of book ends at the gate. "How are things going tonight?"

"It's quiet tonight... for once. We've not had to shoot a zombie since this afternoon."

"That's good... that's good. But if you wanted to kill zombies, you should have come with us. How long have you guys been on duty here?"

"All day, sir."

"All day? How come you haven't been relieved?"

"We're short on manpower so we're doing 12-hour rotations."

I knew from experience that you could not keep that kind of a schedule up for long. It would cause fatigue and burn out. "We'll see about that. Here... Hey, girls, give these guys something to drink."

I saw April toss each man a Gatorade and something else. The soldiers instantly brightened. What was that? I looked at the cans April had tossed... Bud Light.

"You guys are not going to have to pull guard here much longer." I pulled out, heading into the base.

The Specialist that had been at the gate turned to the Sergeant. "Who was that?"

"That was the Governor... the new Governor."

"And the girls?"

"Daughters, I guess." The Sarge looked a the Gatorade and popped open the beer instead. "I like this new Governor." He looked over at the Specialist... and put the Gatorade in his hand and took the beer. "But he didn't know you were under age."

We drove to one of the barracks building. The guard had set one aside for my use. It was empty of people, but the bunks were ready with clean sheets and blankets... rows of them. Foot lockers all had a couple towels on top. We unloaded the food and drink and carried them inside, then brought in some ammo boxes and our gear.

I was about to pull out my Becker Companion knife to slice some meat, but thought better about it. I didn't think I wanted to eat a sammich made with the same knife I'd used for zombie slaying. I pulled out of my pocket, the Cold Steel AK-47 knife I had clipped there, and started slicing. I made sandwiches for myself and for the girls. They were hungry and we ate and drank in relative silence. After we had eaten, the mood had lightened up considerably.

"So you really are the Governor then, huh?" Jen said, less as a question, more of a statement.

"You thought I was joking?"

"No, but it just didn't sink in until those soldiers saluted you."

"Yup, the Salutes make it official." Joy agreed.

I looked over at April who was chewing some beef. She just shrugged. "Don't look at me, I took you for your word. How else would you have a M-ATV? Most of the military hasn't even seen one of those." She said matter of factly, then kicked her boots off and put her feet up.

I was impressed that she knew what a M-ATV was. There was something about April that didn't jive. She wasn't just an accounting student. Not many of those had FN SCAR rifles, and knowledge to run them.

I started reloading all my magazines and suggested to the girls that they do the same with what they had. We went over cleaning and maintenance of the weapons with Jen and Joy. April of course had no problem with her SCAR.

With bellies full, the guns cleaned and readied, now I could relax. I pulled off my boots and picked up a towel. "I need a shower."

"There are showers here? I want one!" Joy exclaimed.

"Hey, I called it first." I held up a finger. "You girls can have it when I'm done."

I picked up my bag and went to the showers, but before I went in, I turned, "After." Innocent eyes just blinked at me. When I went inside I distinctly heard giggling.

I stripped my clothes off and tied the towel around my waist, then started to unwrap the bandage around my chest. I could feel the bandage sticking to the wound. I hadn't changed it since early that morning.

"That looks bad." Jen said. My knee jerk reaction would have been to cover up and act modest, but I had no idea how long Jen had been there, and frankly I just didn't care.

"It's not that bad. I had a doctor sew me up yesterday."

"What happened?"

"Zed tackled me, I landed on a sprinkler head. That's how I got the rake marks on my face too."

"I'm surprised you let one get that close."

"I was taken off guard... it happened. Now, are you going to just stand there and watch me or did you have something in mind that I'd say no to?"

"I just wanted to say thank you. Really... thank you. I don't know what we would have done if you hadn't shown up."

I nodded. "Well, I did what anyone would have done."

"I don't think so, but still, thanks."

I turned on the hot water. "I'm taking my shower now. Bye bye."

Jen turned , "I'll help you bandage back up when you're done." She walked out and I took a long, hot shower thinking about state issues and my wife, and why there were no doors to the showers.

I changed into clean skivvies and went to my bunk. True to her word, Jen applied a fresh bandage to my wound and didn't say another word. As soon as she was done, I pulled on a t-shirt and crawled into my bunk. I fell asleep almost immediately.

Getting my Girl Squad

I awoke with a start. I didn't know where I was. My ribs were on fire. I didn't hear the familiar sounds I was used to hearing in the night. Something was wrong. Instantly my hand behind my head, under my pillow, where my Glock rested. It was there. I grasped it and then held still, listening.

Memory and reality flooded back to me. I was at Camp Williams. I was in a barracks. I was on a bunk. There were three women in the same room. It was in the middle of the night. Early morning.

Slowly, quietly, I sat up and swung my legs off the bunk. Both feet on the ground. As I stood, I looked around. Through shadows I saw two people on the same bunk near mine. Long hair, blond, and long hair dark. In the other bunk, long hair, auburn, was laying on her side, breathing deeply but otherwise unmoving. Everyone was safe. Everything was fine. No threats. No moaning zombies. No blood.

I walked to the latrine, barefoot across the cold, hard floor. I used the bathroom and washed my hands, then ran water into my cupped hands and washed my face. The barracks had no mirror to look into. No moment of self reflection. I just felt tired, heavy, and full of remorse. I walked out across the barracks, past the bunks and went to the window facing north. From here, I could see out over the Veterans Cemetery where my Grandfather was buried... where I helped carry him to his resting place. Beyond that, the Salt Lake Valley. Normally it glittered with millions of lights, now, it was almost completely dark. In some places there were lights, some electric, some fire. All completely quiet.

I felt someone come up behind me, silent as a cat. She put an arm around me and her head against my shoulder as I stared out across the ruined city. I turned my head slightly and saw that the hair looked dark red in the strange light. She smelled of softness. "I've never seen Salt Lake so quiet." I whispered, looking back out the window. I felt her head turn, and her breath on my neck.

"I don't know how to tell you... but you saved my life." April whispered so quietly, it was as if her voice went straight from her brain into my mind. "I was going to..." I felt her whole body shudder, and heard a small sob. I didn't say anything.

"Then you pulled up in front of the store."

"It's okay, Sunshine." I lied. *Nothing was okay*, I thought as I looked back out at a dead city. I was surprised though. April had seemed so tough to me, so together. Now here she was weeping on my shoulder like a little girl. I put an arm around her and held her. So tough before. Now, at this moment, she seemed small and frail. She broke down into a full cry. I put both arms around her and held her tighter for a few moments... she shook in my arms as she cried, like a little girl.

"Hey now. You are a strong woman, April. I really respect that. You'll get through this. We'll all get through this, together." I kissed her on her forehead like a father.

"Now go get back into your bunk and get some sleep. We have work to do tomorrow."

Obediently she stood up straighter, looked at me with a sheepish smile and turned to go back to her bunk. I turned back to the window. I heard her crawl into bed and the rustling of the thin, woolen military blanket. I let out a sigh and looked at my watch. 3:33AM. Up in the sky the stars were visible. Not especially bright due to some of the lights at Camp Williams, but probably the best SLC has had in 80 years. I searched the heavens for signs or signals or omens. I saw only distant points of light, cold and unfeeling. I returned to my bed.

Some time later in the night, my nose was filled with the smell of softness, and I felt warmth against my forehead, just briefly, then suddenly it was gone again. I didn't move, didn't open my eyes. But I thought, "you're welcome." Then I rolled over onto my side.

Hours later I felt the sunlight of a later-than-intended morning warm my eyelids. I rolled over and pulled my hand up to my face. With one eye cracked slightly I looked at my watch again. It was after 8:30AM. I hate mornings.

I threw off my blanket and swung my legs out. The floor felt cold still, just as I remembered it. I looked over at April's bunk. It was made tight. I looked behind me, Jen and Joy's bunks were made as well. Their gear was gone. All the gear was gone. I had my ruck at the foot of my bunk. I didn't know if I was ready for another day, especially not one that started out with a curious beginning. I looked at my clothes in my ruck, the ones I'd worn yesterday, then the clean ones I had left. I quickly got dressed in my last pair of clean clothes. BDU pants in desert camo, "DCUs" as they called them, a long-sleeved Under Armour shirt, under which was fresh wrappings around my chest.

I went back to my bunk and sat on my footlocker as I pulled on socks and then my boots, my ancient black combat boots that I had been issued when I first went to Fort Benning. Lacing them up was like an old unbreakable habit I wish I had quit a long time ago. Beside my ruck lay my shotgun and my tactical vest. I pushed myself into the vest again, but left it open. I slung my ruck over my left shoulder, and my shotgun I slung in a low ready under my right shoulder. I walked outside through the door facing the east, facing the rising sun. It was bright and I had a second or two of my eyes adjusting to the new light before I could see. There was the M-ATV, parked where I had left it. I walked over to it and threw my ruck into the back.

I looked up and saw three figures approaching, silhouetted against the morning sun. The three figures walked with a sway in exactly the way men don't. I looked at them as they came nearer. It was a stunning sight, beautiful ladies, each with a fully automatic weapon slung casually across their backs. They were smiling in unison. One could easily fall in love, but I was suspicious. When they got closer, "You guys are up to something."

"They have hot food here!" Jen was excited. "Here! We got you some breakfast!" She had a plate of eggs, hash browns, and grits.

"Hey, thanks." I just realized that this was probably the first time since the uprising started that they had a hot meal.

Joy held out a cold can of Diet Coke. "They didn't have regular."
I took the plate and the can of soda and looked at the M-ATV. With a standard Humvee, you can eat your chow on the hood. With the M-ATV that's not really happening unless you are freakishly tall. Luckily there was a picnic table just a few feet away.

"You girls already ate?"

"Oh yeah, we're stuffed. The chow hall was great. Everyone was so nice to us! We just said that we were your body guards and they let us in and gave us all the food we wanted. It was cool."

"They treated you right?"

"Yeah, they were very nice."

"Good... good."

April handed me a note. It was from Whiskey Six's pilot. He said that they had recovered the three bodies of my body guards and that they are in the morgue, waiting for disposal.

Disposal? I'd see to that later.

The girls sat down around the table. April smiled at me sheepishly. I just gave a slight nod to her. There was nothing to talk about on that account. I ate my breakfast with the plastic fork and drank my Coke as the girls talked about the day before and what they might do today.

That's when I cleared my throat to get their attention. "You girls have passed yourselves off as my body guards. You are not beholden to me... you owe me no duty." I looked at April when I said that.

"You guys are welcome to escort me while I'm out here in the Salt Lake Valley, but I'm moving everything back to the Uintah Basin. That's where I am going. You can come with me. Or you can go do whatever you want to do. You're free to make your own choices."

Jen had a look of panic in her eyes, Joy seemed relieved, and April just looked down at her hands. "You can do what you want."
"The Governor needs body guards. I'll do that, if that's okay." April said without looking up.

"That's fine with me, April."

Joy looked at Jen and back at me, but didn't say anything. "Joy, you can take a truck if you like. You can go where ever you want." I could tell that she wanted to stay with Jen, that was obvious, but Joy's response though was what surprised me.

"I'm with you. No matter what."

Jen smiled, "Me too."

Joy seemed relieved. She was worried that Jen had maybe wanted to go.

"Okay then. You're my team." I held out my hand over the center of the table. April's hand was the first to cover mine, then Joy's, then Jen's. "It's official now." And with that, they went from being girls I saved to being my Body Guard Team. I wasn't sure that I needed one, but it gave them purpose.

"And Jen... no more trying to sex up the Governor. I'm not a Clinton."

The girls laughed and joked that if April or Joy had tried, it would have worked.

Having finished the last of the grits and eggs, I retrieved the sat-phone from the M-ATV and started making some calls. First was to my family. We had left a sat-phone at Ogre Ranch.

Everyone was okay, kids missed me, wife loved me... everything was good there. "Where's Zack?" I asked.

"He's still in bed... with Rosa." My wife was frank and I wasn't surprised about that bit of news. "When are you coming home?"

"I've got to get some things organized."

"I see you are still at Camp Williams."

"How do you see that?"

"Zack showed me the Blue Force Tracker. I'm looking at it now. You've been parked there since late last night."

Ah... "Keeping tabs on me, eh? Did Zack tell you about what happened yesterday?"

"Yes. You had a big fight and your body guards got killed... I'm sorry... "
"That's why I didn't want Kilo coming with me. Things are not stable out here. Not yet."

"He can handle some zombies, he's fine. He even got up early and he's

124

doing great."

"Sweetheart... did Zack tell you about the guys from Evanston?"

The line was quiet... then really slowly she said, "What guys from Evanston?"

I laid it out. "He killed some people. So did Zack, so did I. Humans. Real people. Keep an eye on him, make sure he processes this right."

"I will. I knew your body guards were killed. I didn't know how. I don't like the idea of you being alone out there."

"I'm not alone. I have a new security team."

"How did you..."

I held the phone out. "Say hello to my wife, girls!"

"Hello!" They all sounded out with cheer.

"Ah... they are all women? Are they good looking... of course they are... you watch it, Hill Boy!"

"I'm fine... Yeah, and you remember Jen from Wind River?"

"Hey Teach!" Jen called out.

"They are survivors. They fight well."

"Oh, I know. Women will protect you better then men. They'll fight harder for you."

I looked at the girls around the table. She might be right.

"Okay, I've got some other calls to make... Three Hundred Plus!"

"Three Hundred Plus.... now promise me."

"I'll come home safe, I promise."

I hung up and called another number. Nightcrawler got on the line, "Governor Ogre."

"Hey, Mike. How is it going up there?" We talked about everything going on and what I had in mind, then I hit him with the question. "Now talk to me about big ordinance."

We talked for a while and my plan was coming together. I hung up the sat-phone with a big smile on my face. I took off my glasses and put on my sunglasses again. I was so happy I gave Jen a pat on the back as I laughed to myself.

Joy looked at me with a raised eyebrow. "You can be really f'ing evil."

A couple soldiers were approaching. I recognized them from before. Specialist Meyers and Speedy, the female trooper that had Zack at gun point. I stood up, "Specialist Meyers, good to see you again... And PFC Speedy." As they got closer I looked at Meyers collar, the Specialist emblem was gone, replaced by a Bar. Speedy's collar had three stripes on it. "I see you guys got some promotions. Did the Captain promote you?"

"He did, just before he put a gun in his mouth." Lt. Meyers held out a fist. "How's the Governor this morning?"

I gave him a fist bump, "I'm doing just fine, Lieutenant."

"We've got some good news, in bound, right now."

"What's going on?"

"The 19th SF Group is coming back from Afghanistan."

This was good news. "That's great!"

"What's left of it."

I could hear an aircraft and looked up into the sky. A C-130 flashed past, low overhead in a hard bank. The pilot was probably checking the area out around the flight strip before committing to setting the bird down.

"Let's go welcome them home."

I threw the paper plate and empty can into the trash and we all climbed into the M-ATV. Meyers and Speedy climbed into the very back, standing up. I could hear him talking into his radio, ordering some trucks to the air strip.

The air strip was across the highway, in the training area side of the camp. We drove up as the C-130 taxied back from its landing. Humvees and an MRAP and a couple Deuces pulled up besides us, waiting for the plane to come to a stop. I climbed out and stood in front of my truck as Lt Meyers and Speedy climbed down.

The C-130 taxied right in front of us and turned away so the ramp was close. It opened slowly and as it lowered, I could see people standing inside. I counted heads, twenty two men. Dirty, haggard, but standing proud. There were a couple stretchers with men laying in them. Guardsmen rushed forward, including Lt Meyers and Speedy. Salutes were thrown, hands shook, and gestures were made.

I stood waiting at the M-ATV. April came up, slightly behind me. She had her SCAR slung in front of her, just in case. The litters with the injured men were carried out of the plane to one of the Deuces, and the members of the 19th stepped out into the Utah morning sunshine.

Lt Meyers approached with a tall and lean 19th member behind him. The SF guy wore a Lt Bar on his collar, but the look about him said that he had worn it for some time. Lt Meyers introduced the man. "Governor Hill, this is Lieutenant Anderson."

Since I wasn't a member of the military, I didn't salute, but I held out my hand. "Lieutenant, I'm glad you and your men made it back."

Lt Anderson shook my hand, "We're glad to have finally made it. We've been fighting our way home since this all started."

"It's taken you some time then."

"We were in Afghanistan when things started. Chinese cargo planes landed in Iran, Turkey, UAE, Saudi Arabia, in the Stan... At Kabul. Sick people, infected people got out of the planes. The Middle East is now officially back in the stone ages."

"So China orchestrated this."

"They did, but it backfired on them. China is completely wiped out. Hong Kong, Beijing, gone."

"How did you guys get out?"

"We confiscated a plane and flew into Turkey, took another plane from there and made it to Ireland. We lost most of our men in Ireland. The whole island is crawling. We barely made it out."

"How many did you have before?"

"One hundred eighty five when we landed in Ireland. Fifty when we left. It was a bitch in New York." Anderson looked at April, "Sorry, Mam. New York was completely infected but we took a 747 from there and made it to Hill Air Force Base... got there this morning. They were kind enough to give us a lift here."

"We're very glad you made it. We can use you guys, big time. Take your men to one of the barracks, settle down, relax. You can write a report later... if you guys like, you can take some Humvees, go see about your homes."

"That's our plan, sir."

"I want everyone back here tonight. 8PM. If you guys have family – bring them. If you guys find survivors, bring them. Now go take care of your men, let them know."

"Yes, sir."

Anderson jogged off. I looked at Meyers, "Did you catch that?"

"What happens at eight?"

"Briefing, orders. We're going to throw down tonight."

"You have a plan?"

"I have a big plan. We have a lot of work to do."

"What do we need to do now?"

I started telling Meyers what I had in mind. As I explained, he was nodding his head. When I got to the big part, his eyes got big. "No way!"

It took Meyers some time to let it all sink in.

I looked at my girls. They needed to get kitted out better if they were going to be seriously used as my security detail.

We went to Supply and got them BDU pants, tactical vests, radios, good EarPro and EyePro, boots, tactical holsters that worked. I still had some NVGs but we grabbed a couple more, along with a few more LAW rockets... because, well, I love the damned things.

The new uniforms gave the girls a more serious look. Hair pulled back into pony tails, caps, Wiley X sunglasses, armor plates in the vest/carriers. Pant legs, tucked into their boots. Everyone had their big knives on their belts. They really looked like a security detail now.

The problem with this is that I have a firm belief that the female posterior looks absolutely amazing in BDU pants. Stunning even. April's... well... Some things can go without saying.

Jen protested the loss of her .500 Magnums, but we turned them in to Supply along with all the .500 Mag ammo, in favor of a pair of SIG P228's in 9mm. She loaded up on magazines and we grabbed an extra crate of 9mm ammunition for her. She pouted in the M-ATV as she loaded up magazines and got them ready.

"How do you use this?" April asked, holding up a LAW. I grabbed a dummy LAW and traded her for the live one. "Take it with both hands, like that... now pull it firmly, all the way out. Good. With the sights up. Now put it on your shoulder."

"It's very light."

"It is, but the live unit is heavier... but it's still light. Easy to use. Easy to miss with too."

I explained the use of the sights, how to use the brackets, where to aim.

"Now to fire it, you pull this tab out. That cocks the mechanism. Then depress this, the trigger is under the rubber, just crush it down." The dummy LAW "clicked".

"There, that was the shot."

"That's easy!" She beamed.

"Easy to use, that's the whole idea. And it packs a pretty good punch."

"I want some."

"Sure, go grab some more.

FIVE

Prepping for the Big Bang!

After talking with Zulu, aka my brother Zack, we devised a simple thing. The concept of the "Thumper" from the movie "*Dune*" was a good idea. Combine that with the radio-controlled car I had used in the mall, and we had something that would attract massive numbers of zombies in a real hurry. The Rabbit. Recordings of screams, combined with flashing lights and other noises would be played from a remotely controlled or robotic platform. The Rabbits would then be dropped off in different areas around the Salt Lake Valley. The Rabbits would converge in a large open area just west of I-15 in between Midvale and West Jordan. The area was large enough, but I wished it was larger. For the digital recorders and the playback, we made a run back to Cabela's.

When we pulled up, there was a small truck parked out front. A Ford Explorer. There must be people inside. I made note of the vehicle as I climbed out. "We'll need someone to stay here... Man the Sixty."

"You mean, Whoa-Man the Sixty."

I looked up at April. "Absolutely."

We did a radio check, and everyone's comms worked. I unlimbered my shotgun as Jen and Joy did the same with their M4's. In case of problems, I directed them to put in the EarPro. We didn't know who was inside or what they were doing... or if they would be hostile or not.

Joy led the way. In uniform, with hats and sunglasses on, the two girls looked similar. Joy's black hair however, was a strong contrast to Jen's blond. Joy went through the entrance and I followed, with Jen coming in behind me. I didn't see any movement. The new EarPro we snagged amplified sounds that were normal, but dampened loud sounds, like gunshots. Because of this, we heard someone in the store, near the gun counter area. We spread out and knelt down with weapons at the ready. Someone was breathing hard, arms loaded with rifles, like they were cord wood. He was straining to carry them all at once, and didn't notice us. I decided to be helpful and offer a suggestion.

"A shopping cart would make it easier."

The man screamed, and promptly dropped half the rifles he was carrying. All Brownings. A collector, perhaps.

"You really should only take what you need, someone else may come in later and need something to protect his family or something."

"Fuck you! Who the hell do you think you are telling me what to do?"

Joy instantly struck as fast as a Mongoose, she darted in and raised the butt of her rifle, about to deliver a smashing blow to the guy's head.

"JOY! STOP!"

Joy didn't hit the guy, but came real close. She sneered at the man, "Show some respect for the Governor."

The guy froze, then thought for a moment. "Uh... I guess I don't need all of these..."

"Do you?"

"Huh?"

"Do you need them?"

"Some of them."

"Good. Take the ones you need... leave the ones you don't... Be fair to other survivors. That's all I'm asking."

"Yeah, yeah, Okay..."

"Do you have ammo for these rifles?"

"No."

"You'll need ammo."

"Yeah."

"Okay, don't forget it.

"Okay..."

"We cool?"

"Huh?"

"Are you cool... are you going to cause me or my Security Team any problems?"

The Man looked at me, then at the girls. "N, n, no, sir."

"You aren't going to go into Salt Lake are you?"

"Yeah..."

"Stay away from Midvale, okay?"

"I'm going up to Logan."

"Good, that's good... now, go along."

The man hurried out the door with a bunch of rifles as the girls and myself continued to where the hunting calls were.

The radio squawked to life. It was April. "There's a man out here pissing himself."

"Are you pointing my M-60 at him?"

"Yeah."

I had to laugh, "Move the gun barrel away from him and wave him by."

"Got it."

A moment later I could hear through the radio the squealing of tires. "The guy decided to leave."

"Roger that, Alpha, keep an eye out." That's too bad. The guy forgot the ammo.

"Joy."

"Yeah?"

"Were you going to hit him?"

"Yeah."

"Let's not hit people unless they try to hit you or me."

"Okay."

"A protection detail protects my life, not my tender sensibilities."

Joy was smiling, "ah... okay."

We found the hunting calls. The ones we wanted were from FOX PRO. The ones that allowed the use of memory cards or were otherwise recordable. We gathered up a total of 25 of the units, from what they had out on the shelf and from what they had stored in the back. This would be enough. Using shopping carts, we pulled the units back to the M-ATV and started to pile everything in.

"One more thing." I said as I went back inside. The M-ATV only had so much room for everything, but this was important. I grabbed a Yeti cooler, tan colored, a large one. I took it out to the M-ATV, "Make room for this in the back someplace."

I ran back inside, upstairs. The power had not failed here, and the fridges had kept everything cold. Meats, cheeses, elk roasts and boar brats. Unfortunately the bread was all bad. There was some mustard and that was it. I grabbed it up and carried it out.

"You must really love deli food."

"Yup. I hate being hungry."

"We need ice."

"It's coming."

Ice, lots of ice, and drinks, lots of drinks. "You know, you girls could help... most of this is for you."

"You want to make us fat?"

"More cushion."

Jen raised an eyebrow. "Oh Really?"

I went back inside. I came out pushing a shopping cart full of ice and bottles of water and other assorted beverages. We got it all loaded up "These little deli raids are going to run out real quick. We've been lucky this stuff has been kept cold. It probably wont last long." I climbed in the driver's seat, "so go ahead and dig in if you get hungry or thirsty." This was the best thing about the Yeti coolers, they are expensive as hell, but nothing keeps stuff cold as long.

I looked at the BFT screen after I fired up the engine. I had a message. Zulu. "Thinking about going to the SLC Airport. Document the start of the infection here."

I messaged back. "Cool. Look for survivors, leave my kids at home. Use caution. The Thumper idea. Try to test it. I think it will work, I'm going to use it for something big."

I sent a message to Mike at HAFB. "I need all the EOD Robots you guys have, and any other robots you have around there. Anything remote control that can be driven from a distance. The Big Package we talked about... we need it ready to go. Soon."

All the girls got in positions, Jen behind me, Joy beside me, April above me. "Everyone ready?"

I cracked open a Mountain Dew and took a swig, then put the M-ATV into motion.

"Where to, boss?" Joy asked, while checking the action on her weapon.

"The Capitol Building."

The drive to SLC proper was about an hour. April had pulled herself down from the Up Top position and was sitting behind Joy. We listened to Nightwish's second album as we took the freeway exit and followed the streets into the city.

One of the things I remembered seeing, driving through down town Salt Lake City... Was Temple Square. In the midst of the utter chaos that had become Salt Lake, was this oasis of peace. The gates to Temple Square had been closed and men in suits stood behind the gates. They wore sunglasses and held P-90's. I drove around Temple Square and saw there were a lot of men in suits. The zombies could clearly see the men through the gates and would normally be piling on the gates to get to fresh meat. However the zombies stayed clear of the gates. In fact, they didn't even cross the street towards the gates. I pulled up to the south side gate and stopped the M-ATV. The men in suits just looked at me. I got out of the truck and walked up to the gate.

The men smiled, one of them said, "Good to see you, Governor Hill."

"Good to see you guys too. You need anything, any supplies?"

The men just smiled, "We have sufficient for our needs. Thank you. Is there anything we can do for you?"

"Pray for us."

"That is already being done."

"The First Presidency?"

"They are fine, Sir." Again, said with a confident, peaceful smile. As he said that though, he took a step back, indicating that the conversation was over and that I was dismissed. I nodded and got back into the M-ATV and continued to the Capitol.

Flesh-eating Politicians

I couldn't believe the number of walking dead that were all around. If we had to park and walk in, this would be impossible. Instead, we pulled into the east side, where the underground parking was. I pulled up to the key pad. The M-ATV isn't really drive-through friendly, so I had to open the door and half climb out to reach the key pad. "April, pull the M-60 down."

April scrambled up and started to take the gun down as I typed in my access code. "45 357 9" The gate started to roll up, just as zombies from the street started shambling their way to us.

"It's down!"

I pulled forward, slowly. The top of the M-ATV just barely fit. We pulled in and stopped. The gate started to come down but not before two zombies got under. I jumped out of the rig and pulled my shotgun up to my shoulder. As soon as the zombies recognized fresh meat, they charged.

Cara, my Mossberg 930 SPX 12 gauge, lived up to its name. The name is Gaelic for "Beloved" and I really did love this gun. Cara spoke twice. One blast crushing the upper torso of the first zombie, knocking it down flat. The second blast removed the head of the other zombie. The first zombie was on the ground, writhing, trying to find my legs. I shucked two shells in from the pouch attached to my vest's belt. I took aim at the zed again, trying not to think about how this one reminded me of one of the staffers here who was always cheerful and helpful. Boom! I reloaded one more shell, then did a ghost load so I had a full nine shells on tap. From deeper in the parking structure I heard moaning from more than one zombie.

I wanted to work my way in, instead of driving straight up to the entrance. The Girl Squad flanked me.

"Remember where we parked, everyone." Jen quipped.

We started moving, and didn't get more than a dozen steps before at least twenty zombies came at us at a full-tilt run. Dead, white, fish eyes. Bloodied hands reaching out. Moans of hunger and desperation coming out of blood-soaked mouths. Bursts of fire from full auto weapons. Empty brass tinkling on the smooth concrete floor. Bodies falling. The zombies got closer and Cara spoke again.

BOOM! BOOM! BOOM! BOOM! BOOM! BOOM! BOOM!

Then all was still save for the echoing of the shotgun's reports. I reloaded as we walked. Seven shots fired, seven shells reloaded.

As we passed the bodies, more of those broken faces looked like people I had seen and dealt with. Fellow legislative workers who had made it into the parking area before they turned, having been bitten inside. The offices of the

Legislature were going to be ugly.

A few more zombies jumped out at us, but the girls dropped them. They were getting better.

There was a door that led to the office's lower levels. We went through, moving quickly into the hallway. At the far end of the hallway were several zombies bent over a body, they were face down into it, absorbed in the feasting. We stopped and I took the rifle from Joy's hands, who obliged by hitting the quick disconnect on her single-point sling. I raised the weapon to my shoulder and sighted through the ACOG. "Psst!"

One of the zombies looked up I shot him first, before cutting lose on the others. In a couple seconds, all the zombies were down. I handed the rifle back to Joy. "I think I like my shotgun best for inside.'"

We continued through the hallway until we got to the next set of doors. Before I pushed the next set, I looked down at the body. A Senator from central Utah. I don't remember his name. It wasn't important any more, but I remembered that he was a good guy. I pushed the door a crack and looked in. It was dark. This is why I made sure we all had NVGs. These were not the very latest generation but they were good. I put mine on and helped the girls with theirs. "This is cool!" Joy whispered. Yeah, it was. I had to agree.

We pushed inside, slowly, working our way along the walls to the right. From here we could go right, into the office buildings, or left into the Capitol. Office building first. I lowered my shotgun on to its sling and pulled up the pistol. It was much quieter. Through the goggles, the Tritium inserts in my pistol sights glowed like beacons. This is one advantage of my Warren Tactical sights... the "Straight 8" configuration of the tritium with the brighter one on the front sight post; it made sighting with the Glock much easier than normal 3-dot type sights.

I spoke in the softest of whispers, knowing that the electronic EarPro would pick the sound up with no problem. "Let's see if any Senator's are still alive in here." If there was one, he was then the Governor of Utah and I could go home. Let him or her deal with the mess.

We went in and started checking offices. We'd open a door and a zombie would lurch forward, only to be shot in the head. Sometimes we would open the door and find just a body or two. What we didn't find, were any survivors.

We worked our way down the hallway, up the stair case, down another hallway. We would enter a new floor and I would shoot all the zombies in the hallway so it was clear and we could work the offices. We cleared all three office buildings and found nothing. I had stopped in my office, sat in my chair. I really liked that chair. It was leather, with studs, it tilted and swiveled. It was dark red. My desk was big, wood, and one of those desks that put barriers between you and whoever comes to see you. "Power Desks". I've always thought they were for cowards to hide behind, not for getting work done. Come to think of it, I hated this office. Loved the chair, but hated the office.

"I'm getting really low on ammo. Let's get back to the truck and reload." We made our way back down into the parking garage. Near the truck, the outside of the gate, there was a zombie reaching through, he was tall and skinny and his arms both reached long into the structure. He looked like he wanted to say something. His mouth opened and closed, his eyes, while white and dead, looked pleading. I came closer, but stayed out of reach. The zombie made strange sounds in the back of its throat. "K, k, k, k... mmm-mmm."

"Did you hear that?" I turned to the girls. April was tilting her head, looking at the zombie.

"K, k, k, k... mmmmmmmm."

"Is he saying kill me?"

"He couldn't be. Zombies have no intelligence left."

"What about that film '*Land of the Dead*' where those zombies used guns and pumped gas?" April asked.

"Or that one about the slave zombies?" Jen offered.

"You mean '*Fido*' where they were more like pets than slaves." I corrected her. "But bad zombie movies don't really teach us about zombies, they are just some dude's idea to make his movie different."

"Oh, well what movie teaches you what you need to know?" Joy asked with a hand on her hip.

"*Zombieland*." I said flatly as I turned around and pulled my side arm.

"K, k, k, k... mmmmmmm." The zombie uttered once more. This time, I got the distinct impression it was pleading for death.

A single shot to the forehead and the zed slumped against the grate and hung there by the arms. I thought about the zombie's sounds as I reloaded magazines. I'm not sure what that meant, a zombie with some sort of intelligence left... but it made me all kinds of uncomfortable.

Once all the magazines were reloaded and my shotshell pouch was refilled with 00 Buck, we were ready to go again, I paused, drank a big pull on a Gator-Bull.

"Are we ready for this again?" I looked at the girls. They looked tired.

Jen asked "Why are we doing this? Seriously, what's here that is so important?"

"There might be a survivor in the government... A senior congressman... someone..."

"So?"

"So... that would mean that they are the Governor, not me."

"But you have control of the Utah National Guard, you're calling the shots."

"I know, that's why... I've got to make sure. Before I do what I'm going to do, I have to know."

The girls got quiet. They knew what my plan was, and they understood. April turned away. "Just so you know, I didn't stay with you to body guard the Utah State Governor. I stayed with you to body guard you. If we find someone in there, they will have to get their own security detail." She picked up her SCAR rifle and slipped her head and arm through the single-point sling.

I picked up my shotgun again and reconsidered. The Capitol building itself, was large. Inside, under the dome, were two chambers: the legislative and the judicial. There can be hundreds of people inside on a busy day, and the morning of the uprising was certainly busy. Outside, as we pulled in I counted at least six different news vans and cop cars surrounding the building. So far we've seen no police, no reporters, no camera crews. That meant everyone was inside... in there... under the dome. I detached my shotshell pouch and threw the 930 SPX into the M-ATV. I needed more firepower than that. I opened the back door and reached in. The M-60. I pulled it out and the familiar weight felt good in my hands. I checked the belt that was in it and grabbed a couple others and looped them around my neck. I pulled the charging handle all the way to the rear and opened the feed tray cover, laid a belt in carefully, and shut it. Just to be sure, I gave it a light slam with my fist... for luck. The Hog was ready.

"Let's go."

Through the parking garage, through the doors, down the hall, and this time we took a left. April and Joy led the way with Jen taking up Tail End Charlie. Our NVGs were the only way it was possible to see anything. The darkness was complete. There was the option of an elevator or stairs. We opted for the stairs. I swung the Hog up and covered the stairs above us. April went wide around, giving me room to maneuver the Hog. Joy stayed closer to me. Jen was right behind me. We could hear shuffling, soft sounds above us, nothing about the sounds were normal. April saw the first zombie on the stairs as she sliced the pie. She fired a three-round burst and the zombie fell. She quickly ran up the flight half way and her gun barked a couple more times. Joy dashed forward and her gun was firing. I chugged up the stairs with the Hog but when I got up to where I had sight, the zombies in the immediate area were down.

We came up into the main floor of the capital building. The white marble floor was washed in blood, pieces of meat, and shredded cloth that used to be people's clothes. The floor was slippery and I had to look down as I stepped on something soft. It was a human hand, torn from the wrist. I looked around and didn't see the wrist it came from. There was light coming from open windows and we were able to pull our NVGs up. We moved to a large pillar and I peeked around it. The main floor was wide and long, the full length of the building. To one side, I had the east entrance and the gift shop for tourists and freshmen congressmen. I dropped a couple hundred bucks in there myself my first time here after I got elected. To the right, I looked down the hall and saw a lot of zombies. Some in police uniforms, some of these zombies still had rifles on slings hanging off of them. These zeds were tore up the worst. Probably because in life, the officers put themselves between the zombies and people. They were shredded. I whispered, "take them" and the girls opened up with careful aimed fire. Zombies started dropping before they realized what was happening, then they surged. In mass the zombies turned and moved toward us. I unwrapped the belt from around my arm to let it just drape over the arm.

"Stand back, Girls!"

I opened fire.

The Hog chewed up zombies, with each round cutting through several of them at once as the gun spat out brass and links. We walked forward as I fired, moving into the center of the building. The girls picked off stragglers and wounded zombies. Soon, the whole floor was cleared as my gun ran dry. Above us we could hear a chorus of moaning. There were stairs that went up to the next level so we followed them. At the base of the stairs I knelt down with the Hog's bi-pod legs extended. Again, I pulled back on the charging handle, put the gun on Safe, opened the feed tray cover, and laid a new belt of ammunition in the tray. I shut the cover, gave it a lucky smack with my fist, and hoisted the Hog back up.

The stairway went up behind another set of stairs, that went back overhead... a set on each side of the room. The girls instantly started firing as we quickly moved around and up onto the next set of stairs. The Hog was hot, but ready to go and when I had a good number of zeds in front of me, I opened up again. The gun ran like a machine, and again, zombies were cut down as they came forward. Jen pulled me as I walked backwards up the stairs. April and Joy cleared the stairs above us. Zombies from around the atrium and others on the floor we had just left, surged up after us, but the Hog didn't let them get far.

I pointed, "In there!" The State Senate Chambers. The big doors were made of heavy wood and frosted class. Joy pushed the doors open and we filed in. The doors shut and I stopped shooting. Smoke wafted up off the barrel and action of the gun. We moved in and found a number of zombies that were already rising from their previous kills. I set the Hog down and pulled my pistol. The zombies inside were slower, but had been no less effective in getting blood all over. The girls checked everywhere, stepping over dead zombies as we moved. They pulled open doors, even checked behind desks. Nothing. I picked the Hog back up and leveled it at the frosted door. Shadows moved on the other side of the glass. I opened fire again and blew the door out. Zombies were cut down as I pushed forward to the door and cleared the area around it. The gun ran dry again,

"Reloading!"

The Girls turned their guns up to loud as they took over, outside the door and in both directions, zombies were dropping. I got the Hog fed again and pulled it back up. Small offices surrounded the Atrium as we moved around the upper floor. Soon the hundreds of zombies inside the capital were now gone. Gunsmoke filled the space, as did the smell of blood. But the zombies were done.

I put in my last belt and the M-60 was ready for more work, but nothing was apparent. We moved out to the court side of the joint, and found a few zeds in there, but that was it. Joy finished them off and we were essentially done.

We had no luck finding any survivors holed up anywhere in the buildings. The State Capitol was a tomb. Part of me was relieved, that I was still the Governor. The other part of me was disappointed. I wanted to go home. I was tired. The walk back to the M-ATV came after a detour to the office of the Governor. My office now. It was big. The desk a massive monolith of dark lacquered wood. In a cabinet were some flags. A small Utah State Flag and a US Flag. I took both of them. As I was leaving, I stopped and went back to the desk. I dropped the heavy M-60 machine gun down on top of it and walked around.

The chair was big, leather covered, and impressive. I sat in the chair. The girls looked at me, then at each other. I pulled the NVGs off my head and leaned back with my eyes closed. This was my office now. My chair.

I didn't like it.

On the desk were some papers, reports of the spread of the infections. First reports were of a new strain of rabies, others about Chinese ties to flights that went to Seattle, Portland, Boise, Vegas, Denver. Airliners to some cities fell out of the sky en route, but somehow those cities were infected anyhow. No corner of the country was untouched. I went through page after page. Other countries were infected as well. Africa, Australia. Europe was reported to be heavily infected. Then the reports stopped. That was it. In just a matter of hours, the infection had spread faster than wild fire.

I put the papers down and didn't touch anything else. Back at the M-ATV we ate chunks of meat and cheese for lunch. The girls were all facing away from the gate, and I understood. The zombie at the gate was still hanging there, staring, mouth hanging open.

Jen tried to lighten the mood. "So how do you make a proper Gator-Bull?"

I was happy for the change of subject. "Take a Gatorade, chug down this much, to here. Then pour in a Red Bull. Now you get your refreshing, thirst-quenching electrolytes, and you get your caffeine. They should bottle this."

Jen took a Gatorade and cracked open the top. Tilting her head back, she chugged it down to the mark. Then very carefully – more carefully than necessary – she slowly poured in a can of Red Bull, and put the top on the bottle.

"Now just turn the bottle over a couple times to mix it. Don't shake it. Yeah, like that. Done."

April held her hand out and Jen passed the GB to her. She drank about a quarter of the bottle nonstop. "I can see why you like this."

"Like? Best damn drink on the planet."

Joy sampled it, then shook her head, "No... it's not. I'd rather have a Pepsi."

I put some mustard on the last bite of a wild boar brat and really wished I had a bun and some kraut.

Time to go.

We had to get the Rabbits ready.

Thumpers, Rabbits & Horses

Back at Camp Williams the frustration was high. The little EOD bots were too slow. This wasn't working. The only thing that worked so far was the Thumpers. The girls, a couple guys, and Speedy all had fun shrieking and screaming into microphones. The FoxPro calls worked like a champ. The problem was moving them.

I had a solution, but I didn't like it.

It was seven o'clock, and the briefing was in an hour. I printed out maps and overhead sat views. Once that was ready I sat down.

Lt. Meyers shook his head. "You can't do that. It's not right."

"What else can I use?"

"Goats."

"You can't ride goats."

"Llamas then."

"Nothing else works."

"Cows... you can ride cows."

"Have you ever seen people riding around on cows?"

"But horses are smart. They're intelligent. You just don't like horses."

"No, I don't. I hate horses. One bucked me off into a patch of cactus down in Arizona. But that doesn't have anything to do with this."

"Can't we use motorcycles... strap a bunch of cats all over it?"

I laughed at that one, "I'd love to do that.... that could be fun... but we both know that nothing else works. It has to be horses. They can do it."

April came in, she had a plate of hot food for me. Salisbury steak, potatoes, gravy, and a roll. "Thanks, love."

Why would I say that? April paused, and turned away with a very slight smile and walked out the door. I took my glasses off and rubbed my eyes. That was a mistake.

Meyers watched April go, not catching my sudden problem. It was a knee-jerk reaction. Meyers whistled, "That is amazing."

"What's amazing?" I asked, not looking up and already knowing his answer.

139

"BDU's must have been designed for women, not men."

"I think you're right. Okay... now... where can we get the horses?"

"Wait, I thought we were going to use cats on motorcycles."

"Meyers!" I started eating.

"You know, we could take a bunch of cows and tie them behind a Humvee."

"I'm still waiting for a better idea." I said through a mouthful of steak and potatoes.

The briefing went well. Using the maps I had printed out, I showed the locations of where I wanted the Rabbits to start. I demonstrated the Thumpers.

"Sounds like my last weekend in Vegas." One of the soldiers said. Some men laughed.

"If this works, this will make the rest of our job much, much easier."

"I'll need volunteers for the Rabbits."

"What are the Rabbits? Bikes? Jeeps?" One of the men asked.

"Horses."

The room erupted.

After some heated discussion, the same conclusion I had made was reached by everyone. The only thing we had that would work was horses.

"Before we start, we put up a scaffolding here." A pin placed in the map showed the location. "Volunteers will ride from their start points, to this point. Then get on the scaffolding and climb up. At the designated time, Whiskey Six will make a pick-up and get you guys out of the area."

I looked around the room. "Now, who are my Rabbits?"

PETA's Gonna Hate me for this!

We had found the horses on a ranch near Lehi, not very far from Camp Williams. It had taken some time to get our volunteers ready. Some had to learn how to ride a horse. Most however had already been good riders and had stepped up.

Brad was one of the volunteers. He didn't like the idea of using horses, but like everyone else, he understood that nothing else would work as well And this had to work.

Another WTA Member and Staffer had showed up, and volunteered to run Rabbit. Supernaut, who had showed up just after the briefing, driving a brand new Land Rover filled with band members, some girls, and gear. Music equipment and instruments were strapped to the top. He said he had seen the activity at Williams as he drove over Point of the Mountain, and decided to stop in. "I never flew in a helicopter before."

"That's the easy part, Tom. Have you ever rode a horse before?"

"Yeah, a couple of times. But I'd prefer to use my Harley. Wasn't there a plan to use bikes and cats?"

We had found horse trailers, enough for everyone, and hooked them up to Humvees. Everyone had their locations. The Humvees would drop off the Rabbits and then move to high ground as the Rabbits made their runs.

The estimated time of the run from start locations to the destination spot determined when each run would start. Timing was important. The rabbits couldn't run too fast, they had to lead the zombies. Yet they couldn't let themselves be pulled down. Once they started, their only safety was at the top of the scaffolding.

The humvee's pulled out of Camp Williams, some taking different routes, some seemingly following others. They fanned out across the valley.

About 45 minutes later I looked at my watch. The Rabbits were running. I looked over at Whiskey Six, and the crew was pulling the mini guns off the bird and getting it ready. It was going to be crowded on the flight back. The air crew was going to stay behind, leaving just the pilot to fly the bird, alone. Not just because of the weight, but because just in case this didn't work. If the bird went down during the pick-up... well, they wouldn't even have time to know something went wrong. Whiskey Seven was doing the same thing, getting ready for a heavy lift.

I pulled up my binos. Over head I saw the shape of an aircraft circling the area at high altitude. The plane moved out over Midvale and started flying a racetrack pattern from Midvale to West Jordan.

The Thumpers attracted zombies out from all their hiding places, then they saw fresh meat riding on top of all that living flesh. They would give chase. They would follow. All of them.

The men on horses, including one woman, Speedy, had a dangerous game. They had to converge into the target area at the same time, giving enough room for each other to climb up the large monolith of scaffolding to the top. The horses would stay below, as bait for the zombies, keep their attention, attract more zombies, get as many zombies into the same area as possible. If timing was off, and one rabbit got there too soon, the other rabbits wouldn't be able to get to the scaffolding.

I heard Whiskey Six start up. I turned around and looked at the pilot. He gave me a thumbs up and pulled up on the collective. The Blackhawk lifted off the ground, turned towards Midvale, then tilted forward as it accelerated away. Whiskey Seven gave me a thumbs up as he took off. I returned the signal and wished them luck.

I wanted to be out there on a horse, this was my idea, this was something I should have done. However everyone protested. April, Jen, Joy, Zack, Meyers, Anderson, even my wife, who actually dropped the F-Bomb when she declared "No f'ing way, Hill Boy!"

Their excuse was that I was the Governor. I think the reality was that they saw that all the horses hated me. It was as if they knew what I had set them up for. They wouldn't let me ride them. So the horses protested me as well. I felt helpless.

"Joker One Nine, Joker One Nine. This is Ogre."

"Go for Joker, Ogre."

"Can you see the Rabbits, Joker?"

"Roger that, Ogre. We have multiple rabbits in view. They are moving to target. Over."

I put the radio down and looked at the BFT. The Rabbits were not on the screen but Joker and Whiskey Six were. That didn't tell me anything. Whiskey Six flew high, going around the target area.

"Whisky Six to Ogre, Whiskey Six to Ogre."

"Go for Ogre."

"I've got Rabbits in sight. The plan is working... zeds are following... Lots of zeds. It's like a flood."

Some of the Rabbits were converging, riding together as their paths merged. The horses were sweating up a froth. The zombies, overly excited, ran faster than anticipated, but the horses kept ahead of them.

One soldier got caught. He was being pulled down off the horse, used an Uzi to get the zeds off of him, the ones that were grabbing at him, but others started pulling the horse down. There was no saving the horse, so he jumped off and ran. For all he was worth, he ran. He had two miles to run. He was the first up the scaffolding.

The Rabbits made it to the scaffolding within moments of each other, scrambling up as if their lives depended on it. Because it did.

"Whiskey Six going in for the pick-up."

The horses, now without riders, ran looking for a way out. They were completely surrounded. The Thumpers were still screaming, the horses panic was complete, they bucked and kicked and cried out as the zombies fell upon them. The blood, the chunks of meat flying, zombies surged in, climbing over each other to reach the horseflesh.

Whiskey Six flared and came to a hover just beside the scaffolding. Everyone that could, climbed in the helicopter. When Six pulled out, Seven dropped in, picking up the rest of the Rabbits. Everyone was on board the helicopters now. When the Blackhawks got out of danger range, they signaled they were clear.

Per the plan, a chute opened up behind the C-130 high overhead. I watched through binos as a sled was pulled out from the back of the plane. As it fell away, something on the sled fell off of it. The C-130 immediately banked left and turned into a circling pattern to watch.

The large, 21,000-pound object was GPS-guided directly to the scaffolding. Just before it hit the ground, it released a high pressure mist of flammable vapor, which a split second later, detonated.

All the zombies in the area were instantly obliterated.

Inside the C-130, Outbreak watched the chute deploy. Having loaded this monster, seeing it get yanked out of the plane like it was nothing more than a tin can was almost shocking. "The MOAB is falling with style." He said into the aircraft's intercom system. He looked out and saw the sled being pulled away and watched the MOAB fall separate and free. It was on the way to the target. The chute would end up pulling the sled all the way to Draper, landing on the Chuck O Rama and crashing through the ceiling. Outbreak hit the button that closed the door. The plane banked as he went back to his station and grabbed his camera.

On the ground, as the MOAB detonated, the zombies that had filled the area were shattered by the blast. An estimated 40,000 zeds were instantly vaporized and another 40,000 were shredded to pieces. The horses, mercifully, were also vaporized, a quick and painless end to their terror. Nearby buildings, apartment complexes and some houses, which had been cleared of any survivors, were flattened by the concussion.

From my vantage point, I looked out across the valley through my binos and watched the huge mushroom cloud rise up. The cloud was visible from across the entire valley. It was shocking enough to those who knew it was going to happen, but even more shocking to those who didn't.

To my left, Lt Meyers whistled. To my right, April whispered, "My God." I nodded in agreement. "Most impressive. Good work everyone." I said over the radio. But no one was listening. Everyone was staring at the mushroom cloud.

"The Ogre nuked Salt Lake!" I heard on the radio, but I didn't know who said it.

I thought to myself, *Yeah, I guess I kind of did.*

I turned away from the horror show and walked back to the M-ATV. The blast was imprinted permanently into my mind now. I'd never forget it, and I didn't need to watch it anymore. Joy had been standing up in the truck's turret. Jen was eating something, sitting on the hood. I climbed in and said a prayer of gratitude that the plan worked without a hitch. This could have been a disaster. But since it worked, a good portion of the free roaming zeds were now gone. Most of what remained were the zeds that were trapped inside houses, apartments, garages, or behind fences. Some zeds didn't make it inside the blast zone, but the odds were now in our favor overall.

I was asked if I was going to want to do this in Orem or Provo. No, we'd come up with a different plan for Happy Valley. I had an idea about commercial-grade chipper shredders like the utility companies use for clearing trees and stuff. Maybe mount a Thumper at the front of one at the intake... where workers would feed a branch into. Take the safety mechanism off, let the machine pull in whatever zombie tried to reach into the Thumper. Done. The zombie mulch we could just use for fertilizer or whatever. Maybe use it as hog slop. The shredder idea was already in play for corpse disposal. Why not just use it as a two birds, one stone sort of thing?

All I knew at that point was that I was tired.

I gave the Guardsmen their orders to convoy as much military hardware, supplies, stock piles, and relocate everything and everyone out to Vernal, Utah. The Apaches and support were going to be fielded right by Ogre Ranch. They could land in the field in front of the ranch while all the supporting hardware and personnel would be quartered in the cleared out scrap yard next door.

April climbed into the M-ATV and rode shotgun as I turned the truck in the direction of home and hit the gas.

Maybe I was overly protective. Since Mrs. Ogre forbade me coming with her, or my Girl Squad, I assigned four squads of Guardsmen to escort and to aide my wife and her team of "Power Shoppers". They had Willie driving the lead truck in a convoy of six 18-wheelers and four armed Humvees. The alternate mission, should any be found – bring back survivors.

The wife rolled out at 8AM. Zack rolled out an hour later for Europe. I tried to convince him not to go, but there was no talking him out of it. I wrote in a notebook "Ten Bucks says he goes to Venice." He'll be fine, so I wasn't worried about his going. If I hadn't tried to talk him out of it, he would have thought something was wrong.

I spent the day with my boys and my ever-present escort of body guards. We read books, kicked our feet up and listened to music, played on Zack's X-Box (*Mercenaries 2*) and watched movies. The boys and I played kickball in the field, between the parked Apaches. I worried about my wife, but was keeping tabs on her with the BFT in one of the guard Humvees. I was relieved when I saw the convoy making its why back to the canyons, meaning they were on the way home. I was finally able to relax. April grilled a ton of elk kabobs.

Later in the evening, Joy wanted to watch a scary movie that freaked the boys out and they went downstairs to watch something lighter. Jen was completely freaked out and started giving everyone foot massages.

So when the wife came back, I was laying back on the couch, snacking on elk kabobs with a cute blond giving me a foot rub, and a good-looking girl on either side of me. She walked in, looked at us, raised an eyebrow, and ordered Joy to scoot over. Dirty, hair a mess, some blood on her, and a wicked grin on her face. No one was killed, but it was close. She also said she never wanted to do that again. All the trucks were loaded with food stuffs, and it was being unloaded now. The mission was a success.

I handed her a kabob. "What are you watching?" She asked, not sure about the foot rub thing.

"*The Changeling*."

"Never seen it."

"It's good." April whispered.

My bride responded by saying, "Jen, bring me some toenail polish."

By the time the movie was over, all the toenails in the room were red.

My wife can't watch a scary movie without doing toenails, mine included. I made sure to wear nice thick socks and shoes until the red was gone.

It was very late when the movie was done, so I retired to the bedroom with the wife while the girls made themselves comfortable on the couch. April however took Zack's empty bed.

SIX

Helping Neighbors

*T*he question was simple and spoken as a thought out loud to themselves. John, my friend on the Sheriff's department just muttered it under his breath. "I wonder how they are doing over in Craig." The question kept me up all night. The thought of China actually starting this on purpose gave me worry. We needed to consolidate survivors. First thing in the morning, even before the girls on my couches or family woke up, I had packed the M-ATV myself and loaded up extra supplies.

We rolled into Vernal and stopped at the hospital. We might need some medical supplies, basic medicines. I was given plenty. A friend of mine, a medic named Ivan came out and asked what we were doing. "Health and Welfare check on the rest of the Uintah Basin, Dinosaur, Craig, maybe cut up north to Baggs, Rocksprings... Check out Manila and Dutch John... make sure everyone is doing okay."

"You might need some extra food, clothing and stuff."

"We might."

"You might need a medic too."

"You want to come along?"

"I think so."

I had Guardsmen, Ivan and a couple other EMTs, and other folks who wanted to help, who could turn a wrench or fix an electrical line. I had no intention of making this an all-out excursion, but that's what it turned into.

Some of the food we had taken from SLC was loaded into a Deuce and a half. The M-ATV led three Humvees and the Deuce. I guessed a show of force was good, but not too much force. We wanted to show that we had organization and resources, and an offer to help, not that we were invading.

When we passed through the Raven Ridge check point, Dinosaur, Colorado as visible. We could see some of the houses and buildings had burned to the ground. Bodies lay in the streets. Crows and coyotes scattered as we approached. I had heard reports that Dinosaur was lost. The sight of it shocked me. We tried to call for survivors. We found only zombies, which we put down. Just outside of town, the last house, someone came running out. April swung the M-60 over, but held her fire. "HEY! STOP!" It was a teenage boy, still human.

"STOP WHERE YOU ARE!" April commanded.

As I pulled up to a stop, Joy dove out of the M-ATV covering the kid with her rifle. "Put your hands on your head, down on your knees!"

The boy complied.

I came running around the truck, "Are you injured? Are you hurt?"

"No, no!" The boy was frightened.

"Are you bitten?"

"What?"

"Did you get bit by a zombie?"

"No, I'm okay."

"Is there anyone else in the house?"

"My Mom."

I pointed at the house and Joy nodded and brought the rifle back up to her shoulder and started moving to the house.

"She's in her bedroom – don't open the door! She ain't right."

Jen pulled up behind Joy and they entered together. April came up, "Are you hungry? Thirsty?"

"Y, y, yes..."

April and I checked the kid out. He had cuts, bruises, but he was otherwise unhurt. April gave him a cold water bottle and an MRE packet that she had sliced open for him.

Our group's medic, Ivan, came up. "So how is he?"

"Seems okay, hungry, dehydrated, freaked out... but okay."

"I'll put him in the Deuce, keep an eye on him."

"Sounds good."

"What's your name, kid?"

"Jared."

"Come on, Jared. Let's get you out of here."

From inside the house we heard a three-round burst from an automatic rifle. Jared jumped at the sound, but had no other reaction. I looked at April who seemed numb to the human tragedy we'd just witnessed. She looked at me.

"One of these days, I want to stop by my folk's house."

"Where's that?"

"Prescott, Arizona."

"We'll go there."

"Thank you."

April turned back to the M-ATV and climbed up into the turret and put her goggles on.

Jen looked at April, she opened her mouth to make a crack, but I cut her off. "Don't give her a hard time, Jen."

We got rolling again and didn't stop until we reached the city of Craig. Some areas showed signs of a good burn-down. One house was still smoldering, which meant that it had burned fairly recently. Some cars and trucks littered the road, not as many as I'd expected. There were relatively few bodies as well.

Then we found it. A barricade of sorts, made up of cars and trucks and chicken wire. It was a at least 12 feet tall, and it blocked the street completely. We went down the next block and found that it too was blocked. Some zombies milled around the barricade. Our bullets would pass through the zombies, and could go through the barricade. We didn't know what was on the other side, so it was best not to shoot. Another block, another barricade. We found that a large section of the town was barricaded. On one block, we found evidence of someone having watched *Mad Max*, as part of the barricade was a bus that would be able to be rolled away if someone wanted to "open the gate".

We stopped a block away, not sure if it was safe to approach or not. I sat behind the wheel and thought about this situation. If they built this fortification, people inside could be safe. Or they could have trapped themselves inside with infected, and that would mean everyone is dead.

"Might as well go see if anyone is at home."

I opened my door, but Joy put her hand on my arm. "No. You stay... I'll go see if anyone wants to talk."

I looked at her. "You sure?"

"I can't let you."

"Nope, you can't make first contact." Jen agreed. She was searching the radio waves for any signals, none found.

"Well, how do I know they won't just kill you too?"

Joy unzipped her tactical vest and unbuttoned her shirt to show off a bunch of cleavage. "Odds are in our favor..." She winked and climbed out.

"She is sooo going to get shot."

Joy tossed her hair as she swayed her hips while walking up to the bus-gate. She had keyed her microphone and was broadcasting so we could hear her through our radios. "Haaalllooooooowwww! Anyone in there?"

Suddenly movement to her left. A zombie sprang up and charged her. She swung her rifle up and got a round off into the zed's stomach but it tackled her anyways. Jen screamed. April charged the M-60, but held her fire. Joy tumbled and rolled with the zombie, got a leg under it, and kicked it off her. The zombie went flying. Joy rolled up to a kneeling position and drew her bowie. As the zombie came back, Joy leaped back, swinging the big knife. The zombie fell and the head rolled away.

A few seconds later, a head peeked up over the top of the wall. "Who are you?"

"I'm from Utah, with the Governor of Utah." She poked her thumb back over her shoulder. "We came to see if you guys had any survivors, needed any help or supplies. So... do you?"

I spoke to no one in particular. "She should be an Ambassador." I shook my head.

The guy at the wall said something I didn't make out. A moment later, the bus started moving and Joy motioned for us. Our convoy rolled slowly through the gate. We fanned out as much as we could. All the troops in the vehicles got out and formed a perimeter. The guy at the wall climbed down.

"So who's the Governor of Utah and what is he doing in Colorado?"

"I am. This is a good-will tour. Spreading some good news."

"Yeah, what's the good news?"

"You are not alone."

"Yeah, I heard that before from some guys from Utah."

Great, I come all this way, and I get Mormon Jokes... then again, I did set him up for it. "Who's in charge here?"

"No one."

"How many survivors?"

"We've got about two hundred."

"Supplies?"

"We're getting really low. If you guys think about raiding us, you've got a fight on your hands."

I detected movement on roof tops. Men with rifles.

"So the barricades were not to keep the zombies out, I take it."

"No, not so much. We've had other troubles."

"So you guys need some help and some defense."

"That would be nice. Know where we can get some?"

"You're in luck, we deliver."

After some more discussion and a meeting of all the Craig Alpha-Male Types, we formed an agreement. We would give some supplies in turn for their cooperation and support. The man on the wall, Daniel, was now the leader of Craig's survivors. Some of those survivors were members of Colorado's Guard. Now members of mine, as state boundaries didn't really mean too much anymore. The armory in Craig had some trucks, some water buffaloes, and a few rifles, already in the hands of the survivors. They didn't really need that much in the way of protection, but supplies were a different matter. We gave them half of the food in the Deuce, and promised more.

"Have you heard from anyone in Rangely?"

"I was in Rangely 2 days ago."

"What's the situation there?"

"I barely got out alive. My buddy Nathan had come with me. He's still there, probably standing around moaning and stuff. There is no one left."

"Sorry... What about Steamboat Springs?"

"Dead, totally. A couple folks from there made it here."

"Any other hold outs anywhere? Anyone that might need our help?"

"I don't know."

As I walked back to my truck, I saw two little kids, peeking out from behind a stack of tires. I took a knee, "Hey you." They were cute kids, cleaned, cared for, smiling. I looked back at Daniel and smiled. I could see they were doing pretty good here. One of the kids came out, not shy at all.

Aaron says you're the President."

"Oh really?"

"He says you are. Are you?"

"No. I'm just the Governor of Utah. I'm from Vernal."

The kid cocked his head, "Did you sell my dad a gun?"

I had to laugh. "I probably did."

The kid turned to the other kid, "See... he's not the President."

April brought over a couple sticks of beef jerky. "Do you boys like Jerky?"

They did, and took it from April's hand before she could say another word. The kids ran off, chasing each other.

"Jen, get on the horn with my wife and set up a weekly supply run to Craig. They are now part of us."

"What's us?" Daniel asked.

I didn't have a name for us, hadn't thought it out that far ahead. "We're what's left."

We shook hands and got back into our vehicles. Joy gave Daniel a list of radio frequencies to communicate with Vernal, the new Capitol of Utah. Ham radio worked just fine, phone numbers, if the phones came back on line, we'd string a line between cans if we had to.

We rolled out of Craig, having expanded our little empire.

From Craig, we went north, into Baggs, Wyoming. The survivors there were better off than Craig, but threw their lot in with us when we promised them electricity. Their power had been out since day one. We got some linemen to restring some power cables that had been knocked out by a crashed semi.

Strange Fire & Amazing Grace

*W*e continued north again until we hit I-80, where we turned west. Normally, I-80 was a busy interstate that crosses the USA, a major channel. Now it was empty and quiet. There were very few vehicles of any sort, and those we saw were abandoned, had driven off the road to stop on a gully or ditch. The drive westward was long, but we hit Rock Springs just before dark.

We pulled into a small gas station. A couple of the Guardsmen instantly pulled out a pump system and tapped into the gas station's underground fuel tanks. They quickly ID'd the diesel and we began to top off our vehicles. South of us, we saw a thick pillar of smoke. We had seen it coming into Rock Springs, miles before we got there. The smoke was thick and black, painting a dark streak against the sunset.

"What do you think it is?" Jen asked. I could tell she was uncomfortable. Like Baggs, Rock Springs was without electrical power and this time of the evening, with the sun just disappearing over the horizon, the city should be lit from all the lights. Instead, we saw some fire lights. From the direction of the smoke, we saw the glow of a huge fire. What made it all the more unsettling was the shrieking and wailing sound that we could just barely make out. We had rolled in with the lights of our vehicles off, and we were using red filters on flashlights to keep a low profile. We had learned that like moths, zombies would come to lights, but not red light. This was to our advantage. Red light didn't carry as well as blue or white, so it kept a lower profile while the guys topped off all the tanks. The Deuce was almost dry when we pulled in, and it had big tanks, and we had a slow pump. This was going to take a little while. I grabbed my binos and walked away from the trucks to look at where the smoke had come from. I couldn't see anything.

"I really want to know what's going on over there." I said to myself. April walked up behind me, "We'll be gassed up and ready to go in about ten minutes."

I shook my head. "Nope. I think I want to talk a stroll."

"Shit." April didn't say that very often, but she meant it this time. I went back to the M-ATV and tossed the binos in. Instead of reaching for my shotgun, I grabbed my M4 and made sure the suppressor was locked on tight. Then I checked my ACOG. The green chevron glowed nice and bright. I threw my arm through the single-point sling and looked at April.

"Well?"

She climbed up into the truck and pulled out her SCAR.

I whistled to the LT that was running the Guardsmen. "Give me two hours to scout on foot before you come looking for me. We'll hold up for the night in that motel over there."

"Yes, sir. Governor... er..."

"Just call me Ogre, keeps everything simple... and don't salute me. You don't salute the Governor and you especially don't salute in the field. If there were snipers about, you would have just told them who to shoot."

"Yes... Ogre. Sorry, sir."

"Damn it, Man..."

The LT went back to the trucks.

Joy came up, with Jen right behind her.

"I want you girls to stay with the trucks. Stay alert. If I get in trouble, I'll pop this." I held up a star cluster flare. "If you see this green flare, you know to come running. We should be back in about two hours. We'll be staying the night in that motel over there. Pull the trucks up to form a blockade at the front. Have the Guardsmen clear out the rooms. Jen, I trust you can find me a comfortable bed?"

"No problem with that, boss."

I turned and started walking south. "Hey, you need your night vision!" Joy called out.

I pointed to the full moon, and without turning back, "Don't need them." April followed me with her SCAR slung at a low ready.

We walked across a bridge that spanned a small creek that was almost dry. During spring run-off, the creek would be a decent river. The moon overhead was bright, as were the stars, making the night plenty bright enough to see clearly. The night smelled of burning wood, hickory, but otherwise clean.

"You know what I am not smelling?"

April sniffed the air. "Dead meat."

"There is no stink.... the rotting meat and death smell." The smell of decomposition had been so pervasive almost everywhere we went, the absence of it was a surprise. Up until now, the only place that didn't have it was in the Uintah Basin. There were no bodies in the streets. Abandoned cars had either been pushed to the side or were parked. I saw broken glass, a lot of it, some white, some red; indicating that there were collisions, but the cars had been moved.

Up ahead, I saw a tall, lean figure walking across the street. I took a knee and sighted on the figure. It wasn't shambling, but just walking across the street. A human guy. A live guy. A guy with what looked like a long gun over his shoulder, but he seemed casual as he turned south.

We were not so casual. We moved in a crouch, walking, running, stopping and listening, sticking to shadows. As we approached our objective, we could better hear the mysterious noise.

"What the hell is that?" April whispered.

I recognized the sound and the song. "Bagpipes... that's *Amazing Grace*... the song. *Amazing Grace*."

"You're kidding."

"I think I know what's going on here."

We sneaked between some houses and came to a spot where we could climb up onto a roof to get a better view. We could see the source of the sounds, and the glowing light. A huge bonfire. The biggest I had ever seen in my life. On the fire, I could see the shapes of skeletons. They were burning the dead. The bodies of the dead and re-dead were mixed with timbers and wood pallets and crates, stacked up to provide a complete burn. Then I noticed where it was. They were in the center of a cemetery. A fitting place. There were hundreds of people gathered around the fire, and a bunch of guys in kilts playing the pipes. This was a funeral service.

"Come on." I said. We climbed down and walked into the cemetery. No one seemed to have noticed strangers in their midst.

The sound of the pipes touched me. I stood there, head bowed, paying my respects. April whispered, "Where is my EarPro?"

"Shush."

After *Amazing Grace* the Pipers played "*Going Home*". A sad song, one fitting the occasion.

A woman looked at April and I. She did a double take. "Who are you?"

"I'm George Hill. This is April Peterson."

"How? Where?" She was genuinely shocked.

"I'm the Governor of Utah, April is one of my body guards. I'm going around the Uintah Basin finding survivors."

"How?"

"We walked."

The woman was still in shock. "I have soldiers, we drove in from Baggs and my boys are refueling the trucks now."

"Harold!" The woman shouted. This attracted attention, most of it unwanted. April took a step back and took her weapon off of Safe.

A large man, Harold, came up. He was wearing the work shirt of a local oil company that I was familiar with. I held out my hand.

"Harold, I'm George. I'm from Vernal."

He smiled, "Yeah, I know you. You're that gun guy that won an election down there."

"That's me."

"What are you doing here?"

"I was just telling this lady here, that I've been going around looking for survivors, checking out things, getting people united, seeing what they had to offer, what they need."

"You came at a bad time."

"Yeah, I know. A few weeks ago would have been better, but I wasn't the Governor then."

"Governor?"

I looked at Harold, "Yup, Governor of Utah."

"The Governor of Utah is some guy called The Ogre, a total nut job that took over the place and nuked Salt Lake."

I could see that urban legend was also one of the zombie apocalypse survivors. "I'm the Ogre, and it wasn't a nuke. It was a fuel-air explosive called The MOAB."

"No shit?"

"No shit."

He looked at April. "Then this is one of your sex slave escorts."

"Yes... no!" I shook my head, "No, she's not a sex slave, or anything like that. She's one of my body guards."

April was bristling.

"Where's the others?"

"With my trucks, along with my soldiers."

"Soldiers?"

"Yeah, I have the Utah National Guard under my command, and we've been looking for survivors, killing zombies, and establishing contact with other communities."

Harold scratched his beard. "Well I didn't vote for you."

"No... I was elected in Utah."

"This is Wyoming."

"Yes, yes it is... but you are neighbors." Harold didn't seem to quite get it. "Say, Harold, who's in charge of Rock Springs?"

"Bill Simpkins."

"Take me to him, please?"

Harold led April and I to where Bill was sitting at a table eating some corn bread. "Hey, Bill. This is the Ogre that nuked Salt Lake and running Utah now."

Bill's eyes went wide and he froze. I held out my hand and smiled, "Bill, pleased to meet you. I'm George."

We went through the whole sales pitch of what I was doing, why, and a promise to not nuke – or MOAB – Rock Springs. The contact wasn't one hundred percent amiable. They had a hard time believing what I was telling them. This was taking longer than I had hoped.

April was on the radio with Joy as the 2-hour mark approached. "Come pick us up, we are... uh... Just drive south until you hit the bonfire."

When the M-ATV pulled up into the light of the fire, it looked ominous, intimidating, and ferocious. It tipped the scales in our favor, especially with Jen manning the M-60 and Joy jumping out of the truck with her M4. Rock Springs was now on board.

After shaking more hands, organizing some supplies, and basically just showing the folks of Rock Springs that they were not alone, the funeral turned a great deal more cheerful.

Ogre Goes Airborne

Back at the motel we had a planning meeting over the hood of one of the Humvees. We had a road atlas from a gas station. I marked red circles around the towns we'd hit. Going around one town at a time was taking too much time. We needed to fan out.

The LT asked a good question, "So what kind of government are we setting up here? What kind of system are we using?"

"Until we can reestablish our Constitutional Republic – one that is based on the US Constitution – we will operate in a very simple feudal contract system. We establish regents and hold them accountable. They control their area, but answer to us."

Those who had studied history nodded their heads.

"Tomorrow we're going split up, and we're going send out vehicles in different directions. We need to find people, make sure they are okay, and bring them under our banner."

"Why?" A soldier asked.

"Because we're still Americans, and we need to people together. It gives people hope, help, and we just might need them."

"For what?"

"Because this zombie plague was unleashed on us, and the western world on purpose. China did this to us. They did that for a reason. Think about that. We need to be ready."

There were no more questions about why.

"Each one of you – yes, even you, private. Each one of you is now an ambassador of Utah. Each of you represent Utah and me. I want you guys to take a truck – find one that runs – and spread out. If you find people that need help, call Ogre HQ and we'll send what we can. Or bring them back."

We talked about different things for a while longer, everyone picked a direction to go, and everyone knew what they were going to do. Once we had that established, I stretched and looked at my watch. It was midnight thirty.

"So which room is mine?"

"Ours." Joy corrected.

I gave her a stern look. Jen put her hands on her hips. "Hey, we're your body guards, your majesty. You have to be in our sight at all times."

I was too tired to argue. "Fine... fine... Which one?"

"That one. Upstairs, center." Joy pointed.

We went upstairs and into the room. Because of the lack of electricity, the room was very dark, but I could make out two double beds.

Jen quipped, "Do they have free Wi-Fi?" She pulled out some small candles and put a couple on top of the TV, one in the bathroom, a couple on the little round table. The candle light flickered, but put off enough light so we wouldn't be tripping over each other.

"I could kill for a hot shower," Joy was serious about that threat.

"I just want to get horizontal. I'm freaking tired." And I was serious about that. I took my boots and socks off. "My feet hate these boots."

Jen unzipped her tactical vest. "I can breath again."

Everyone peeled out of the tactical gear, stacked rifles, and got comfortable. April claimed first watch and pulled the chair over to the window by the door. She could see out with little problem. Outside, the Guardsmen were pulling security duty in rotations, making sure no one or no thing caused any trouble with us or our vehicles.

I kicked back on the bed and closed my eyes.

"I'm taking a shower." Joy said.

"It'll be cold." Jen said.

"You could warm it up."

"I hate cold showers, they make my nipples hurt."

"Your nipples make me hurt."

"I'll pass on the cold water."

A moment later, I could hear the water running. A shower curtain being pulled, then a small squeal. A few seconds after that, I heard the rustling of clothes, the bathroom door opening and closing, the shower curtain being pulled, and another squeal.

"They never get too tired do they?" I said out loud.

April sighed, "No, they don't."

"They must really love each other."

"Joy loves Jen, a lot."

"Jen doesn't love her back?"

"She does, but not like Joy loves her. Jen just needs sex. Everyone does."

I didn't catch the meaning of that statement, but instead thought about Rosa and Zach. Zach never really cared for Rosa, but Rosa evidently needed that physical contact, which is why she found someone that just wanted the same thing. Zach wasn't really even bothered by it. Maybe he was though. Maybe that's why he went to Italy. It's hard to say. I felt sleep pull me into the mattress. I dreamed of flying. Then I dreamed of my wife.

In the morning I rolled out of bed, slightly disoriented as I found my way to the bathroom. The candle was out, so I used my little Surefire Defender and set it on the counter pointing up. I relieved myself, washed my hands and looked at the shower. My face was covered in stubble, as was my head. I didn't have my razor with me, so I had to pass on shaving. There were towels though. Some on the floor from last night, but a couple left. I considered the situation for a moment and decided to go for it. I took a cold shower. After the shower I toweled off quickly. My bag was still out in the M-ATV. I pulled on my dirty clothes again and went out of the bathroom. Jen was sitting in the chair.

"Morning, boss." She whispered.

"Morning."

Wait a second.

I looked at Jen. Then I looked at the bed I was sleeping on. April was laying there, facing away from where I was sleeping. She was wearing her oversized Oakland Raiders football jersey and not much else. Oh crap. I had a small panic attack. No, it was cool... she was asleep... nothing happened. It's cool. Regardless of anything happening, I was uncomfortable. Had to get out of the room. I grabbed my socks and boots and went out the door. I sat on the steps as I pulled on my foot gear. I would change clothes, and socks, later.

I went out to the M-ATV and climbed in to grab my pack. I noticed the BFT flashing a message box. I pulled out a pair of socks and started changing them as I hit the screen. It was from Anderson, the 19th Special Forces leader.

Military Vehicles approaching from the east, they are two hours away from the Raven Ridge check point. Shutting off our BFT to help hide our locations. Anderson.

I checked the time on the message. It had come in just moments before. I honked the horn. Jen was already standing on the balcony, keeping an eye on me. "We've got two hours to get back to Vernal! Get the Girls out here!"

They scrambled, grabbing gear and guns. I ran back up and grabbed my kit as well. We piled into the M-ATV, and we headed back to the highway.

"There is no freaking way we will get there in time." I growled.

"What's going on?" Joy was scared and didn't know why.

One of the Utah Guard sergeants came to me, "What's going on?"

"There are unknown military vehicles approaching Vernal. I'm going back now."

"What do you want us to do?"

"Continue the planned missions, but stay in touch." I fired up the M-ATV's big engine.

"Yes, sir."

I gave the Sarge a nod and pulled out. We hit the highway at full speed. I was pushing the M-ATV as hard as I could, but this thing was no sports car. "Who's coming?" Joy asked as she was holding on for dear life. April was still in her Raiders night shirt. "How long is it going to take to get back to Vernal?"

"I don't know Girls... I don't know." In the distance off the freeway, I caught a glimpse of something. I decided to go for it. "Hang on." I pulled off the freeway again and ran the truck through the shrubs and across a gully. We caught some air but the M-ATV handled it just fine.

Jen was bounced out of her seat, she wasn't holding on. "Where are you going?"

"There!" I pointed. I could see the tail of an aircraft sticking up over the sage. The M-ATV took air again as we jumped a ditch. We crashed through a fence and the next thing I knew I was driving on tarmac again... on a run way. I angled the truck towards the parked planes.

"You know how to fly?" Joy asked.

"No. I was hoping you did."

"I can't fly."

"Me neither."

"I hate flying!"

I pulled up to a stop in front of several small single-engined aircraft and jumped out. Piper Cub ... No. Cessnas were parked in a line. 152. ... No. 182 ... Maybe. I checked it. The fuel tank was almost empty. Damn it. Piper Archer ... Maybe. I looked into the cockpit. Dead guy in the seat. Pass. Beechcraft T-34. That might work. I jumped up onto the wing and slid the cockpit back. No dead guy, that's a plus.

Suddenly the sound of rifle fire ripped through the air. I looked over to the M-ATV and saw that Jen was laying it down. Zombies coming from the main building of the little airport. Joy opened up as well. The zombies were pouring out of the building. I checked the fuel and the plane was topped off. I looked at the other planes. The only ones that I had flown before was the Cessnas. I had never flown a Beechcraft before.

The zombies were running flat out. I looked over at April who was scrambling up into the M-60. I looked back into the plane, the model was a T-34 Mentor, an old military trainer. I had only seen them from a far. Now, I'd be flying one.

Automatic gunfire punctuated my thoughts.

I climbed in and examined the controls. Landing gear. Throttle. Central stick. I can do this.

"Who's coming with me?"

No one heard me. April was rocking the M-60. I jumped out of the plane and ran to the M-ATV. "April! Grab your gear. Get in the plane!"

"No way! I hate flying."

"Fine, I'll go alone." I grabbed my vest and M4. "You guys meet me back... "

"Fine... Damn it!" April cussed as she slithered out of the turret ring and grabbed her clothes, vest and SCAR.

"Joy!" I was trying to get her attention. During a mag change I told her to take the M-ATV and Jen and meet us back in Vernal.

"Roger that, boss. As soon as we can!" She opened fire again. I shrugged into my tactical vest as I pulled the wheel chocks from the little trainer. I found the fuel drains and opened them up and let them run for a moment. Hopefully there was no water in the tanks, and if there was – it drained out. Jen had scrambled up into the turret and opened up with the sixty again. I climbed back into the plane, holding the rifle behind my right shoulder against the seat. It wasn't comfortable, but there was no other place for it.

April threw her tactical vest on as she jumped in. "This thing is so tiny!"

"I've flown smaller."

April didn't say anything so I craned my head around. She looked pale. I grinned. This was going to be fun. I found the switches I needed, flipped them, got the power on in the plane, and hit the starter. The T-34 was an old classic warbird. Not a fighter, but what a lot of pilots learned to fly fighters in. It could even drop training bombs. The engine turned over with a very high-pitched wine, evidently from a big electric motor. Then I noticed the little tag on the dash. "T-34C Turbo Mentor" Wait... Turbo? This thing wasn't a piston engine bird, it was a little turbo-prop. The sound of the engine was similar to that of a helicopter engine... because under the bonnet wasn't a normal engine, it was a little jet engine that spun the prop.

"COOL! Hey, April, you might want to shut the canopy." I said as I pushed the throttle forward. The engine's pitch changed and I could feel the plane start to move. More throttle and the plane was rolling. I steered with the peddles as I fought with the seat belt to get strapped in. April was doing the same thing, but more frantically. I rolled the plane behind Joy and the M-ATV and angled it to the runway. Just like a Cessna. This was going to be cake. I shut my canopy.

Without slowing down I rolled onto the run way and pointed the plane at the far end. "Here we go." I said as I pushed the throttle to the stops. I noticed the throttle response was sluggish compared to a piston engine, but when the power came on, it came on big. "Oh yeah!"

The plane picked up speed with a lot more authority than I was ever used to. I kept an eye on the end of the runway, making sure we kept pointed at it. The little Mentor felt like it was getting lighter, so I looked at the speed. We were going over a hundred MPH. Here we go. I pulled back on the stick and the little plane practically leaped off the ground.

"Oh sweet Mary and Jesus..." I heard from the back seat. After a moment "I think I peed a little."

The plane was gaining altitude eagerly, but I didn't need to fly too high. I checked the gauges and everything looked good. There were little lights over three little tabs that read "L. Main Gear" "R. Main Gear" and one that said "Nose" On the lights was a marking that said "Up". I looked next to these lights, and saw a fat lever marked "Gear" with an arrow pointing up or down. I pushed the lever up and held it. I could hear a new electric motor sound and pretty soon all three gear lights lit "Up". I noticed the airspeed was picking up a lot faster now. It must be up. We were about 2,000 feet as I banked the plane and turned.

On the ground we could see the M-ATV driving away from the parked planes. Blond hair was in the turret and the gun was still firing. The M-ATV headed to the airport's gate, passed the gate, and was now headed to the highway via the roadway and not my more reckless route.

"The girls will be fine." I said as I backed the throttle down off of max power.

"I'm not really worried about the girls right now. I'll worry about them later. After you put me back down on the ground safely. Really safely."

"That won't be a problem. This old bird flies really good." I looked at the compass. We were going North West. Wrong direction. I turned the plane again, in a tighter bank, putting on a few Gs. Then I dropped the nose and flew directly over the M-ATV as it was turning onto the highway, then pulled up and waggled the wings.

"Please, for the love of all that is holy, don't do that again!"

"Do what?"

"Everything you did just now."

"You mean..."

"DON'T DO IT! I have a rifle, a pistol, a big knife, and two frags."

"Take it easy, girl. I was just teasing. I don't want you to get sick on me."

"Might be too late."

"Can you hold it?"

"I think so."

"Okay, this flight won't be too long. We are going really fast."

"How fast?"

"Look at the ground."

I had the plane in a climb and we were gaining altitude quickly. I didn't want to get too high, as I'm strictly VFR only. But the cloud ceiling was not a concern. There were almost none in the sky. I leveled off and let the plane continue to accelerate. It stopped at 300 MPH. The hills below us rolled passed quickly. I checked the compass. We were heading directly South. I turned, very gently, to head south east. I wanted to fly over familiar ground. It wasn't long before we saw water.

"Look at this, April. That's part of Flaming Gorge."

April looked "It's fantastic."

After a while the sensation of speed fell away and we were just cruising. A part of me wanted to fly lower, buzz the canyons, follow the nap of the Earth. The other part didn't want to die, either from hitting the ground or having April run a bowie knife through the back of the seat. I decided not to die and kept the plane nice and level. Just thinking about that made my back itch. I pulled my sunglasses out of my tactical sunglasses case holder on my vest and switched my eyeglasses out for sunglasses. If I was going to be flying, I had to look cool.

Below us the narrow strip of water started to get wider as it snaked around. We were flying without conversation and this was unusual. Normally there was always something being talked about, or some music. The only sound was the wind and the engine. I looked at the fuel gauge. It had hardly moved at all. I think I love this plane.

At the top of the cockpit, on either side in the canopy, were little mirrors. I angled one of them to look at April. She looked like she was daydreaming as she stared out of the window. She was strikingly pretty. "How are you doing back there?" I asked.

She brushed her auburn hair away from her face. "I've never flown before."

"Really?"

"It's beautiful up here."

"It is."

"I love it."

"I'm glad."

April got quiet and stared back out the window again. Below us we cruised directly over the Flaming Gorge dam. I could see the highway. 191. A few minutes later I could see Red Fleet. Then Steinaker. I remembered that this was where it all started. Seemed like a hundred years ago. In my truck on 191 heading into Vernal we first heard the reports of the first zombie attack.

I heard a sniff and looked back at April. She had tears in her eyes. "Hey, if you're still not wearing any pants, you might want to put them on. We're almost there."

I pulled out my radio and turned it to the frequency the 19th SF guys used. "Ogre to Anderson."

Nothing.

"Ogre calling for Anderson."

"Anderson here, go ahead, Ogre."

"Where are you located at, right now?"

"I'm on highway 40 at the Raven Ridge check point."

"Roger that, I'll be there in a few minutes."

"I thought you were in Rock Springs."

"That's affirmative. Out."

I banked the plane to the south west and found highway 40 under me as we flashed over Jensen. I followed 40 west from there passed Blue Mountain on my left, and then I saw Raven Ridge.

"Okay, George, now let's not screw up the landing." I said to myself as I pulled the throttle back and let the plane start to slow. Nose down, descending. Throttle back more. Speed coming off, 180, 170, 160... Landing gear. Down. Locked. We're good. 120. The highway was almost perfectly straight here to Raven Ridge. Plenty of room to work. A little cross wind, so I gave it a little peddle. The plane had a slight yaw... no problem. The road was coming up. 100 MPH. 50 feet. 40 feet. 90 MPH. I pulled the throttle back all the way. 80 MPH. 30 feet. 20 feet. 75 MPH. 10 feet.

Touch down.

The plane was still very light... it wanted to bounce a little, but it stayed on the ground. I let the plane carry some speed as we ran along the freeway. I could see the barricade and a number of vehicles to the south side of the highway, near the ridge. I taxied up near the gate, used the peddles to turn the plane and pointed it back west to get it ready for take off, then I killed the engine. I looked in the back seat. April's eyes were clamped shut.

"We're down, safe and sound."

"We are?" April looked around.

"You're safe."

I opened the canopy and unbuckled. Anderson walked up laughing as I climbed out of the little trainer. "What in the hell is this?" He asked.

"Oh, this? A little thing I picked up in Rock Springs. Thought I'd take it for a spin when you put out your mayday. I had to come running all the way down here. No in-flight snacks though. That was disappointing." I was laughing too.

"I didn't know you could fly. How many hours do you have in this thing?" I looked at my watch. "What time do you got?"

"You're kidding."

"She's a fast little plane."

April was slow getting out of the plane, but once she was out, she was ready and at my side like a pro. I was glad to see that.

"So what do we have coming our way." I asked Anderson.

"We're not sure, at least ten military vehicles. The folks in Craig reported that they blew through non-stop, hell bent for leather. They didn't get a good count, but they said some of them were tanks on wheels."

"Tanks on wheels? That would make them LAVs or Strykers. And we don't know who it is?"

April asked, "Do we have anything that can stop them?"

Anderson looked at her and said flatly, "No."

"Yes we do." I grinned and grabbed the satellite phone from the check point security. Anderson just stood there. Evidently he didn't know what I knew. "You're staying with the guys at the Western Park, right?" I dialed a number.

"That's right."

"Okay."

"What's wrong with that?"

"No, nothing. It's cool. Seriously. You are going to love this." Anderson raised his eyebrow.

Kilo answered the phone. "Hey."

His phone skills were Gold Medal. "Morning, son. How's it going with everyone? Good, good. You holding down the fort? Excellent. Okay, now listen close... I've got a bit of a situation here... so I need you to do me a big favor. Go out onto the front porch and tell me what you see."

I heard him shuffling, then walking. The door opened, I could tell by the chirp-like squeak it always makes. "I see military gunships. I see pilots playing football. I see Tango riding his bike. I see birds."

"Okay, okay... Okay... Listen to me... Go give the phone to one of those guys playing football."

"Kay."

A few moments later, "Hello?"

"Hello, this is Governor George Hill, who am I talking to?"

"Sir, this is Captain James Hancock."

"Captain, I need you and your comrades over here, Buster. I've got unknowns approaching us from the east. At least two armor, plus a number of trucks."

"Roger that, hold on a second." Suddenly there was a great deal of shouting. I had to hold the phone away from my ear. I could hear running. "Where is over here, sir?"

I told him where and he gave the phone back to Kilo, who said, "Hey."

"Where's your mother?"

"She's... uh... I think she's in town. She's getting trucks ready to send out to Craig and places. I don't know."

I smiled to myself. Good. She won't worry about me scrambling the whole field. "Okay, my boy. I'll be home in a few hours."

"Cool."

I hung up. I walked up to the pass in Raven Ridge. We'd see them coming from Dinosaur. "If I had a TOW or two or three, I'd put them up over there on those rocks."

"We have Mortars, but they are only 60mm's."

"That won't do anything to the armor."

"Might button it up."

"Doubt it."

"It's better than harsh language." Anderson admitted.

If it's one thing I know, it's killing armor. Anderson had something else though. "Where are our Fifty Cal rifles?"

Anderson turned and pointed. "There. There. There. There. And there."

Okay, not bad if we had someone break through. We needed them stopped before they breached the gate. "Move that Deuce over here. Right behind the gate. Call the Fifties down. We need different positions here."

I pointed out the positions, "There. There. There. There. And there."

Anderson nodded in agreement. "I like it."

If we can get them to stop here, even for a moment, we can put rounds into anyone unbuttoned or into their prisms and camera lenses. If we have to. We don't have to stop them. We just have to hold them for while. Delay them.

"SIR!" One of the men called to us.

We turned around.

"We've got company!"

Relatives from Out of Town

Back at Ogre Ranch the Apaches lifted off the field, hovering just feet above the ground. They were heavily armed with rocket pods and Hellfire missiles. One by one, they turned towards the highway, accelerating down the road and climbed into the air, heading eastward at full military power. The Apaches split into groups. Some angling to the north, others to the south.

On the porch of Ogre Ranch, my boys stood watching the gunships take off. They were cheering the big angry helicopters, accept for Kilo who was grimacing. He knew why the Apaches were taking off and he wasn't comfortable about it.

At Raven Ridge, I was really wishing I had a bigger weapon. We ran up to the barricade and took up positions. The first vehicle was just coming out of Dinosaur. I looked at it through a set of Steiner Binos... it was a

Stryker. One of the Mobile Gun Strykers that had the 105mm Cannon on the top. The turret was swinging side to side, scanning for targets. When the turret found us, I swallowed hard.

Then the second Stryker came out of Dinosaur, it had a huge Gatling on top that was already aimed right at us, it pulled up next to the first Stryker. The 3rd Stryker took up another position besides the first, another mobile gun.

"Crap!"

The Strykers slowed to a walking roll. A moment later, an MRAP came around the bend, it had a flag tied to an Antenna. I couldn't make out what was on the flag. Behind the MRAP was a collection of Humvees and other vehicles including a couple dirt bikes.

One of the Guardsmen was on the radio, trying different frequencies, trying to contact the incoming vehicles but was having no response in return.

The Strykers kept coming. There were almost at the Utah/Colorado border.

From this distance I could hear music coming from the Strykers. In the first Stryker I could see someone standing up in the turret. Large, muscular, wearing leathers and gargoyle-style sunglasses. His head was shaved and his long braided goatee was flapping in the wind. He held a huge rifle in one hand, his other hand was fist on his hip. Another bald-headed, goateed man was in the turret of the MRAP.

"Oh no. " Anderson grumbled.

Suddenly a group of Apache gunships flashed past overhead, swooping down on the Strykers, popping flairs and chaff. Along Raven Ridge, out of view of the convoy, the other Apaches lined up, waiting to pop up and unleash their Hellfires. Through the binos I could make out the flag. It simply said "Chillin The Most".

I started laughing. "NO WAY!" I jumped up. "Everyone stand down." I grabbed the radio, "Ogre to all units, Stand Down. I say again, Stand Down!"

The Apaches stayed on station but uncovered from behind the ridge. The other Apaches broke off their attack run and started circling. I started walking towards the incoming vehicles. I could hear biblical curses being shouted by the man in the Stryker, holding his rifle up over his head like one of the Sand People from *Star Wars*. I had to laugh at my brother. He hated almost everything that was modern or that might contain a battery. He hated batteries more than almost anything. His cursing was epic as he scanned the skies, waiting for another flare run by the Apaches. Then he saw me. His curses changed their tone, but now it was directed at me. He climbed out of the turret and walked along the barrel of the 105, then dropped off of the muzzle as the Stryker came to a halt.

"Was this your idea of a welcome, brother? Have your infernal birds shiat suns upon us? This is it, eh?"

"Now don't hold it against me, Musket, I dinna know who you were or yer intentions." I said, slipping into the appropriate accent. "And besides that, ye scared the bejeesus out of my men."

"Aye, I guess I can understand. I'd have probably done the same if those birds had proper front stuffers in those pods."

We laughed as Musket threw a bear hug on me that lifted me off the ground I could feel and hear things cracking inside me.

"Easy, little brother, my ribs are broken." He let me down.

"I dinna break anything more did I?"

Catching my breath, "No, I'm good."

"Alright, ye'll be alright then."

Josh came running up and threw another hug on me. "I am glad you guys made it!"

"It was a hell of a ride. Sorry we're late. Pushing through Denver was more of a challenge than anyone expected. Did we miss anything?" Josh was grinning ear to ear, then he nodded. "Who's this?"

I turned around and April was standing behind me, her sunglasses on top of her head with a bemused look on her face. Her SCAR slung casually, but with her hand still on the grip. "Brothers, this is April, one of my body guards. April, these are my brothers."

"Aye, she's a bonnie lass, brother Ogre. When she's done with your body, she can guard mine! Then I could guard hers all night!" Musket growled. April moved so fast, it was a blur. Her boot connected with a solid punt to Musket's junk. He grabbed himself as he fell over onto his face, saying only one word, "Bollocks!"

I had to laugh. April looked at me, unsure if it was okay to have defended her honor. I winked at her and she just gave a slight grin back at me. Suddenly I was surrounded by family. Ruth, Josh's bride, my mother and father, and faces I remembered from Virginia, Josh and Zach's battle brother's from their service.

"Guys – let's move this reunion back to the homestead. Josh, you remember how to get to Ogre Ranch?"

"I think I still remember."

"If not, April knows."

I looked up at the Apaches that were flying circles. I held up my hand and gave them the Thumbs-up sign. They peeled off and headed back west.

My mom had taken April's arm, "So you help keep my son safe?" She pulled April into a hug and they started talking.

"Let's get going. I'm hungry and tired. I gotta beat those Apaches back to the ranch or I won't have room to land myself."

"Land?" My father asked.

"Yeah, I have a T-34 Mentor, C model. I flew it down from Rock Springs after I heard you guys were seen passing Craig."

"The Turbo Mentor? That's a good little plane."

"I'm not getting back into that." April shivered.

"Okay. You don't have to. Come on, Musket." I helped pick Musket up off the ground.

"That woman is a Banshee... I dinna see it coming... infernal woman."

"April can ride with me." My mom said in a tone that was more of a "That's decided then" rather than as a suggestion. "We have a lot to talk about! Let's do it in a more comfortable setting!"

Five minutes later I had Musket in the back seat of the T-34. "My sweets..."

"You'll be fine, Musket," I said as I flipped the switches for the batteries and the generator. "You'll forget all about your stones in just a moment." Then I hit the starter.

From a hundred feet above them as the T-34 passed overhead in an aileron roll, April could hear Musket's scream, "AaaaaarrrrrrrrrggghhhhhhH!" She smiled to herself as she braced herself to listen to mother's stories about young Ogre. At least, she thought, I am not in the air.

Due to the nature of the Girl Squad's responsibilities they remained at Ogre Ranch while the new guests, namely all the friends and family that had shown up, had to spend the night next door.

While I was happy everyone was here, safe, sound, and unbitten, I was pensive. This was too good. I laid in bed unable to sleep, and after I watched the clock tick past 2:30AM, I decided to get up and get some fresh air.

I walked through the living room, where Jen and Joy lay on the couch sleeping. They made it back in the night and were very tired from the long drive and the pack of zombies that they found shambling towards Manila. I went outside.

April was sitting on the porch. "Hey." She said.

"Hey."

"Can't sleep?"

"No," I stretched. "Something is bothering me and I can't put my finger on it. How come you are not sleeping?"

"Standing watch. In half an hour I'm waking up Jen for her watch."

"You know, I have a dog, a house full of shooters, and a front yard full of Apache helicopters. I think it's safe to say that you can stand down while we are at Ogre Ranch."

"I don't know."

"April – Go get some sleep. Besides, I want to be alone for a bit." I walked down the stairs from the porch and out into the alfalfa field which was now an airfield.

April stood up and walked into the house. "Good night," she said quietly as she shut the door.

The T-34 I flew in was parked nearby, surrounded by Apaches. The pilots were impressed with the little plane and those that could fly a fixed wing, wanted to take it up. I made them a deal – they agree to help teach me to fly a helicopter – they could fly the T-34.

The ground crew however was most excited. They explained that they could fit Hydra Rocket Pods under the wings on the hard points, and turned the T-34 into an A-34, making it a little attack plane. "Go for it!" I liked the idea. I also had them put a Garmin GPS unit in the cockpit because the thing needed some navigation help.

I looked at the little airplane and contemplated the future. I needed a plan, and to make a good plan, I needed to think. I do my best thinking while driving. I looked around and my eyes settled on something that I've not driven in what felt like a very long time. My old Chevy. The keys were in my pocket, as usual. They always are.

Climbing into the old Chevy was like putting on your favorite old jeans, comfortable, familiar... it just fits. I fired up the engine and checked the radio. The Talk Radio Station was quiet, but the Classic Rock Station was playing "*Shine On You Crazy Diamond*".

I pulled out of the ranch and headed up the highway to the plateau. The moon was just a sliver, but the stars were out in force tonight. I pulled off the highway and shut off the truck, but left the radio playing. Something about sitting on the tailgate. In the sky, the stars looked peaceful. After a while of watching, I was able to pick out a couple satellites. Normally there would be an Airliner visible.... or two. But there were no flights. It was quiet in the sky.

While sitting there on the tailgate, looking at the stars, I decided I needed to slow down. Things were happening too fast. People were coming in, and these people would have to be entertained, fed, occupied with productive work. We could keep raiding the big cities for some time, but eventually it would all run out. We needed food production. Zombies drained ammunition, more would have to be found, and eventually more would have to be made. Life would have to be reestablished. I wondered how they did it in Europe after The Black Plague killed off so many people. Then again, that was over the course of years while the zombie uprising happened practically over night.

Headlights behind me. I could almost feel them more than see them. The vehicle was quiet, so I knew it wasn't a military rig. I turned around and could only see headlights. I heard a door shut and a figure approached. Tall, lean. A Deputy Sheriff badge. It was Joe.

"So what's this shizz about you being the Governor of Utah?"

"Everyone else had better things to do... like standing around moaning and looking for brains to eat. I was the only one left. What are you doing up?"

"Working. What are you doing up?"

"You're working?"

"Yeah, we're doing our regular patrols... keeping the schedule. Keeping things normal."

"That's a good idea. Who's was it?"

"Sheriff's."

"Ah. So how are things in town? I've been running around too much."

Joe came over and sat down on the tailgate. "They are always beautiful, aren't they?"

"Yeah, especially at night it seems."

"Things are going pretty well. Better than you'd expect."

"That's good news."

"There has been some suicides. Remember Randy Oaks?"

"Yeah, what about Randy?"

"Sucked off a 12 gauge."

"He didn't have a shotgun."

"Yes he did. You sold it to him last year."

"AH! Yeah... Winchester. "

"Yeah, that Winchester."

"His wife had left him... no kids... so his big old house is empty?"

"Yup."

"Do you think anyone would mind if I put some people up in it?"

"I don't think anyone would object."

"Any other situations like that?"

"You want me to make you a list?"

"Actually, yeah."

"I'll bring it by tomorrow."

"Right on, Joe. Thanks."

"No problem. Thank you."

"For what?"

"For help keeping things together. The power... getting that back on was great."

"What else could I do?"

"Suck off a shotgun, like Randy. A lot of folks did."

I shook my head. "No, I'm not done yet."

"What are you going to do?"

"I think I'm going to go hunting."

"Hunting zombies again?"

"Elk."

Joe jumped off the tailgate. "Not in season yet."

"I'm disbanding the DWR."

Joe shook my hand and laughed. "They should make you King," he said as he climbed into his truck and continued his patrol.

"King, eh? King George. Now I have a plan." I said to myself as I got back into my own truck and headed back to the ranch.

The Undead Elk

The next morning I went next door. The old guy that lived in the house adjacent to my own wasn't happy with the new folks running around, and he wasn't happy with me because of it.

"I've got a trade for you."

"Trade what?"

"Houses."

"I don't want your house. Mine's bigger."

"I'll trade you for Randy Oaks' place. It's closer to town where you go every day... bigger... almost double the size of yours. And he's got that four-car garage."

"It's not yours to trade."

"Randy killed himself. He had some back taxes owed so his place belongs to the State of Utah... and since I'm the Governor... and since he has no family to give it to. It is mine." Honestly, I had no idea about Randy's tax status. But it sounded good.

"I'll think about it." The old guy turned and walked away.

The old guy was back two hours later. I was sitting in the cockpit of a Blackhawk, Whiskey Seven, when he walked up to the chopper. "I'll take it."

"Excellent! Thank you."

"You can have all my stuff. I'll take Randy's."

"That's fair enough," I said to his retreating back. About 20 minutes later, the old guy was out of the house with a couple suit cases and he was gone. So now we have a place for Josh and Ruth.

Mom and Dad were sent to a smaller house up the street. It was a nice place, newly built. Slight case of blood stains on the wall where the owner used a .30-06 on himself. A little Spackle and some paint would fix it right up.

The house on the other side of Ogre Ranch from Josh and Ruth's new place was a nice little house. Simple place. Quaint. "Cute" as the Girl Squad called it. The owner had disappeared but his truck was found in Heber. He wasn't coming back. Which meant that The Girl Squad had their own place. They were happy to take it as it beat my couches and sharing the bathroom. They pulled out crates of old porn magazines, after Joy looked them over briefly. She declared Jen's hooters to be better. I didn't make a comparison, but would have bet money that Joy was right. April insisted on new mattresses. We'd make arrangements for that next time we went out to The Big Dead City.

The next morning I woke up very early. Finally able to break away to hunt some elk. I took my twins with me, my wife and of course, one of my body guards had to come to. April insisted. Jen and Joy stayed home in their new place. "Getting it fixed up."

Echo and Bravo wore their camo clothes and the boots I liberated for them from Cabela's. Each of them were armed with a Browning X-Bolt in 7mm-08 topped with Zeiss Rapid-Z scopes. They each had a nice pair of binos. Swarovski 10x32 EL's. My bride had a Sako A7 in .270 Win topped with a nice Swarovski Z6, and she wore her SHE brand camo. April wore her usual tactical gear over a t-shirt and BDU pants. She was armed with her SCAR as always. I wore my favorite jeans, long sleeve King's Camo shirt, and I was packing my Remington 700 in 7mm Rem Mag.

We drove my old Chevy up to the top of Grizzly Ridge and we got out and started walking.

"You guys talk softly. We don't even want to make a sound. That's one of the fastest ways to bust your hunt."

They all nodded. "We know, Dad."

We went up trail that soon went back down hill before it opened up into a clearing. "This is where the elk will start coming through. So I want you to find a good hiding spot."

Rolled up at the top of our day packs were Ghillie Capes. We pulled the hoods up and let the capes roll down, then took up our positions. The sun was going to be coming up in just a few minutes. We didn't have to wait long. We were hunting spike bulls for the meat, so we didn't need trophies. The area we hunted had a bachelor herd of small bulls and big spikes in it.

They came in to the clearing cautious at first, smelling the air. They were good-sized bulls but instead of the classic branching antlers, only had straight prongs. It's good to take them out of the gene pool before they pass on inferior genetic traits. So I didn't feel bad about our taking them out of season. Especially since there pretty much were no more seasons anyways.

A small group of spikes came in and got comfortable. There were six of them. I whispered to my boys really quietly, "Take them together. Bravo, you take the fat one on the left. Echo, you take the biggest hog there on the right."

They took their rifles off safe and carefully aimed at where I had taught them. "On Target." They both said within seconds of each other.

"Okay, take them in three... two... one... Fire."

Both rifles bucked at the same time and the .284 caliber bullets lanced out and hit both bulls. At the sound of the shots, four bulls instantly bolted for the trees and disappeared. One of the bulls started kicking like a rodeo horse before it fell over sideways, still kicking into the air. The other bull ran in a circle around the clearing before it fell.

"Good Shots!" We stood up. Momma was high fiving the boys and I ruffled their hair. Bravo and Echo were all grins.

We approached the closest spike as it was still breathing. Echo pulled out his Ka-Bar knife, holding on to one of the spikes he straddled the elk's thick neck and pulled the knife hard through the meat, severing the jugular. The elk kicked for a moment, but Echo stayed on it until it stopped.

Bravo's elk was stone, cold dead, with its tongue hanging out. The SST bullet had entered the elk's side, expanded as advertised, and turned the heart tissue into blood pudding.

"Good job boys!" We did our war dance, all of us hopping and hooting in circles when suddenly something came into the clearing. It was a huge bull elk, massive rack, thick muscles, and ... milky white eyes.

We stopped dancing.

"April..." I said as I unslung my 7mm Rem Mag.

April pulled her rifle up. The elk shook its head and bugled a sick sounding shrill cry that made my blood run cold. It charged. April fired a volley of shots that did nothing. The beast was going straight for April and it wasn't even slowed by the SCAR's 5.56 rounds. It crossed the clearing before I could get my rifle up.

The elk was almost on top of April when she rolled to the side. Blood was pouring from wounds on its flanks, not April's rifle hits, but large tears in its flesh. The thing was on top of her and she used the SCAR to block the biting mouth that was going for her throat. My rifle was almost on target when a shot rang out. A .270 slug passed through the neck with little effect other than making the zombie elk turn from April to my wife. It lowered its head and gnashed its broken teeth as it leapt. The creature was too close to aim at this point and only a shot to the brain would finish it. Instead of aiming I lunged, knocking my wife to the ground and spearing the elk through the mouth before pulling the trigger on my 7mm Rem Mag. The elk's head came apart, but the momentum of the corpse carried it. I was knocked backwards and flattened, the rifle torn from my hands. Then it was quiet for a moment before Bravo and Echo both ran to the elk and emptied their rifles into it.

I picked myself up and looked at my boys. They were standing over the dead creature making Hero shot poses. I started to laugh until I reached for my rifle. "Ah crap."

The barrel was bent a good 30 degrees, the stock broken, and the scope dented. I threw the rifle down. "Freakin hell!

My wife was pissed. "Oh sure, pick up the rifle before you help me up." I reached out a hand to help her up but she pushed it aside. "I'm fine." Great.

I looked over at April who was brushing dirt off of herself. "You okay?" I asked her.

"Yeah... that was close.... but I'm okay."

"You didn't ask me if I was okay!" Wife was getting pissed.

"Hey, you said you were fine."

"You care more about her and your damn rifle than you do me!"

"That's not true and it's not fair."

"If you want her, you can have her... if you haven't already." She snarled.

"Debbie..." I tried to talk to her. "That was a great shot. You hit it in the neck!" She turned her back on me and walked away to go get the truck, cussing me as she went.

"What the hell did I do?" I shook my head. "Boys, come on, we got work to do." I ignored the ranting. When she gets pissed, she's like a hurricane. Nothing you can do to stop it, so best just get out of the way and take cover. We gutted the two spike bulls and got them loaded up into the truck.

"Take them over to the meat guy on 500 East. Tell them we want these things processed into burger, sausage, steaks, the whole nine yards." I reached into the Chevy and pulled out my 870 Police Tactical and shotshell pouch. Then to my boys, "Get on the radio as soon as you can and tell Joy where we are."

"Where are you going, Dad?" Bravo asked.

"That elk didn't get zombiefied by itself. We need to find out how."

"How are you going to do that?" Echo asked.

"It was bleeding before it got shot. I should be able to track it."

"We can help you."

"I know you can, boys. But we've only got hunting rifles for you, and we don't know what's out there. I need to know you guys, and Momma are safe." They nodded understanding, even if they didn't like it.

Echo marked the location on the GPS. "Okay Pops, be careful." Bravo tossed me a couple Gatorades and two Red Bulls.

"I will. Now get that meat processed for everyone."

I looked at my wife. She was glaring at me while she fired up the Chevy. She pulled out and headed back down off the mountain. I stood there, watching them leave.

"What did you say?" April asked hesitantly.

"I have no idea what happened."

"You have great boys."

"Yeah," I said as I turned back to the zombie elk body. I checked the shotgun to make sure it was loaded and ready, then put it on Safe and topped the feed tube off.

The zeddified elk had been torn up. Something got to it, bit it, and it looked like it started eating on it before the thing turned and got away.

Look at this." I held my hand like a claw and held it over some of the marks. It matched.... almost. "Looks like a human zombie got it."

"A bite mark here... yeah... it looks human here too." April observed.

"One zombie couldn't have taken down a bull elk."

"Then we have some work cut out for us." April tried to sound chipper, but failed. Regular zombies are one thing. This was new territory.

I stood up and unlimbered the shotgun, setting it so it was loose in front of me. "Yes we do."

We followed the blood trail through the brush pretty easily, across rocks and spots of shale and saw that the trail went up over a ridge. We had travelled about three miles already, along a trail that meandered north. Over the ridge we came into a thick area of Aspen, where the blood trail ended.

"Now what?" April asked.

I looked around. There was blood, splattered, with flecks of meat on bushes that were knocked down, as if a large weight pressed it down. "I think this is where the elk was taken down."

"This is where the elk was attacked by zombies."

"So where are the zombies?"

"How do we find them?" April looked around.

"Stand over here. This is where the thing went after it was attacked. It was heading south."

I started in the center and walked in an outward spiral. There were marks from the elk, deep, tearing at the ground. It fought. There were other marks, not nearly as deep and these didn't tear the foliage. I continued my search. I found tracks, but couldn't tell if they were coming into the bloody spot, or going out. Then I found one... a print. A shoe print in a spot of earth made muddy with elk blood. At least I thought it was elk blood. It was going into the spot. Okay, maybe it was coming in. I found another pretty good sign. If this was from the same zombie, it was a very long stride. I tried to match it. "Running." I said to myself. Okay, so this is where it came in to attack.

Searching further, I found another print. It was on the other side of the spot. Another print showed a good-shaped imprint, this one was going away... much closer. It was walking. Slowly. "Gotcha!"

I turned to April with a grin. "This way." We walked in the direction of the zombie's travel for about 200 yards through the Aspen when April whispered. "There is something over there." She pointed.

Through the thin, white trunks of the Aspen trees, I saw movement... something blue. It was about 60 yards. Not too far. I pulled the action release on the shotgun and gently eased the pump back until the shell started to tip out. Using my finger, I pulled the shell out and slipped in a slug. "Get ready."

I braced the shotgun against a tree and lined up the shot. I am zeroed for a bit farther away so I held a few inches low on center of mass. I slapped the trigger and the shotgun roared. The sound of the slug impacting the zed was clearly audible. The zombie fell down and out of the line of sight. I shucked the empty hull out and chambered another shell. We kept our eyes and ears open, and kept our weapons at the ready. The sound of crashing came from up ahead and something red was darting through the trees, heading for us. I leveled the gun and unleashed a torrent of Buck Shot. The red thing was knocked down but was still moaning.

I rushed the red thing and put another shell through its head. An instant before I pulled the trigger, it registered that this had once been a woman, and her shirt had once been white, tucked into a skirt. We went over to where the blue thing had fallen and we found a mess. A zombie with a balding head wearing a blue jacket hand its spine blown out right below the shoulder blades. It was trying to drag itself with its arms. When we got close it lashed out. Another shell ended it.

April covered the area as I reloaded.

"I think that's it." She said.

I was looking at the zombie. The jacket was some kind of uniform, but I couldn't tell what it was. I was most pleased with these Remington Slugger loads. The accuracy was great, but the effect on the target was amazing. Normally, I don't really care for Remington ammo... but dang!

"Let's go see where they came from." We went back to the bloody spot and followed the direction the attack came from. This trail was not as easy to follow as the blood trail was, but it was workable. Especially since there was an occasional foot drag. Shambling. It's amazing how something that's shambling so clumsy-like can instantly turn into an Olympic class sprinter at the mere sight of fresh meat.

We followed the trail for another mile when I spotted some-thing. White. We took a knee and I told April to use her SCAR for this one, but to hold on a second until we ID'd the target. The white thing was moving between the trees, not giving us a good look.

"This might not be a good idea.... but what the hell." I whispered to April, who looked at me with a raised eyebrow.

I coughed.

The white thing turned out to be another woman in a white shirt. She had a skirt on, but her shirt was ripped open, she ran towards us. April fired one hushed shot and the zombie's dash ended in a face slide.

We went and looked at the zed. She wore the same outfit as the other woman. But this time, the shirt was less thrashed even if it was torn open.

"She's a Flight Attendant." April moved the shirt with the barrel of her SCAR, exposing the word "Southwest" on it.

"Then that would make that guy in the blue jacket a pilot, maybe." I said.

"Which means..." We both said at the same time.

"We have a plane down." I finished. April smiled.

We walked through the trees in the same direction we had been following and came across broken trees, scraps of metal, and an engine. It was huge. There were bodies all around. Some had been eaten on by some coyotes, but no other zombies. There were a lot of empty seats, but in looking at them, they had not been buckled.... the plane was mostly empty. I found a ticket. "Salt Lake International to Denver."

Someone was missing a plane.

"I thought they had grounded all the planes."

"They did. This one must have taken off before the order was issued. Here, look at this."

April came over and looked. "This guy is still strapped in, but look at the head."

"Someone took a chunk out of his scalp."

"I bet the plane was in the air, someone or some ones turned, and the zombies got into the cockpit."

"How far away is the Salt Lake Airport?"

"By jet? Less than half an hour... 20 minutes maybe... I don't know... How fast does a jet like this fly?"

April shrugged. "So you're saying they turned real fast. Or were turning when they boarded the flight."

The plane was broken into sections. The front section with the cockpit gave us a good clue as to what happened. The door between the cockpit and the cabin had claw marks all over it. It had been ripped open. There was blood and pieces of fingernail stuck in the door and bulkhead. There was a body in the left seat, strapped in. It was shredded. The other seat, the belt was ripped, but there was no body there. This was the one we met in the woods.

From here, we followed the wreckage backwards, all the way to the tail, which was laying almost sideways on the ground. In the last section there were only a few seats. Several bodies were laying about, one was hanging awkwardly, still strapped into the seat. Each one of these had a shoulder holster. A couple of them still held weapons. SIG handguns. I climbed up the tilting floor up to the bathroom door... Something told me to open it. I don't know why I did it. The latch was shut, and "OCCUPIED" was indicated. I swung my shotgun around and put the muzzle near the latch and fired. As soon as the latch was blasted off, the door sprang open and the body of a woman fell out. The thing did a rag-doll fall to the ground. Whoever this person locked in the bathroom was, all these men around died protecting her. April looked the body over as I climbed down. "Looks like she died of a broken neck... probably because of the crash."

"How do you know that?"

April pointed to a piece of cervical vertebrae jutting from the back of the neck as the head had been bent over sideways. "Ah, yeah.... Ouch... that might do it. So who is this lady?"

She was wearing a business pants suit, no purse, but a name badge and an access card was around her neck. The card said "Sarah Jennings" and under that it said "Cheyenne Mountain Directorate." On the back of the pass was written "I'm Late, I'm Late!" in very small letters.

"What's Cheyenne Mountain Directorate?" April asked.

"I think that's the new name for the big NORAD base in Cheyenne Mountain in Colorado."

She looked like she didn't understand. "It's a big base they built under a mountain. Supposed to be able to survive a direct hit from a nuke."

"So she worked there."

"Well, she was going there. Something important was going on. 'I'm late, I'm late.' A password. A code or something. From *Alice in Wonderland*. It goes I'm late, I'm late, for a very important date."

"What does that mean?"

"No idea. But this explains why the plane was in the air after the FAA grounded everything."

April nodded. Just then the radio crackled. "...ovenor... Joy to... Gov..."

"April to Joy, we are getting you.... come in Joy."

There was a pause.

"... last location... pick up."

"Joy, this is April. We are on the way there, over."

"Roger, April! Standing by!"

April pulled out her Garmin Vista HCX GPS and marked this location, while I cut the card from around the neck of the dead body.

"Let's hustle."

We jogged through the brush back to where the Chevy had last departed. That's the spot my boys had marked so that is where Joy was, with our ride back off the mountain.

After a while, April slowed down and stopped. "Hold up." She doubled over, catching her breath, unzipping her vest. "Not used to the altitude." She said with a grin. I stopped too. I was pushing myself hard, and I was more than happy she stopped first. From my pack, I pulled out a Gatorade, slammed some, and handed it to her. She drank deep, letting some pour down her chin and throat.

"How much farther do we need to go, probably another quarter mile?"

April looked at the GPS. "Just about, yeah."

"Good."

I called Joy on the Radio, "Governor Ogre to Joy."

"Joy here."

"We are on the way back, almost there. Stopping to take a breather."

"Roger that, Big Gov. We're waiting.... but please... take your time... don't want you out of breath."

"That's a negative, Joy. Senior Security Escort Alpha is the one out of breath."

"What are you doing?"

April threw the GPS at me. "We'll be there soon enough, Joy. Stand by." I laughed as I let go of the radio key.

"Hey, don't get mad at me. I'm not the one that's not used to high altitude!"

April stood up and walked up close to me. Her eyes were looking down and her voice was soft, "Debbie said you could have me, if you wanted."

"She was just pissed off. That's all. She'll get over it."

"You don't want me?"

"That's not even the question. I'm married. That's all there is to it."

I drank another gulp of Gatorade. "We've got to get back. If we don't, they'll come looking for us." I picked up my shotgun and turned away. I started walking.

April caught up with me and took my hand. "Hey."

I stopped and looked at her. "Yeah?"

"You can have me. I've given myself to you. I'm yours. Your wife even said so. If you don't want me here, or now, you can have me whenever you like. However you like."

I swallowed hard.

"April, my wife says some rash things sometimes. She didn't mean it that way. She was saying that I have to choose."

April stood there, looking at me.

"If I choose, then someone is going to get hurt. I don't want to hurt anyone." I turned and started walking again.

"You would choose her.... because she's your wife."

I didn't say anything, but kept walking. I came to the blood trail that I had followed earlier, and soon I was entering the clearing where we had started.

The M-ATV squatted in the center of the clearing. "Here they be!" Uncle Musket roared. Josh came around the truck with a look of relief. "What took you so long?"

"We had a ways to come. We found something."

Musket had been sitting on the hood of the truck, "Some things are a blessing to find... others a curse... what discovery have you?

"I have no idea at what point my brother started talking like this, but it went back a long way. He was born in the wrong era. On the wrong continent. His perfect time and place would probably have been Rourk's Drift, but I could never be sure.

"We found a puzzle."

Josh raised an eyebrow.

"A plane crash." April said, standing beside me. Musket moved casually but quickly behind Josh. He was afraid of no man. Unfortunately, April was a woman... and this meant he couldn't hit a woman... unless she was a zombie or mutant and then that was different.

"What was in the plane?"

I held up the access card and explained what we had theorized.

"I don't know about you lot, but I don't think this has anything to do with us. We should leave it be." I looked at Musket and nodded.

"I agree, brother. It's just an interesting mystery at this point. Too late for anything to be done now."

Joy had come around and was standing on the other side of me. She had something in her hand. It was a piece of folded paper. I opened it. It was a note from Kilo.

WTA is up.

"Sweet." I thought, until I read the next line.

AZ group in bad shape.

"Crap."

Uncle Musket rode in the turret. As much as he was all about the muzzle loaders, the old M-60 was the least offensive of the modern weapons. "It needs a side hammer. I can't trust anything without a side hammer. The empty cases from this one might make a good powder measure."

April rode shotgun and Josh in the back on the passenger side, with Jen in her usual spot right behind me. Joy was in the very back, sitting on top of the ice chest, pulling out black cans upon request of my brother.

While we drove off the mountain, Musket was telling us glorious old stories that stopped making sense after he started in on his umpteenth can of Guinness.

SEVEN

Precious Metal: Gold, Silver & Lead

Ogre Ranch had become something of a military outpost. Helicopters, Humvees, Deuces, my M-ATV, Josh's MRAP and Strykers, and LAVs. Out in the field, in a corner near the road, we put up a large canopy with some picnic tables under it. Mom, Sarah and Debbie put out a spread. Potato Salad, baked beans, biscuits, and grilled elk. There was plenty of food, enough for an army. Which was great, because we had one. Our own, plus the pilots and crews supporting the helicopters.

Uncle Musket is one of the best story tellers around when it comes to keeping kids enthralled and entertained. He even had our father laughing. During the meal, Debbie would hardly look at me. She was still angry. April kept her distance, but stayed close enough if I needed her. Jen was playing with some of the kids, the new ones we had picked up and my own.

I was sitting in a camp chair, laughing at Musket who was now showing us his interpretation of the art of belly dancing, while Josh and his crew were helping themselves to more beans, and demonstrating why they were called the musical fruit.

After everyone had eaten their fill and Musket sobered slightly, I called the guys around. We had some planning to do.

"Guys, the whole western world rebuilt after the black plague. It took some years, but the world moved on. The same will happen again. Here. Now. Normality will be restored."

The guys all nodded. Almost everyone here was a student of history. "During this time, there was only one form of currency that was recognized. Gold. Gems. Silver."

Musket started grinning ear to ear.

"We're going to need some, fellas. A lot of it."

"What do you got in mind, Ogre?"

"I think we need to go get it. We'll go into town tomorrow... do some collecting. I'm not about to be worried about survival. Look at us... we're surviving well enough. We need to worry about the future."

April, who was always within earshot came up. "We go into town tomorrow... we need to sort something out. I got two things."

"Oh? What's up?"

"The M-60 you're so fond of. We're almost out of ammo for it. The belts for the M-240's don't feed in the 60. We've only got two belts left. I suggest we mount up an M-2. We've got plenty of ammo for one of those. Tons of it." She jerked her head over to a pallet sitting outside of the tent.

"You're probably right. And the increased fire power would not hurt a bit. Okay, and the other?"

"I never had real jewelry before. I get first dibs."

"Fair enough."

April smiled and walked back to the table to pick up a roll to nibble on. Josh nodded towards April and whispered, "She's in love with you. You know that right." It wasn't a question. "When we first got here, my wife picked up on that. She's always close to you."

I knew it. "When I found her, she had pretty much given up on life. She was about to put a bullet through her own head. She's stuck to me ever since. Not like that's a bad thing, either. She's very good at fighting zombies."

Josh looked at me, eye to eye. "She's pretty good looking too."

"Yeah."

"Debbie has been pretty upset. She can see what my wife saw."

"I know." I looked over at April. Everyone did too. She was wearing some ACU pants and a long-sleeved black t-shirt, tucked in under a pistol belt. Her hair was pulled back into a lose pony tail. She was gorgeous. April turned around and saw all the guys looking at her. "WHAT?"

Musket smiled at her, "We were all just admiring that fine arse of yours."

April point a finger at Musket, "I'm going to kick you again for that. When you don't expect it."

Everyone laughed, but just the same, April went around the table to keep an eye on everyone. I turned back to Josh who poked me in the ribs.

"You need to be careful with that one."

"Yeah, I know."

The next morning, before sunrise, we saddled up the M-ATV and all the Humvees. Josh's MRAP rode in the rear. My boys Bravo, Echo and Tango were riding in the MRAP accept for Kilo who drove the second Humvee with Jen and one of Josh's troops. We were in Salt Lake before 9 AM. All our units spread out across the valley according to the plan. We hit the jewelry stores and cleared out the counters.

Along with the jewelry shops, I hit some banks. Some had open vaults after getting through the locked glass doors. LAWs make great door knockers. Some had open access to the safe deposit boxes. These were surprisingly easy to get into with large pry bars, cutting tools, and no one to hit alarms. The worst were the shopping malls. I tried to avoid them, but took the Fashion Place mall and we ended up clearing out its jewelry stores.

By 9 PM we had hit every joint in the phone book. The haul was vast, and the MRAP carried the majority of the loot. The suspension was riding low. It was a long day and we had killed a lot of zombies along the way.

We rallied at the Hilton hotel near the airport as it was too late to drive back to the ranch. The hotel had power and lights and everyone got rooms. The front desk had a sheet under the keyboard that told employees how to make key cards. I followed the instructions and made cards for everyone. For myself and my body guards, I made "Security" cards, that could open all the doors. Just in case.

Somewhere along the way Josh picked up an X-Box and a stack of games. The hotel lobby had a huge plasma TV. The couches were pulled over and it was party time.

Musket found that the hotel had a bar.

"We had a good day." Josh said as he put his feet up on the coffee table. "Kick it! Relax."

Everyone was happy, except for me. I just felt tired. I went up to the top floor and went into the room with my All Access Pass Key Card I had made down stairs at the desk. The suite had a TV, but nothing was on. Could have done a lot of things, but instead I took off my boots, my vest, and just relaxed.

April had said she had to do something and excused herself. I showered, then I was going to bed. I laid down, pulled the sheet up, but not the blanket. Then I closed my eyes.

Ambushed by a Weasel

*T*he next morning everyone was up early and wearing their war-gear. When I came out of the hotel, April was up on the .50 running some Slipstream weapon lubricant through the action. She smiled at me, but didn't say anything. Jen was checking things out on the BFT, sending and receiving status reports. My boys, Bravo and Echo were standing on top of a Humvee's hood, using some binos, checking out the city, which was stone silent

"Everything is doing fine, boss!" Jen reported. "We're almost ready to roll." She climbed out of the M-ATV and headed over to Kilo's rig. Kilo had found a nice leather jacket and leather gloves to match. He came out of the hotel with a strut. "Ooohh... Hot!" Jen said as she climbed in the oversized jeep. Tango had climbed up into the turret and was ready on the M-240. He wore his goggles and gave me a thumbs up.

"Where are we heading to next?" Josh and Musket came up with the rest of the crew out of the hotel.

"Happy Valley".

"Orem, Provo? We'll need another rig for the loot. We can't put anything else in the MRAP."

"Musket can drive the MRAP."

"No, that baby is mine."

"Fine, you can drive your MRAP until we find a Suburban or something. Musket can drive that."

Musket stood there with a large shotgun type muzzle loader in one hand like it was a toy. "If I must."

"Alright. Let's roll."

As we came into Happy Valley, coming off Point Of The Mountain, at the Alpine exit, one of our units peeled off, another at Lehi, then another in American Fork. I took the first Orem exit.

Operating in Happy Valley was more risky than in the Salt Lake Valley, as there were still zombies roaming the streets in pockets of large numbers. I was considering organizing another MOAB-RABBIT operation, but no one was interested in riding, or in the horse sacrifice. The motorcycles strapped with cats might do it. I kept an eye on the status of the units my boys were in with the BFT.

I pulled up in front of a Mountain West Jewelers. Zombies were all around the small strip mall. I told April to hold on the .50 but to use her SCAR. She had the advantage of being high up and out of reach, while having the perfect angle to administer inter-cranial V-max injections. When the ratio of shamblers to still lumps tilted to our favor, I opened my door and jumped out with my M4 up and ready. I engaged any zombie that was within sight, going through two magazines and a half before I turned my attention to the door of the store. The door was locked. Plan B. I shot the locks. No joy. Well, so much for trying be subtle. I blew out the whole front window then jumped in. Like Burglers, we used Pillow Cases to collect the sparkly stuff. The glass cases could have been smashed, but that made picking out the jewelry much more difficult. It was easier to go behind the counter, open the back, and slide out the trays one at a time. Some stores had locks on the cases, which were fortunately not very resistant to 5.56mm. We were about finished when I decided to poke my head into the back. The girls were taking the loot they had out to the M-ATV. Gold Chain was wrapped on fat spools. And there were a lot of spools. I took it all. The sack I had was heavy. I was about to come out with it, when I heard something out of place. A male voice.

"Looks like we have some jewel thieves here, Johnny."

"I wonder where they got these guns."

"Best looking girls I've seen in a while, that's for sure.

I peeked out and could see two guys. The two I could see were armed with shotguns, long barreled hunting type shotguns. Benellis, from the look. I knew there was a third from the sound of the voices, but I couldn't see him. They were holding my girls at gun point.

"Man, they got a lot of stuff in this rig! I'm keeping this thing."

"I get that Fifty Cal!"

"I'll take the girls."

I set the sack down and crept out of the back room, staying low.

"Who are you?" One of the voices demanded.

"I'm none of your business," April growled. From my vantage point I could see her face. There was blood on it. They must have hit her as she came out of the store. "But if you leave now – we'll let you guys live."

The men laughed.

April continued. "Except for you, weasel, I'm going to kill you."

This made the other men laugh like it was the funniest thing they had ever heard. I moved slowly, having to set down the M4. It was too heavy.

"And how are you going to do that, bitch?" The weasel spat and then kicked April hard in the stomach. April screamed as she fell, and she started crying hysterically. She rolled over onto her side and tucked into a ball to avoid the weasel's kicks. All the men were occupied watching her. She saw me through the glass as I moved behind a counter right next to broken out window. I held up my hand. Five Fingers.

Four Fingers.

April's cries turned to laughter.

Three Fingers.

"Is that the best you can do, big boy? You're nothing, you pencil dick." April growled, getting everyone's attention.

I sprang with my Glock drawn and ready. I fired once into the first guy, once into the second guy, then gave the first one what I thought was four more, but turned out to be six and then another four into the second guy.

The Weasel spun to face me, but I grabbed the barrel of his shotgun as I stepped inside. He froze when the hot muzzle of the Glock's suppressor pressed into his forehead.

"Move and die." I said flatly.

April stood up, slowly. "Kick a girl when she's down. You are such a bastard! "

"He called you a bitch too." I offered.

The weasel's eyes were wide with fear. "I, I..."

He never finished the sentence. April pulled out a small fixed blade knife from behind her belt buckle. A Becker Necker she wore in appendix carry. The draw was so fast, I didn't even see it coming. April pulled the razor sharp knife across the throat, opening it into a wide smile that revealed a severed wind pipe.

April whispered into the weasel's ear, "I told you I was going to kill you." Her voice was ice cold.

I held the shotgun by the barrel as the guy let go of it with one hand, grabbing at his throat. Blood poured from between his fingers. April backed up a few feet and let the guy stagger. I yanked the shotgun away from him, and the weasel fell to his knees. He tried to say something when his eyes rolled up and he fell over like a toppled Jenga stack.

April stood there with the knife in her hand, still up at throat level. Her eyes were blazing. Beautiful and frightening. Especially when her eyes turned from the fallen thug to me. Then her eyes softened.

"Are you hurt?" I asked her.

"No... I'm okay. I just had to keep the attention on me so you could make your move."

"How did they get the drop on you guys?" I looked at Joy who was still visibly shaken. I had sent a handful of rounds within inches of her. Joy looked at me, speechless.

"They were up on the roof. They jumped down and caught us by surprise." April sounded like she was apologizing.

"I'm just glad you girls are okay." I held on to April for a second longer. You sure you aren't hurt?"

"I'll be fine."

"So that was all acting."

April smiled. "I'm very talented."

I had to laugh. "Indeed." I went back inside and grabbed the sacks I had left and threw them into the back of the M-ATV.

Joy hadn't moved. "You okay, Joy?"

"I... I thought you were going to shoot me... You looked so... angry." There was no explaining my look. I don't know what I looked like. "I wouldn't let anything hurt you if I could stop it, Joy."

Joy's eyes got a little moist. "I thought..."

"Come on now. I would never hurt my girls."

"You came through the window shooting... looking like the devil... Bullets going right by me. It just scared me."

I gave Joy a hug. "You're okay now?"

"I'm okay."

Joy climbed into the rig and sat there quietly.

"Hey," I said to April, "Get Joy something to eat and drink out of the cooler. Let's let her rest a bit."

April climbed up into the back of the M-ATV to the cooler and started digging around. I picked up the two shotguns. They were both Super Black Eagle II's, a very nice shotgun if you are hunting things with feathers. I threw them into the back of the truck and checked out the other guy. He had a Maverick 88 and a bandoleer full of 12 gauge #7's. I threw those in the truck as well.

"You want a Gator-Bull?" April asked.

"Yeah, I'll take one."

April drank a long pull on the Gatorade and popped open a 12 ounce Red Bull and poured it in before she tossed it to me.

"Thanks." I knocked it back and drank a long gulp of it. As my head was back, I looked up at the roof. Now, if I was up there with two of my buddies... what would I be doing up there? They had to have been there before we pulled up.

"Anyone got a ladder?"

We rolled down the strip mall to the end where we found the thugs vehicle, a Ford super crew truck with a ladder in the bed, leading up to the roof.

"Okay, I'm going up. I want you guys to stay here, keep your eyes open. Maybe one of you should man the Fifty."

April tilted her head. "Excuse me?"

"I mean, 'Whoa-Man' the fifty."

"That's better."

I climbed into the back of the truck. It was full of cases of beer and bags of Little Smokies. I thought this was very odd considering there were no Tail Gate Parties going on that I knew of.

I went up the ladder, slowly, with my M4 ready, making sure nothing was up top waiting for me. Once on the roof I walked around. Nothing really struck me as out of place. There were no open skylights that they may have tried to drop down through. No burglary tools. Then I found the other ladder.

I walked over to it. The ladder was extended out and reached from the roof over to the top of a high brick wall of a neighboring property. The wall was too tall for the ladder, even from the back of a truck, but the wall was close enough to be bridged by the ladder. Okay. This is strange. I looked at the property, but couldn't see into it because of trees. I did make out a roof through some branches, but couldn't make anything of it. Part of me wanted to walk across to see what was up. The other part of me said that I really didn't care. I pulled the ladder back and left it on the roof. As I turned, I heard someone say "Thank You."

What? I turned back to the wall. There was a guy standing there, looking over the wall from the other side. He was about the same age as my boy Kilo. "Uh, your welcome."

"I was going to have to shoot you if you tried to come across."

"I'm not one of those guys."

"Good... they have been trying to get in all day."

"I'm George Hill."

"Mark Price... my dad is on the Utah Jazz."

"Ah... sports fans."

"Yeah."

"So where is your dad?"

The boy's eyes dropped. "He's gone."

"I understand. What about the rest of your family? You are not all alone are you?"

"They are all dead... but I'm not alone. My girlfriend is here."

"Are you guys okay? You have food and water and stuff?"

"Starting to run out I guess."

"Do you have a car?"

"Yeah, but where can we go?"

I filled him in on his safe zone options and suggested he pack up some stuff and get to one, at least for a while. He could always come back to his home again.

I went back to the M-ATV. "Did you find anything?" Joy asked from the turret.

"Those guys were trying to get into the house of one of the Jazz players. I found his kid and told them where to go."

"What about the Jazz player?"

"Dead."

I climbed into the truck. "How's my kids doing?" I asked April. She was looking at the BFT and turned it in my direction. "Looks like they are doing fine. Josh's unit has been moving along, hitting different stops. Kilo and Jen's unit finished at one stop and have just pulled to a stop at another."

"Other units?"

"They all seem to be fine."

"Right on. Let's hit our next target."

We hit a couple small jewelry stores before we pulled up to the biggest target in Orem. The University Mall.

"I hate this place even more now than when we were last here."

The body of the kid Jen shot through the head was still in the parking lot. Dried blood and a hole in pavement where a .500 magnum slug blasted through marked the spot, but the body had been pulled apart by dogs. Next to the body was a shopping bag. We parked the M-ATV and April got out and picked up the shopping bag. It was full of jewelry. She handed me the bag. I looked at the body, "Thanks kid." I didn't remember the name.

"Do we have to do this?" Joy sighed as she climbed out of the truck.

"Let's do this quick."

"I thought you burned this place down."

"I didn't try hard enough. Come on."

We went through the door with our weapons up and ready. The zombies were scattered and easily dispatched. We ran along the mall to the jewelry stores, finding the bodies of the kids that had tried to loot the stores before, finding their bags of goodies and scooping up the rest that the kids had passed over.

On our way back through the mall, April stopped at the Victoria's Secret store. "Just a second. What color, red, white, pink?"

186

"The candy wrapper doesn't matter."

"Black then."

April went into the silk and lace shop and Joy and I laid down some suppressive fire down the hallway into the Mervins where a number of zombies were milling about. The Thumper I had built out of toys had gone silent, but the zombies were still around with nowhere else to go.

The urgency we had before was gone so we took our time. Joy and I were playing a morbid game. Fire a shot, if it was a good headshot and dropped the zed with one hit you got a point. I was winning 6 to 5 when April came out with a new handbag that seemed full over her shoulder, her SCAR in her hands. "I'm ready to go now."

I rolled my eyes. "Come on."

We worked our way back. "Hold on a sec." I was in front of the knife store. I looked into the cases for the large Chris Reeve Sebenzas. I always wanted one, so what the hell. I grabbed all of them. "Here." I gave one to each of the girls.

"Nice." April nodded as she flicked it open with the thumb stud. "Oh... smooth."

Joy flicked her wrist and snapped the blade open. "Love it."

I was disappointed the fire I had started before only burned for a bit and then went out, but holding the Sabenza, I was glad at least that these were not ruined. The food court looked like it could have actually have been cleaned out and reopened for business.

A small, shrill moan came from down the hall. "Oh my God." Joy gasped.

When I turned, I saw the thing. It was a toddler when it was alive. Now it was a zombie with a hand missing and half of a leg eaten to the bone. It shrieked at us as it gimped along slowly because of being hobbled. Its milky white eyes looking at us, pleading from the hunger. This was the single most disturbing thing I'd ever seen. April raised her SCAR. "I can't."

I looked at the zombie child as I raised my M4. "Mercy on us." I pulled the trigger. The zombie child's head exploded into chunks of flesh and blackened blood. The body fell down and was finally still. I lowered the M4. "Let's get the hell out of here."

We headed down the hill from the University Mall, into Provo. We pulled into the Albertson's parking lot and Joy and April got out and looked around. I was looking at the other units, getting ready to climb out when I heard some shouting.

I looked up to see April raise her SCAR as a tracer flashed past her head. The memory of Hudson getting shot in the head suddenly came to mind, and without thinking jumped out of the M-ATV. Joy was reaching out to something when I came around the truck.

"STAY LOW!" I shouted.

Joy was also yelling "COME ON!" But she wasn't talking to me.

April was firing rapidly, but they were aimed shots. I couldn't see what she was engaging. A round pinged off the fender of the M-ATV and ricked off with a buzz. A close one.

Suddenly two girls raced into Joy's arms, knocking her over. What the hell? I brought my M4 up and moved over to Joy. There was a man in a cowboy hat and a woman with long, blond hair tied in a braid. The man had an SKS rifle. The woman had a Hi-Point Carbine.

"What the hell is going on?"

"They came out of Albertson's dragging these kids." April started to explain. "When the kids saw us, they screamed for help and started running. They said these were bad people."

The kids were screaming. One had a red hand print across her face. The kids didn't look like either of the adults that were shooting at us.

What the hell is wrong with people today? I raised my M4 and put the chevron center in the cowboy hat, then yelled. "STOP YOUR SHOOTING! PUT DOWN YOUR WEAPONS!"

The man's response was to hold his rifle over the hood of station wagon and fire off a string of rounds. I figured as much. I pressed my trigger and felt the gun buck but I don't think I even heard the shot. The bullet put a small hole in the front of the hat, but a red plume of spray came out the back. The man instantly dropped. The woman screamed and pointed her weapon at me. Time slowed to a crawl I'll be honest. I hesitated. She fired first. I didn't know Hi-Points could go full auto, but hers did. I felt rounds impact my M4. When I went to pull the trigger, my gun didn't fire. I felt rounds impact my tactical vest, and heard a ping as one of the rounds clipped one of the magazines I wore up front. Since my M4 Malfed, I transitioned to my Glock and brought it up. April screamed as she fired. I looked over at her as she shot. I watched her finger pull the trigger and then the gun recoil and brass fling out of the mechanism. I looked back and put the front sight of Glock on target and started to pull the trigger again. I fired until the slide locked back and I went for a reload. I felt very tired.

The gun and magazine started to get heavy, but I got the gun reloaded. The slide release was difficult. The blond woman with the Hi Point was falling.

Joy started screaming as she scrambled to me. I looked down at myself. There were a couple holes in my vest. One over the magazine, and another right by my zipper. *Not again.*

April was calling my name, but I just stood there. That chick freaking hit me. The hole by the mag looked funny, but the hole by the zipper wasn't funny at all. Blood had welled up in it and started to flow pretty good, but I didn't feel anything. The fatigue I felt was overwhelming. I've never felt so tired before. Wait, yes I have. Last time this happened, but those hits were lower. April grabbed my arm. Joy grabbed my vest. April was screaming at me. I felt very heavy, like I wanted to lay down. The ground came up at me, but I didn't hit it. The girls caught my fall and lowered me down.

"Call the other units! Call for help!" April ordered and in a flash, Joy was gone. April started pulling my gear off me.

I could hear the kids crying.

"Oh sweet Jesus." April said. I could feel her tugging on me, then her pressing on me.

Blue sky.

Clouds.

I didn't black out, but time distorted. I heard the voice of my boys.

"DAD!"

Then I could see their faces. The looks of fear on them. I was so proud of them.

"These kids... Bravo, Echo... You need to take them back home. Get them out of here, get them safe. I'll be okay."

"Dad – no..."

Josh's face pressed in "Start an IV." He said to someone. I felt pressure on my arm.

"Jimmy... these kids... I want my boys to take these kids home."

"We'll do exactly that, George. We got them... the kids are safe, your boys are safe. Don't worry."

April's face came into view. Her eyes were red, she had tears. She leaned in close and whispered, "I love you."

I didn't know what to say, so I pulled a Han Solo line. "I know."

"What the ... ?" Josh exclaimed.

April kissed me.

"My boys..."

"Will be fine, bro. I'll see they get on their way home." Musket said.

Kilo said in a way that defied argument, "I'm staying with my Dad. He didn't tell me to go anywhere."

Musket in a command tone, "Bravo, Echo! Come with me."

They put the two little kids in a Humvee before Bravo and Echo climbed in. Musket jumped into the driver's seat and they peeled out of the parking lot.

I felt myself being rolled over. "No exit."

A slap on the face, "Stay with us, Governor."

I didn't respond. I wanted to, but I felt 300 miles away.

Bullets in my Chest

*M*usket pulled up in front of a motorsports shop. Out in front, there were parked a couple funky looking cars that looked like they were made out of pipes. Sand Rails. Each one had two seats. Musket ran inside and found keys and in the shop section of the store, gas cans. He filled up each tank and put a five-gallon can inside each Sand Rail. Bravo fired up his unit and the engine purred, ready to go. Musket picked up one of the children and put the kid in the passenger seat and strapped him in.

"You know how to make your way back, eh?" Bravo nodded. Musket then patted Bravo on his head. "Now that's a good lad! You don't have to make it all the way to the ranch now... you just have to make it to the check point and them men there will help ye get the rest of the way home. Here." Musket pulled out a P-90 and a pouch full of spare magazines, all loaded. "This will be easier to shoot than that thing while driving..." He pointed to the boy's AR. "Now off you go! Drive!"

Bravo nodded and hit the gas, roaring in the direction of Provo Canyon. Musket turned to Echo and said the same things, giving him a P-90 as well. "Don't let your brother beat you home, Lad!"

"Hell no!" Echo hit the gas, leaving Musket alone in the parking lot. Musket looked after the last Sand Rail as it streaked out of view. "They be fine boys as there ever was." He crossed himself. "May the good Lord see them home safe."

Musket drove back to Albertson's.

When he approached, "My boys."

"They'll be home in no time. I sent them off in a couple buggies. Sand Rails they are called. Wicked contraptions made of left over plumbing. Infernal sprightly they are. They'll be home before you."

The ache in my guts became sharp. "This hurts."

"I got it."

Anderson had some forceps in his hand. They were clamped onto a copper slug. It was a bullet, the one that was in me. "Mag caught the other one. This one just missed the liver. Lucky bastard." One of the things Anderson was really good at, "Battlefield Medicine."

I had enough morphine in me to numb the pain, but that was about it. He did some more work on my insides before announcing that I was stable and ready for transport. As soon as the chopper gets here.

Bravo and Echo jetted up Provo Canyon like a couple slot racers. When they came too near a zombie, they would fire a burst at it as they squirted away. They made it to the checkpoint in no time, and there, inside the safe zone, they stopped, refueled the tanks from the spare cans and made sure the little kids had a drink and went potty.

"Where's the Governor?" One of the guys asked. They had heard radio chatter. "How is he?"

"He's going to be fine." Echo said "He's had worse. Helicopter is picking him up."

Bravo sounded optimistic. "He got hit with a 9mm. You can't kill an Ogre with a 9mm. Can't happen."

The boys jumped back into the Sand Rails and launched in a cloud of dust and gravel.

The blackhawk set down as gently as it could. I recognized Whisky Six smiling at me, "I'm always saving your ass, Governor."

"Took you long enough to get here, Rotorhead. I knew I should have called him a zoomie." I could only whisper, but he heard it... he grinned.

"He'll be fine."

April and Kilo climbed in the helicopter and Whiskey Six lifted up off the ground, tilted forward, and raced to the canyon.

I woke up and looked around. I had fallen asleep after the helicopter ride. I remember being wheeled in to the hospital. One of the docs there I had sold several guns to. "Hey Doc."

I don't remember anything after that. I didn't so much black out as get knocked out. But once knocked out, I stayed out. I was tired. I felt pretty good, all things considered. Until I tried to move. Okay, that's not such a good idea as I had tubes in me. I looked at the IV bag which was almost empty. I looked at the second little bag hanging with it, it was on a slower drip.

I laid back down and looked up at the ceiling. I was pissed. Going over everything in my head, replaying the situation, I saw where I made my tactical error. I hesitated. I could have fired, but I didn't. Then she fired, and I was hit. Because I hesitated. I felt like I had let everyone down.

Where was I?

This wasn't a hospital room. This wasn't my room at the ranch. I ran my left hand over my torso. I had a bandage wrapped around me. There was a compress under it. I very carefully pulled my IV out of my hand and rolled over to push myself up. The room was spartan, the bed I was in, a chair, which was small, uncomfortable and empty. A small table with a pitcher of water and a cup. In the corner was a table with some of my clothes on it. My DCU pants, boots, a black t-shirt. On a peg above this table was my gun belt, with my holstered Glock 23. A window that was open with the blinds angled to let in light. There was a simple tract light in the ceiling. The carpet was grey and industrial looking. I was in a smock.

Screw this. I stood up and was surprised at how strong I felt. Or more accurately, how not strong I was. I felt like a kitten. The water pitcher was heavy, but I got a cup poured. My mouth was dry, the water while not cold, tasted very good. I made the 15-mile hike across the small room to the table where my clothes were. Instead of picking them up, I pulled the wheeled table back to the bed so I could sit down again. Out of breath.

Come on, Ogre. Man up! I worked at it slowly but got dressed, leaving my bandages on. Once dressed, and my Glock 23 back on my hip, I felt better. I went to the door. Metal handle, not a nob. Stainless. Cold. I was about to find out where I was. All I had to do was push the handle down and pull the door open. Which I did after taking a deep breath.

Outside of the door was a hallway. Left ended in a dead end. To the right, there were a couple other doors to the right of the hall, and windows to the left side. I looked out of the window and could see that I was up stairs. The sky was half dark. It must be morning. Across the street was the hospital. I was in the Sleep Clinic. That explains the comfortable bed. And why it was so quiet.

I walked slowly down the hall to the end where it opened up into a small lobby. Lounging in one of the chairs was my wife, she was leaning on her hand, eyes closed, and I could tell she had been crying. Kilo was there, sacked out across two chairs, sprawled out like only Kilo can. April was there and she was in another chair, curled up into a ball, knees tucked into her chin. A Doctor came out of a door and stopped.

"Governor Hill! You should not be up."

"But I am."

The doctor came and took my arm as if to lead me back to my room like a child. He pulled my arm but didn't budge me an inch.

"I'll lay back down when I'm ready, Doc."

I walked over to Debbie and touched her face. "Hey, Love." I wanted to lean down and kiss her forehead but I wasn't quite up to that yet. Her eyes opened wide and she looked at me.

"Hey you." She stood up and carefully embraced me. "It's about time you woke up." She gave me a kiss. "Let's get you home."

"Good, I'm kinda hungry for some breakfast."

"Honey, it's past dinner time."

Kilo woke up and jumped to me. "Dad!" He hugged me. "I thought you were going to die!"

April stood close by but refrained from contact, but she was smiling. I looked at Kilo, "I've had worse." I gave him a hug back. "You okay?"

"Yeah, I am now."

I looked at April. "You okay?"

"I am now."

"Come on guys, let's go home. I'm tired and hungry and I want to be in my own bed."

I looked over at the Doc. "Hey, why am I over here and not over there."

"Your body guards insisted on getting you out of the noisy place the hospital became when you landed. Reporters."

"We still have reporters?"

"Vernal Express... they are quite full of themselves now. They interviewed everyone. That came back."

Back!

"Where is Bravo and Echo? Did they make it back!?"

"They did, with a couple more kids. They are okay. But I'm not – When did you let them drive dune buggies?" Debbie was putting on her fierce mom face.

"I didn't. Musket must have."

"I should have known." She shrugged. "So why did you send them away so fast?"

"I didn't want them to watch me die if I was going to."

Down stairs and outside I looked around. Where was my truck? My M-ATV? I was led to a large, black SUV. A Tahoe with blacked out windows. April opened the door, she was holding an HK UMP. I carefully climbed in, with Debbie right behind me. Kilo got into the driver's seat and April rode shotgun.

On the way home, Debbie broke the silence. "There is a Sergeant Ferguson from back east... One of the Carolina's."

"Oh? The Sarge finally made it. Good. I've been waiting for him. I have a job for him."

I was going to say something else, but instead fell asleep again.

Sergeant Fergusen Arrives

The next morning, I was really sore. All over hurt. The pain killers that I had been given were no longer in my system. Instead of taking narcotic-based meds, I took a mix of Tylenol and Advil, which helped a lot, but didn't have that "I'm kinda high" feeling. I could deal with some aches if I had a clear head.

I was sitting on the porch of Ogre Ranch in the big, ugly, blue recliner. I had on my sunglasses and a British style driving hat. Debbie had made me a breakfast burrito, but it wasn't as good as Rosa's. I missed Rosa all of a sudden. Debbie had made a good try at making them like she did, she used all the same stuff... the beans, the eggs, the peppers, the cheese, even the potato.... but it was the tortilla that was lacking. Rosa's hand-made tortillas made all the difference. I'll have to find her again and ask her to come back. After Zack left, Rosa went out and found another guy to cling on to. One of the soldiers, but I didn't know which one.

Along with the BB, I had a Cherry Coke Zero. I was a contented Ogre, really I was. This wasn't bad. Breakfast on the porch, looking out at what had become an Airdrome.

Debbie had gone over to the school. Zombie uprising or not, the kids had to be educated, and we had a lot of young kids around lately. So with the kids gone, Debbie gone, it was quiet.

I watched one of the soldiers throwing a football to Kilo, who was the only son who wasn't at school at the moment. At the foot of the steps to the porch, Jen sat on a stool with an ipod in her ears. I could hear the music she was listening to from here. Joy was cleaning weapons on a folding table we had set up out under a tree. April was cleaning out the M-ATV.

"Check this out." She said as she brought out my M4.

"It never failed me before... not once." I felt remorseful.

"No, it didn't fail you. It saved you. Look."

She held the rifle like I do. "See this?" "Now look at where the bullet struck." She popped the pin on the back of the M4 and hinged it open. Inside the receiver was a slug, buried in the trigger mechanism, with damage going into the upper as well. The gun was effectively ruined. "See, you were aiming at the guy, so the shot from the woman came in here. See. Hold the rifle."

I held the rifle like I was shooting. Then she pulled the rifle out of my hands. "The bullet's vector would have gone straight through your heart." I thought about it for a second. If I had also used the old way of shooting it, with the rifle held higher – same thing – I'd have been dead.

"The other round, it hit my vest, but didn't penetrate."

"You had one of my HK mags, stainless steel filled with brass." She pulled the mag out of her cargo pocket. The bullet was stuck in the mag. The mag saved me.

"That was one of my mags." April grinned. "That round would have been through your liver. My mag saved you too."

I thought about this all and took it into consideration. None of this changed the fact that my hesitation is what could have gotten me killed. I was very lucky.

"I'll need a new rifle now."

April turned, "Hey Joy, you done with his rifle, Girlfriend?"
Joy tossed the rifle to Jen, who in turn tossed it up to April, who handed it to me on bended knee. "Your rifle."

It was a Remington ACR. As I took the rifle, I noticed April was wearing the ring I had given her, the one with the diamonds around a ruby... it was part of her take from the mountains of gold and jewels we scavenged from Salt Lake to Provo. I didn't expect her to be wearing it. I raised my eyebrow and nodded at the ring. She gave me a sly smile and took the Rock River from me and started taking off the accessories I had on it. I put on the ACOG, the suppressor, the Magpul AFG, but left off the light. Instead, I asked, "Do we have a spare Surefire X300?"

She nodded and fetched the smaller, lighter tactical light from the M-ATV. I nodded. "This is nice. You know, a girl has never given me a gun before."

"Your wife never gave you a gun? Seriously?"

"Never."

She made that little "huh" sound that was full of judgement that all women can make.

"You know, not that it matters. I always got my own guns.

"But you liked it when we gave you this one."

"Yeah, I kinda did. It was nice. Thank you, Girls. I mean that."

"Thank you for not dying on us."

"No, no problem. And I'll even forget that this is the same ACR I snagged almost a week ago."

"You were not supposed to notice that." April bent down and kissed me.

I picked up my coke and changed the subject. "Give this to Kilo. Tell him I want it zeroed."

April gave the rifle to Jen, who carried it out to the field to where Kilo was. Just then a man rode past on a horse. I'd not seen him around here before. He did a double take, then wheeled the horse around and trotted up to the side of the M-ATV and jumped out of the saddle. He then threw the reigns around the rear view mirror of my truck. Who the hell? Ah... recognition hit me.

I called out, "Yeah, go ahead and tie him up anywhere. Oh, and George Straight called, he wants his hat back." Curious as to why a large black crow landed on top of the M-ATV and acted like he expected something to happen.

April was standing at the top of the steps, full body guard mode. Joy had a new toy in her hands, not pointed, but in a low ready. Looked like a short barreled Remington 870. April held up her hand. "And who are you, Friend?" The way she said friend sounded less of a salutation and every bit of a challenge.

Sgt. Ferguson opened his mouth, but I spoke first, "April, this is Sergeant Ferguson from the Cherokee Nation... and he is late! Come on up, Neil, pull up a chair! Forgive me if I don't get up. I had an unfortunate event. I was playing catch with some bullets. Word has it, so have you recently!"

I waved him up and April stepped aside, letting him pass. As he walked past, April whispered something into his hear. I couldn't hear the words, but it sounded cold. She casually walked a few steps that put her at clear angles so if something happened, I was out of the line of fire.

"She's being overly protective since I got hurt. Forgive her. She was almost out of a job." Then I turned to April, "He's cool, Love. I trust him. Get him a Dr. Pepper."

April walked inside and I turned back to Neil. "So are they really calling me Hiroshima Hill back east? Seriously?"

The Sarge threw his head back and laughed.

"It wasn't a nuke."

Uncle Musket's Pub

After speaking with Sarge, I told him I had some work for him to do but I'll talk to him about that over supper. I had things to line out before I commissioned him. He seemed occupied and kept eyeing that big crow. I think I'll get old Killswitch out in case that thing comes back. My Savage 93R17 is really good at popping crows. But anyways, I had other things to worry about.

I sent for Anderson and his staff. I needed situation reports. I felt some-what out of touch. Sleeping for a whole day does that. I had my laptop booted up and went to WTA to follow how everyone else was doing. AZ had some messed up situations as the zed count was still very high.

Anderson and his S-2 and S-3 sat down with me and we went over the ramifications if certain scenarios played out and what we could do about it. The Nuclear Power Plant in AZ was checked out by one of the WTA members and he carefully cleared the place of zed infestation there. While in there, half the board was one big flashing red light. Not being a Nuclear Engineer, he bugged out. That's problem 1.

Problem 2 was that a small armada of Chinese warships was intercepted by the 7th fleet and got into a tussle. They slugged it out and chewed the fleet down to a fraction of what it was, but only a few vessels of the 7th remained, and they ran straight back to the US at flank speed. Where they are now, or their condition, no one knows. Last observed, the Chinese warships were heading to San Diego.

"What can we do to stop them?" I asked.

"What do we have?" Anderson shrugged. "Some Apaches, some armor and Arty, an old fighter Trainer. At Hill we have some heavy lifters, some fighters, 2 F-18 Super Hornets, a bunch of Falcons, four F-22 Raptors, and an Eagle. Not really enough to hold off a fleet."

"If they are going to San Diego, they are going to dock, off load troops and gear. Can we stop them there? Swim under them, put some charges on them, and sink them in place so other ships can't get to the dock. Or is that something only SEAL's can do?"

"That's a possibility." Anderson bristled.

I stood up, slowly. Anderson and the other officers stood up as well.

Anderson, I want you, the rest of the 19th and half of every Guardsmen we have to go to Hill for air transport to San Diego.

Call in every one you know from other State Guards. We will stop the Chinese before they can get their feet dry. Conventional or unconventional if we have to. I'll take some men and we're going to Arizona."

"But, sir. We don't have enough men."

"I have a plan. I'm going to send an ambassador and if this works out, you will have more than enough. Now, you have your orders, son. I want you on the move by 0600."

"Yes, sir!" The officers then left.

The next day I was coming back from the school where I helped organize the kids reading program. It was important that the children have a sense of normality, structure, stability, and routine. School was a good way of doing that.

Going to the school, I went down the block and not down the highway. Coming out of the school I went straight to the highway where I saw something out of place.

"What the hell is that?" I pointed to the large log cabin that was now out the end of the field that wasn't there the last time I had looked.

The girls looked at each other and shrugged. "It's a cabin." Jen offered.

"Why is it on my airfield? Joy, pull in there."

I climbed out of the truck and looked around. A cabin. A big one. Magically grew out of the ground right here. WTF?

Above the door I saw the cause and the reason. A small sign carved out of a plank of wood, painted, and set swinging above the door. "Uncle Musket's Pub".

"Oh good hell!" I suddenly had both a headache, and a bad feeling about this. But I went in anyways.

Inside was a hardwood floor, picnic tables with a random assortment of chairs. On one wall was a long bar – well stocked. Above the assorted bottles was a huge blunderbuss. Behind the bar, wiping it down with a white cloth, was a smiling Uncle Musket.

"Come in, my brother the Governor! Pull up a chair and sit your perforated arse down now! What will ye be having to drink? Or eat? We've some fine sandwiches."

A girl came out of the back – I didn't even know there was a back – wearing a rough skirt and a linen shirt that was open low with a small leather thong tied just so to barely keep the shirt from popping open in a massive "wardrobe malfunction". The thong looked like it was under a lot of strain.

"Where did this place come from? And where did you get it? Where did you get a serving wench?" Just then another one came out from the back.

"Wenches? What the hell, Musket!"

"Now calm yourself down, brother Ogre – or you'll pop a stitch and you'll have blood shooting out all over my floor that I just finished cleaning."

One of the wenches smiled and ran a finger along my cheek as she walked past. April bristled and balled up a fist.

"Musket..."

"I just found it all alone sitting in a field and thought I could put it to use. So don't be getting all worked up like you do and start using my Roman name or I'll start using yours, and then we'd have to go to blows and all that and our poor old sainted mother would be ever so disappointed in her lads. So just relax yourself and your Valkyries and let my girls take care of you lot."

He had a way of making his point. I had to laugh. "Sounds good to me. What do you have to eat?"

The Serving Wenches brought out a plate of meat and cheese with a round loaf of bread. It wasn't long before The Girl Squad was relaxed and we were all enjoying the food.

"So tell me... have you slept with your Serving Wenches yet?"

"Slept with? Nay, brother. I would do no such thing. On my honor!"

One of the Wenches laughed as she nipped Musket's ear. "But I shag them each at least twice a day!"

Musashi strolled in. "Hey, this place cleaned up nice."

"You knew about this?"

"Yeah, I helped him set it up. I got the chairs."

"How did you guys..."

"Halliburton."

"Ah, yeah... they can do anything." I nodded.

Just then a number of servicemen came walking in, each one of them reaching up and rubbing the Brown Bess rifle that hung above the inside of the door. "Praise the Musket!" They each said in turn.

"The Musket welcomes you!" My brother bellowed as he went to the bar and started pouring drinks.

"I gotta go." I was laughing again as I started to walk out the door. One of the wenches stopped me.

"When you leave, you rub the musket and say Peace to Musket." She smiled.

"Peace to Musket!"

Uncle Musket grinned, "Peace, brother!"

I walked out and after me, the girls followed the new tradition.

I spent the rest of the afternoon in the pilot's seat of Whiskey Seven. Jason Jones was the pilot and my instructor. Going over the systems, system checks, procedures, and giving me the whole rundown of the aircraft. I had two hours of stick time in a UH-1, so JJ explained that I'd have little problem with a Blackhawk if I could keep a Huey in a hover and keep it straight.

While talking with JJ, I had people coming to me with reports, questions, I even had to sign authorization forms for some things. So learning was slower than I wanted. However much was accomplished.

Wyoming, Eastern Colorado, Idaho, Montana, all of the Utah Safe Zones, and Eastern Oregon had joined forces with me, what little government they had left. But forming a new government to build from what is left, has been seen as a good thing. Especially when democratic elections will be held as soon as we have reached a stability. Utah at least, is getting under control. Sheriff's from across the state have been in conference, and establishing order. I authorized a joint building project between three of the remaining oil field companies to build a refinery. We need to be able to process our own oil into fuel.

Survivors from outside the safe zones, are getting fewer and fewer. Ogden is still crawling with the undead and the Air Force has secured the base and fortified it. There are so few people left, and cooperation has been necessary for survival. The Ute Tribe has been a big help. Other tribes, have declared their independence. Foremost are the Navajo. They must be reached, reasoned with, and brought in as member or our new Coalition of Western States. Someone needs to go talk to them. Someone I can trust.

Someone was talking to me. "Huh?"

"I said... Are you ready to light this thing off?" JJ said, looking as cool as humanly possible with his hairless baby face. No pornstash like Outbreak, so he's no where near as cool.

"I thought you would never ask!"

As I hit the starter, I glanced over to the ranch house. I had spectators. A lot of them family. A lot of them friends. I noticed by Sarge a short, little guy standing beside him. At first I thought he was a kid, but he struck me as very old. The main rotor started turning. Slowly at first, but in moments it was spinning at full speed. Everything looked good.

"Very nice, Governor. Now, let's pick it up just a few feet and hold it."

I pulled up on the collective as I gave it just a little throttle. The Blackhawk resisted at first, like the ground was holding on to the wheels. Then it seemed to just step into the air like it had been waiting and eager to do so. I felt the peddles now, as the bird was off the ground. Left, then Right, then back to the left. Getting the feel for it was a lot easier than a UH-1. The Blackhawk was a much more stable aircraft.

"Impressive, sir. Okay, now let's get higher, then turn the aircraft to face the other way. Nice!"

I let the helicopter slowly rotate in the air as we climbed a few more feet skyward.

"Let's move forward about one length of the aircraft."

We went through simple motions in the bird. Forward, back, turning, sliding to the side, moving backwards. JJ was putting me through the paces, and I was able to make the Blackhawk do just that. We ended up flying over the ranch, around Vernal, then back to the ranch, where I set the chopper down gently, right where I took off from.

"Man, that was awesome!" I was excited and felt like a kid. JJ gave me a high five as we walked away from the chopper. He headed to Musket's pub, and I headed back to Ranch House. It was almost supper time and I was hungry, and hurting as all my pain meds were out of my system. I didn't want to try to fly with any pain killers in my blood. Had to have a clear head. I walked slowly as I was also very tired. I got a little dizzy all of a sudden and almost stumbled. Before I could blink, April was at my side, grabbing my arm and keeping me steady. Debbie was on my other side.

"Come on, Flyboy." She said. "You've had a busy day." I was led to the blue recliner on the porch where I was eased down into the cushions.

April scolded me. "I can't believe you. Shot one day, now your buzzing the joint in a Blackhawk. You need to heal."

"That's my man." Debbie said with pride.

I looked out from the chair and watched mechanics crawling over the chopper I had just flown and prepping it for another flight when it was called for. There was a book sitting on the end table next to me. *The Hobbit.* I started reading.

A couple hours later, I woke up to Debbie smiling at me. "Dinner is ready, babe. You want to eat?"

"Yeah, I can eat some."

Dinner was a spread of fried chicken, corn on the cobb, and biscuits. Family gathered, grace was said, and everyone dug in. Family and the friends too, this was a special meal. I leaned back in my chair and smiled.

Kilo brought over my ACR, "This thing is sweet. I want one."

"Is it zeroed?"

"Dead nuts on."

Sarge finished his chicken and wiped his hands on a napkin before he sat down next to me.

"I didn't know you could fly, Ogre."

"I had an Ultralight when I was younger and learned by not killing myself."

Sarge nodded, "Pardon me for cutting to the chase. You said you had a task."

I filled him in about the Navajo situation and how we needed their alliance especially with the Chinese at our door step. I had two Ute tribe members willing to go down with him, both guys from the Ute tribe's police department, both good men, both able to handle weapons. Ray and Yazzie. Both tall, both armed, and both with amiable natures. They would be a big help.

Sarge nodded.

"Time, Neil, is running out. I need you jet-moto ASAP on this. I was going to fill you in after supper, but you beat me to the punch." I motioned to Joy who handed Sarge a heavy velvet bag. Stuffed. Sarge looked inside and saw that it was full of diamonds. His eyes went wide.

"For their cooperation, give them this. Tell them it's out of my deepest respect." Then I handed him one other thing, a single thin metal ring. "If that doesn't work, hand them this." The ring was the pull pin from a fragmentation grenade. "Then you tell them that Salt Lake told me no." I looked Sarge in the eye as I said that. He knew I wasn't joking around and the stakes were very high. "Clear?"

"Yes, sir. Crystal."

"Do you need anything else, before you go?"

"I could use some more ammunition."

"Absolutely, ambassador."

EIGHT

Arizona on my Mind

It was a week later and I had not heard from Sarge. He must have been down with the Navajo by now, and I was getting worried. But worry had to be pushed aside. The calls for help from our friends in Arizona became pressing. It was time to go help them out. Drug Cartels had started taking over the place, and then the power plant was becoming a concern. They had tried to stabilize it, but it was looking like it was going to fail. This gave me an idea. I had promised April we would look into her family, and I couldn't let that slide either. Our convoy was already set to roll out.

"You are not fit to run off to Arizona." Debbie scowled at me. "We've enough problems here."

I was standing on the porch, watching soldiers check out the helicopters. The Apaches were getting ready to leave for San Diego. Some of the 19th had already left. The bulk was leaving early in the morning. Here it is, not quite a month of me being the Governor and I've essentially declared war on China. Things are not as I had wanted. But then again, the Chinese are the ones that decided this. They did this.

The Girl Squad had decided that one of them would be within ear shot of me at all times, even here at Ogre Ranch. Jen was close at hand and when the sat phone rang, she picked it up.

"Hey Sarge! Uh huh... Hold on."

She brought the phone over to me, "It's Sarge."

"Thanks, Jen."

"Yes, Sarge."

He filled me in on all the good news. He didn't let me down. I knew he wouldn't. Something told me that he was the only one who could get it done. The Navajo were one of, if not the largest surviving populations in the country. They had to be allies. If they were not, then they could end up being enemies. The AIM movement had a huge resurgence since the zombie outbreak happened. This problem had no solution until I found that Sarge was coming. There was strong magic about the Sarge. An energy. The same energy that was with the two men I sent with him.

He was going to San Diego to help out there, and he'd be back as soon as he could. "Be careful, Sarge. Keep your powder dry."

I hung up the phone and watched the first Apache spin up. All but two of them were going to go. Two were staying for local support. That and they needed some engine work. This meant that none were covering our run to Arizona.

"I have to go. I can't sit by, Debbie. You know that. We've got Chinese invading the coast and some Cartel trying to move in on Arizona... and you know I've got a beef with those jackholes."

"I know," Debbie admitted, sullenly. "You always have since I've known you. I remember you got shot by one of them before we got married."

I handed the phone back to Jen who took it and went back to her chair where she had been reading a paperback.

"We're going to be leaving tomorrow morning. First light." I turned to Jen, "Go get the security team ready."

Jen got up and headed to Valkyrie House as the last of the Apaches lifted off and headed west.

"Go ahead, call them the 'Girl Squad'. Everyone else does." Debbie sat down in the recliner. "Your devoted battle maids. I've heard all the talk. All of it."

I sighed. "You used to be devoted to me too, Debbie." I turned and looked at her. "Even if you... can't... I still come back to you. You are still mine... and I'm still yours."

"I don't know why."

"I'll come back home, safe."

"Promise?"

"Promise."

The next morning, as the sun was rising over Ogre Ranch, the group was ready. All the rigs were fueled up, armed, and everyone was on board. I looked up to the Ranch House, and on the porch stood my family. We had said the goodbyes and had all the hugs. I waved one last time and pulled out.

Raymond Seeing Red

In a little town called Beaver we pulled off the freeway for a refuel. There was a truck stop here with the happy omen of a fuel delivery truck parked near by. I pulled in and climbed out. April slowly turned the M2, scanning the area. Nothing moved. It didn't look like there was any power, but that was not a problem. The other trucks pulled in, Josh's Cougar being next in line. The other rigs queued up and soldiers jumped out and brought up the pumps while others started opening the underground tanks.

Suddenly the door to the truck stop opened, and a man walked out, putting on his sunglasses. He was tall and lean and strangely hunched.

"How are you all going to be paying?" He said with a hiss as he walked to the guys with the pump.

Something didn't feel right. I snapped my fingers and pointed and April spun the fifty cal over to track the strange tall man. "We can pay you with some food. Coin is useless."

"Food." The man said to himself, his walking pace increased. I didn't think he repeated what I said.

"Hey," I shouted. "Stop right there." My pistol was in my hand and aimed center mass. The tall man stopped, then his head pivoted in my direction. The way the man moved wasn't quite right. My safety came off. The Guardsmen nearest the tall man had been crouched by the pump, but were now standing up, backing away and pulling up their rifles.

"Hungry... Food is good... Food is fine."

The man was acting very strangely and unsettling. Small jerks and twitches. His fingers seemed to be in a palsy. I looked him over carefully, there were no bite marks visible, and his clothes were not exactly clean, but there was no blood evident on him. Maybe he had a medical condition that had worsened since any normal society was a thing of the past. Maybe. But I doubted it.

"What's your name, mister?"

"My name?" He had to think about it, "Name's Raymond."

"Take your sunglasses off, Raymond. Let me take a look at your face." Raymond moved his head side to side, slowly. Deliberately.

"I said take them off."

Raymond turned around and started walking back to the store. I nodded to the soldiers who were looking at me. "Take him down."

The troops were instantly a blur. A double flying tackle crushed Raymond into the ground, but Raymond fought, struggled to get away. He punched. He kicked. He screamed. And then he bit one of the men before he was flex cuffed.

"Strong as hell for such a lanky dude!" One of he soldiers said. The other soldier was in a panic.

"The fucker bit me!"

"Don't worry... he's not a zombie. He's just a creepy bastard." The first Guardsman stood up and reached out and pulled the glasses off Raymond's face. Raymond's eyes were solid red.

"I feel sick." The bitten trooper said.

Raymond had some blood in his mouth from the bite. He started to laugh. "Boy tasted real good."

"Nutcase!" The trooper kicked Raymond who snarled back then started laughing again.

The bitten trooper started twitching then retching. A moment later he was vomiting blood. "Medic!" One of the other troopers said. The Guardsman's eyes started to get pale.

"No!" I shouted to them. "Stay back!" I raised my rifle and pointed it at the sick guardsman. I knew what was happening but I couldn't believe it. He was turning. The man... the what was once a man, started snarling and clawing at himself. When he looked back up, his face suddenly went slack and his eyes opened again. They were completely pale and dead.

Suddenly the zombie's whole upper torso erupted in blood splatter and chunks. The echo of the shot thundered in the truck stop. April had fired one round from the fifty, then swung the big gun over to Raymond again. Raymond was laughing. "You can't get all of us!"

What?

We looked around and found that we had been surrounded by shamblers. White milky eyes staring and unblinking as they moved closer from all sides.

"You'll pay now. Food is fine I said." I looked at Raymond and saw that he was standing again, still cuffed, but defiant, and laughing. The sound of a truck backfiring was heard at the same moment Raymond's head just evaporated. Musket's Brown Bess belched smoke as he tilted the gun up and started pouring powder again from a paper cartridge he ripped with his teeth. Then he was pushing another ball down the barrel with the ram rod and before you could say Jack's your Uncle, he was shouldering the big musket again.

As soon as Raymond died, the zombies that had been standing there, charged like race horses when the gates opened. Everyone opened fire at once.

The number of undead that surrounded us was surprising. The whole town must have been turned. Also surprising was how close they came. I thought about this but couldn't make sense of it. I ran my ACR dry and reloaded. Thinking would have to wait.

With gunfire in every direction, the mass of zombies still pressed in as they cared little for their falling comrades or for their own wounds. I scrambled up onto the back of the M-ATV to get out of reach as I picked my shots. The ACOG, while normally excellent, was a handicap at these ranges. I let the ACR hang from the sling and instead drew my new pistol. Since my Crusader M4 was retired I thought I'd retire the Glock 22 as well. Now I was packing an M&P 9mm, just like Kilo (who was at home this time) and my Girl Squad. The higher capacity was nice, and today it was more than welcome. When the pistol ran dry, I used my big Becker to hack off anything that reached for me.

Musket was yelling his curses while reloading again. He was half out of the turret and wearing a thick leather vest, bare arms, and heavy gauntlets. One zombie was trying to crawl up the side of the MRAP and Musket with his Brown Bess in one hand and a huge caplock pistol in the other, roared in anger at the affront. He cursed the zombie before smashing its head in with the stock of the Brown Bess. He fired a shot into another zombie's face with the pistol, then flipped it again and smashed one more. The empty pistol was then tucked into his belt and he drew out a fresh one. All the while his stream of curses never wavered. Impressive work.

Josh's RFB rifle spoke with authority, his .308 TAP rounds found their mark every time. He was shooting left handed out of the passenger window while Cappello's FS2000 was working from the driver's seat. I couldn't see the other troops, but from the volume of fire that was being put out, everyone was engaged. April was being stingy with the .50, saving ammo. One round would blow several zombies apart if they were lined up, and she was looking for those shots. Jen and Joy had the truck's doors open partially, and firing from the gaps.

As quick as the ambush started, it was over. I climbed down from the truck and walked around. Immobilized zombies moaned and reached for me. In return, I shot them in the head. Zombies that still twitched received a shot to the forehead.

"What in the hell was that?" Josh asked. He had come up beside me as I was looking at the headless body of Raymond.

"I don't know, but he wasn't a zombie. He could talk, knew his name, or made one up. He spoke to us... he stopped when ordered... he withdrew. That's not zombie behavior."

"His bite turned Cook in a matter of seconds." Josh observed. "Normally a bite takes an hour or two to change a guy."

"This was different, for sure. Did you see his red eyes?" I asked.

"Eyes... both eyes were filled with blood. Totally red." Josh kicked Raymond and then spit on him. "Well, we know one thing now," I said. "Red eyes... shoot them first."

Then it clicked. I looked up at Josh, "Did it seem like maybe Raymond had the other zombies in control?" I questioned what had played out in my mind and I was left with only one thing. "A master zombie."

"I don't know, bro. But if I was to guess, I'd say they worked together. That was a coordinated ambush. Because guess what the zombies didn't do?"

"They didn't moan until after Raymond blew up. They stayed quiet and moved slow."

"Yeah." Josh turned back to the MRAP and shouted to the men. "Come on boys. We've got something to talk about real quick." He started to brief the men.

April came up besides me. "Good work on the fifty."

"Thanks... uh... Can we get gassed up and rolling? I don't like this place."

"I don't like it either," Joy said flatly.

"I thought you would love Beaver, Joy."

She stuck her tongue out at me, then winked. Jen flushed red.

The fuel pumping commenced and we were almost topped off again when April came up. "How many people lived in Beaver?"

I shrugged, "Maybe two to three thousand, perhaps. Counting all the surrounding area."

"I would have thought that Beaver would have come out okay in this... good distance from anything. The isolation would have helped... but we've got about three hundred dead zeds here. That's a pretty steep percentage. And that's just here."

I got her drift. Beaver is pretty much wiped out.

"Can we please get the hell out of here now?" Joy pleaded.

"Yeah, let's get moving." April agreed.

I looked over at Josh who was shutting the lids on the underground tanks. "We good to roll?" I shouted. Josh gave the thumbs up.

"Saddle up!"

It was almost midnight when the convoy approached Cedar City. The barricade across the freeway was lit by a couple fires in 55-gallon barrels. The city only had a few lights. Power was not on here.

I pulled up to the gate as the convoy stacked up behind me. The men at the gate held up rifles. One walked forward, "Governor Hill?"

I climbed out of the truck and approached the gate. "I am."

"I'm Officer Grossman, Nick Grossman."

"Pleased to meet you, Nick." I shook his offered hand.

"You guys are a little late."

"Had some problems in Beaver.... so... you going to let us in?"

"Sure. Once we get a doctor over here to check you all out. He's coming. Beaver huh? We sent some men over there to check things out. They never came back."

"It was completely infested. We took care of the bulk of it, shouldn't be too much of a problem now. You could probably check it out now for yourselves, search for survivors. We didn't have time, but I don't think it would do any good." I left out the situation with Raymond on purpose. Mainly because I didn't quite know how to process it myself. Telling someone who hadn't seen it with his own eyes, well, I don't think anyone would believe it.

Musket came up, "Do they have a tavern?"

"I don't remember them having anything wonderful, Musket."

"I'm afraid there isn't a beer left in town," Nick said. "We've got some folks working on a still, but I think it's mostly for fuel, not consumption."

"Bollocks." Musket wandered off grumbling.

I laughed and turned back to the officer. "So, Nick. How have things been down here?"

"Pretty rough as you can imagine. The breakout happened pretty slow, but it made up for it in volume. We fought for days before we got it under control."

"How many casualties?"

"Man, I don't know."

The doctor finally arrived. The man was tall, bearded, reminded me of Hawkeye from *Mash*. You could tell that his face was used to smiling, but he wasn't smiling anymore.

He checked out my Girl Squad, then me. A quick look in the eyes. Then at the wrap around my middle. "What's this?"

"Gunshot wound."

"When did you get it?"

"A couple days ago in Orem."

"You need medical attention."

"I got it... I'll be fine."

"I wouldn't be so sure... and you are up running around, fighting undead." The doctor shook his head.

"I'm doing what I have to do."

"We're all doing that."

"I hope so."

The doctor checked everyone else out. Once everyone was cleared, we got back into the trucks and rolled through the gate. I was tired, I hurt, and I was hungry. I also felt sticky. There was a copper taste in my mouth. I knew I needed rest.

"Let's stop there." I nodded to the Holiday Inn just off the freeway.

"We need to keep rolling." Joy was looking at the map.

"I need to stop." I looked down at my shirt. It was bled through.

Joy looked at me and her eyes went big. "Oh man, April!"

April pulled herself out of the turret and crouched in between the seats. She looked at the shirt, then at me. "Are you feeling light headed? Dizzy?"

"No, I'm feeling okay. Just tired."

"We're stopping." April ordered.

I pulled in to the parking lot of the Holiday Inn and stopped. Jen jumped out, "MUSKET!!!"

I climbed out of the M-ATV and suddenly felt very heavy. The blood had run down my chest, stomach and pants, and I was bleeding pretty good. Musket and Josh ran up.

"I need to stop for a rest, brothers."

April called for one of the men to go after that doctor again.

"No. I'll be fine. I just need to lay down. Bumping around in that truck hasn't done well on me."

Josh protested. I held up my hand, "I'll be fine."

April and Joy helped me inside. We went up a flight of stairs where April blasted the lock on a door off and we went in. The room was clean. Double beds. Another TV that didn't work. I laid back and closed my eyes. "Jenny girl... can you be so kind as to get my boots off for me?" Soon I was rebandaged and relaxing.

"We'll get you something to eat... what would you like?"

"I've not had a pizza in some time."

Joy laughed. "I'll see what I can do." Then she went out. Jen and April were talking quietly while I was laying there, thinking about things. Then I heard the door open and I looked over in time to see Jen slip out the door and quietly shut it behind her.

April walked around the bed to the table where she pulled off her guns and her tactical vest. She took off her boots, then unbuttoned her pants and pulled them off as well. Wearing only a Guns and Roses t-shirt she walked around to the bathroom. I closed my eyes again. I heard water running in the shower.

A few minutes later the water was off and April came out again. No longer in the black t-shirt, but in a towel instead. It covered her, but was very short. She casually dried her long dark hair with another towel.

"I'm thinking about cutting my hair shorter."

"It would look good no matter how you wore it. I'm sure."

April checked the bandages again. She smelled like peaches. "You need to relax. You can't heal if you don't relax."

"I'm completely at peace."

"Uh huh."

Some time later, the doctor came in. I had torn a couple stitches during the fight in Beaver. The doc closed them with some Super Glue and tape. He had to save his stitching threads, he explained. But this should close the wound again.

Family Reunion

*I*n the morning I checked the bandage again. The doc was right. No more blood. I'm good. Jen agreed and helped get me wrapped up again. "Make it tight." I said. "So I don't pop a stitch again."

As soon I was dressed and ready, I went outside. I could smell bacon. Some of the boys had been grilling on a Hibachi grill. They had snagged some of the small grills and charcoal from a local store. It was an easy means of cooking on the go. They had some thick cut slices and offered me some, which I gladly accepted. April handed me a Gator-Bull, and I called that breakfast. "Man, this hits the spot. I'm starving."

"Didn't you have dinner last night?" Musket asked.

"Too tired. That and I didn't feel like eating. Doc came by and glued me shut again."

Musket nodded and poked at some charcoal with a stick. Josh walked up. "You feeling better, Oh Great Ventilated One?" Josh asked.

"Yes, I do."

"I would think so. I reckon he was well taken care of what with three lovely nurses seeing to his every need." Musket quipped. Josh smirked.

"You guys have a problem?" I said, eating my bacon and not looking up.

"Oh, no problem... but..." Josh said, but I cut him off.

"Then let's get this circus back on the road. We've got a long way to go." My brothers were taken back. I turned to the soldiers. "Mount up!"

One of the soldiers looked at the grill that was still hot. "But the Hibachi..."

"Strap it to your hood. It'll be fine. Let's roll, boys!"

Moments later, we all climbed into the trucks.

"You shouldn't be harsh on your brothers." Jen said. "No matter what; they are your blood."

"I know. I just don't want to..." I fumbled for words. "Address certain issues with anyone right now."

"You can address them with us." Jen said.

"You mean undress them?" Joy quipped.

"I mean I don't want to talk about it."

Before we hit St. George, we took a cut through Zion's National Park to Kanab, Utah. From Kanab we crossed into Page Arizona, and from there, we made it to Flagstaff where we had to refuel again.

"Just where are we heading?" Capello came up and asked. Capello was tall, lean, with a muscular build and good natured. Always upbeat. I knew Josh sent him over. I was getting the treatment, evidently.

"Prescott, then down through Phoenix, to Buckeye."

"What's there?"

"The Cartel is down there. I aim to put a stop to them. They have taken over Buckeye and are using that place to stage raids into Phoenix. We are going to end them."

"How are you going to do that?"

"I have an idea."

"What is it?"

"Can't tell you yet. If I told you now, you would tuck tail and run."

"Yeah right," Capello laughed, but it was more of an uneasy laugh. "You going to nuke them like you did Salt Lake?"

I didn't say anything and the smile went off Capello's face. He went back to Josh and I caught a glimpse of them whispering together.

The trucks were taking on fuel, and while that process was under way, Jen had the back canvas top of the M-ATV pulled up so it was open. She was rooting around the Yeti cooler looking for something. "What are you hunting for?"

"I'm out of Sunkist. And we are out of ice. It's just slush in here." Jen was terse. So was I, so I wasn't in the mood for it. "I'll see what I can find." I shouldered my ACR, grateful that it was lighter than my Rock River. April was asleep in the back of the M-ATV, Jen was pissy and Joy was no where to be seen, probably doing her business. I walked to the gas station's little store. The power was on, but the door was locked. I had a key. The suppressed key took four rounds to unlock the door. It pushed it open with some effort. There was a body that had been laying in front of it. I pushed the door open far enough that I could step over the body. On second thought, I put a round through the body's head. Didn't want anything coming up behind me. I checked out the small store, looking behind the counter, then I opened the men's room door. Empty. I then pushed open the door to the women's room and the smell that poured out was overpowering. Even having become more acclimated to the smell of death, this was too much. I wanted to puke. The woman was sitting on the toilet, head back, she looked like the girl in the closet from *The Ring*. "Oh hell." I retched. The woman's head fell forward and then slowly lifted. Dried lips peeled back from her teeth and she moaned a shallow dry moan. One arm lifted and long bony fingers uncoiled from her fist to reach out for me. I fired one shot. Her arm fell back down, and her head snapped back and then she was in the very same position where I first found her. I shut the door. Sunkist, there was a couple 12 packs. Mt. Dew, a couple 12 backs, and a 4 pack of Guinness. I grabbed them, leaving Pepsi behind. Unfortunately there was no Gatorade or Red Bull. Can't have everything. I carried them back to the trucks, giving Jen the Sunkist then I took the Dew to Josh. Musket was sitting on top of the Cougar.

"Hey."

He looked down at me but didn't say anything. More treatment. "Here." I tossed the Guiness up to him. He caught the pack with one hand, looked at it, then nodded and went back to looking off in the distance. Fair enough. I walked back to the store. The ice cooler still had ice in it. I pulled out six bags and carried them back to the truck. "Here. Now cheer up. Sunkist and ice. Just like you wanted."

Jen took the ice, "At least I get something." She muttered.

"What's that supposed to mean?" I had no idea where she was coming from.

Joy came up to the truck. "Oh, Sunkist." She cracked the box open and pulled out a can. "I love Sunkist. Anything with the word kiss in it works for me." Jen dumped the soda and the ice into the cooler.

"Are we ready to go yet?" I asked out loud.

Joy popped open the can and volunteered, "I'll go see if everyone's ready."

I climbed into the driver's seat, carefully. Jen dropped through the turret and climbed into the front seat. She sat there looking at me for a moment that came in real close and whispered in my ear. "Thanks for the sunny kiss." She kissed my cheek and climbed up to the .50 Cal and put on her goggles.

April was sitting in the passenger seat reading a map. She looked over the top of the edge at me and smirked.

Joy climbed in. "Ready to roll out, boss."

"Huh, what?"

"Let's go." She motioned with her head.

"Oh, yeah." I got the M-ATV moving again. We headed further south on the freeway. Intel had the Cartel camp in Buckeye, just west of Phoenix. I decided going through Phoenix, as bad of an idea as it was, was even worse now. We turned off the interstate and headed to Prescott.

"Turn here." April said. I went ahead and took the next left as directed. It didn't take long before we pulled to a stop in front of a wide, low house made of adobe and bricks.

"This is it." April sounded excited. I looked around the trees surrounding us and didn't see any movement.

"April..."

She dove out of the truck and ran up to the house, excited like a school girl. I jumped out and followed, with Joy and Jen on our heels.

April burst through the front door. "Mom! Dad!" The house was quiet.

"April, maybe we should check the rooms for you." I offered but April sprinted through the house. The back door had been left open and wind had blown sand and dust inside.

"Mom! Dad!"

I motioned for Joy to follow April. Jen and I searched around the house. It was completely empty.

"Where could they be?" April seemed confused. There was an attached garage, but there was nothing inside. "They must have left."

"Maybe they went into town?" Jen offered.

We loaded back up and got back onto the freeway. A few miles later we pulled into Prescott to find a warm welcome. Ron, Hyrum and Jesse were standing there waiting for me. I climbed out of the M-ATV and clapped hands with my friends. "Took you long enough to get here!" Jesse said.

"I always meant to get down here sooner. Hey, where's Terry?"

Hyrum looked down and played with the hem of his kilt. Ron looked away. I looked back at Jesse who just shook his head. "I thought for sure..." I stammered.

Jesse sighed. "He was trapped downtown when everything happened."

"Shit."

"What is this thing?" Hyrum nodded to the M-ATV.

"I don't know. It's called an M-ATV. Outbreak gave it to me."

"It's hideous." Hyrum announced.

"I kinda like it." Ron said, holding his Steyr Aug.

"Yeah, you would, you like weird things." Jesse said.

The Girl Squad had been hanging back a bit but had now come forward. We made the introductions and for some reason, no one called them hideous.

"Where is Khorne? Hyrum asked.

"He's actually in Italy right now."

"Italy? But it's the peak of the tourist season."

"What can I say? The man loves that Italian stuff."

Musket, Josh, and the other guys made their way up from their trucks. More introductions were made, shakes and laughs.

I put an end to the levity. "Time to get down to business. What's the situation?"

Hyrum started to fill me in. While we were talking I saw an old Jeep Wrangler pull up. There was a woman driving it that had a familiar look to it. When April turned around and saw it, she bolted. "Mom!"

I smiled and turned back to Hyrum. "What's that about?" He asked.

"Family thing."

A few minutes later April timidly came to me, she had watery eyes and streaked eyeliner. "This is my mother." I stood up.

"It's an honor, Mam." I held out my hand to the woman, who instead threw her arms around me and squeezed me.

"Thank you for saving my girl. Thank you!"

I didn't know what to say.

Cartel Zombies Unchained

The next morning I was looking through my binos watching six Cartel thugs standing around a Lincoln Navigator with Arizona plates.

I made a mental note about the guys, their clothes, weapons, mostly HK G3's. Make that Seven. Another one just came out from behind the big black SUV. He was zipping up his pants. I turned my head and whispered. "They seem to be waiting around for something."

Joy took my binos and looked through them for a moment. "No one seems to be in charge, so these guys are probably just soldiers."

"That's what I was thinking."

"They must think they are big time now. Lots of jewelry on, nice clothes, dressing up like they are kings. Arrogance. Pomp. Totally full of themselves." Joy was reading them like I did.

I got my rifle ready. My .338 Lapua topped with a Nightforce scope slid forward into firing position. The laser rangefinder put the range right at 900 yards. Well within range of the big rifle. This was the 98 Bravo that I snagged from *Get Some Guns* some 8,000 years ago it felt like. It was suppressed, and I had only shot it enough to find the scope dope out to 1000 yards, so being inside that range was helpful. I looked at my dope book that I had quickly worked up, double checked the range, and started making my adjustments. I gave another MOA's worth of adjustment for the lower altitude. Then I started looking at wind signs. Here the wind was very still, but further down range, I could see I had about 3 or 4 MPH of wind. The wind was quartering so that meant it was half value. I'd adjust for 2 MPH of wind and call that good. With my scope dialed in I then tucked in. Through the greater power of the Nightforce, I got a good look at the Cartel guys. The big SUV partially obscured the Mercedes and I watched the men walk around, smoking and joking. They were waiting for something for sure.

Our position was in a curved rock wall, with little dust. The sound, being suppressed would be hard to detect from this range, and if they did hear it, they would have no idea where it came from because of the distortion of the sound. Behind me, a draw through the wall allowed for an egress from the shooting position, one that offered both cover and concealment from the Cartel. It was also one of the many such cuts in the wall that would make tracking us hard to do. This was about the most perfect firing position that anyone could ask for.

"There." Joy whispered.

I looked up the road, coming from Phoenix was another big SUV, even from this distance, I could tell it was another Escalade, this one was white. As it approached, the Cartel men stood at, well, not attention, but at least in a more respectful posture. I watched through the scope as the white SUV pulled up and stopped. The guys in the white SUV stepped out, all in sunglasses, open shirts, and more gold chains than anyone should own, let alone wear all at once. One in particular wore more chains than all the rest. His hands glittered in the sunlight from what must have been fists full of rings and bracelets. The man was darkly tanned, with his long hair slicked back in a way that would have put him as a top villain in a *Miami Vice* episode. I didn't like him. I kept the cross hairs on this one. There was some discussion, then one of the guys pulled someone else out of the white SUV. This person was in cuffs or his hands were tied behind his back. I couldn't tell.

"Looks like a prisoner." Joy said.

"An exchange?" Josh was looking through his binos. I had given him a set of Swarovski EL's, because my poor brother had nothing but Bushnell Permafocus binos. That just wouldn't do.

"Don't know yet."

Out of the black SUV, one of the guys pulled out a long pole with something on the end. "What?"

Another guy popped the trunk of the Merc and the end of the pole was shoved in. They pulled a guy out of the trunk. I could see this guy had a collar and a chain, like a dog. The pole kept the guy at a distance, just like an Animal Control Officer uses. "It's a zombie." I said.

We watched as one of the soldiers took a spike and a sledge hammer and anchored the end of the chain to the ground, then they released the zombie's neck. We could see it flail around, stumbling, trying to get to the men. They were having a good laugh about it. Soon the zombie just stood there, leaning against the end of his chain, arms hanging at its side. I didn't think it would have been possible, but even from this distance, I could hear the moaning that this one zombie was making.

The man with all the gold around his neck was gesturing with large waves of his hand. Then he slapped the prisoner so hard the guy fell over. Everyone laughed. Suddenly they put the pole around the guy's neck.

"Are they..." Joy swallowed. "No."

The men pushed the captive into the circle of the zombie's area and without hesitation, the zombie fell on him. They unhooked the man's neck and stood around. They were cheering and laughing as the captive was torn to pieces. The man in gold raised his hands and everyone cheered as another person was taken from the SUV. I could see long, blond hair on this one. She was forced to kneel before the man in gold. The sermon started up again. Wild, broad gestures, just like before. I chambered a round from the magazine and flicked the safety off. Just like before, the man in gold struck the captive. She fell over hard.

"Sending." I said.

The guy with the pole moved to slip the end over the woman's head. That's when I fired. I chambered another round as Joy said the one word I loved the most. "Hit". The man was still standing with a hole through his upper torso, a little on the left, so I think I blew out his aorta. The man froze in place, then slowly fell. The other men just stood there. I fired another shot. Goldie threw his arm up into the air, probably a nervous reaction from the impact of the 250-grain slug. Goldie fell down and I chambered a third round as I watched the Cartel thugs looking around. Some of the guys were taking cover from the shooting on the wrong side of the cars, not knowing where the shots were coming from. "On the way" I whispered and pulled the trigger again. This man was struck lower than I had planned. The man spun and staggered from the shot to the abdomen. He almost regained his balance but it was too late. He was standing within the zombie's ring. The zombie hurled itself at the wounded man. I chambered another round.

One guy was looking through the window of the Merc, searching. He had a pair of compact binos. I sent another 250-grain slug flying. The round cut through the window and shattered it. I didn't see the man inside again. By this time, the guys were diving into the vehicles. I fired quickly into the engines. One round each, then another.

"Reloading." I dropped a magazine and Joy handed me another. I locked it into place and chambered another round. Somehow, the Merc was able to start and I watched it lurch forward. I fired into the driver's side of the windshield. The car surged forward into the black SUV and stopped. Fish in a barrel. No one was going anywhere.

Soon it was over and no one moved save for the blond woman and the zombie. The woman struggled to get up on her knees, then up onto her feet. She started running. The zombie who hadn't cared about anything other than its meal suddenly snapped to attention on the running female. The woman was running in our direction, and could see panic in her face. The zombie lunged against the chain, rebounded and lunged again. The stake in the ground moved. The zombie threw itself against the chain once more and the stake started to give. I was about to fire when the zombie's last lunge broke the stake free. My shot missed.

"Damn it!"

"Come, George." Josh growled. "Hit it."

The zombie was after the woman like a patriot missile. The zombie's path curved in behind the running woman and I had no shot. "Damn it."

Joy had worry in her voice, "Guys...."

"I don't have a shot – GO! GO!"

Josh and Joy were up and running, weapons in hand. Joy was faster, she pulled ahead and I saw Josh tuck his head down and lean into it. He was keeping pace now.

"Come on!" I yelled, watching the woman and zombie through the scope, hoping for a shot. Joy was yelling at the woman, but I couldn't hear. The woman made a course correction towards Joy, just a little. I could now see the zombie behind her again. It was much closer now, but I didn't have a shot. I reached up and started pulling back on the range, I estimated 500 yards and set the turret.

What happened next was almost too fast to see. Joy grabbed the running woman and pulled her down to the ground, a split second later Josh ducked his head launched himself, his RFB rifle out in front of him. The collision caught the zombie high in the chest and I saw the zombies legs going up into the air. The zombie flipped in the air and landed on its back. Josh rolled away from the zed and suddenly I had my shot.

"Sending." I said to myself. The zombie rolled over and was about to leap at Josh who was still picking himself up, when the round struck the zombie in the upper spine, exiting the top of its head.

Josh looked at the zombie for a second, then fell back down, out of breath. "YES!"

I looked through the scope at everyone. Joy was giving me a thumbs up. She was okay, and so was the blond lady. Josh held up a middle finger. He was fine too.

I stood up, picked up the Barrett and put it over my shoulder. It took a minute to slowly make my way down the hill to where the action was. Josh was helping Joy get the woman on her feet. They walked back to the SUVs. As I approached Josh was putting finishing rounds into one of the Cartel thugs.

"You know, it sure would have been nice if you hadn't ruined all three of them." Josh said to me. "Not that I'm complaining. I'm sure you had a good reason."

"No. No reason really. Just didn't want anyone running off. Who's the girl?" The blond woman was wearing a police uniform, but she had no gun belt on. There was a tear where her badge used to be. "You okay, Mam?"

The woman sobbed.

"I can't get these flex cuffs off of her." Joy said. The cuffs were put on so tight, that they were cutting into the woman's wrists. Her hands were blue. I pulled out my Sebenza folder and slid the thin, hollow ground blade between the wrists and nylon ties, then levered the blade up. The cuffs were super tough, but the knife split them easily and her hands were free.

"What's your name, Mam?" I asked. She only sobbed. I looked at Joy.

Joy knelt down on her level and put a hand on her shoulder. "You're okay now... you are safe. Take a deep breath. There... What's your name?"

"Rebecca. Rebecca Hallbrook."

"You were a police officer?"

She nodded, pulling herself together. "Phoenix Metro. For about six months."

"What happened? Why did they take you?" Joy asked.

"I don't know. I was down town... I came out... and they were outside. They pulled guns on me."

"Why did you approach them? They were Cartel."

"They were the first living people I had seen in days." Rebecca rubbed her hands and wrists. "How was I supposed to know they were Cartel?"

"Profiling?"

She laughed and wiped her eyes. "You're funny. Who are you guys?"

"I'm George, the Governor of Utah. This is Joy, one of my security detail. And this is Josh, my brother. We came down to take care of some business. Namely to decapitate the Cartel operating here and run them from this area."

"Excuse me for calling bullshit, but why is the Governor of Utah down here? Where is the Arizona Governor?"

"That's what I'd like to know. Hold on a second." I picked up my radio. "Ogre to Valkyrie One."

"This is Vee One, Go ahead Ogre."

"We've got Nine Tangos down, one zed, and three vehicles."

"You had a busy day."

"And we are a little tired, if you catch my drift."

"Roger that, we are on the way."

"10-4."

I looked at Rebecca. "You look hungry."

When the M-ATV pulled up April jumped out and walked over to me.

"We've got everything ready, boss."

"Good. Get Rebecca here something to eat and drink. She's hungry and dehydrated."

"Certainly." April sounded glad to help.

Josh picked up the best three G-3 rifles and an AK-47. Joy helped pick up magazines and rummage around the SUVs for more.

"That .338 did quite a number. Check this out." Josh got into the black SUV and turned the key. The sound that came out of the hood sounded like a train wreck. "Totally ruined."

"My bad." I smiled and patted the 98B. Great rifle. I found the corpse of the Goldie and checked his pockets. An iPhone. A wallet full of credit cards, each with a different name, a Colt 1911 in Nickle chambered in .38 Super. Nothing useful. "Let's burn them." I nodded at the bodies and the three vehicles. "Send up some smoke. Get some attention."

I had finished pouring the gasoline over the vehicles, and inside them, I touched them off with my Zippo.

"Come on, let's get going."

Phoenix Goes Nuclear

*B*ack at our base camp, we had a doctor take a look at Officer Hall-brook. Other than some bruising and dehydration, she was fine. Still shaken, but she'd get over that.

Hyrum, CXB and Capello came up to me as I was looking over the topo map of the area. Compass in hand, map oriented, spotting scope set up. I was studying the terrain. "What's the situation?"

Hyrum shook his head. "It's not good. At least, I think It's not good. You tell me."

"What do you mean?"

"Every light in the control room is flashing red. The cooling pools are empty. One of the reactors is even shaking." Capello said. "I didn't even know it could shake."

"The worst yet, the computer system says it's going to go critical mass." Hyrum emphasize the point. "So I think this isn't a good thing."

I looked at the map again. "That's what I was expecting... and it is a good thing. The timing is perfect."

I looked at Capello. "Is everything set?"

"Everything's ready." He handed me a small box.

Hyrum looked at me with shock in his face. "What are you going to do?"

Jesse and Ron came up.

"What's going on?" Ron had his Aug and a dire look on his face.

It was time to explain myself. "We're going to have a nuclear incident and there is nothing we can do about it."

I looked at CXB, "Is there anything, any possible way we can stop it?" He shook his head and rested a hand on his big revolver.

"Since we can't stop it... we can use it. Use it to our advantage." I pointed to the map.

Hyrum held up his hand, "Hold on a second. You're going to just let it go up? This place will make Chernobyl look like a Fisher Price set! You can't do that!"

"Dude, I'm sorry. I left my Nuclear Reactor Repair Manual back in Utah. You don't know how to fix it. No one knows how to fix it. All I know about reactors is what I've read in Tom Clancy novels."

Hyrum turned away. "Shit!"

"Since we can't stop this from happening, we can make it happen when we want it." I tried to explain, but the big Scotsman kept his back to me.

Jesse looked at the map. "I think Ogre's right, Harm."

All morning, our men had been searching for survivors, destroying Cartel soldiers and leaving our messages. We found only a few people left in the city. Phoenix had been wiped out. The only things that walked in the city were Cartel and zombies. The messages left on the dead Cartel members, was one they could understand.

We control the Palo Verde power plant. We have cut off the power. It will come on again only if you give us 500 million dollars in gold.

The Palo Verde power plant stopped generating power. We didn't have to flip any switches. It went out on its own. This was expected, so we used it to our advantage. Phoenix went dark and now the Cartel thought we did it.

Around the plant, we parked military trucks. The crappiest ones we had, old Deuces, a couple Cut-Vees, and police cars. Dead bodies were propped in the cars. Some were stood up in windows, using brooms and mops as braces. Once that was done, everyone raced back to a safe distance and made their way back to our location. If the wind would stay in the same direction we should be just fine.

We had given everyone radios and created a lot of chatter, laughing at the Cartel that they had no control, that their soldiers fought like "little girls." We even questioned their sexual orientation. We taunted them over the radio mercilessly. We even insulted their mothers. Everyone on the radio spoke of all their troops, waiting in the power plant in case the stupid Cartel tried – dared to try to come take over the plant.

The taunting worked.

We watched from miles away through high-power spotting scopes, as hundreds of vehicles from Phoenix headed to the power station. The parade included military humvees, Lincoln Navigators, Cadillac Escalades, and some funky armored cars.

The convoy was just pulling into the Palo Verde complex when I pulled out the long antenna from the little box. I flipped the safety cover open and there was the switch. I looked at it for a moment. Small, chrome plated. Innocent looking, really. I flipped the switch.

A moment later from our vantage point, we saw a blinding flash of light that lit the entire area. Four seconds later we heard the explosion. The shockwave from the blast was impressive. I picked up my spotting scope and looked at where the plant was. It was gone. The Cartel thugs and all their vehicles were gone as well. Above the plant, the mushroom cloud was rolling into a gigantic ring.

"My God!"

The radio crackled, "The Ogre nuked Phoenix!"

"Let's get out of here. Back to Prescott."

I turned and walked back to my M-ATV. The Arizona contingent just stood there, looking at it. Taking it in. The immediate fallout would bathe Phoenix in radiation. A massive dose that would kill everything pretty quickly. It would be a long time before it was safe to return. If there was any Cartel left, they were welcome to what was left.

In Prescott, we celebrated and relaxed and good food was eaten. We raised our glasses to Terry after we read his note, which Jesse found when he found Terry's body. Terry didn't make it out of his building, but he died human, and he died the way he wanted.

We held a fair election amongst all the survivors in attendance, all two thousand two hundred nine of them. The voting was almost unanimous. Given Harm's performance in the Battle of Prescott, he was universally applauded. Wielding a stop sign like a battle axe, while wearing a kilt, cutting a swath through an undead horde... that stands out. I'd have voted for him as well, if I was from Arizona.

Hyrum protested. "No! I didn't volunteer for this! No way."

"No but you voted for Jesse, so it's all fair and square. Casting a vote meant that you were in."

"This is some bullshit." Hyrum grumbled.

I stood up, "Don't get your kilt in a twist, Hyrum. You will get used to it and the voting was fair and square."

Everyone was smiling and cheering and clapping. CXB and Musket fired shots into the air in congratulatory salutes. I held up my glass. "It's official! Hyrum is now the democratically elected Governor of Arizona!"

Hyrum's protests subsided. "Okay... Okay... I'll do my best. That's all I can promise."

I shook his hand. "That's all anyone can expect, my friend."

"I'll try not to blow up as much stuff as you've managed to. What's the score now? Two nukes?"

"It wasn't... well, the first one wasn't a nuke."

Jesse was grinning, "Speech!"

Hyrum pointed the official finger, "Maybe you should be writing a speech of your own, Lieutenant Governor!"

Jesse took a step back, "Now wait a second. Arizona doesn't have Lieutenant Governors."

"It does now." Hyrum looked at me, "I can make appointments, right?"

"Absolutely."

"Done!"

Adding to the Celebration was the news from San Diego, which was short and sweet.

Chinese forces destroyed. We have prisoners. Casualties moderate. Remaining Utah units returning. – Sgt Ferguson.

We left the party on a high note. My convoy pulled out of Prescott, heading back to Utah.

NINE

Catching the Red Eye

Our path cut through St. George. One reason was that I wanted to reduce the zombie population there, since I'd lived there for a while long ago. The other reason was that we picked up a radio signal. We tried to tune it back in, but we couldn't get it. We took this as an indication that someone was there, some place. Other reasons aside, this was reason enough.

We rolled in with all of our vehicles in two columns, taking two lanes. April, the expert with the M2, was in the turret, and even before we got into the city, she was already busting off rounds in one- or two- shot bursts of accurate fire, blowing zombies apart as we found them. She was making noise on purpose. We wanted to draw them out. Make a racket and attract as much attention as we could. We'd attract the attention of the dead, but hopefully of the living as well.

Uncle Musket's Brown Bess added to the thunder with his distinctive backfire sounding reports. He was loading charges extra hot, because there was a lot of additional smoke and noise.

It didn't take long before the undead gathered ahead of us and shambled to us. When they got within about two hundred yards, the shambling turned into jogging, and then running. They came at us straight in, which is a mistake when heading into a .50 BMG. They didn't know that though.

April tapped the trigger a few times, shredding zombies by the bunches. .50 BMG has a greater effect on a zombie corpse than it does on normal living tissue. Zombies came apart like ripe pumpkins from the shock of the big rounds. This made headshots really not so necessary. The moaning they were putting out was attracting the zeds faster than the .50 was destroying them.

Then it stopped.

The zombies stopped moaning. All at once. They seemed to lose interest in us, turned and went back the way they came.

"Josh to Ogre."

I keyed my radio, "Go for Ogre."

"Did what just happened, happen? Or am I smoking crack?"

"Unknown on the crack thing, but something did happen."

April ducked down into the truck and said what I was thinking. "Raymond."

I looked back up at her. "I know." I didn't like this. We should be getting piled on. Instead the zombies were pulling back. Totally against their nature. I keyed the radio again, "All units, stay extra alert. We have a Red Eye here."

"A Red Eye?" Rebecca Hallbrook looked at us. Rebecca had come with us. She had family in Cedar City and we were going to drop her off. In the mean time, she had my Mossberg 930SPX and my shotshell pouch on her belt, along with an M&P and some magazines.

"We found a new kind of zombie," Joy explained. "They have red eyes, blood red, no visible iris. They seem to be able to control other zombies. At least that's what we think. The one we found.... other zombies acted differently... like these are doing now."

I pulled forward and we entered St. George. The men in the convoy used 5.56mm rifles to engage individual zeds as they came visible. Up ahead I saw a man walking across the street. Not shambling. Not lurching. Not twitching. Just walking. "There!" I pointed. I hit the gas and raced the M-ATV up to where I had seen the walker. He was wearing dark pants, and a clean white shirt. When I got to the area where I saw him, he was gone. Nothing. April was panning the M2 around the area. She didn't see anything either.

We drove around the city and as we did, our feelings were getting hurt. The zombies seemed to be actively avoiding us. Great, now the zombies were giving me The Treatment. We didn't find any evidence of anyone living here. That needs to be said right now. St. George seemed to be completely quiet. I pulled up to a stop and climbed out, "You should stay in the vehicle, sir."

When Debbie gets stern, she calls me by name, using my middle name. When the Girl Squad gets stern, they call me sir. I looked over at Jen who was sitting in the shotgun seat. She had her hand on my arm. The firmness in her voice was matched by the concern. "I'll be okay." I said.

Jen answered flatly. "I'm coming with you."

"Me too". Joy said.

April stayed up in the turret with the fifty. Rebecca would stay with the truck. She climbed out and stood at the open door. The rest of the convoy had fanned out through the small city. The mission was simple. Shoot zombies, find survivors, find Red Eyes and either attempt to capture, or if unable to capture, shoot... a lot.

I walked down an alley between some houses, with Jen and Joy flanking me.

"So he's really the Governor of Utah?"

"Yup." April said as she looked down at Rebecca.

"I thought the Governor was..."

"Dead."

"Ah... So you guys working for him... you're his body guards."

"That's right."

"So you were State Police?"

"Nope. I was... I was a student."

"I thought a Governor's..."

"They got killed."

"So he got you guys as replacements."

"They lasted a couple days. We've been rolling with the Governor ever since."

"Why?"

"He saved my life. Saved all our lives."

"So."

April looked down at Rebecca again, "He saved your life too. Made sure you're okay. Giving you a lift home. And he's letting you use his favorite shotgun. He didn't have to."

Rebecca looked at the shotgun and was about to say something when April cut her off, "He's a good man. Show him some more respect."

Rebecca squinted her eyes and tilted her head a little while looking April over. "There's something else isn't there?"

April looked at her ruby ring. "You are full of too many questions for a stray we just picked up."

Rebecca bristled. "No disrespect, it's just that we had heard a lot of rumors about him. I wanted to know the truth. Like how he runs around with his personal love slaves."

"We're not slaves. We can do anything we want. Even leave if we want. He doesn't own us." April's voice was terse. "And he hasn't touched any of us. So you can just shut up now. Shut up and keep your ears open. This isn't a safe zone." April pivoted the turret, tracking a zombie up the street. Rebecca nodded and turned around, looking down the street. "So you love him."

"That has nothing to do with anything."

Rebecca stayed quiet and kept her eyes open.

I rounded a corner and caught a glimpse of the walker. He turned around another house. "Come on, double time." I ran to the house and went around the other direction, Joy and Jen following me.

When I came to the corner of the house, I stopped and shouldered my

ACR on my left shoulder, then sliced the pie, keeping my self behind cover as much as possible. He was coming this way. When he was close enough, I jumped out with the ACR up and on his chest. "STOP RIGHT THERE. DON'T MOVE."

The walker stopped, with a surprised look on his face. He raised his hands slowly as he let out a quiet hiss. He was wearing sunglasses.

"One move and I'll end you." I snarled. "Jen, Joy. Very carefully, cuff this guy."

As soon as I said that, I flipped the rifle around and smashed the buttstock into his face hard, sending him sprawling. I remembered how quick Raymond was and how fast the bite took effect.

Joy was on him instantly, grabbing his arms and throwing a set of S&W hinge cuffs on him, just like I had showed her. She had practiced on Jen and had the technique down. I had declined the offer to practice on me.

One of the tactical items I always carry with my gear is duct tape. Something I learned way back when at Ft. Benning. "Always, always, always have duct tape." My drill sergeants were never wrong. I tossed the roll to Jen who pulled off a length, bit it with her teeth to rip it off the roll, then stretched the tape across the guy's mouth as he tried to bite. Duct tape was more useful than flex cuffs with a guy like this.

"Take off his sunglasses." I wanted to see this guy's eyes. Jen flicked them off his face. His eyes were the color of open wounds. Red all around with small black centers.

"Ogre to the Bronze." I said into my radio. The Bronze was Josh's code name.

"The Bronze here."

"Bagged a Red Eye here, Over."

"Roger that, we are 10-17 to your 20. Out."

I looked down at the strange thing in cuffs. "Get him up on his feet." Jen and Joy lifted the thing to its feet. "Let's get back to the truck."

All around us, we could hear moaning. Then the sound of the .50 opened up. Single shots at first, then a couple full auto bursts. "Hurry!" We started a jogging pace, half dragging the Red Eye with us.

Zombies fell in behind us, and I fired a salvo of shots into them, slowing them down. Zombies in front cut us off.

Radio chatter from different units was all the same, "They're everywhere!" "They are all over us!"

I pulled the girls to a stop and slammed the red eyed creature against the house, then I shoved the barrel of my ACR under the Red Eye's chin, hard.

"Make them stop or your brains get to paint this wall."

The zombies kept coming. "Three. Two..."

The zombies froze in their tracks. "Good... Good... we have an understanding. Now send them away."

The zombies backed up and then became disinterested. The .50 cal went silent as did the radio chatter. Everything was quiet now.

"Ah... so you have a self awareness... a sense of self preservation. That's good. Because the last one of you freaks we found, he didn't." I looked into the red eyes. There was a tangible feeling of hatred in them. Hatred and rage. This was the stuff that would give Stephen King nightmares, if he could see these eyes. I wondered if Stephen King was still alive. I doubted it.

"Now, we are going to go for a little ride. Would you like that? We're going to where we can talk, okay?" The eyes stared into mine. "Nod your head if you understand me."

The thing nodded, slowly.

"Come on."

We made it back to the truck, but we could see a lot of zombies standing around. Some seemed uninterested in us. Others stood there, staring, breathing hard and leaning in, like they were sprinters waiting for the starter pistol. At their feet were chunks of zombie bodies, others that had April's handiwork all over them, or they were all over. However you wanted to put it.

As we came into view, April waved us over, "Hurry! I can't believe this; they were coming and then they just stopped."

"I can. Because of this guy."

"How?" Rebecca asked.

"This guy controls them. Somehow."

Josh and other trucks came racing up the road. The MRAP not caring who or what was in its way. It ran through dozens of zeds that were in the road.

We put the Red Eyes into Josh's MRAP. He had some room, then we drove to Dixie College, into the middle of the big field in the center of the campus. We pulled Red Eye out of the truck and dropped it into the grass.

"Go find us a chair for our guest." One of the soldiers ran off.
A few minutes later, we had the Red Eye in the chair, more duct tape kept him in it. Legs taped to legs. Arms to the back of the chair. He wasn't going anywhere.

"So tell me... what's your name?"

The thing didn't say anything.

"Oh, please, excuse me." I grabbed a corner of the tape on his face and ripped it all off quickly.

The zombie hissed and bared its teeth.

"Now, where were we? Ah... Name. The last guy we meet that had eyes like yours and liked sunglasses like you do; he had a name. His was Raymond. So what's yours?"

The zombie-guy looked at me and hissed again with a Billy Idol sneer on his lips. "I'm the only thing holding them back."

I smiled, "That's the only reason I've not made you into modern art. Not that I care about them. We've got more than enough firepower to handle them all. We've taken care of bigger cities than this. Zombies don't scare us. But you... You are interesting. You are different. So I'm not just going to shoot you in the head. So you can answer my questions and be nice... or I'll end you real quick just like I ended Raymond. You understand me?"

The Red Eye looked at me and slowly nodded.

"That's good. Now, what's your name?"

The Red Eye looked down... shook his head... "Johnny. My name was Johnny." Johnny spoke with a strange hissing sound that came from the back of his throat.

"So you can control the zombies, you remember your name, you don't want to die... this is good." I looked at April who just shrugged her shoulders.

"Hungry... Johnny is sooo hungry." He sniffed the air. "Meat.... blood and flesh... hungry..."

"Oh, you're hungry? I don't have any zombie chow... I have some water. Do you want a drink of water?"

Johnny shook his head. "You want something else to drink? What do you want to drink?"

"Meat." Johnny said.

I stood up. "You know, I saw a *Ren and Stimpy* cartoon like this. I'd be laughing my ass off if we were not living in a horror show. I'm kinda thirsty myself. You wont mind if I get a drink do you?"

April drank down some orange Gatorade and then poured some Red Bull into it. She handed it to me after turning the bottle a few times to mix the solution. Rebecca eyed the bottle. I caught her look as I opened the bottle and drank some of my favorite beverage in the world. "The Orange is the best, isn't it?" April nodded.

I looked back at the Red Eye. "Johnny, Johnny, Johnny... I tell you what, Johnny. I'll be honest with you. I don't want to kill you, Johnny. I've no reason to, so I'd rather not if I don't have to. So I'm going to make a deal with you. You help me... and I'll let you go. Do we have a deal?"

Johnny's head sagged.

"A deal, Johnny. Do we have one?"

Johnny's head nodded.

"Good. Good. I'm starting to like you, Johnny. You're a good ghoul. I'd let you come over to my place and play X-Box. You remember an X-Box?" Johnny just sat there. "No? Oh man, you're missing out. Lots of fun. But the X-Box wasn't my thing. I like other stuff. I like killing zombies. I really do. But you are not a zombie, are you, Johnny?"

Johnny sat there with his head hanging.

'So what are you Johnny? How did you get this way?"

"Bite. Bite me. Zombie bite me."

"Really? A bite. And you didn't turn into a zombie... you turned into this."

Johnny just hung his head more.

226

"So how do you control the zombies, Johnny?"

"Think about... them."

"You think about them and they do it?"

"Yessssss."

"Anything. Anything at all?"

"Ssssssss... yessssss."

"Okay... I have a plan, Johnny. You help me out with this plan – I'll let you go."

Johnny looked up at me.

"If you do what I ask... I promise I'll not kill you, and I'll let you go. We got a deal?"

It Slices, It Dices, the all-new Zombie Shredomatic

The zombies lined up like it was a Soviet bread line. One by one, they walked up, stretched out, and reached into the machine. The machine did the rest. The zombie was instantly pulled in and through the shredder, to be spit out the other side in a spray of red mist and small chunks of meat and bone.

We found the machine parked besides one of the small streets where the power company was trimming tree branches away from power lines. Industrial Chipper Shredders made for great zombie processors. The pulp that came out the other side was collected in a garbage truck where we would dump the contents into a safe place.

The only one that didn't like this was Johnny, who would howl every time a zombie was pulled through the machine... which was a lot.

When the last zombie went through, we shut the machine off.

"Good Johnny. Good boy."

Johnny tried to kick in the chair, but had no luck.

"Oh, you're right. A deal is a deal Johnny. I promised I'd let you go. Didn't I?"

Johnny nodded.

"Okay, I'm going to cut you loose, and you're not going to try to bite anyone... you are going to walk that way... Okay?"

Johnny nodded again. I pulled out my Becker Companion knife and split the tape to the chair legs. Johnny stood up.

"No, Johnny... I didn't say I'd take the cuffs off of you. Or the tape. That wasn't part of the deal."

He grunted and shrieked.

"You best run along now. I would if I was you."

Johnny turned and faced me. "See that big guy over there? He didn't make a deal with you like I did."

Johnny took off running with the chair still taped to his arms as Musket slowly measured his powder charge.

Capello looked at Musket's loading process. "Tight weave?"

"Silk" Musket said. "Another fifty yards."

Capello nodded.

Johnny had made it across the parking lot and almost to the street when Musket's gun backfired in an eruption of smoke and fire.

The ball of led entered Johnny's neck at the base of the skull, crashed through the vertebrae, blowing bits of bone and sinew out, ripping flesh and tendon out. Johnny's head flew across the street, but his body dropped right there.

"Impressive shot, Musket."

"A day's work to be sure, but tis a labor of love, I assure you that."

We were packing up the gear and getting ready to roll when I noticed something. A glint of light. "Look up there." I pointed.

April shaded her eyes with her hand, "What's up there?"

"The airport is there... but something else."

I reached back into the M-ATV and found my binos. The glint on the plateau was gone, but movement remained. It was too far for my eyes or my binos to see. One thing I knew, I've not been up there, and neither had anyone else in my party.

"Let's go."

I drove up the plateau and before we reached the top, we came to a barricade of vans and trucks parked side by side.

It was a simple matter of taking off the parking brake, putting it in neutral, jumping out, and letting the vehicle roll down the hill. We watched trucks and cars roll, bounce, careen, and smash into houses.

Once clear, we drove on. Okay, we rolled all of them, taking bets which one would either go the farthest or do the most damage. What can I say? We had fun.

I drove up to the top and as we got up there, we saw someone on a horse galloping away as fast as the horse would run. I hit the gas and followed. As I got closer, I could tell that the rider was female. She was good. She cut the horse to the left, crossed the runway, jumped a marker, and left me in the dust. April pulled out of the turret, "Don't scare her!"

I slowed down.

She ran the horse into a hanger, jumped off, slapped the horse as she pulled a lever action from the saddle.

"April, get back up there, take off your hat and goggles, smile big."

The girl took cover behind some tool boxes. April got back up into the turret and turned on her charm. "Hey there!"

The girl didn't immediately shoot.

"Jen, you want to say howdy?"

"Sure thing."

Jen opened the door and slowly stepped out. "You're pretty good on that horse. Very fast. That's good riding."

"Leave me alone!" The girl said. To emphasize the demand, she cycled the action of her rifle.

"Easy now." Jen held her hands up.

"We just want to make sure you are okay."

"I was fine before... I'm even better now."

"When was the last time you ate anything?"

Silence.

"We have food. Water. I think we have a cold soda."

April jumped to the cooler and dug in. "Jen."

April tossed a can of Sunkist and Jen caught it. "Sunkist. These are my favorite. And it's ice cold. You want it?"

The girl stood up and lowered the hammer on her Winchester 92, then put the rifle over her shoulder. "You have no idea how much I love Sunkist."

I turned to Joy. "What?"

"Sunkist is good stuff. Don't underestimate it."

"What is it with orange soda?"

I looked at Rebecca, who shrugged her shoulders. "I like the diet version."

Jen had given the can to the girl who was now drinking it like it was the first thing she'd drank in days.

"What's your name?" Jen asked.

"Stacy Roth." She held out her hand. Jen shook it. "Nice to meet you, Stacy. I've got some folks that want to say howdy as well."

"You said you had some food?"

Jen laughed.

Stacy had long, straight red hair and blue eyes. She was wearing a plaid shirt, blue jeans tucked into tall cowboy boots, brown, leather chaps, and had a big silver and black belt buckle with an NAA Mini revolver in it. Her brown hat was hanging from around her neck. She was a true cowgirl. She was young. Probably 16 years old, and from the way she rode, probably been riding all her life.

I stepped out of the truck. "Stacy, how long have you been alone?"

"What do you care?"

"I worry about everyone. We want to make sure you're okay." I had an MRE in my hand. "Here's some food. It's kinda gross, but its food."

She took the MRE, flipped open a Buck 110 knife one-handed, and cut the bag open. I watched her eat the crackers in about a minute flat. She had been alone for a while now.

"Where's your family, Stacy? You've been alone for at least a few days."

She nodded. "I was waiting for my dad. He was supposed to have been here." She told us she had talked to him a week ago and that he was going to fly home to St. George to get her. He was a pilot with the Air Force. Flew a fighter jet, a Strike Eagle. He was in California. Stacy was here at the family ranch with her Mom, but she was bitten by a zombie. She ran to the stable and got her horse and came to the airport to wait for her Dad. That was a week ago. The small terminal had vending machines that she busted into, but she was down to her last pack of Famous Amos cookies.

"Where's your ranch, sweetheart?" Jen asked.

"Hurricane." She said, pronouncing it like "Herkin" the way they say it here.

"You rode your horse all the way from there, up to here?"

"Where's a Herkin?" Jen asked.

I pointed. "Across the city, up the freeway a bit. That's a good ride.

"How did you get away from all the zombies?"

"I was faster and I'm a crack shot."

"I believe you. Jen, get her another Sunkist and make sure she's okay. I'm going to make a phone call."

Joy tossed me the sat-phone and I started dialing as I walked away from the girl.

"Sarge, this is George."

"Yes, sir."

"Man, stop being so formal. Hey, you're still in Cali, right? Good. I found a girl here in Saint George. She was waiting here for her Dad. She said he's a Strike Eagle pilot."

"Air Force, then."

"Yeah. The name is Roth. He was alive a week ago."

"Lot's happened since then."

"I know."

"I remember seeing some Eagles when this furball started, but I've not seen them for a while. I know some jets zoomed up north as soon as we had this in the bag here. Maybe he went up there. The Chinese had some boats heading for Seattle. But I don't know anything else."

"We've never lost an Eagle in a fight before. So I'm hopeful. Ask around. Find him. If you find him, tell him we're taking Stacy back to Ogre Ranch, we're going to take care of her until he can come get her."

"And if..."

"Then find out what happened. This girl deserves to know."

"I'll see what I can do."

"She's a neat girl, Neil. Total cowgirl. Horse and everything. You'd like her. Born in the saddle."

"A daddy's girl. I'm on it."

I hung up the phone with a knot in my stomach. I had a real bad feeling about this. I walked back to the girls. "Stacy, let me show you something. It's called a Blue Force Tracker."

I explained who I was, where we were going, and that I had men in California that were looking for her Dad. I explained about what happened in California.

She agreed to come with us with one clear condition.

Two hours later we were on the freeway heading north. With a horse trailer behind the M-ATV.

We pulled into Ogre Ranch just after 1:00 pm. Off in the distance, I could hear the sounds of engines racing and soon a pair of sand rails came into view. The drivers were wearing gloves, motorcross helmets, and they had P-90 SMGs strapped across their chests. The SRs roared up besides the M-ATV, passing the other vehicles and slid sideways to a stop.

I jumped out of the truck as the drivers climbed out of the SRs. "My boys!"

Bravo and Echo pulled off their helmets, "Dad!"
They about knocked me down. "We were up on the plateau and saw you coming."

"Yeah, we had a race getting down. I won." Bravo boasted.

"You cut me off at the corner! You cheat." Echo protested.

"Guys, guys... neither of you won."

They stopped and looked at me like I was crazy. "I won. I got here first and I'm even pulling a horse trailer."

They laughed, "Yeah right, Dad."

"Where's your momma?"

"She's at school."

"Tell her I'm home." The twins jumped back into the SRs. "Oh, hey... Where's Kilo?"

"He's at the depot, on their X-Box. Or he was."

I looked up the road to the depot and saw the tall figure of Kilo, walking with his hunched shoulders and his long hair coming my way.

The Girl Squad was climbing out of the truck. "This is Ogre Ranch, the home of the Governor of Utah." Jen was explaining to Stacy. Stacy looked around for a minute, then walked to the trailer and opened it up. A moment later she was in the saddle. "I'm going to take Taco for a ride. Where's some water?"

Jen looked at me. "There's a trough behind the Valkyrie house. She can stay there with you guys. I don't think Stacy would be comfortable in a house full of boys... teenage boys."

"Ah, I don't know... I'd have loved it." Jen looked wistful.

"Yeah, that's why she's staying over there. Way over there."

"Ah, same reason we're over there and you're here." Jen said as she giggled and started walking up the lane with her tac vest in one hand and rifle in the other, walking besides Stacy who was trotting her horse over to the Valkyrie house.

"You can come over any time, boss. We'd love to have you." Joy said as she unzipped her vest with a wicked grin on her face. She grabbed a few things out of the truck and headed up the road to the house.

"She's right, you know. They would." April stretched like a cat and tossed her goggles onto the turret seat. "Me too, right about now. Well, after a bath." She picked up her SCAR and then leaned in to me. "Or during."

She turned with a wry smile and headed up the lane.

Kilo walked up to me. "Hey Dad." He just stood there.

I gave him a hug. "How are you?"

"Cool," He said. Leaving it at that. "Who's that?" Kilo nodded to the Stacy who was trotting across the field now.

"Stacy Roth. She might be with us for a while." I looked over at her. Her Dad's a pilot, he might have gone down in California. We're looking for him."

"She's cute."

"Yes, she is. Adorable."

"She rides well."

"Yup. Very fast. You should go talk to her. She could use a friend. She's your age. Maybe take her around, introduce her to the Hughe's girls."

Kilo smiled. "I can handle that." He walked out into the field.

Josh, Musket and the others were parking at the depot. I could see them walking to Musket's Pub and I watched as the Serving Wenches ran out to meet Musket... all three of them.

I turned back to the ranch, walked up the stairs and looked around. The house was empty. Debbie called and said she was glad I was home safe and she would see me tonight.

Back out on the porch I saw dots in the sky just over the horizon. Apaches returning. Kilo was on the back of the horse with Stacy and they road by, both smiling. I sat down on the steps and watched the Apaches come in, one by one. There were only eight of them.

Battle of San Diego

*M*ajor Roth set the throttles to full military power and let his F-15E Strike Eagle climb at an easy rate. He banked the aircraft a few degrees to the right and let its flight path curve out to sea. As soon as he went Feet Wet his radar lit up. His wingmen were a pair of F-18 Super Hornets, which were lagging behind. "Gunslinger One reads Five Bogies at Angels 9. I have lock. Fox Two, Fox Two!"

As soon as the Eagle found the enemy, they were well with range. ECM reduced his radar's capability or he would have seen them much further out. His systems gave him an audible tone indicating his weapons saw the enemy. He flipped the switch removing the safeties and pulled the trigger, twice. Heavy missiles dropped off the rails and their motors ignited. Within seconds Major Roth watched as his missiles streaked out in front of him, flying straight and true.

He couldn't see the enemy aircraft, but they were out there. In answer to his two missiles, tiny dots became visible ahead of him. He goosed his engines into afterburner and rolled his aircraft. Streaks flashed past his cockpit. Vapor trails from Chinese missiles, fired without getting lock. They were nervous.

The F-18's both called shots and fired. Roth looked at his radar and saw his missiles intercept and destroy two Chinese aircraft. SU-33's.

"We got two of them." In the back seat, his weapons officer was reading the radar and keeping an eye open all around the airspace.

"I want more." Roth spoke with a cool even tone, laced with ice.

"Looks like the Hornets both got one. Hold on, they're locking us up."

Roth's instruments suddenly blurted out warnings. They had radar lock on him. "Dropping chaff."

Roth rolled his plan again and pulled Gs, going into an inverted dive. He breathed and grunted fighting his own body weight. Missiles went past the Eagle, missing him, but reacquiring other targets, the Hornets. The missiles were almost to the Hornets when they exploded, white hot fragments tore through the Hornet's cockpits and intakes, shredding impellers and pilots alike. The fragments didn't stop until they passed through fuel lines. One Hornet exploded instantly, while the other one trailed black smoke and flame as it carelessly fell into a parabolic arc that ended in the Pacific.

Roth pulled his Eagle out of the dive and back up into the fight. He then killed four more Chinese fighters.

His back-seater got excited, "We've got the Cherry On Top, Man! Look, 11 o'clock on the horizon."

Roth banked his plane a little for a better look. "Their carrier!" Roth counted only three escort ships. "Tally Ho!" Roth point the plane at the carrier and dropped the nose.

"Arming the Harpoons. We've got locks, positive on the carrier." The Back Seater worked his magic, then said what Roth was waiting for. "Safeties are off."

"Fox Two." Roth pulled the trigger again.

Nothing.

"Fox Two."

Nothing.

Roth kicked the side panels of his Eagle, "Damn it!" He pulled out of the attack run.

"They're armed! They just didn't release."

Roth looked back at his wings, the warheads of the Harpoons were just hanging there, like personal insults. "Screw it! Going to guns."

Roth snapped his Eagle around and dove back for the carrier at full afterburner. As soon as he was in range, Roth pulled the trigger and held it down. He could feel the 20mm Gatling firing and watched his tracers lance out to the big ship. The ships erupted in fire of their own. Glowing softballs arched up to him in long chains that he was able to evade as he kept his fire on the carrier's bridge. He could see his rounds shredding the bridge and people diving... and dying. Roth grinned as he pulled out of the run and he flashed across the deck of the carrier, releasing chaff and flairs. The deck crew scattered, running in between the planes with red star on the wings that covered the carrier's deck. Roth saw that each plane was loaded heavy with ordinance.

The Eagle passed the ship and he leveled out, his back seater was laughing. "Nicely done!"

This laughter was cut short. The Eagle flew over one of the escort ships. On the ship the Chinese version of our Phalanx tracked the Eagle. When it was in range, the Gatling gun opened up, sending high velocity HE rounds into the American plane.

In the Eagle, Roth laughed too, until he saw flashes from the corner of his eye. His plane shuddered and he suddenly felt sharp pain in his arm and blood splattered across his cockpit. He looked down and saw that his hand was still on the throttle, but it wasn't attached anymore. There was a 20mm hole through his left leg.

Every warning light in his cockpit was on and everything was buzzing. "EJECT. EJECT. EJECT." Flashed repeatedly on his main screen. His HUD was gone.

Roth looked in the mirror so he could see into his back seat. He was going to tell him to eject, but it was too late. The body back there no longer had a head and he could see that the rear half of the cockpit canopy was gone. Roth was suddenly filled with rage. He wasn't done yet. The fight wasn't over. He banked his wounded Eagle and came around for one more pass. He skimmed the tops of the waves, unable to pull any more altitude. When the carrier came around in front of him he leveled out and pulled the trigger again. Nothing. But the warheads hanging off the pylons under his wings were still there, still armed. Roth looked at the carrier as it grew in his cockpit.

"Stacy..."

All Smiles and Cleavage

I woke up in the morning just before sunrise. Others were asleep. From the fridge I pulled out a gallon of OJ, made from frozen, not fresh. Dang it. I poured some OJ into a big glass.

Need caffeine.

Poured Coke into OJ.

Better.

Eyes still not focused I shambled like a zombie out onto the front porch so I could watch the sunrise shine across the valley. I could feel the caffeine entering my blood, waking up my brain. Before my morning jolt, I'm a zombie.

I stood there looking at the APC parked right in front of my steps next to my M-ATV. I sipped my OJ and Coke and thought about how I might have an addiction problem if I think that this crap tastes good. Shut up, I argued with myself, it's good for you and it has caffeine in it!

WTF is this APC? I didn't remember it here yesterday. You know, Sunkist has some caffeine in it. Does it? Well, it used to. I think. Maybe the girls all like it because it's better than OJ and Coke. My inner dialog continued while I walked around the strange armored fighting vehicle in my front yard. WTF is this? It's not one of mine. Let's see... I have Strykers... yeah, they are over there. I have LAVs... they are over there... I have a couple M113 Gavins, there they are. I don't have this. What is this? I looked in my glass at the OJ and Coke and decided next time to just leave out the OJ. I set the glass down on the steps and climbed up on top of the strange APC. Hatches are all shut. The MK-19 was empty. I climbed down and found the rear door unlocked so I opened it.

Art.

Lots of Art.

Khorne has returned. So... this was a Centauro. It had to be because he wouldn't bring anything back if it wasn't Italian. I went back inside, in his room, in his bed. That wasn't Khorne. He wasn't here.

I was still waking up, finding a man that was not with his APC was something I couldn't do on an empty stomach. There was no breakfast here ready. I don't really like cold cereal. I need protein. At least three animals have to die before I can call it a meal. I walked across the field to Uncle Musket's Pub.

"Praise the Musket." I muttered as I entered. The busty Serving Wench was all smiles and cleavage. That's a lot to take in first thing in the morning. I sat down to a table and just said "Breakfast." I heard snoring from the corner and saw Musket, in a hammock, in a night shirt, with two wenches with him. He smiled in his sleep. I think I would too.

Breakfast consisted of stone-baked bread with strawberry jam, sausage, eggs, bacon, gratuitous views of ample cleavage, cheese, grits, orange juice, and Mt Dew. I was stuffed and feeling much better.

About the time I finished, Josh's voice praised Musket. I turned and saw my brother, "Hail brother!"

"Don't start talking like Musket. I can only handle one." I laughed.

At this point, Musket tried to roll out of the hammock and managed instead to dump himself unceremoniously on top of a rudely awakened tavern wench, who said "Again! I can't take any more right now!"

"Nay, you wanton woman... I'm just trying to get... Hey, let go of me clothes, woman! No! There's guests in my house! Evil succubus! Who hired you? Hands off my Musket!"

I turned back to Josh, "So, anyways... Did you catch a glimpse of that new APC in front of the ranch?"

"No, what is it?"

"I think it's a Centauro. It's like a sleeker LAV but with a tank turret on top."

"Sounds like a Centauro. Those are Italian. That means Zack's home. Where is he?"

"I don't know. Haven't seen him." I said as I popped the last bit of bacon into my mouth.

Uncle Musket joined us at the table. "Breakfast, wenches! For my and me Kin! But not this one, he's already eaten. He couldn't wait. No manners at all."

"You were snoring."

"No common decency."

"You were asleep in that... fishing net thing."

"Well, I hadn't planned to fall asleep in it."

"Two at once?"

Musket grinned. "Three. You should try it."

"No, I don't..."

"You have the opportunity if you just asked, lad!"

Josh just shook his head. "You're both pigs, you guys know that, right?"

"What did I do?"

"You considered it."

"No, I... I... Okay, well you got me there."

Musket laughed, then looked over my shoulder. Zack walked in the front door. We all stood and cheered, "HEY!"

And then a nun walked in behind him. We stopped. She was very pretty. Fresh faced and innocent looking... and she was holding his hand.

"Zack. Good to see you brother!"

Josh gave him a hug. We all did. Then I turned to the nun, "Hello, I'm George. Pleased to meet you." I shook her hand. It was small and delicate, and it felt like I could break it. She smelled like jasmine and lilacs.

At that moment a tavern wench walked past with her jugs leading the way. The Sister blushed. "How does she not fall over?" She said it with an Italian accent. "That is obscene."

"Only if you stare, Sister!" Musket hooted.

All four of us at the same table at the same time. I couldn't remember when this last happened, but it only took the end of the world as we knew it to make it happen again. We stayed at the table well past lunch telling stories and laughing.

April came into the pub, searching me out. She came to the table, looked around at the four brothers with the shaved heads, epic goatees, and beautiful women surrounding us. "There are four of you. I didn't see the horses tied up outside."

"The apocalypse started some time ago, sweetheart", Musket smirked. "You might not have noticed it staring at my brother so much.

April flushed and handed me the sat-phone. "It's that Ferguson guy from one of those Carolina's. Says it's urgent."

Then she bent down, "You're definitely the best looking." She said in a whisper loud enough for everyone else to hear before she walked over to the pub's bar where she sat and eyed a wench up and down. "What do you take for the back pain?" The wench winked and went about her business.

"Is that the Missus Ogre?" The nun asked.

"Nay," Musket said. "That's one of his bodyguards. He has a three-piece set of them."

She turned to Zack, "I can be your bodyguard."

Josh, who was working on a mug of orange juice suddenly choked and spewed OJ out the sides.

I excused myself from the table. "Yes, Sarge! What's the news?"

The Sarge told me everything about Stacy Roth's father, the carrier, and that because of him, the carrier was sitting on the bottom.

"When I get back, I can help out with her... take her riding. She sounds like the same age as..." He coughed. "I'll do what I can. I got to go."

"That'd be a big help, cowboy. Thanks," I said as I hung up. When I turned back to the table, everyone was quiet.

"I've got to go find our new little cowgirl," I said as I walked out of the pub. April pulled herself up from the bar and followed me out.

"Not the news you wanted to hear, was it?" She asked.

I looked at her, "No, not at all. Her Dad is dead. Crashed his fighter jet into a Chinese aircraft carrier.... sank the carrier."

April was quiet.

"Hey, I'm going to have to tell her... and when I do, the young lady is going to get on her horse and ride off and she's going to keep riding until she about falls off. So before I tell her, I want you to go to the Comms tent over there, get a small GPS transponder, and stick it to the back underside of her saddle. So when she makes to disappear, we can find her."

April nodded. "Okay."

"Her Dad is going to be watching over her, but I'm sure he would not want us losing her. She's probably going to head up into the mountains, or back to her home in Hurricane."

April headed to the tent and I went to find where Stacy was.

"Hey Dad!" It was Kilo. He was wearing a wool sweater, with jeans and his long hair. He looked like one of The Boys from the beginning of *Boondock Saints II*.

"Yeah, what's up?"

"You've always said you hated 5.56mm."

"Yeah."

"Why aren't you using a .308? Uncle Jimmie packs a .308."

"Well, 5.56mm is cheap.... er... I see you're point."

"Look what I found." Kilo had a small box in his hand. I opened it and it was an ACOG with a 762 drop reticule in it. "I thought you'd like it."

I smiled, "Yes, I do. Thanks."

"Where did you get that tank?"

"What tank?"

"The one parked in front of our house."

"Ah, it's a Centauro. That's Zack's."

"It's cool." He said, as he started to walk away. "Oh, ah... I left you something on the seat of your M-ATV."

"Thanks. Oh, where is Stacy?"

He smiled, "She's eating lunch in the depot."

"Can you go get her for me?"

"Sure."

I didn't want to tell her anything yet until I knew the transponder was in place so instead of heading to the depot, I went to the M-ATV to see what Kilo had left me.

It was a Springfield M1A SOCOM 16. I raised my eyebrow. The stock was aftermarket. A Sage EBR set up with a collapsible stock. Where did he get this thing? I decided not to question it, but accepted it gladly. He had a new vest for me too – with Ballistic panels in it, and it had pockets sized for the .308 magazines. There was a note.

"With Love, Your Girl Squad."

Under that,

"And Kilo!"

I picked up the M1A. Wow, it was brand new and not nearly as smooth as it would be. I took the gun apart at our weapon cleaning station which consisted of a couple big fishing tackle boxes filled with cleaning supplies and bore snakes and such and a folding table. I first used MPRO-7 cleaner on the gun and relubed it generously with Slipstream Styx. I hand cycled the action several times then all of a sudden, there it was... that Slipstream feeling. Super smooth. NICE! I lubed up all the trigger group parts and reassembled everything back into the Sage stock and felt confident that this weapon was suitable. Especially with the ACOG on it. I'd need to test it before I rolled with it, get it zeroed... but I was pleased with it.

April walked up to me with a smile. "I see you found your little care package. I hope you like it."

"Yeah, I love it. It's great. Where did you get it?"

"The rifle, Kilo had. We found the Sage stock in Arizona. And we had the vest made. Dragon Scale armor is what's inside. We were told that it was good. We want to keep you safe."

"Thanks."

"It's our job." Then she kissed me on my cheek.

"Am I interrupting something?" It was Stacy.

"No. Not at all. I needed to talk to you." I looked over to April, who nodded. So the GPS transponder was ready. "Sit down, please."

"Okay."

"I had our guys in California look for your Dad, you know that. Stacy, your father was an incredibly brave man. He was key in defeating the Chinese invasion."

"Was?" There was horror and pain written all over her face.

I told her the story as Sarge had told me. As I guessed, she went to her horse, swung a leg over it, and took off at full speed. She headed up into the mountains. I looked over at April, who was crying.

"I need to get away myself." I said as I stood up. I jumped into the M-ATV and fired it up. As I did, April got in. "Me too."

I drove up the Ballistic Testing Zone One and saw that Zack and his Nun were there, shooting. So I continued past and headed to the "Super Secret Training Area". The M-ATV had no problem climbing up to where my Chevy even has a hard time getting to. I drove across the area and parked the truck. I set up some targets on the target stands I'd made years ago when I was a simple trainer. I pulled out the new rifle and set about getting the thing zeroed. After the first shot, I knew this rifle was pure win. A few more shots, and with April spotting, I had the ACOG dialed in perfectly. No malfunctions of any kind. I emptied the magazine, speed loaded another one, emptied it and repeated it. Not even a hint of a jam. "This gun will do nicely."

"I think it fits you."

"It's a little loud, but I think we have a suppressor for it." I said. "Come on, let's get back."

April took a step towards the target stands. "Leave them."

We climbed back into the truck and I looked at the BFT. Stacy's position was indicated on the map, still moving, heading high up into the mountains. "Hey, where was the government airliner crash, the one with all the zombies?"

"I think it was..." She was studying the map. "Right here."

"Okay, now look where Stacy is heading... if she continues..."

"She'll ride right up to it." April finished my sentence.

"Not good."

We drove back to the ranch and found Jen and Joy. "Come on, let's go!" April ordered. She had become the de facto leader of the Girl Squad.

"Where have you guys been? We were looking all over for you. No one knew where you were."

"Zeroing my new rifle. Come on, Stacy needs our help."

The girls grabbed their rifles and jumped in. As we drove, April filled them in. We drove the same route that Stacy had taken then were able to break off and take a faster trail heading closer to where the crash site was.

We got there and climbed out of the truck. The BFT indicated that Stacy was still coming, so we moved through the trees to intercept. The trail was well defined and we made sure we were between her and the crash, so she wouldn't see it.

We heard the horse before we saw it. It was plodding along. Stacy was half out of the saddle, laying on the horses neck. She was still crying, sobbing softly. The horse saw us and came to a stop, whinnying. Stacy sat back up and looked at us. "How did...?"

Jen was good with her, so she took point on this. "Because this is where I would have gone." Jen walked up to Stacy and reached out to her. She slid off her horse and Jen gave her a hug.

"It's going to be okay, Stacy."

We left Jen and Stacy so they could talk. We walked back to near the crash site. It was funny that we ended up back here as I had been thinking about this place more and more lately.

"This is where we found that security access card."

"Yup." I said. I still had that security card and it felt like it was getting heavier.

"We need to go there. Maybe there is some of the Federal Government there." April was making too much sense.

"I know. We need to. We've found nothing so far, no one has been reached. I don't know if there is anyone left."

"What about Air Force One?" April asked.

"Well, the protocol would be to get in it, fly away from trouble, head to a safe place."

"Which could be Cheyenne Mountain."

"Could be."

"When are we going?"

"Soon." I determined.

After a while Jen called us and we walked over.

"Stacy is going to need a ride back to the house."

Joy volunteered to ride the horse back while Jen stayed close to the young lady. I was grateful for that, fearing I'd have to ride the horse back down the mountain, and I hated horses.

Joy took off and we walked back to the truck skirting the crash by a good margin. In the M-ATV, Jen cradled the girl, who was still sobbing. She continued to cry off and on all the way back to the ranch. I dropped them all off at the Valkyrie House and then checked Joy's progress on the BFT. She was coming along and I didn't worry.

I went to the ranch house and walked up the stairs. Debbie was reading a book to our youngest. "Where have you been?" I explained the Stacy situation to her and that she had run off and we had to go find her. I left out the part that we had her bugged and intercepted her.

"Is she alright?"

"No, not really. But I think in time she'll be fine."

"Musket called for you."

"He used a phone?"

"No, he yelled across the whole damn field."

"What did he want?"

"He said the defendant wanted an appeal."

"What?"

"Which word did you not understand?"

"Defendant and appeal."

"You better go find out."

I walked over to the Pub and found a bawdy dinner crowd. Musket was sitting in a tall chair at the end of his longest table.

"It's about time you showed up, we've been wait'in for ye."

"What's the story?"

"This lad here did a terrible thing."

He explained the "court proceedings" and then his judgment. The defendant asked for an appeal.

"Okay, let me think about this for a moment."

The house got quiet. I made a show of deep thought.

"Okay, here's the thing. If you trade someone for a can of beer, and you open the beer, it's your beer. You can't trade back. Skunky beer or not, your satisfaction wasn't a part of the deal, just that you would get a can of it."

"So that be it then?" Musket asked.

"Not just yet. Now, if the person who offered the beer knew the beer was skunky and intentionally made the trade for the purpose of defrauding... Well, that's different." I looked to the defendant. "Did you know the beer was skunky? Don't lie to me, because I'll know it."

"N, n, no, sir. I didn't know. I got that can from another trade."

I shrugged. "So there it is."

"So that be it then?" Musket asked.

"That's it. Trade stands." I confirmed.

"Case closed." Musket banged his beer stein on the table and everyone in the house cheered.

One of the Wenches came up, "have you had supper yet?"

"No. What do you got?" I asked.

"Spam, baked beans, eggs, sausage, and Spam."

"You've been waiting to say that, haven't you?" The Wench smiled.

Some eggs and toast is fine, thanks."

Musket led the pub in a round of old Muskety ballads. Perhaps they would have made sense better if I was less sober.

I noticed Jen had come in. She was talking with one of the Wenches who was crushing apples in a big wooden press, collecting the juice in a bucket. After a while, Jen was leaning over the press, with her sleeves rolled up, twisting the large, wooden cross member.

I sat there admiring her curves, and the way she moved. Her breasts were no where near the massiveness of the Tavern Wenches, but they were ample enough, and when Jen bent to work the press, they looked inviting. The shape of her hips was complementary as well. As she pressed the apples, she would look up at me and smile. I smiled back but shook my head. It was time to go. I got up and left the tavern. "Blessings to Musket" I said as I walked out the door.

TEN

Mysterious Visitor from the North

I woke up early the next morning, got breakfast, and walked out through the airfield. I was trying to decide what to do with Cheyenne Mountain. I found a security card. Not a written invitation. However, I really couldn't explain the draw... it felt like I was being pulled.

Whiskey Seven was sitting there and I found myself doing a Pre-Flight. Per SOP, the bird was topped off, so fuel was good. I went through the check list as I thought about what it would take to run to Cheyenne. The place was no hop and a skip, but it really wasn't that far. And once there, the welcoming party would be a concern, or would I just find big, sealed blast doors? If I did find a welcoming party, would they be hostile?

I strapped in as I went about the rest of the check list.

A tap at the window. It was Jones, my Helo Instructor. "Going for a Solo?"

"I guess I am." I said as the engine started to spin up and the rotors started to turn. "You coming or are you going to stand out there?"

"Go ahead... I'm going to go eat breakfast at Musket's." Jones walked away.

The rotors got up to speed and all the instruments looked good. Once satisfied, I pulled up on the collective and felt the Blackhawk lift up off the ground. As I looked around the bird I glanced into the back and was startled to see Jen sitting back there, smiling peacefully as if she was just waiting.

"How long have you been back there?"

"I've been in here as long as you have." Jen smirked. "You seem preoccupied. What are you thinking about?"

"Cheyenne."

"Who's she?"

"Cheyenne's a place."

"Wyoming?"

"Nope, Cheyenne Mountain. It's in Colorado."

"Never heard of it."

I was scanning around the bird as I let it climb straight up a hundred feet, then I turned south and flew over Uncle Musket's Pub, over the school, and out over the Utah Desert.

"I was flirting with you pretty hard last night," Jen said. "Then you walked out."

"Yeah, I did."

"That hurt. I didn't think it would, but it did."

"If it makes you feel better... I wanted to... But I can't. You know that."

That seemed to brighten her up. "You and April and Joy are..." I didn't know how to define this, very special to me."

She smiled and looked down. "I understand."

"I intended to fly alone here."

"Oh, I'm sorry..."

"You might as well climb up here and take a seat." I nodded to the empty seat besides me. She was delighted. Once in the co-pilot's seat she strapped in and put on a crew helmet. "So where are we going?"

"Nowhere. I'm just thinking." I said as I let the Blackhawk drift lower to follow the contours of the desert.

"Look at that!" Jen blurted.

I looked as a herd of antelope passed below us. I picked up the collective and put the bird into a banking climb. The helicopter responded gracefully. We found ourselves flying over Vernal, over Naples, then we turned and circled around to Red Fleet.

The radio came to life, it was Josh. "There is someone here to see you. You better get back here as soon as you can."

"Roger that, I'm on my way."

"How long do you think you'll be?"

"Not long."

"She seems impatient."

"Who?"

"You'll see." He laughed. "You won't believe me if I tell you."

"Try me."

"No way, bro. Just get here."

I pointed the bird straight for Ogre Ranch and poured on the power. Soon I buzzed over the ranch, looking down on it, looking for vehicles. I didn't see any new cars or trucks or anything. Wait. Sitting in the middle of the field was a new helicopter. A huge chopper with more blades than any I'm used to seeing. It was a Super Sea Stallion with huge fuel tanks under wing pylons and a long lance projecting out the front, and an air-to-air refueling probe.

I came back around, and set the Blackhawk to hover over where I took off from, then eased the bird down until it lightly touched ground. Once landed I shut down the engine.

Jones ran up to me. "Great landing, sir!"

"Thanks, Jones. I had a good teacher." I slapped him on his back. "So who's here to see me?"

Jones just laughed. Joy and April jogged up to me. April had a fresh shirt for me, tactical vest, and my new Sage M1A.

"So when is it my turn?" Joy asked.

"So who's here? Am I in for a fight?"

"Fight or not, I don't know, but I want you looking like you're ready. They're in the pub waiting for you." April said.

I looked at the Stallion and saw the markings. There was a logo of sorts. It looked like The Great Seal of Alaska but it was different. Under it were the letters R.O.A. I didn't know what that meant.

"Come on." I said, getting tired of the mystery. I ducked my head through the sling as we walked around the helicopter and headed to Musket's Pub.

As soon as we came into view, two guys wearing standard contractor uniforms straight out of the EOTAC catalog, complete with vests and sunglasses, turned to us and one spoke a few words into the mic that was clipped to his shoulder, then they turned to square their shoulders to me. Huh. They considered me a possible threat. Hence the war-gear that April, Joy, and now I was wearing. We walked confidently to them.

"Your weapons, sir."

Without breaking stride, "This is my house... so fuck you." I walked around to Musket's Entrance and met two more contractors standing on either side.

Inside, Josh, Capello, Zack, his corrupted Nun, and Musket were waiting, quietly. A small group of guests were waiting as well. The Wenches were wiping off already sparkling counters and tables. I banged through the door with a contractor in each hand. I dropped their unconscious asses to the floor on my third step.

Musket raised an eyebrow and gave a slight nod of approval of my entrance style. The guests turned, some reddening as they saw that I was fully armed and their security was laying on the floor. "You guys have a lot of balls coming in here and telling me that I have to leave my guns outside. What fucking idiot thought that was a good idea?"

"I did." A woman's voice that I recognized, said clearly and without reservation. The woman pressed forward through the group and held out her hand. "Sorry, I didn't mean to offend. I just wanted a meeting on an even playing field."

It was Sarah Palin.

I stood there. Sarah Palin. WTF is she doing here? "Then you are sadly mistaken, this isn't an even playing field. It's my field. Remember that."

245

"Do you know who I am?" She said.

I hate people that say that. Seriously. How arrogant. Bitch.

"I know who you used to be, Missus Palin. But I don't know who you are now. I've not heard anything about the GOP lately, so you have me at a loss."

I coughed and at that moment, my weapon came up as did the weapons of the Girl Squad. "Your security can drop their weapons."

Musket and Josh collected the weapons from the Secret Service looking guys that were with Sarah Palin.

Sarah just smiled, with her hand still out. Now that I had the home field advantage, I went ahead and shook the offered hand. She really was as pretty in person as she was in the news. Same hair. Same glasses. A bit more practical in dress. She had an FN Five-seven pistol on her hip. While holding her shooting hand, I gently plucked the pistol out of the holster and tossed it to Musket, who looked at the plastic weapon with great disdain. Okay, so she wanted to be armed but expected me to be disarmed?

"It's nice to meet you, Missus Palin, so far away from Wasilla, Alaska."

"Far only in distance, but not in purpose. Or so it seems."

"The Chase... go ahead and cut to it."

"We need friends, Governor Hill. And quite frankly, so do you. I think me and you need to become BFFs. Best friends forever, don'tcha know."

I'm usually pretty good with handling strangeness. However Sarah Palin standing in Musket's Pub, saying we need to be BFFs has to be some of the strangest I could think of. I looked back at the door expecting to see a walrus wearing a Viking helmet come lumbering through. There was no walrus. So I'm not on crack.

"Friends, Huh?"

"Friends that can work together... without getting in each other's way... and can help out when needed."

Ah. Here comes the nitty gritty. "Let's have a seat, Sarah. I think we have a lot to talk about."

"Do you have a map?" She asked.

The meeting lasted for hours before we both sat back. A more casual posture both physically and politically. Sarah was shockingly smart and ambitious. I had no choice but to stay on her good side.

Sarah was now filling me in on generalities. "We've only had relatively minor problems with the outbreak of this contagion. Anchorage and Fairbanks. Anchorage was the bigger problem for a while, but we have it locked down and everything is under control."

"That's good. I figured Alaska would come through everything pretty well."

"We can take care of ourselves. And evidently so can you even though you were hit much harder."

"Sarah, what you want to do is..."

246

"I'm not asking for permission, Ogre. I just don't want you in our way. We will then be in a better position to work together for our common good. You agree... and we'll back you up. Our full support."

"The US Constitution, Sarah. We still live by that. We both still live by that."

"Of course, that's not a question. The only thing we are doing is firming up states rights and drawing a new map."

I looked down at the map. Having no problem with the plan, no reservations. I picked it off the table and held it up. "Take this over to the school and start making copies."

Capello took it and headed out the door with it. What I did have, was reservations about what this meant in the future when Sarah Palin had this completed. She would become very powerful. And I knew she would become a problem in the future. But there was little I could do now.

I stood up. "We have an agreement, Sarah." We shook hands and photos were taken. People were free to mingle now and the Pub was no longer the quiet and tense place it was only moments before.

We made history here. After all, we just redrew the map of North America. While I was talking with those that had just become my Chiefs of Staff, I kept an eye on Sarah. But something about her... I didn't trust her. While I was talking to my guys I noticed her glances my direction and the conversations seemed to be mirrors. This was an uneasy accord.

Alaska was already rolling, floating, and flying troops through the parts of the Yukon and Northwest Territory of Canada, and British Columbia. A massive land grab that would be completed within a matter of days, even if the fraction of Canada's military tried to stop it. There was nothing I could do to stop her if I wanted to, so just staying out of her way was easy to agree to. Our defense against the Chinese sent a message that we had military power. Never mind half of it was shear luck and the sacrifice of a single F-15. Then there was the rumors that I had nuked SLC and Phoenix. She felt we had strength and I didn't break that illusion for her. What military units were left from around the country were making their way to Utah, and what was the Utah Guard was quickly becoming the biggest military engine in the lower 48. But much of it was still unorganized. She, on the other hand, had a lot of actual military strength, organized, and without the disruption we had faced. She was flexing those muscles. Not for defense, but to gain power. If it came to blows between Utah (meaning the lower western states) and Alaska. It would be a meat grinder. And neither of us wanted that.

After the Election that they were going to have up there in a couple days, Alaska would become a separate nation with my official recognition and support. The Republic of Alaska. Which is why their helicopter had "R.O.A." on the side. She was rolling this ball, my support or not. This is also why she thought she could insist on disarming me. An attempt to put me at the disadvantage. I put us on an even playing field. In her mind, Utah and the

Coalition of Western States was still quite powerful.

I looked over at the bar, where Sarah's husband stood. Near the bar, in the corner, a band was setting up. Tavern Wenches, four of them, were bustling about the pub with food and drink.

"We need an Uncle Musket's Pub back in Wasilla." Sarah observed. "I like this place."

"Be careful what you ask for, lassy." Musket said.

While the band played and everyone was relaxing, I pulled my staff aside. We were sitting around the table making plans for a run to Cheyenne Mountain, when Sarah Palin came over from her table.

"The rumors I've heard about you are quite unfair. You're not the monstrous dictator people have made you out to be."

"I only turn green and rip off my shirt when I'm asked to disarm."

She laughed. "I see that. And these are," She said, indicating to my body guards, "professionals."

I glanced at April who nodded slightly.

"They don't look like strippers."

"I assure you, they are very good at their jobs. They have fought with me through more oceans of zombies than I care to remember."

"You fight yourself?" She seemed surprised and even looked shocked.

"Lead from the front, Sarah. The view is better. My first security team was killed in action just a few days after everything started. We had a run in with some gunmen from out of state. This team has been with me ever since. They are devoted, loyal, and I trust them with my life. Obviously. How many zombies have you fought?"

"Me? None. I try to stay as far away from them as I can."

"Don't like to get your hands dirty?"

Sarah shook off the idea of fighting zombies. "Hey, I'm not afraid to get out there and get my hands dirty. I just don't like to put myself at unnecessary risk. I owe it to my people that I stay safe. I can't lead them if I'm dead."

"You mean you can't rule. There is a difference."

"What would happen to everyone here if you got killed? Huh?"

"I'd imagine one these fellows here would pick up the ball and run with it. Life goes on. It will go on after I'm gone."

She stood up. "Just as long as you stay out of my way... I don't care what you do."

I stood as well. "Just as long as you stay out of mine, and you uphold your end of the bargain, I don't care if you lock yourself in a castle." Everyone at the table stood with me.

Her eyes narrowed, "I think we understand each other perfectly." Then she smiled. "We are going to be best of friends."

Sarah Palin snapped her fingers and then she, and her people walked out of the pub.

"You know what, guys?" I asked after the last of them had gone. "I don't think I trust that woman."

Musashi shook his head. "Not as far as I could throw her."

"I wouldn't trust her even that far." Musket said.

The newest bar maid walked past, unlike the others this one had blond hair. She was well endowed like the others and dressed the same. I'd never seen her – or any of them before. I looked over to Musket, "Where do you find these woman? Seriously."

Musket laughed, "They come to me lad, they come to me!"

With the increasing popularity of the pub, the workload was increasing as well. I didn't ask where the meat, cheeses, and bread came from. Or the beverages. But I imagined he had a good supply of it.

"So when are we going to Colorado?"

"I have some admin shit to do now. Today is shot to hell, tomorrow, I won't be done... so the next morning we'll go."

"Good. I need to run to Salt Lake." Khorne said, looking at his nun. "I need to pick up a few things."

"That's fine. But be careful. I'll need you in Colorado." I headed out the door.

I took about 3 steps outside of the pub when a Humvee pulled up in front. Two men stepped out wearing Army ACUs, two more wearing the Air Force equivalent. Pistol belts on, with pistols. Uniforms were pressed. Boots, polished. All four men were top Brass according to the emblems on their uniforms.

"You gentlemen must be from Lewis-McChord." I said. My Girl Squad flanked me. Brass in magazines trumps brass on collars.

"That's right." One of the men said. The stars on his collar indicated that his rank was Lieutenant General. "How did you know that?"

"You and this guy are Army. Those two are Air Force. And Lewis-McChord is the only joint base in this geographical region. And we've both had a slight case of Chi-Com Invasion. So, it was an educated guess, General. How can I help you."

"We're looking for Governor George Hill. We were told this is the best place to find him or to wait for him."

"You found him."

"You're the Ogre?"

I held out my hand. "And you are Lieutenant General Watson, US Army, head honcho of Lewis McChord, and commanding officer of the First Brigade of the 25th I.D." He shook my hand. "And this is Colonel Rain, commanding officer of the 1st SF group." I shook Rain's hand.

"You seem to know a lot about us, Governor Hill."

"I don't know your Air Force associates." I said, not explaining anything any further.

Watson turned and gestured to the first Air Force officer nearest him. "This is Brigadier General Clark, US Air Force. He commands all Air Force Assets in the Pacific Northwest. He arrived at Lewis-McChord about three days before the late unpleasantness erupted. He is now the acting commanding officer of both the 62nd Airlift Wing and the 446th, another pack of bus drivers. Previous commander got a case of the zed... had to be replaced."

"Ahem..." Clark cleared his throat, "But we have really big buses." I shook Clark's hand.

"And this is Major General Anthony Williams, he commands a little organization called the Western Air Defense Sector. We just found him two days ago. He was stuck in Anchorage for a time, but we are glad to have him back."

"Western Air Defense Sector? I'm not familiar with that."

"I used to be a fighter jock, now I pilot desks for a living. I appreciate your help, Governor Hill. Your sending of the fighters we had at Hill, when you did, made a huge difference in our little misunderstanding with the Chinese."

I had to laugh. "Misunderstanding? Yes, they thought we would let them in. We had to clarify that."

"Precisely. They attacked San Diego, Seattle, and made a go for Alaska as well."

"How far did they get?"

"Not very. They made a parachute drop into Alaska, but that was crushed, their boats never made it to the shore. In Seattle, they almost started getting one ship unloaded. Almost. And we heard they had a carrier in the San Diego area."

"Had is the correct word, General Williams. That was taken out by one of your boys, Major Roth. An F-15 pilot. He died in the action. His daughter is here, we are taking care of her. Last I heard she was teaching my oldest son how to ride a horse."

"Major Roth, I knew him..." The General said. "Strike Eagle Driver."

"That's correct." I said.

"He was a good man. He would be happy to know his girl was still riding. She was a rodeo champion, you know."

"I didn't, but I might have guessed." I told him how I came to find Stacy.

He laughed, "That's Stacy Roth alright. You're lucky she didn't pop you."

"Well, fellas, I just had a conversation with Sarah Palin, Commander and Chief of the Republic of Alaska... we have a great deal to discuss."

"Yes, that's why we came." General Watson said, his face taking on a more serious pallor. "You know what she's doing, now. The woman is insane."

"She may be, but then again so are we all." I motioned that we go into the pub, and we did. Took another table, and the serious discussions began. I had a copy of the new North America Map, which showed the Republic of Alaska, the Coalition of Western States, and they filled me in on trouble brewing from back east.

"The Mighty Miss is the border line." General Watson said. "There is no more Federal Government, as such there is no more US Army, US Air Force or any of that. However, we are still here. And you are here."

I nodded, "Yes. So what did you gentlemen have in mind?"

"The military operates under civilian control. That is the way it was designed. Right now, you represent what is civilian control."

"Wait, so what you just said is that I am your boss."

"We hoped to come to that agreement. Because there are problems coming your way, and that means our way."

"What problems?"

"Some rogue elements back east that think they can come in and federalize everything they please."

"I have a problem with that."

"We hoped you might."

"What can we do about it?" I asked.

One of the Air Force Generals pulled up his brief case. "Satellite images. Human intel. We've got their names, we've got their numbers."

I sat back. "Knowing you guys, I would be shocked and painfully disappointed if you guys did not have a plan for all of this."

The SF General laughed. "You are perceptive, Governor Hill. We have a few ideas rolling around."

We spent hours talking in detail. It was truly scary what an SF General was capable of when he decided to take the gloves off.

"And all we need is a green light from our civilian leadership."

"General, you have my full authorization. Not only that, but you have my blessing. Get it done. Fast."

The General sat back with a grin. A frightening grin. He pulled out what looked like a blackberry, pressed a few buttons and said "Tiger, Tiger, Tiger." Then he looked at me. "Governor Hill, It's already started."

Part of me had cold shivers run up my spine. The other part made me feel very happy that these men were on my side.

"So there is no Governor in Washington State?"

"No sir. There are no elected officials left other than two county Sheriffs. As President of the Coalition of Western States, we were hoping you could make an appointment until proper elections could be organized."

"Is Washington that bad off?"

"It is. Our bases held together alright, but the civilian populations..." General Watson looked down at the table. "Ninety Five percent casualties in the Sea-Tac area."

"I used to live there." I said, quietly.

"We didn't know that."

"I used to go on camping trips with the Boy Scouts to Ft. Lewis all the time. That's where I decided that I wanted to join up. I have always loved the Pacific Northwest. Lots of friends."

"You still have a lot of friends there now, Governor Hill."

"Just call me Ogre."

"We've heard a lot of rumor about the Ogre in Utah."

"I didn't nuke Salt Lake."

"We know that. A MOAB. That would have been one hell of a sight to see."

I explained the plan. "Riders on horses, they had recordings of people screaming. They played the sounds while they rode through the city, getting a whole hell of a lot of zombies to follow them. The riders then climbed up a scaffolding structure we built, and helicopters picked them up. The horses were left behind, keeping the zombies there, making the zombies pack in. Once the helicopters were clear, I had a C-130 drop the MOAB on that spot."

"Unbelievable. And then in Arizona?"

"Nothing I could do about the power plant. It was going to go up no matter what. So we got the Cartel to meet us there."

"But you were not there."

"No, but I was watching."

"Goddamn! You should have been a General."

One of the Air Force guys shook his head. "Couldn't you have used something other than horses? Like cats strapped to motorcycles?"

I laughed. "That idea came up. But horses work out the best. No, I don't think I'd want to be a General, at least not in this life. I think Commander in Chief is better." I said, folding my arms behind my head.

Everyone at the table had a laugh, "Well, I'm glad you are on our side, Ogre."

"After seeing your plans, I'm thinking the same thing. Now, something has been bothering me... and I have a little problem."

I told them about the crashed jet in the mountains, the access card, and the strange feeling I'd been having about Cheyenne Mountain. The Air Force Generals looked at each other.

One of them leaned in, "I don't know anything about it... but there was a project. Classified like I've never seen before. They had something cooking there. Something big. Something that scared people. A project that I think was called "Fire Eye". I only saw those words on a folder that was covered up as soon as I walked into the room, once."

"What's the condition of the facility now? Is it locked down, buttoned up, what?"

"We've no idea. We've been unable to make contact."

"I'm going there... day after tomorrow."

"I would advise against that." One of the Generals said. "It's not a good idea."

"Do you know something that you're keeping from me?"

"No, Ogre. I'm not. That's the problem. We don't know. There could be anything there now."

"Well, then we should find out... and be ready for anything."

Don't Tease the Zombies

After the officers from Lewis-McChord left, I took some time to eat some dinner. Let them get good and gone, and hopefully no more guests today. I was afraid to step outside. No telling who would show up.

Outside again I turned to one of the soldiers who was constantly running around. I spotted one with a "I'm doing something" act going on.

"YOU! Come over here." I shouted.

The man ran over and saluted, "Yes, sir!"

"Damn it, man! Never do that again," I pointed at him. "I'm not an officer. See that hilltop there?"

"Yes, Governor."

"And that one there?"

"Yes."

"And that one over there?"

"Yes."

"I want Air Defenses on those hill tops ASAP. Go tell whoever is above you to pass it on. I want it up before it gets dark so I can see that it's there. I also want some up at the Vernal Airport. Do you get me?"

"Yes, sir."

"Damn it!"

"Sorry, sir." The man ran off.

This is getting stupid. Fighting zombies is bad enough. People have to go and make things worse. Chinese. Federal Bureaucrats. Sarah Palin pulling some shit.

I released the Girl Squad for the rest of the evening. However, once I did that, they talked to each other briefly and April lingered near the M-ATV acting like she was taking care of things.

Debbie stepped out onto the porch as I was coming up. "You've had some interesting visitors today. What's going on?"

I climbed the steps to the porch and sat down in the blue recliner. "Where do I start?"

"The very beginning is a very good place to start." Debbie said, quoting a line from *Sound of Music*.

"Sarah Palin is invading Canada, making Alaska its own country. Someone back east is stirring things up, and now we've pretty much established the Coalition of Western States as a power. I don't know if we are our own country yet, but it's feeling like it. There is no Federal Government anymore, so... that leaves us potentially vulnerable. I've just locked that down so we are in a better position. Palin thinks we are a military power. And with her ambition... it's good she thinks that. We basically made a treaty to stay out of their way, they stay out of ours and we'll help each other if called."

"Is that all?"

"How was your day?"

"I've got about 300 kids, most of whom no longer have a family. Zack's nun-friend helped out for a while, she's really good with kids... but I need more help. We've got the school acting as an orphanage."

"Is that all? I think I'd rather deal with Sarah Palin on a power trip. I can get you some more help. I'll work on that tomorrow. We've got a lot to handle, but we can do it."

"What choice do we have? You sleeping here tonight or at the tavern again?"

"My bed sounds really good tonight."

"I was hoping you would say that."

Ten minutes later the arguments started up again, all the old arguments, I walked out of the house again. I looked at the M-ATV and considered jumping in it. Instead grabbed my gear, some binos, and a couple ammo cans. I jumped in my Chevy. April climbed into the passenger seat. "Where are we going?"

"Cheyenne Mountain."

April got on the radio and within moments Jen and Joy were running down the lane, half dressed but with gear in hand. They piled in and we headed out as the sun started going down.

"It's a little late to get started." Jen said, shrugging into a shirt.

"You volunteered." I said. I put a CD into the player and let the sounds of Pink Floyd fill the truck as much as possible. We crossed into Colorado, and once in Dinosaur, turned south to Rangely.

The town of Rangely had its boom and bust cycles, before the great uprising. Now, it was a ghost town. There were few lights on, but mostly the people here were shambling dead. I drove slowly through the main street. The zombies here were sluggish and didn't seem to care about anything. I suspected that if I was to stop the truck, they would take a much greater interest. I didn't stop.

"Look at that one." April pointed to a man wearing a white shirt and tie, covered in dried blood. But what was interesting about him was the hole the size of a grapefruit blown through his chest. Bone was visible, rib and spine, but the zombie was still upright. Tough bastards.

"I wonder who did that to him." She voiced the same thought I had.

"I went to the police academy up there." I said, as we drove past the road that led up the hill to Colorado Northwestern. I was curious about the school, but not enough to make me turn.

I continued out of town until we came to the turn off that would lead us to Grand Junction. It was now almost completely pitch black outside. The only light was from the headlights of the truck. Overcast, no stars, no moon, just an eerie vibe as the road wound up the canyon, through trees, passing an occasional elk that watched us go by.

"So why didn't we take the time to get a full expedition together?"

"I needed to get away. Besides, they will come. My brothers will come. I know they put a GPS transponder in my truck. They'll find me if they need me, they know where I'm headed, and they know that I know when to expect them. I'm not worried."

"They don't seem to like us much."

"You did kick Musket in the junk."

"No, that's not what I meant. I meant us... That we're with you all the time."

"Like they have room to talk. We are all not without our own sins. None of you were a nun were you?"

We drove a while longer before she said anything again. "Remember the Shoguns of Japan?"

"I'm not that old."

Jen snorted

"From your history... " Joy said.

"Yes, what about them?"

"You are one of them." April said. "Some of them had bodyguards who were women."

I thought about that. "Shoguns also served their emperor... so if you are correct... Who am I serving?"

"It wasn't a strict comparison." April said.

Maybe not, but it got me thinking. What if someone was pulling my strings? The thought was disturbing enough to keep it stuck in my mind for the rest of the ride into Grand Junction.

We stopped to rest for the remainder of the night outside of Grand Junction in a little town called Rifle. There was a small motel with only a couple zombies walking around. We pulled into the back and parked behind the dumpster where no one could see the truck unless they knew where to look for it. We then dispatched the few zombies quietly before moving in. We found the keys at the front desk and went up to a nice, quiet room. Two big beds, a nice couch and chairs, and a small table. Joy tried the shower, but the cold water only trickled.

"It's fine." I said. "We only need to rest for a while."

The girls grumbled but soon fell asleep, Jen hadn't even taken off her tactical vest.

The next morning I woke up to the sound of a shriek, then girls laughing.

"It startled me."

"You were scared."

"I was taken off guard."

"It got you."

"It only startled me."

I sat up. Outside the window was a zombie who's head rested against the glass as it stared in. Evidently Jen went to open the curtains and got a surprise.

Before the girls knew I was awake, I took out my pistol and fired a shot. The sound was muffled, but it was loud enough to make them jump. My round put a small hole in the window, and a hole though the zombie's head. It fell down outside with a muffled thump.

"Stop teasing the zombies!"

We hit the road not long after.

Cheyenne Mountain

"*I* think this is as far as we should go." I said as I pulled off the winding road into the trees and found a place to hide my old silver Chevy. We got our gear out and then unrolled the camo netting. Using my Becker Combat Bowie for its true purpose, field work, I lopped branches to put on and around the truck to further hide it. Discovery by unwanted persons could mean they are alerted to our presence or that we could possibly lose our ride out. Either way, it's best the truck stays hidden.

Getting into a military compound is sometimes a piece of cake. Or it can be damn near impossible. I've read detailed reports in the past of attempts to infiltrate Cheyenne Mountain. The only successful attempts have been by going through the front gates, using Human/Social Engineering to bluff, bluster, and deception to get in. Sneaking in through other means, has always resulted in failures. Hopefully things will be different considering the circumstances.

We left the hidden truck and made our way through the woods, going up hill, working our way to a location where we could observe the main gate. I don't know what's there or not, but driving straight up to the front door and saying, "Hey Guys!" just felt like a bad idea. So we drove along back roads that didn't lead to the Cheyenne Mountain, instead heading along one that went past it. Past, so as to not be under observation, but close enough to make a run on foot. It seemed like the best plan.

The girls were doing very well, learning to walk quietly, learning to step carefully, to put the foot down softly and to roll the weight transfer from one to another. It's a chicken walk kind of motion. Funny to look at, but it works. The night was dark thanks to an overcast sky. No stars. No moon. Almost pitch blackness under the trees. Our NVGs were the only reason we were able to make any progress.

We had three miles to go. We could move quicker being farther out, but more cautiously as we closed in on the objective. An hour later we came to a path that was probably an overgrown utility line trail. I couldn't see any lines overhead. We cut up the trail a little and sure enough, we found a tower. Steel cables hung off it limp and powerless. I pulled out the GPS unit, and got down on the ground. I pulled my ghillie-cape's hood over my head and over the GPS. I turned the brightness down almost all the way to reduce any light emissions from under the hood. I found my location easily, found my truck's location and then followed the terrain features to the area where I wanted to go, but the map had zero detail for. I knew I was going in the right direction.

I turned the GPS off and waited for it to shut down completely before I lifted up off the ground again. Whispering, "We're going the right way... about a mile to go."

A hundred yards further I sensed movement so I signaled a freeze. The girls stopped, frozen in place, not moving, not making a sound. Up in the trees ahead, something was moving. Not wanting to give away our position, I slowly pulled out my suppressed pistol, the Glock again. I had switched back because I was just flat out disinterested in 9mm. The tritium glowed like a flare in the NVGs for a moment before the system adjusted. The shape in the trees moved towards a wider gap, and then I was able to make it out. A White Tail deer. A nice buck. Healthy looking. I stayed quiet and the deer kept walking past, taking its time. It stopped suddenly and sniffed the air, then looked around. It walked away quicker, going on its way feeling less at ease, but unable to locate any threats.

The girls and I were camo'ed up in some digital camo we got courtesy of the US Marines. I had my Ghillie Cape as well. I looked back at where they were. Even with the NVGs on, I couldn't see them until one of the girls smiled. Her teeth just appeared like the Cheshire Cat's grin out of nowhere. It was Jen. After a moment, her silhouette and that of the others became more apparent. "Deer," I whispered very quietly. Jen nodded. At least I was pretty sure it was Jen.

After a while we came to a slight rise and I dropped low. The glow of electric lights back lit the terrain. Crawling up to the crest, I moved very carefully and slowly peeked over the edge. There was the famous arched entrance to Cheyenne Mountain. Fences, Spotlights, and sandbagged emplacements. At the emplacements were some heavy weapons. A Carl Gustav at one, and a .50 cal at the two others flanking it.

Driving up would have been a huge mistake.

I pulled up my NVGs and used my Leupold Mojave binos. I love these things. People were sitting by the emplacements, a couple guys at the entrance. All armed with military weapons, but these guys were not military. Long hair on some, others were bald, facial hair. Black leather, brown leather... jackets, gloves, silver chains. Tats. Lack of discipline... smoking at guard posts... Occasional nips at hip flasks. A biker gang. I didn't care about which one. Doesn't matter. They should not be here. I counted heads. Nine of them. Three of us. A couple trucks were parked inside the fences, some bikes... all of them Harley's and custom choppers. I kept looking. Watching for patterns. This didn't seem right.

Then it hit me.

This was all fake. None of these guys were fat. None of these guys were even slightly over weight. No one had a finger on a trigger. I bet the flasks held water.

Shit. If these guys were acting...

I pulled back. "We've got to move."

I stowed the binos and pulled the NVGs back down. "What's wrong?" April asked in a hushed voice.

"Someone knows we're coming."

"Those bikers?"

"If those guys are bikers, then my name is Donald Duck. Come on."

Instead of going downhill and around the way most folks might go, we went uphill. Following deer trails. Heading into the secured zone instead of away. When we came to a fence line, we followed it until we found a spot where runoff washed out some of the earth from under it. A small crevasse that allowed us to shimmy under. Once through, we worked our way closer. A radio squelch caught my attention. A soft voice, hushed, then quick steps. A patrol. We got low and quiet. I used my Ghillie cape and the girls huddled behind me, half in a rut. A hand on my leg... it was trembling. I held it, squeezed it... after a moment the trembling stopped. The patrol was five guys and I watched them break cover heading to the fence, but then they cut the wrong way. They went down hill. They were looking for us, but missed where we came through.

I have to admit, even though they went the wrong way... they were good. They moved like ghosts. I stayed still for a moment longer then continued. I had an idea where I was going, but didn't know for sure, so I was hoping beyond hope I could find it.

Following a line of brush we moved up the mountain away from the patrol, heading in what I hoped was the right direction. There was a soft glow on the eastern horizon. Dawn was coming. Time was against us. If we didn't find it soon, they would find us.

Wait. I saw something. There. Concrete. Painted Concrete. Down hill, below us. It reminded me of a smaller version of the back door to the shield generator on the forest moon of Endor from *Star Wars*.

We moved very carefully to the small maintenance door. We could hear a thrumbing sound and I could smell exhaust. This was it. The facility was being run on generators, this entrance allowed access to the exhaust should it become obstructed or if they had to evacuate. Military base or not, OSHA requires these doors to be unlocked. From the inside. There was no handle on the outside... but there was a seam. Around the door were numerous cigarette butts. This was a good sign. In fact, this told me that it was very likely that any alarm on this door would have been bypassed for workers to step outside for a smoke without the bosses knowing.

"How did you know this was here?" April asked in a whisper, her lips almost brushing my ear.

"I read a lot of stuff I shouldn't." I whispered back. I pulled out my Becker Companion, a knife whose daddy was a crow bar. I was able to wedge the blade in, pry a little, and soon had the door open. The door was utilitarian steel, covered in cheap OD green paint. Up above the door on the inside, ran the wires for the alarm; they were bypassed with a quick disconnect so they could rearm the door alarm for inspections, and then disable it again at will.

Security always fails at the lowest levels. We went inside and closed the door behind us, quietly. We were in Cheyenne Mountain. We were in a small room that was lit only by the green glow of the "Emergency Exit" sign.

Still whispering, "I need to borrow something." I reached out to Joy's face, brushed a bit of hair off her face... she smiled softly... then I plucked a strand.

"Sorry, Love." I whispered. I took the strand and slipped it up into the top corner of the door so if it was opened, the hair would fall so I would know if anyone came through this door. Maybe this would give me a warning that this exit was compromised. Hopefully the current security would take it for granted that this hidden door was still hidden and that since the alarm didn't go off, it was never opened.

"Okay, let's find a place to hold up and rest for a bit." We went further in and found that this room we entered was a small chamber that was reached by a ladder. I looked straight down where the ladder disappeared into blackness even the NVGs couldn't penetrate.

"I don't want to go down there!" Jen was whispering, but she was genuinely frightened.

I turned to her. "Jen, you are going to be okay." I touched her face, then kissed her softly on the forehead. "I'll go first to make sure it's okay down there. Then you follow. I'll be there waiting for you."

"Okay. I just don't like the dark... like that."

"It is pretty creepy." Joy whispered.

"Yeah... reminds me of something." April was thinking out loud.

"The Mines of Moria." I whispered slowly... then shuddered as I started down the ladder.

"You know that didn't help me." Jen breathed. "Not at all."

The ladder was very long and I was getting tired by the time I reached the bottom. Climbing up it... just for a smoke break? No wonder that door was never inspected. Who would think anyone would do that? But then again, I have seen smokers standing outside in blizzards, shivering, just for a puff.

As I came out of the access tube, the ladder ended in a large room full of industrial supplies, lockers, tool chests, and clip boards hanging on the walls. One of the large generators was below us, and there were large fuel tanks full of diesel near by. I didn't know how those tanks were filled, but thick pipes went along the ceiling through the walls while smaller lines went down to the generator. A green light off in the distance indicated where the door was at. Beside the ladder was another green light with an arrow pointing up. Boots, legs, a nice bottom, an M4... came down out of the tube above me. It was Jen. "You're doing good, babe." I said quietly. She nodded as she looked around.

Joy came down next, then April.

"Let's ditch some of our gear here after we take a break." We were all very tired and as far as I knew, we were in no rush. Anyone looking for us would have to assume we were still outside somewhere, probably moving away.

We went around the fuel tanks and found a nice wide corner hidden from view. We pulled off our small day packs, set down our weapons, and leaned against the wall.

"I can't believe this." April whispered.

"What?"

"I'm in Cheyenne Mountain."

I almost laughed as I pulled off the NVGs and turned them off. The blackness was almost complete. "Why?"

"I love *Stargate*." April admitted.

"Really?"

"It's so cool."

"I didn't know you were a geek at heart."

I felt a light punch on my shoulder. I could hear moving as the girls got comfortable. April to my left, she stretched out. She always makes the same tiny little moan when she stretches out when she's tired. Jen was on the other side of her. Joy was on my right. It was from the right that I felt a body snuggle up against me, curling up almost into my lap. A hand on my leg. I held the hand and it felt the same as the one on the mountain side; it was Joy that had been frightened out there. She still was. I put my arm around her and held her, stroked her head. After a while, she relaxed.

An hour later, I woke up three sleeping beauties. "Come on girls. Time to go to work."

Joy was still half on my lap, and I don't know how she did it, but she twisted like a cat and kissed me on the lips before she stood up. That was nice.

I got up, feeling stiff from sitting on concrete floors, leaning on concrete walls. I put on the NVGs and got back into the game. We stashed our packs and my ghillie cape in the lockers.

At the door, I could hear no sounds from the outside, so I pushed the door handle down slowly, then pulled it open just a hair at a time. Bright white light flared my NVGs, making me blink. I pushed them up onto my head and let my eyes adjust before I moved the door anymore. A hallway. A long hallway. Doors at different intervals. I opened the door enough that I could peek down the other direction. Same thing. Above the doors were brass number plates, but no indication what the doors led to. It was quiet in the hallway. No movement. The floor was industrial type flooring, not tile, large squares. A darker shade of grey than the light grey on the walls. Fluorescent lighting was above. Between the doors the walls had stupid motivational posters or cheap prints of landscapes. This could be in almost any building.

I led the way out, took a right, and then glanced at the door I'd just exited from. 881. No other information. I walked past a number of doors, crossed the hall to 874 and stopped. I listened. *What the hell?* Inside was an office with filing cabinets, a desk, computer. Papers on the desk were some personnel files, work assignments, employee assessments, new employee manual for HVAC technicians. Manuals. And maps showing where critical HVAC junctions were. But also it showed the layout of the place. With descriptions to go with the numbers.

Outside the room, we heard foot steps and voices. We held our breaths and didn't even dare blink. The sounds went past the door and down the hall. The voices were talking casually, but under the casual tone, a clinking sound. Weapons over other tactical gear. Security of some sort. How often they patrolled, I didn't know. But if it was regular it would be avoidable.

I looked at the maps. What the hell was I here for? What do I need to find? I studied the map carefully.

There.

A room marked "Facility Security". The room wasn't too far, considering. Through a few corridors and cut through a commons area – piece of cake. Especially since we knew where we were going which was a 100% improvement of our circumstances.

"Come on."

We carefully made our way through the corridor, moving quickly, but as quietly as possible. The M1A Sage with an AAC suppressor was not a light gun to carry, but the benefit of it became apparent when just as we reached the door at the end of the hall, it opened. A wiry man with a leather biker jacket and an MP5SD came through. His eyes were down, looking at his iPod Touch. He looked up, startled. I used to play baseball a lot. One of my favorite things was an unexpected bunt. I did that with the rifle, holding both ends, I used the side of the rifle to bunt the guy. He had Picatinny marks across his face where his nose was and his eyes rolled back in his head as he fell.

I grabbed his feet and pulled him back into the hallway and into a small office. Computer cables made up for a lack of rope and while not ideal, served to make for a good hog-tie. He would eventually wake up and work his way out, but we would be long gone. Hopefully.

We were about to go to the door when we heard voices. I looked through the door and saw it. The guy's iPod was on the ground.

Quicker than I have seen anyone move, Joy darted out, snagged the iPod and dove back into the room. I shut the door just as the other door opened. The voices passed. They were talking about making people disappear in Vermont, New Hampshire and New York. Survivalists and Gun Owners. These guys laughed about it. "Crazy wackos." One of the guys spat.

"Worse than the zeds."

After a few moments, we moved out again in a single file. Cheyenne Mountain is a lot bigger than people think. We crossed the commons area that had benches and tables throughout the room. Piled in the center of the room were bodies. Zombies and victims of their hunger and rage. Limbs pulled apart, zombie heads blown open, blood splatters and drag marks. The place stank enough to make us gag. Across the commons area, we came to the security office.

We crouched at the door, got tensed up, and made a dynamic entry into the empty room. No one was here. The room had monitors, computers, and checklists on clipboards. The monitors showed views of the outside and other of rooms inside the facility.

"Shit."

"What's wrong?" April leaned in to see what I was looking at.

"That." I pointed.

"Shit!"

The monitor showing us the view of the main gate gave us a clear picture of a Humvee pulling a truck in tow. My truck. Armed men were around. One of the guys, you could make out that he was issuing orders, pointing and gesturing. Then other men ran off with their weapons in their hands. None of them ran into the facility, so they don't know that we are in here. That's good for now. It's going to be trouble when we go to leave.

I looked at the other monitors. Several were set to switch views every few seconds so I almost missed it when I glanced up at one just a split second before it switched. A man sitting in the corner of a room.

"Wait, what was that?"

We watched. A room full of crates. What is it – Military Installations and crates?

A room set up like an operating room.

A room full of people standing. What?

A morgue.

A laboratory.

A man sitting in the corner.

"Where is that at?" Joy asked.

"Let's see..." I checked the camera number against a list, and the list against my little floor plan.

"Got it. Come on."

"Wait a second... I can't leave this." Anyone that came in here would be able to use this system to find us. I used my suppressed pistol to put out the monitors. One round each. "Now we can go."

We worked our way through a maze of hallways and came to a door that was locked. A security panel beside the door was lit with a blue back light.

"Please Swipe Card."

I have a card. The woman from the plane crash. Her card was in a cargo pocket and I fished around for it. Ah... I swiped the card.

"Password."

On the back of the card the woman had written "I'm late, I'm late."

On the keypad I typed, "RABBIT."

The door opened and we went through. Medical type rooms like what you would find in any normal hospital. It looked like no one had been in here in a while. I doubted the men running around had access to this part of the facility. "Spread out and look for anything interesting."

April gave me a "Are you serious?" look.

A few minutes later, "Check this out." Jen found something. We went in the room Jen had found. It was an observation room, looking into another room, which probably had a two-way mirror in it. There was a man sitting in the corner. He wore slacks and had on a white jacket. His head was down. His hair was matted and unkempt.

Under the observation window was an intercom system. I pushed the button. "Hello."

The man jerked in surprise then slowly stood up. When he finally looked up at the two-way mirror, we instantly knew there was something going on here. The man's eyes were blood red and he was inhumanly gaunt. Skeletal. Joy pulled her rifle up, ready for anything.

"Where is Doctor Sandberg?" The Red Eye said with a hiss.

"He's no longer here. Who are you?"

The Red Eye tilted his head. "If Doctor Sandberg isn't here then who are you?"

"I asked first, buddy."

The Red Eye looked around the room, then it seemed as if he looked at each of us through the two way. "I am Christian."

The way the Red Eye stood there was creepy. His body was completely still save for his head.

"Why are you in this room, Christian?"

"For Science." He hissed the word, stringing out the sound.

"Can you explain that for me? What's going on?"

"They wanted to know why... Why I am still... cognitive." Christian held up his arm to the glass and pulled the sleeve back. There was a chunk of his forearm that had been bitten out. The wound was blackened and rotted like spoiled meat. "I didn't turn like others."

Christian explained that they got information from agents inside China on biological research. Samples were smuggled out and sent to the CIA. China was working on something and the CIA wanted to know what it was.

Christian was working on other research. He was a doctor conducting AIDS research. Something happened in the laboratory. Contamination. Infection. Panic. During the panic, one of the infected jumped on Christian's co-worker and he fought him. Christian was bitten. But Christian didn't turn... not for days... then he turned differently.

"AZT." He said. Christian was on AZT. He had HIV. The disease he was researching. They thought that the AZT in his blood helped prevent his turning. Christian however, didn't think that was the case.

"I stopped AZT a year ago." He said.

"So what other drugs are you on?"

"You are not doctor. They already ask all questions... check their work."

"So what do you think kept you from changing like others that got bitten?"

"I prayed."

Huh? Faith? That took me by surprise.

"... to the Dark One."

"You prayed to Satan?"

"Lucifer came to me. Called me brother. Said he would save me if I promised him."

"Promised you what?"

"To give my soul to him... to spread his work." Christian was getting agitated.

"What's his work?"

"Infection."

Okay, that was drastically uncool. Jen grabbed my arm. "I don't like this."

Christian stepped to the glass, pressing his head against it. "OOOohhh.... I can smell you.... girls... GIRLS! Ssweeeet fleeesh!"

"Christian, you need to be nice." I said. I wasn't going to put up with anymore of that.

On the other side of the glass, Christian moaned and whimpered. "Sooo hungry... please."

"Please what?"

"Let me have girl!"

"Which girl?"

"You are not even funny." Jen said.

"I want this one." He pointed right at April, "She's Sssspecial..."

"Fuck yourself." April gave the Red Eye the middle finger.

Christian smiled, his dried lips pulled back from his teeth, enhancing his skeletal appearance. "Sssssooo sweet... Let me have this girl!" He yelled.

"No." I started to feel very uneasy.

"LET ME HAVE GIRL!" The ferocity Christian displayed took me by surprise. He started banging the glass. "MY GIRL!"

Suddenly Christian laughed and raised his hands up. April started choking. "MINE!" Christian roared. The glass started cracking and April was pulled against it by an invisible force. She tried to scream, but couldn't. The other girls however, had full capacity to do so and did. Christian's eyes were glowing now.

"She is mine!" He said in a voice that was completely different than before, with no hissing, just a clear deep voice.

Christian put his hand out to me and simply opened his palm. It felt like I was hit by an NFL linebacker. I was thrown back across the room, hitting the wall halfway up. When I picked myself up off the ground, Christian was laughing in a deep booming voice.

That's it. I pulled my Sage rifle up and fired one single round. The bullet smashed through the glass, through Christian's head, and splattered the room with blackened blood and brain matter. Christian fell backwards, twitching. The force that had held April against the glass released her and she fell to the ground.

"April!"

She was shaking and taking in air with big gulps... then she reached out and grabbed my shirt and pulled me close. "Shoot." She gasped, "Sooner."

I held her for a while. "You okay?" I asked her.

"No... I'm not."

"Me neither." I said.

"What the hell was that?" Jen asked.

"Some sort of super zombie?" Joy asked.

I shook my head. "No... this was different." Inside, I felt sick. Being in the presence of this Red Eye was different than Nathan or Johnny, the other Red Eyes I had encountered. This one was older... had been a Red Eye longer. Maybe that had something to do with it. Or maybe not.

"Come on... Let's get out of here."

We went out of the room. The girls were quiet. We went into the lab area. "What was the name of the doctor he said?" Joy asked.

"Sandberg."

Joy pointed. A small office with "Dr. Sandberg" on the door. Inside we found a laptop amongst other things. The battery was dead and it wouldn't turn on. I flipped the computer over and used my knife to break the plastic that held the screws to the hard drive cover, then pulled out the hard drive.

"Why didn't you just take the whole Laptop?" April asked.

"I don't like Macs."

"What, you don't like the best computers?" Joy asked.

I looked at her. "They are only the best if you put Linux on them."

We walked past other observation rooms, the people inside were in various states of dismemberment. Some were zombies. One particular zombie was crouching just below the glass. The thing was chewing on something. I looked down at it and saw that it had a wide gash across its mid section. Entrails had fallen out and the zombie was chewing on them, slowly, methodically. Its white eyes stared into the mirror as it reached down and pulled up another loop of intestine to eat.

We moved on. In the next room was a group of about twenty zombies all standing shoulder to shoulder facing the far wall, as close to the wall as possible. Blood, tissue, fecal matter, different body parts, and mutilated bodies were strewn out across the rest of the room. I indicated that it was time to go. We almost reached the security door when three armed men suddenly came through with their weapons already up and trained on us. One of the men had railroad track marks across his face. He grinned. "Drop your weapons or I drop you."

We complied, slowly setting our guns down. Once down two of the men came over and kicked the guns aside. They stripped the girls of their side arms. "Look at these bitches. I know someone who would love them." One of the guys said. The tracked face guy came up to me and punched me in the face. I fell back and down. He picked me back up. The guy was strong.

"Who the hell do you think you are?" The guy unzipped my tactical vest and pulled it off me, patting me down for more weapons. The other guys were doing the same to the girls but taking their time with the patting down.

"Nice titties... maybe I'll keep this one." He was groping Jen then suddenly gave her an elbow smash to the forehead that knocked her out. They put April and Joy into flex cuffs.

The two guys started dragging Joy and April down the hallway. "Throw them in room 7 with the crowd." One guy said, then the other said "You bring your camera with you again?" The girls screamed and kicked as they were being dragged back down the hall.

"I'm going to mess you up good." The tracked guy said, cocking his arm back to hit me again.

I reached up under my shirt and grabbed the handle of my Becker Necker knife that I worn under my clothes. As his arm started coming forward I twisted and got out of the way of the incoming fist. When his fist hit the wall, I started working his torso with the knife. Fast stabs as hard as I could. He staggered backward and I swung higher. The short knife intersected the guy's throat and he fell. He was kicking and choking as he was grabbing his neck. I've seen this dance before. I picked up the guy's MP5SD. Jen had his old one, he must have gotten a new one. Since he had a back-up now, and a new weapon, everyone was probably searching for us.

I checked the weapon as I ran down the hallway. The girls were still screaming when I came around the corner. April saw me first and she just went limp, sudden dead weight. The man pulling her turned as I opened up. I gave him half a magazine in one long continuous stream.

The other large guy dropped Joy and started pulling up his weapon. My rounds reached him first, stitching him from heart to head. I dropped the empty HK and ran to the girls. Using my neck knife I cut the flex cuffs and set the girls loose.

"We've got to get out of here. They know we're inside."

Joy started kicking the dead goons, cussing them, kicking them more.

"Joy! Come on!" She was pissed and her eyes showed just how much. We picked our gear up and Jen ... Jen was stunned and bleary. I rubbed her head, feeling for any serious damage. "You with me, Jen."

Her eyes came into focus finally. She smiled painfully "Always with you."

"That's my girl." I helped her up.

We moved quickly, but quietly, keeping our weapons up and ready. We went back through the complex into the commons room. From up ahead we could hear shouting and the stomping of running feet getting louder. We took cover behind the piles of dead bodies, laying in the gore and stink. When the men passed through and went out the door we just came through, we jumped up and ran.

In the corridor of doors just past the maintenance office, two guys were coming our way. I emptied my .308's magazine as we ran, cutting them down. We ran past them, not stopping. I reloaded on the fly.

Door 881. We went through, into the dark room. I didn't bother with the NVGs and just hit the lights. We ran to the lockers and got our packs. Jen was the first up the ladder. Joy was right behind her. I was still putting the Ghillie Cape on as April started up the ladder, leaving me in the room alone. I was about to start up, when I had an idea. I fired rounds into the generator's fuel tanks and lines. Diesel fuel began pouring out across the floor from the tank and spraying out under pressure from the lines.

I climbed up the ladder far enough that everything was getting dark, but not so far that I couldn't hear the spraying fuel which was all over the floor by now. When the door to 881 burst open and men rushed in, I could hear the swearing and could feel the anger in their voices.

I expected any second for someone at the base of the ladder to start spraying bullets up the tube. I pulled something out of my pocket. My favorite trusty old Zippo Lighter. I kissed the metal case and flicked it open. The warm flame illuminated the tube and I could see concrete wall and a steel ladder.

"Burn, baby, burn."

I dropped the lighter and watched the light flicker as it fell, but it didn't go out. One of the reasons I always loved the little classic Zippo. I heard it hit the ground and saw it bounce out of view. Come on.

"HEY! Look out!" Someone yelled. Then I heard screaming and cussing as the flames spread from the Zippo.

I hurried up the ladder. I had forgotten how long the ladder was. I was exhausted when I finally reached the top. My legs were burning with exertion and from the heat coming up the tube. It was getting hard to breath, and was very dark, but for a soft, orange glow from below and the green from the exit sign. We didn't have much time. I went to the door and drew my pistol. The MX6 pistol light I had attached to it was painfully bright, but I could see that the dark hair I plucked from Joy had not fallen. So it should be relatively safe to open the door. But right about now, word had spread to those outside and the guys near the front and the patrols outside would be working their way here.

I stowed the pistol and got my rifle ready. I pushed the door open slightly. It was bright out. That can't be helped. I opened the door more and looked around. No shots, no instant death, no shouting. "Come on. We're going up."

"More up? My thighs are on fire!" Jen protested.

"It's good for you... tone up those legs and that round butt." What I didn't want to say was that I was even more tired than they were and my legs felt like they would give out any minute.

We moved through the brush going for the densest cover I could find. Working our way away from the direction we had come. It wasn't long until we heard banging on the door we had just left. Then gunshots. They were shooting through the door. More shouting. "They're not here!"

Any fatigue I felt was gone now. We made it up to where the treeline ended. From here and above it was rocks where ice and snow scraped the foliage from the mountain every winter. Right now it was just bare rock.

Suddenly there was the hypersonic crack of a rifle bullet going overhead. We dropped and scrambled for cover. Was that a wild shot or was it aimed? Another bullet ricocheted off a rock, close by. My M1A Sage came to my shoulder without thinking. The ACOG's magnification gave me an edge. I saw a couple men climbing up below us. One man was armed with a short barreled M4 type carbine. The other man had a scoped rifle. He was the priority target. He was looking down at his footing. He was about 400 yards but shooting down hill I held on 300 and put some pressure on the trigger. The man looked up as I let the gun buck. My round crashed through his scope, shattering the objective lens, taking the gun out of the fight. My next round took the man out as well. He slumped and rolled backwards down the slope. I quickly turned to the man with the M4, who was going for some cover. I put the sights on him and fired. My round hit him low center mass and he crumpled up, dropping his rifle.

We stayed in the treeline and worked our way westward.

"This would have been a lot easier if we had a ride out of here."

"Maybe if your truck wasn't silver."

I looked back the girls, initially angry. I looked in their faces and suddenly I wasn't angry anymore. I saw young women there. I saw fatigue, fear, and pain. I stopped.

"I'm sorry girls. We've got a ways to go, but we'll get out of this. We just need to be not here."

I looked down the mountain again. Through the trees, I could see movement. Lots of armed men. These guys were like a pack of wolves. I pulled up my rifle again and took a position where I had a good rest. "Take cover... this is going to get nasty." I pulled my hood up and let the cape fall out of the roll. "Get down real low."

I let the rifle do some more work. Four more of our pursuers fell. Rounds came back in our direction, but it was ineffective fire. They didn't quite know where we were exactly. This was an advantage.

I saw one guy with an ACOG on his rifle and he was scanning an area that we had just come from. *WHAM* My bullet blew a chunk out of the back of his head and he collapsed. Another man went to the one that just fell. WHAM! The shot went through his vest and he dropped as well.

April had wormed her way near me and had her SCAR at the ready. She crawled half under my cape and used it as shadow to hide in. Her gun barked three times. Through my ACOG I saw a man fall.

That's when I heard an aircraft. I looked up and saw an ugly aircraft circle over the main entrance. It was an Osprey. "Oh crap." With aircraft looking for us, we would be as good as cooked now. The Osprey's engine nacelles rotated up and the bird came in low over the vehicles. Suddenly machinegun fire opened up. Guys on the ground fired up at the strange aircraft. The aircraft lurched away from the threat and turned around, avoiding fire. Then a gunner in the back opened up with a Dillon mini-gun. We watched as a line of fire reached out and touched the emplacements.

What the hell? Who was this?

The men pursuing us were distracted and we took the chance to break our position and move. "Come on!" I picked myself up and we sprinted along the tree line. Moments late the shadow of a V-22 passed over us. The gunner in the back worked the Gatling back and forth, sending a stream of tracers over our heads into the trees below us. I looked back and saw that we were no longer being chased.

The V-22 circled around and put its cargo ramp back to the slope and hovered there. The door gunner was waving at us. Fist pumping the "Double Time" signal. We ran to the bird and climbed in, breathless. We were all on board and the gunner was searching for more targets.

As smooth as silk, the mountain fell away from us. I looked around inside the aircraft, not recognizing anyone. A guy in a flight suit and tac vest moved through the aircraft to us. His crew helmet's visor covered his face. The man pulled the visor up.

The aircraft was loud so the man was almost yelling. "You must be the Ogre! What made you think you guys could get into Cheyenne Mountain?"

I laughed. "We were in Cheyenne Mountain. Got what we wanted. Got out. What makes you think I couldn't get in?"

"No way." The Marine laughed. "No fucking way."

"He's pretty good." Joy said.

I held up the hard drive.

"What's that?" The Marine asked.

"That's part of a Mac." Jen said.

"He hates Macs." April said.

I put the HD back in my pocket. "I got what I wanted."

The Marine shook his head and leaned back. "How?"

"Can't tell you Jarheads all my secrets."

"So what's on that thing?"

"I don't know yet, but I have an idea."

The Marine in the flight crew helmet held out his hand. "By the way, Ogre.. I'm Louis Q. Pleased to finally meet you!"

"Q?" I laughed.

"Yeah, took some time to find you. I didn't expect it would be on Cheyenne Mountain though!"

"Well that puts us even. I didn't expect you in a Tilt-Rotor."

Q laughed then reached into his flight suit. "I'm supposed to give you this. This is coming from the brass at Fort Bragg and Fort Benning... couple other Forts. I don't know. They seemed to think it was really important to give it to you personally."

"What is it?"

"Hell if I know, man. I just said I'd give it to you, not that I'd read it."

"Bullshit."

"If I knew what it was, I'd tell you. They told me there were no pictures of naked ladies, so I didn't bother looking."

I chuckled and started to open the packet. Q lunged over and grabbed my arm. "Not here... Not now ... Wait until your alone. Keep it secret. Keep it safe."

I don't know what, maybe it was because it was the second time *Lord of the Rings* came up, but I took it as a sign. "You're probably right." I tucked the packet inside my tactical vest and patted it.

Q nodded and sat back and closed his eyes for a moment before he turned to me. "So you really nuked Salt Lake City?"

I shook my head. "What do you think?"

Q grinned.

ELEVEN

Information Overload

*B*ack at Ogre Ranch I plugged the hard drive into a USB adapter, then plugged the USB into Hordecaster, my laptop. Windows didn't recognize the drive, said it was unformatted. I rebooted into Linux.

"Ah, there it is."

Files of all sorts; folders of different projects; E-Books, pictures, music from Conway Twitty and Barbara Streisand. I filtered the files by name and scrolled through.

There was a folder for "Project Fire Eye". I clicked on the folder. It took a few moments to open it up.

"Crap."

There were more documents in here than pages in the Obama Health Care Bill. Debbie came up to me and looked over my shoulder. "What's wrong?"

"Information overload."

"How much of it?"

I looked at the size of the folder and contents. "Thirty two gigs worth of documents."

"That's a lot."

"That's information overload."

"Good thing you like reading."

"We're going to need to divide this up. I can't read all of this alone, not and finish it any time soon. I need thumb drives, a bunch of them."

I passed out 25 thumb drives to everyone in the pub, save for Uncle Musket, who is not allowed near a computer. I gave him one for Christmas one year, a nice laptop. He used the screen as a picture frame. I know he posted on *WeTheArmed*, but I just wanted to know who did it for him, typing out what he ranted while dosed on Guinness.

"Each thumb drive has roughly an equal amount of documents on them. Read them all, take notes, be prepared to give a briefing on what was read to everyone, 24 hours from now."

Everyone groaned.

"Oh, I'm sorry to have given you such an inconvenience. You should have seen what we went through to get this information."

The Bronze held his hand up, "How many Bothans died?"

"All of them."

The next day, everyone was back in the Pub at the appointed time. The twenty five readers plus myself had a long and quiet day full of reading. The briefing went on for hours as everyone summarized their reading assignments. Medical reports, intelligence reports, autopsy reports and clinical trial reports. All the medical information came from doctors that all seemed to be working for Dr. Sandberg. Sandberg was the leading man in charge of not just the CDC, but also the head of the NSA's Hostile Disease Program. He reported to the POTUS directly from what some of the notes indicated. What we learned, first and foremost, was that the US became aware that the Chinese were working on a medical program that would allow wounded soldiers to continue to fight even after being seriously or even mortally wounded. The US started our own program, duplicating Chinese research that we got through the use of human intelligence, namely a Chinese-born American operative that was inserted into Beijing before she made it to the mainland and became a mistress to a high-ranking Chinese official who ran his mouth. The program was a failure for its purpose, but as a bio-weapon, showed startling promise.

The zombie plague is a four-way infection transmitted by blood and saliva. The Z-Plague consisted of four pathogens: one virus and three bacteria strains. What the readers had gathered is that one of the bacteria strains gives off oxygen as a byproduct, a massive amount of oxygen. This strain is a flesh eater which is why shortly after a victim is bitten, they start to get a cadaverous appearance. Another strain produces carbohydrates/sugars in large quantities, but it reproduces slower. This feeds the flesh eater bacteria once its population density reaches a high enough level and the other strains learn to live off the sugars. The zombie body can as a result live for an extended period of time without any food ingestion – 8 months to a year. The third strain's purpose is unclear at this time. Speculation has it that it produces neurotoxins that dull pain receptors, but testing has proven to be inconclusive. All three strains are completely resistant to all forms of antibiotics. The virus attacks nerve tissues, CNS and brain, taking over functions, and essentially burning out and rewiring certain portions of the brain. It tends to leave one part of the brain alone, the Medulla Oblongata. The rest of the brain seems to be cannibalized by the bacterial strains.

The results of the bacterial infections are the hyper oxygenation/profusion of tissues. This is why a zombie can keep going even after the heart is destroyed. However, the zombie will eventually die without a heart, but it takes much longer for that to happen. The clouding of the eyes is actually the bacterial infection coating the inner surface of the eye's lens and ocular jelly. In spite of this "milk-like" appearance, the eyes still function, but at a reduced capacity due to a lesser amount of light transferred through the eye to the rods and cones. This clouding effect happens quickly as the bacteria growth accelerates. These bacteria multiply five to eight times faster than all previous known bacterial strains.

The infection causes severe bleeding of stomach lining and esophagus, uncontrollable fever, and apparent death within hours. Due to the nature of the infection's damage to brain tissues, no "cure" is possible. MRI and CAT scans of the brain on test subjects show that the brain is attacked almost immediately after being bitten. If something could be found to treat an infection to stop it, it would be useless/pointless after 1.5 hours.

If any cure is found, which is probable given enough time, it could be administered in the first hour, the contagion could possibly be stopped. Fire Eye subjects contain all four infections that form the Z-Plague, but the bacterial infections are muted/subdued and do not seem to spread through the body tissues like in other subjects, they tend to grow in the mouth/saliva at a greater density, causing a more rapid infection from a bite. The virus strain is unimpeded and multiplies at the normal zombie virus rate, but takes greater hold, growing tendrils that spread throughout the host body until it in effect, rewires the entire body's CNS.

Fire Eye subjects seem to have influence over the more common zombie through sub-harmonic frequencies or pheromones. This is still being researched by Doctor Nathaniel Christian.

Intelligence shows that the Chinese attempted several Weaponized Infection Trials in Africa. In parts of Zimbabwe, Darfur, Swaziland, and in the Congo. Further testing was also done in western regions of China, but exact locations are not specified.

Western attack plan involved agents of China with a history of diabetes who were given tainted doses of insulin. They were unknowing "Typhoid Mary's". These agents were then put onto flights to all major western cities. Most agents landed in their target cities before self injecting the insulin/contagion. One of the agents landing in California self administered her dose halfway through the flight.

The rest is, as they say, history. The most disturbing footnote was a single comment. "The Chinese beat us to the trigger."

Death from Above

*A*fter the Briefings ended everyone filtered out of the Pub. Sarge was just about to leave. "Neil, you got a second?"

"Every time you say that, Ogre, I end up spending some quality time with the 19th."

I chuckled, "Not this time. I just wanted to tell you thanks. You've spent some time with Stacy, and I've already seen that it's made a difference in her. I just want you to keep that up. It's also doing some good for you too."

"I..." Neil was just about to say something when we heard shouting. We looked at each other and ran outside. We saw people pointing and looked in that direction. Up in the evening sky to the north we saw a fireball. I looked at the Patriot Missile launcher on the nearby plateau, it was missing one of the weapons. A streak of smoke reached out to the fireball.

"What the?" Another Patriot leapt off its rails like a bullet. Then another. "GET ME HILL AIR FORCE BASE!" I shouted to a soldier who dashed off like one of the Patriots.

Missiles from the other launchers tracked then fired.

"GET TO COVER!" I shouted to everyone at the top of my lungs. I ran for the Coms tent. Up in the sky something black was getting larger.

I was just about to hit the deck when something smashed into me, driving me to the ground. "Stay Down!" It was April. The dark object flashed passed us going overhead. We heard a big THUD sound and nothing else.

A soldier ran up with a sat-phone. "I've got Hill on the line!" I snatched the phone.

"Hello! Who is this?"

"This is Major Wilkins, USAF. What's going on?"

"We are under an air attack. I need some fighter cover NOW!"

"Yes, sir! Scrambling now!"

The attack was over as soon as it started. The Air Defense system worked perfectly. "Ogre, look!" Neil pointed.

I followed Sarge's direction and pulled up my binos. A grey canopy floated down slowly. "A chute." How in the hell did he spot that? It's almost invisible.

Sarge picked up his rifle, "I'll go get him."

"No. Sorry, Neil." I looked over at my younger brother, Musket. The fury I saw in him was seething and about to burst. His teeth were clenched tight. "Musket!" He was staring at the chute, breathing hard, like a bull about to charge. "Musket!" I snapped again and his eyes darted to mine.

"Bring him here."

274

"AYE!" Musket pulled a giant flint lock from his belt, and his tomahawk, then bolted forward running in long loping strides that soon had him disappearing across the field and into the foothills of the Uintah Mountains.

The soldier who brought me the sat-phone caught some of my own rage.

Get those Patriot launchers reloaded and rearmed. And get Major Wilkins back on the line and ask him for his excuse why we didn't have a CAP up there and why he let an attack through. I want his report in writing. No, I don't want to talk to him."

"Yes, sir!"

"I want it yesterday, Lieutenant. Or should I call you Specialist?"

The soldier bristled, gritted his teeth, and ran for the coms tent while dialing the sat-phone. I looked back up into the sky. The dark streak that went by. It was there... and went. I took off in a run. In the school yard I found it. It was embedded nose deep into the wall, having slid fifty yards across the playground. The body of the bomb was fat, bloated with large stabilizing fins. The sides of the body were large panels.

I jumped back and pulled April away, who was bending over to get a better look.

"Evacuate the school, take all the kids and get them over behind the church. Take them out the front of the school."

"What is that?"

"It's a cluster bomb. This thing was supposed to have flown over us and opened up like a busted pinata and rained bomblets on us... but it didn't open. Which means it could have a hundred bomblets inside armed and ready to explode."

We backed away and April ran around to the doors and started the evacuation. Musashi and Khorne came up behind me. "Is that?" Khorne said in shock... not that he didn't know what it was, but that it was here.

"Yes it is."

"Who did this?" Musashi asked, quietly.

"I don't know. But we are going to find out. There was a parachute. One of the aircraft that were going to drop these... I think those Patriots got them all, but one let this loose. Musket is on the way to find the guy. I looked over and saw school children being led in groups by April, other teachers, and Debbie.

A few moments later I got the count, everyone was accounted for and no one was injured. We were extraordinarily lucky.

"Josh, make sure no one goes near this thing – and I don't want either of you within the blast radius."

"How big is the blast radius."

"Dude, your talking to Light Fighter here. You guys are the Arty Twins... you know more about this than I do."

"Where are you going?"

"To call Nightcrawler. We need EOD here."

"Doesn't the Sheriff's Department have a bomb guy?"

"Yeah, but this ain't a pipe bomb. This needs an expert."

Five minutes later I hung up the phone with Mike. He was on his way with his team. I didn't know how long they would be, but it couldn't be fast enough. If they drove, maybe 4 hours.

To get my mind off of what just could have happened I pulled out the packet Q had given me on the V-22.

The packet was thick. Inside was a sheaf of documents, photos, statistics, and more importantly authorization codes. Not just any authorization codes... all of them. Including "The Codes."

Holy shit... I've got "The Biscuit".

The Generals at Hood, Bragg, Benning and Riley just gave me the ultimate trust. And if I have this now... that means there is no President.

My breathing became short and labored. "Oh hell."

I didn't even notice that The Girl Squad had taken up a defensive posture in the front yard. I put my head in my hands and couldn't stop trembling. If I had the Biscuit, there was a whole mess of implications to go along with it. It also raised a serious question that I needed answers for. Where was "The Football?"

I started going through the documents. Just before Air Force One went down, the last message was that the crew had become infected. And unlike in the Harrison Ford or Snake Pliskin movie, there was no escape pod. The aircraft went off radar some place near Seattle, Washington, the POTUS's home town. No units had been able to make it there. Closer units didn't even know it was there.

Other information in the packet included intel about what was going on in New England. Surviving registered gun owners, retired police officers and discharged Veterans were disappearing, one by one. They have information that one person is behind this, someone that wants to seize power. The former head of FEMA. Charles Bowdren. There was a photo, complete bio and FBI files. It looked like Charles had been very busy.

I looked at the photo carefully. What I was looking at was the face of a lunatic. This guy had to be stopped as soon as possible.

Khorne came up to me and the girls let him through without question, just a nod. I looked up at him and asked him directly. "Bro, how would you like to go Seattle?"

Two things happened at the same time. Musket had a prisoner. I watched as he marched the man across the alfalfa field that had become our air field. The man's arms were tightly bound behind his back with multiple coils of 550 cord that went all around his torso. A line went from the man's bindings like a leash to Musket's thick hands.

The other thing that happened was a sleek Eurocopter Dauphin streaked in with its high-pitched whine. Like a wasp, the Dauphin buzzed around, looking for a place to sit down. Apaches, Blackhawks, Osprey, Little Birds, and a small trainer were all scattered around the field. It was getting crowded. It finally selected its spot and set down delicately and precisely. The three men that climbed out were completely decked out in combat gear. One was packing an M-249 SAW, one an M4 with a long suppressor, the tallest one was packing a Crusader Broadsword in his hands and he had a large revolver on his hip. All wore sunglasses and they walked in the classic "Cool Guy" walk as they approached, looking like a rock video. The Air Force EOD had landed.

"We could have been here a lot sooner if you had an actual runway here."

"Better late than tomorrow." I shook hands, and threw a hug to Nightcrawler. "Koop, it's good you're here. Tony, Andy... welcome back brothers. I have something special that got dropped off for you."

"That's what we came for. Show us."

"Absolutely, just a second." Musket had reached us. "You found him... and he's still alive."

"Aye, if I done worse I'd have had to carry this sorry blighter all the way back here. I found him hiding under a bush like a frightened rabbit. I found him by the stench of his cowardice; it was enough to make me choke."

I looked at the pilot. I was expecting Canadian patches. The fact that I was looking at an American filled me with anger. "Take him to the wood pile and tie him down to the weight bench."

Our weight bench was right by the wood pile. Chopping wood was a work out like lifting was. So it made sense to put them together. "I'll be there shortly."

"Right."

I led the EOD guys over to the package. We stood by the yellow "Do Not Cross" tape. "That thing flew right over my head. I was standing outside of Musket's Pub and that thing went right over."

Andy looked bored and puffed on his coffin nail. Tony tilted his head and raised an eyebrow over the frame of his sunglasses. Nightcrawler just took a deep breath and ducked under the tape. "You guys stay here for a sec."

He walked over and looked at the bomb. "Hey, Tony. Look at this." Tony and Andy walked over. Mike pointed and Tony knelt down. "Cluster Bomb. Big one. US."

"We could pull it out, take it to a safe location and detonate it."

"Or we could blow it in place. That's the safest bet."

"We can't blow it, it would take out the school."

"Only half of the school; they can rebuild it."

"Ogre could have blown it in place if he wanted to rebuild a freaking school."

"Better to rebuild a school than to get my ass blown up."

The knife hand came out, and Mike pulled it out with authority. "You lock it up, that's your job. Ogre called us to do our job."

"No, YOU lock it up – my job isn't to die!"

"It is, if I tell you it is! I outrank you!"

"You want to die so bad?" Tony swung his leg back, "FINE!" Then kicked the bomb with his boot.

I about had a heart attack as I threw myself to the ground for cover.

There was no great earth shattering kaboom. Instead of being ripped open by shrapnel and hearing the echoing thunder of the explosion, I heard laughter. I looked up. Tony was on the ground, laughing. Mike was bent over. Andy was laughing so hard his cigarette fell off his lip.

"You bastards!"

That sent them into an even more powerful laughing fit. After a while, I picked myself back up, and they explained. "The safety pins were not removed. That's why the bomb didn't open up to disperse the bomblets."

I was alive, because someone was stupid. "This couldn't have gone off unless you packed C-4 around it."

That pain between my eyes again... I rubbed the bridge of my nose. "Just get rid of it, please?"

I shook my head, "I gotta deal with the bastard that dropped it."

Mike grabbed my arm and looked me in the eyes, "I know you're pissed... rightfully so... but the guy is an American. Remember that."

"I know, Mike. That's what is making this hard."

He nodded and I walked back to the wood pile.

Musket was standing there, arms folded, with a deep scowl on his face. The pilot was tied to the weight bench, face up, with his head hanging off over a basket. The man was fearful. Good.

"So tell me..." I said casually as I picked a towel from one of the Wenches that was clinging to Musket. "Where are you from?"

"Piss on you!" The pilot spat. "What are you going to do, water board me?"

I tied the towel around one of his legs, just below the knee. "Nope. I was just making conversation to be polite. I don't care who you are."

I put a thick little stick under the towel and twisted it, tightening the towel up and cutting off circulation to the leg. "You tried to kill us."

I looked over to the Wench. "Bring me three more rags, Love. I need them for the other limbs."

"What?" The pilot seemed confused, in a quiet panic, and in pain. "What are you going to do?"

I picked up my favorite axe. "Do? You want to know what I'm going to do? I'm going to cut off your fucking legs." I laughed. "Then your arms."

Musket threw back his head and laughed with me.

"Then I'm going to cut off your head and stick it on a pole."

"You wouldn't!"

"Now, don't worry... you'll feel all of it. I don't want you to bleed out too fast and pass out before I take your arms too." I said as I tied the rag around the other leg.

"You're being nicer to this one, Ogre!" Musket said.

I stood up. "You might be right. The last fella we had out here... I took off his hands and feet first."

"Aye, the dogs like them." Musket offered. "But I don't know why... must have tasted like chicken shit. Of course, they do lick their own asses... so there is no telling with dogs."

I pulled out my Becker Combat Bowie nice and slowly... letting the steel sing and making sure the pilot saw the blade.

His first leg would be just about numb by now. I pulled off his boot by slicing through the laces. "Yeah, my dogs haven't been fed any flesh since yesterday; they must be hungry. I think I'll take the feet off first. I love it when they fight over the feet."

I used the very tip of the blade, on the back side, to just scratch around the ankle. To the pilot, it would feel like he was being cut.
The pilot screamed at the top of his lungs. "NOOOOO!!! STOP!"

"Stop what? You little bastard. Did you think about stopping before you pulled the trigger on us? Before that bomb hit our school? It was full of kids you know. Did you think about that? Did you think about the children? You almost killed three hundred little kids."

I started the scratching again. The man shrieked. "Please, God, stop! No!"

"If you want me to stop, you gotta give me a reason to stop... because I have a lot of reasons to cut you up like stew meat, then cut your head off. I have three hundred reasons! You know, we have a bet to see if your head falls into the basket face up or face down. I bet a whole can of Coke that you're a face down kinda head."

The man sang like a bird. He told us everything.

I cut off the rags as the man sobbed. He wouldn't shut up. He started telling us about the other pilots and their stories... the ones that got shot down.

"Dude... shut the hell up now."

I did cut some things off of him. His patches. His wings. The flag. "These, you don't deserve."

"Where are we going to put him?"

"Jail of course. Call County."

"County is already here." Deputy John said.

"Take this guy to the jail. The smallest and darkest cell you have."

"What charges?"

"Terrorism. Attempted murder... about 300 counts."

John cuffed the guy after Musket helped untie him from the bench, and took the guy to jail.

I turned to my council.

"Charles Bowdren was behind this. FEMA planned it. This was to take me out or send me a message."

"Did it work?"

"I got the message."

"What did it say?"

"It says that he wants to be at the top of my Fecal Roster now."

"I'm ready to go." Khorne was chomping at the bit.

"No, I need you and Josh to go to Seattle. I need to complete that mission. Find The Football for me. Charles Bowdren made this personal. I'm going to make it such."

I looked at the new Marines that had just joined us, and Q. "What's the range of a V-22?"

Prepping for New England

*T*he next morning we were making preparations for my trip to New England. I looked for my scarf, but couldn't find it. I pulled out my OD Green shemagh instead. Not as nice as my scarf, but probably more manly. While taking care to pack my ruck, I heard voices outside.

"The zoo really needs help."

Zoo? I went outside. The Hogle Zoo. People had been taking care of the animals there since the beginning. A couple soldiers from Camp Williams have been there under my direction to assist the remaining zoo keepers in maintaining the wildlife there.

"We can't go on like this." The woman said. I had never seen her before. She was small, frail, mousy, looked like she was in her late sixty's, but she had a feisty nature about her. She had blustered her way past Joy, who looked at me and just shrugged.

"What's going on, Mam?"

"Who are you? I need to talk to the Governor!"

"Do you have an appointment?" I said.

"Appointment? I have a zoo full of creatures, I'm out of food, and two of the three Guardsmen the Governor sent me have been bitten by zombies and were last seen wandering around the lion cage. I can't find them, and the other grunt is... just rock hard stupid. I had to drive three hours to get out here... so no, I don't have an appointment."

"Take it easy, sister. I was just kidding. Have a seat." I pointed to the chairs on the porch.

She let out an exasperated sigh and flopped down. I went into the kitchen and opened the fridge. A couple cokes. I popped one open and took a sip. Back outside, I handed her a cold Coke and sat down next to her.

"A Coke? Oh, its cold too! Thank you."

I sipped my Coke as she drank her's half gone. She burped a little and laughed. I laughed with her. "Oh I'm so sorry.... I haven't had a Coke since everything happened. I'm just glad the Governor wasn't here." She giggled. "Where is he?"

As I put my boots up on an ammo crate, "Sweetheart, I am the Governor." I took a sip and smiled at the shocked look on her face. "Now you tell me what you need and I'll see what we can do about it."

Her requirements were simple. She needed feed: hay, oats, fruits, and fish. And she needed some help taking care of the animals after cleaning out the remaining zombies that got into the zoo.

"I want to help." Kilo said, he had been listening. I looked up at him, he was standing in the door, leaning against the door frame.

"If you are sure... You really want to help?"

"Yeah."

"Okay then. Take a Humvee."

Bravo and Echo came out onto the porch. "I'm going." Echo said. "Me too." Bravo held up his hand.

"I don't know."

"Dad, we can do this!" Echo gave me his let-me-prove-it look. I stood up.

"Okay boys. You do this. I know you can. Gear up in your full battle gear. Bring plenty of ammo. Wear your body armor."

"Yeah, Dad... we know... You taught us."

I smiled. "Okay. Get a sat phone from the Coms guys. If you run into trouble, call for help. I'll task some SF guys to respond if you need help. Oh, and take this." I pulled out a note pad and pen from the small desk and started writing. "Take this to the County Building in Vernal, upstairs, the DWR Department. Tell them...." I finished writing. "That everyone of them is transferred." I signed it. The letter head of the paper was official Utah State Governor's Office. "to the Zoo and they are to report there by the end of the week and they are to..."

I looked at the lady, "What's your name? I never got it."

"Joyce Rasmussen."

"That they report to Joyce Rasmussen, who reports to you... as a liaison... and you report to me. You are going to have to find the food, get it rounded up and shipped in. There are farmers out there still growing plenty of it, and maybe give a call up to the R.O.A for some fish if you have to."

I handed the letter to Kilo, "It's about time those DWR guys did something useful. They can't manage anything in the wild, maybe they can manage it if it's in cages."

"Thank you, Governor Hill." Louise looked like she was about to cry.

"You can thank me by teaching those boys the business aspect of the operation... how to run it."

She looked at me strangely.

"You don't have the only zoo that needs help. If you have animals that can't be cared for any longer. I want you to just open the cages. The bison, deer, other animals that can graze, just let them go. The lions and tigers, if it gets to that point, you'll have to put them down."

"I shouldn't have to now... with help and with the supplies... we'll be okay."

"Good. Now I've got things to attend to. Thank you for coming to me."

"Thank you again, Governor Hill." The little woman gave me a hug. She stepped off the porch and headed back to her Subaru Outback.

I went back to packing.

When I was ready to go, with my ruck and extra gear and weapons, I looked over at Kilo's Humvee. He was loading his own gear into the back. Bravo and Echo had already done the same. Echo was pulling a bore-snake through his P-90. I told my boys how much I loved them and that I wanted them back here before I returned. I gave them hugs, and then I watched them pull out.

"Those are some fine boys." April said.

"Yes they are."

April turned and looked at the gear. "We're not taking much."

"Nope."

"I thought we would need a lot more."

"Nope. I don't need to take on this guy's whole Army."

The V-22's engines fired up. The screams of the turbine was enough to wake the dead. Q came over and looked at the gear. "That's all you need?"

"Yup..."

"That's not a lot."

"So I hear. Get it loaded into the Osprey and I'll be there in just a couple."

"Roger that."

At Musket's Pub, the three EOD techs were laughing and enjoying themselves. Andy and Tony had tall glasses of Guinness in front of them, half empty. Nightcrawler had a Dr. Pepper.

"So where's the bomb?"

"We took it out of the school and put it on a truck. It's going back to Hill with us. I figure, the people that sent this to you... they might want it back. It's still in perfect shape."

"I like it."

My brothers were already gone... headed to Seattle. They left before sunrise. The Centauro and two LAVs, fully re-armed and rolling heavy. We had them loaded on flatbed trailers for the long haul and they could roll on, roll off as needed. They could have driven the whole way there, but 18 Wheelers would get them there faster. Speed was of the essence.

Even in the absence of Musket, who had gone on the Seattle excursion as well, everyone coming and going paid tribute and rubbed the brass and wood of the old Brown Bess hanging above the door. Failure to comply with tradition meant that the Tavern Wenches really took their time getting to you and they poured your glasses short when they did. The only way to get forgiveness for the sin was to go back to the old Brown Bess, and put both hands on it and offer the proper respect. Those who couldn't reach it, just reaching for it was good enough.

I left the tavern, honoring the tradition as I went and went to the V-22. Jen was at my side as I walked across the field. Joy and April were at the bird waiting. Q was standing by as well.

"Did you guys get reloaded with all the ammo you need?"

"Yes, sir. We are topped off."

"What about refueling?"

"We could refuel in the air, make the flight nonstop, but we're going to make a couple stops along the way. Air-to-air is fine, but you said we needed a lower profile approach."

I slapped him on the back. "Good man."

Q climbed in, followed by Joy and then April. April was wearing an Infidel ball camp with her pony tail pulled through the back. Man, I love that look. Once in and ready the V-22's engines picked up the volume and the aircraft drifted up away from the earth.

In the Osprey with us was a strange ATV that looked like a mini WWII Jeep. "What is this thing?" I asked Q.

"That's called a Growler."

"Looks like a little Jeep."

"It is. Kinda. Over a hundred grand for that little thing."

"You're kidding?"

Q shook his head. "Specially designed to go in the Osprey."

"Oh really?"

Q pointed at the lug nuts. "See those?"

"Yeah. What about them."

"They must be about eight grand a piece."

"What makes them so special?"

Q shrugged. "Nothing."

We laughed. Q pulled out a paperback novel called *The Grimnoir Chronicles*.

I looked over at Jen who was listening to music. I popped an ear bud out of her ear. She looked at me as I put it in my ear then smiled and curled up into my side. We were over the eastern slope of the Rockies when the girls fell asleep. April huddled next to me on one side, Jen on the other. My eyes started to get heavy.

Some time later the Marines started talking. I didn't respond, just kept my eyes closed. After a while, the talk turned to the girls.

"I'd take the short blond. She's got the best tits." One of the Marines said. "Which one would you take?" He asked another Marine. "The dark haired one."

"Ah yeah."

"You know he's hitting that... one of them... Which one's the Ogre's?"

"All of them." I said, opening one eye.

"HA!!" The Marine closest laughed and held out a fist. I gave him the bones and grinned.

"Pigs." April muttered. I kissed the top of her head and looked over at Joy, who had a sly smile on her lips under her closed eyes.

I closed my eyes again and listened to the Pink Floyd Jen had playing. She had turned up the volume on the iPod.

The three Osprey flew east in a wedge formation. After we crossed Kansas our fighter escort broke off. I watched as one of the Raptors slid up beside us, gave us a salute, and then went vertical. The F-22's had been flying high, doing racetrack patterns along the flight path of the slower V-22's.

"There goes our cover. We are on our own now." The pilot announced.

The Zombie Zoo

"When was the last time we were at the zoo?" Echo asked as he unslung his P-90. Kilo had parked the Humvee near the main gate, next to the other two Humvees.

"When we went to the one at Point Defiance." Kilo said.

"It's been a while." observed Bravo.

The young men looked around. In the parking lot were a couple other cars, one of them was a Subaru Outback, the same one driven by the lady that talked to their father yesterday.

"Alright then, let's go." Kilo said as he headed into the zoo while shrugging on the rucksack. Echo and Bravo threw on their packs and followed. They went through the entrance gate and stood near the Zoofari Train Station.

"Hey, I remember this." Kilo said as he laughed.

"You do?" Bravo said as they all looked around.

The zoo was fairly quiet, but motion caught Echo's eye.

"Look, there." He pointed.

A zombie was holding a goose by the head, half of the body was eaten while the rest was being dragged along. The goose must have turned as its one remaining wing flapped occasionally. The zombie turned and looked at the young men. Bravo took a knee and raised his P-90.

Kilo held his hand out, "Wait!"

The shot rang out and echoed through the zoo. The zombie's head broke open in two pulpy halves, and the body fell like a marionette with its strings cut. The goose, finally released, flopped around with its one wing.

"You don't have your suppressor on." Kilo finished.

"Too late, I guess." Bravo said as he aimed at the goose's head. Another shot rang out. The goose's head was obliterated.

"Stop shooting! Put on your suppressor!" Kilo tightened the grip on his

ACR.

"Yeah, put on your suppressor. You're too loud! You'll disturb the animals." Echo said.

The sound of moaning came from all directions. "The animals are not the problem." Kilo whispered. "Come on, we gotta get to a better spot."

The boys ran along the tracks heading to the bison area. Shambling zombies came into view from the direction of the "The Beastro". When they saw the boys running, they too broke into a run, moaning and shrieking as they ran. Kilo spun around and took a knee. He was using an Eotech optic and let the holosight cover the first zed. He pulled the trigger and held it. 5.56mm rounds slashed through the zombie's torso and stitched it up into the head. The next zed was soon in his sights and he pulled the trigger again. That zombie fell too. As it did, the next zombie tripped over it and fell into a sprawl. Kilo lit that one up as well, before it could get up again.

"I thought they had this place secured!"

A zombie from the bison area ran at them and Bravo and Echo both opened up on it at the same time. The zed was chewed to bits by 5.7 fire before a round went through the brain and dropped it. "Aim your shots!" Kilo shouted.

The boys picked themselves up from firing positions and ran again. In the bison compound, a small building provided some shelter, but there was no one around. As they jumped from the track they ran across the compound, sprinting past the bison who didn't seem bothered by the drama. "Seems fine to me!" Bravo shouted.

On the other side of the bison was a large service area. The boys headed to it. As they neared it a door opened up. A small older lady stepped out, "Well, hello gentlemen! I'm glad you made it." It was Louise Rasmussen. "Why are you out of breath?"

Ogre Goes East

"We're are going to be setting down soon, Ogre. Gotta refuel these thirsty birds." Q was instructing. "Get ready. Our boys haven't reached the LZ yet, so we may have to clear it."

"Where are we setting down?" I asked as the girls started to check their weapons, just like the Marines were doing.

"We're going to be outside of Trenton, Missouri."

"I thought we could go farther."

"We can, but this is a good location to refuel; it's safe for our supply to meet us, and safe to gas up. The next stop might not be peaceful. Hell, this spot might be hairy, we don't know yet. Our guy's on the ground should have been there already."

I nodded and checked my M-14. It was heavy, but it was exactly what I wanted. I cleared the weapon, function checked it, dropped some Slipstream into the action and cycled it some more. It was as ready as I was. I popped in a loaded mag, but didn't chamber a round yet, not in the aircraft.

We began our decent into the clouds and our visibility dropped to nothing. The ceiling was low, at 1200 feet and when we broke through I immediately had a sensation of our speed. A hell of a lot faster than a Helicopter, that was for sure. Almost as fast as my little T-34 Turbo Mentor. We dropped to tree-top level, and I could swear I saw the tips of the rotors clip a tree. Then the engine nacelles began to turn up and the craft slowed. Suddenly we were over a field and the bird came to a smooth landing. The cargo ramp dropped and all of us fanned out, checking the area. The other two V-22's did the same.

"Zeds." April said and snapped off two shots with her SCAR. "Clear."

"Clear."

"Clear."

Everyone checked around the perimeter and no more threats of any kind were found. I looked back at the Osprey as the rotors slowed to a stop. For a guy that hated the V-22 project, I had to say that I was impressed with the final product. It flew farther and faster than a Blackhawk, and a hell of a lot more comfortable as well.

"I gotta get me one of these."

Q looked at me strangely and said as he looked back out across the field, "It is yours."

"Alright, spread out and set up a perimeter around the whole field." I barked to the Marines. "I want the whole area secured."

They moved with speed and precision. The Girl Squad stayed by me, keeping their eye out but a lot more comfortable around the Marines. These were some good guys. I walked around the bird, stretching my bad legs and getting blood back in them. Then I stopped. "Can you hear that?" I said to April, who turned and looked.

"Trucks."

I heard a shout. "Friendlies coming!"

The girls heard the Marine, but closed in around me, trying to act casual about it. April looked at me and tilted her head as she had a thought. She smiled and turned away. "What?"

Two Toyota Tacoma trucks ran onto the field. Men in uniforms were in the cab and in the back of the truck. The first had an M2 mounted on it, the second had a MK19. Ruck sacks hung off the sides of the bed and as they circled, I saw Jerry Cans were on the back. The Marines in the back were wearing goggles and face masks. They jumped out the back even before the trucks came to a stop. The girls moved and stood before them.

"It's alright lasses, these men are brothers." The girls relaxed.

The first Marine that approached pulled off his mask and goggles. He was tall, dark skinned, shaved bald, and had tats up his bare arms. He looked like a young Lawrence Fishburn but had a voice like James Earl Jones. He had the biggest smile I've seen outside the Osmond family. "President Hill, sir." He held out his hand. He wore no name tag, no rank insignia.

I took his hand and gave him a strong shake, "Marine."

"The name is Cooper, sir."

The others were smiles and handshakes as well. Introductions to all of them. Cooper leaned back against his truck as he considered me. "What is a guy like you going out on a mission for?" He said in that deep voice.

"A guy like me? You mean, old?"

"No, I mean like V.I.P."

"It's personal." I said. "Someone tried to kill me from a distance, so I'm going to go kill the motherfucker in person."

Cooper and all the other Marines laughed. "Hell yeah!" One of them said. The fuel trucks came in followed by two more Toyotas. They were big Oshkosh rigs, wide, but with a low-profile look. The Osprey crews immediately began to hook up lines to start taking on the juice. Soon the fuel was flowing into all three birds.

"So what unit are you guys with?"

"Unit?" Cooper asked. "Used to be with the 22nd MEU. I don't know what we are now." He turned to his fellows. "What are we?"

"We're Marines, Coop!" One of the others said.

"Oohh-Raah!" Cooper shouted with a smile.

I smiled and shook my head.

"You hungry, sir? Need anything?"

"I'm good... I'm good."

"Uh... any orders, sir?"

"Orders?"

"After we are done here... you take off... where do you want us to go?"

"How many men do you have?"

"Twenty five."

I thought about it for a minute. Send them to Benning, back to Utah. "I want you to retake and hold Cheyenne Mountain. Clear it out completely, every locker, every corner, under every desk. Kill all the zombies in there, kill all the resistance currently occupying it. Can you do it?"

"Sir, yes, sir! I will see that it's done."

"You have your orders, Marine."

"YES SIR!"

Q came up to me, Sat phone in hand but he wasn't on it. "Sir, just got word that our target has moved from New York to some place in Vermont."

"That changes things.... but I think it plays into our favor." I said. "Break out the map."

We looked at the map and I pointed. "Okay, if we fly in, we will be noticed. So we fly here. My security team and myself will go in on our own from here. You guys fly around here, make some distractions, then pull back until I call for either a dust off or air support or both."

Q agreed after some discussion.

We soon took off again, this time heading for Vermont. It was getting dark by the time we reached our destination. As we approached, one Osprey did a pass, checking out the area, then our bird came in for a landing. Once on the ground, Marines jumped out and secured the immediate area. It looked clear. Q nodded at us.

"Looks like you're good to go. Good luck." Q held out his hand. When I took it, he said two words. "Faith and Honor."

"Faith and Honor." I said, then I picked up my rifle and headed out. The V-22 lifted off and soon disappeared into the night sky. The others had been circling overhead, providing cover and keeping an eye with their IR systems. My radio crackled, "Good luck, Ogre!" It was the pilot.

I keyed my Mic twice in acknowledgment and turned to my girls. "Here we go again. You guys ready?"

The girls nodded. "Where are we exactly?"

I pointed, "Just past those trees is a little lake." I pointed in the other direction, "Over there, is a little joint called Bristol."

"Yeah, I still don't know where that is." Jen admitted.

"We're in Vermont. We came here because of the lack of population. While you girls were sleeping, we flew over Bristol and we saw no movement, dead or alive. So we thought this was a good place to set down."

The sky was clear and the moon was bright, almost full. We were dropped off in a field that had been partially cultivated. I didn't know what the crop was, but it was low to the ground, giving us a wide view. We moved next to the treeline and oriented ourselves, and gave our eyes time to adjust.

Joy pulled out her NVGs from her pack. "Save the batteries. It's so bright out here, we don't need them. We just need to wait a little for our eyes to adjust." She looked at me funny but a while later, she agreed. We took the time eat some MREs. We needed all the energy we could get now.

"It's really pretty here, but the stars are better in Utah." Jen said, looking up into the night sky.

I glanced up, the stars were pretty good and the moon looked like it was almost within reach. "Yeah, I guess so." I said, pulling on the last bit of horribly processed food. "This place doesn't feel like home at all." I scanned the area and then pulled up my Gator-Bull.

April put her hand on mine. "We don't have to do this. We can use military..." I cut her off.

"I have to do this."

"I'm worried about this one."

"You weren't worried about Salt Lake, Phoenix, Colorado?"

"Nope."

"But you're worried about Vermont."

"Yes."

"Why?"

"I don't know. I just have a bad feeling about this one. We're way out here."

I knew what she meant. I had a bad feeling that had been growing stronger the closer we got. And about the last five minutes of the flight in, it felt like we crossed through into a whole different world. Something was different. This whole area felt... darker, colder.

"Here, take this." She said and pulled out a tiny little gun. It was a North American Arms "Pug" mini revolver in .22 Magnum. She pressed it into my hand. "Thanks." I said, tucking it behind my belt buckle.

I stood up and stretched and looked at my watch. It was 10 PM local time. I walked into the trees a little way off from our rest spot. I found a nice dry looking stump that looked like it needed watering. Movement behind me. Soft sounds, light, I smelled a perfume. It was Joy. I turned my head as I buttoned up and looked at her. She smiled sheepishly, "Just making sure you're okay."

"Yeah, I'm fine. How are you?"

She stepped close to me, "I could be better."

"What's wrong?"

"Since Cheyenne Mountain... I realized something. I'm really not a bodyguard. It's been you that has been protecting us. Me especially."

"You guys have been fighting very well. I couldn't have made it without you. Hell, I'm the one putting you guys in danger."

Joy bowed her head. "I was scared, at the mountain."

"We all were."

"You weren't." She said quietly.

I looked at her. "When those guys grabbed you and April... I was."

Joy looked down at the ground. "You pulled me through. Thank you." She walked back the way she came. I stood there for a moment, then went back to the others.

Joy was bending over her pack when she glanced up at me and smiled as she closed her pack and executed a flawless Ranger Ruck Up.

"Come on... let's go." I grabbed my ruck and even though it was heavy, flipped it up over my head as my arms slipped through the straps. Jen and April grabbed their civilian packs, which were smaller and lighter and picked up their weapons. I noticed that Joy had a new piece of gear. Her chopped down pump action shotgun rode in a shoulder rig under her left arm. Jen had the same rig, but she had a mini Uzi.

I turned to the south and headed out. Our eyes had fully adjusted to the light conditions and we crossed the field. Off to the west of us, a pair of coyotes slunk through the brush, watching us. I took that as a good sign, as wildlife tended to avoid areas where the undead roamed.

We passed the farm house. It was dark and quiet. There was a dog house, but there was no dog. I caught the coyotes darting into the house through the doggie door. Looks like they owned this place now.

We walked on in a half-range walk, half-jog pace. The next farm house we came to was smaller, and it looked like a fire had burned part of it down. In the grass around the smaller house, there were heavy vehicle tracks. Maybe it was a fire truck. I stepped closer to the house and the wood siding had a lot of holes in it. Small arms fire.

"Someone lit this house up." I bent down. Even in the dark, I caught moon light glinting off brass. I picked it up. 5.56mm. Lake City brass. There was a lot of it. Next to the brass, small black metal clips. "M-249." I said. My curiosity was peeked. I approached the house. Nailed to the door was a sheet of paper. A warrant. The charge was "Treason". I turned the knob and entered. The house had pictures on the wall. Some were shattered from bullets passing through walls. Each one was a man in uniform. Three folded triangles hung on the wall over the pictures. One man wore an Army uniform, the others, Marines. Plaques on the wall, service awards from a Sheriff's Department. Another plaque with a badge on it... This one had a Police Department badge on it and a service award. The man sitting in the chair with a Winchester shotgun wore an NRA hat. Bullet holes had riddled him. The wall behind him had burned. Tracers probably lit it. This guy... this was no traitor.

"What the hell happened here?" April whispered.

"This was tyranny." I said through clenched teeth. We left the house and continued south. We passed a few more small farm houses and ended up on a street that cut through a residential neighborhood of small houses that the girls adored. They were beautiful little homes. All quiet. No lights. There was another house that was surrounded by discarded brass and links. The door was shattered in the frame and another warrant nailed to the remains. We walked all the way to the main street. We saw no people and no zombies. Everything was completely quiet.

"I don't like this." Jen sounded nervous.

"I think we need to find a vehicle soon." I said. We looked around. Off in the distance we heard an engine, then saw the glow of approaching head-lights. "Cover." I said. We jumped behind a picket fence that had a small shrubbery running along the front of it. A truck approached. It was a Chevy Suburban, dark, with dark windows. I watched through the slits in the fence. On the door was the Vermont State Seal. The truck rolled passed and con-tinued west through the town. As it passed a wave of energy seemed to pass over me, through me. Unclean and cold. I looked over to April who shud-dered. We followed the direction the truck went and came to a small used car lot. In the lot were a number of vehicles that would have made a good option for us, but one in particular caught my eye. I went to the office to find the key. The door was bolted, but with a quick application of Bowie Knife, the door swung open. I found all the keys on a peg board.

Back outside I tossed the keys to Joy, who caught them and her eyes got big. "Seriously?"

I nodded. "Just drive carefully."

"Oh hell yes."

Joy looked around and found the car. A Porsche Cayenne Turbo. Joy pushed the button key fob and the car chirped and the doors unlocked. We threw our packs into the back. It actually had plenty of room. Joy slid into the driver seat and purred like a cat. Her hands went around the leather wrapped wheel. "Oh baby... this thing is so sexy!"

I climbed into the passenger seat. Joy looked at me while she bit her lip. "You like the car then?"

She made a sound like a small, quiet squeal. The other girls got in. When Joy put the key in and started the engine, I could see her quiver. Next thing I knew we were racing east out of Bristol following the curving road. "I think I just came," she said.

I laughed. "Yeah, I like Porsches too."

"I used to have one," Joy said. "A little red 924. It was nothing like this."

She gunned the engine. I looked back, the girls in the back seat were both grinning. "Jen. Music." Jen pulled out her iPod and a cord. She crawled up between the seats and plugged the cord into the jack. "I think this is the song." She giggled and ran her hand up my leg as she pulled back into the back seat.

We raced towards Lincoln listening to *Radar Love*.

Boots on the Ground in Vermont

The drive was starting to make me feel a touch queasy. Joy was really hammering it. Cutting the apex in the curves, slinging the big car around, letting the tires prove their worth. We were almost into Lincoln when we flashed past another black Suburban. Joy stayed on the gas as the big Chevy slid to a stop sideways across the road and tried to come around to give chase. It was no use for them. We were gone.

"Take a right up here." We were long out of view from the Chevy when she took a turn and followed a small road. "Shut off the lights and use the parking brake to stop!" The black Porsche disappeared into the shadow. I jumped out and ran back to the highway with my M-14 ready. Thanks to the more mossy ground here than back in Utah, we gave no dust trail and there was no sign we exited the road.

The Suburban roared past our little turn off and disappeared. I walked back to the car. "Come on, let's get going again. This time I drive."

Joy looked slightly disappointed as she handed me the keys. As I was backing out of the trail, "Windows down, guns at the ready. Jen, reach back there and get me something out of my pack, would'ja, Love?"

"This?" She held up a Gator-Bull.

"Nope."

"Ah, you want this." She held up a LAW rocket.

"There you go." She passed it up and I put it next to my right leg.

We made it into Lincoln and passed the main intersection. The Suburban was about a hundred yards up the street as we passed, I saw the Suburban's brake lights come on. We drove on and then I put the car into a slide and stopped in the middle of the road. "Come on!" We all bailed out of the car and ran to one side of the road. We moved back along the way we came and took up a position hiding behind some trees.

The Suburban came around the corner, and I heard the engine revving hard. As soon as the headlights hit the Porsche, it threw on its brakes. I pulled the bolt back on my M-14 and let it fly forward, chambering a round. "Get ready."

Two large men wearing black BDUs and a patch I've never seen before, stepped out of the truck. They both had their weapons drawn and in a low ready. SIG 226s from the look of them. As soon as they walked into their own headlights, I stepped out and moved up to the Suburban. They had left their doors open and the cabin light showed me that no one else was in the truck. I took up a position at the driver's door and April tucked into the passenger side. Joy and Jen hugged the truck, but were low, under the doors.

"Get out of the car!" One of the men shouted to the empty Porsche. "You are under arrest!"

No one got out of the empty car. The men approached the car with their guns up like an 80s police show.

"Where the hell did they go?"

"They must have taken off running."

"They were already running, dumbass."

The two guys turned around and started walking back to the truck. About half way I shouted. "That's far enough! Drop your weapons!"

The larger of the two brought up his weapon but couldn't see where to aim, being blinded by the truck's headlights. I dropped him with one round of .308 to the head. "I said drop it!"

The second man dropped the pistol. "Now take three steps back and turn around. Interlace your fingers behind your head and get on your knees! Do it now!"

The man complied, looking very unhappy about it. "Who are you? Who do you think you are?"

"That's none of your business for one... for the other, you are in no position to ask any questions."

I pulled a flex cuff from my belt and moved up behind the guy. I transitioned from rifle to pistol as I approached. "You get frisky with me, I'll kill you." With my left hand I grabbed the man's fingers, locking his knuckles together. Once I had my grip on him, I holstered the M&P and pulled his arms behind his back. He gave no resistance. Once the flex cuffs were on him, I was able to breath again. I motioned with my head for the girls to come to me. I didn't want to get too far from the guy. Cuffed or not he could still run and that would be annoying.

"The two of you," I said looking at Jen and April, "pull that body off the road, into the treeline." They nodded. "Joy, get in the truck and follow me."

"Can't I drive the Porsche again?"

"Fine. You'll take the Porsche and follow me." She grinned.

I pulled the man to his feet and walked him back to the Suburban. I put him into the passenger seat in the front and had April sit behind him. He got a little frisky getting in, but a brief whisper from April and he suddenly played nice again. I looked at her and she winked at me.

Jen got into the Porsche with Joy riding shotgun. I climbed into the Suburban and pulled forward, around the car, and started up the road. Only a few yards past I saw a small dirt road that peeled off to the left, into the trees. I decided to follow it. The Porsche had no problem following me. The trail wound through the trees and eventually came out into a huge clearing, but the trail continued. We passed a couple other small clearings and the trail eventually came to another pretty good-sized clearing well away from anything. This is where we stopped.

I shut down the truck and pulled the guy out, walking him to the center of the field.

"On your knees."

"I'd rather die standing."

"If I wanted to kill you, you would be with your friend."

"Yeah, you had no problem killing him. That was murder." The man got down on his knees.

"If you will be so kind as to remember honestly, I did ask you guys to drop your weapons. Your friend thought it would be a better idea to point a weapon at me. That wasn't a good idea."

The man said nothing. The girls gathered around. "We should just kill him." Joy said.

"No, I'm not a monster."

"Could have fooled me." The man said.

"I thought you were an Ogre."

"Well, I am an Ogre... but see... that's the big misunderstanding. Ogres are just misunderstood."

"Ogre?" The man sounded confused.

"What do you know of Ogres?"

The man was tight lipped and just stared at the grass in front of him.

"Okay, let's start with the basics." I looked at the patch. FEMA. That actually shocked me, and didn't surprise me at all at the same time. "So what is a couple of FEMA guys doing trying to arrest a citizen out for a lovely drive?"

"You were out past curfew and you were coming from a restricted area."

"When did FEMA get the authority to do this?"

"We're in an emergency situation, or haven't you noticed the dead walking around lately."

"Wow... sarcasm. Last I heard that, it was from a 16-year-old girl. I don't think you understand where I'm coming from." I decided not to do the threat of torture thing. Instead I played another tact.

"I've come a very long way to find someone. Someone important to me."

"Like I give a damn."

"Well, you probably should. You see, I'm looking for your boss, Charles Bowdren. And I think maybe you might know where he is. I heard a little rumor that he's in Vermont. Chucky and I go way back. He shared something pretty big with me and... well... I just want to share something right back."

"Director Bowdren?" The man laughed. Good luck with that!"

"Where is he?"

"Fuck you!"

April cocked back ready to throw a punch, but I stopped her. "No, no no... We're not going to hurt him, Love. He's going to tell us what I want to hear, then I'm going to let him go. I only kill zombies or guys trying to kill me."

"You'll let me go?"

"I'll toss the keys to your truck into the trees, but you'll be able to find them."

The man sighed. "He's in Hanover... in the court house. You can find him there."

"That's all I needed to know. Thank you."

I took the keys and pitched them not too far into the treeline. As the man looked to follow the keys, Joy blasted his chest open with her little 870. The man crumpled to the ground.

I stood there, considering the dead man for a moment. I really had intended to just leave him here, but this was just as well. I know it seems cold, but if he found the keys, got out of the cuffs or however made it to help, he could have alerted Charles Bowdren I was coming.

"Pop the hood on the SUV."

"Why?"

"The thing has On Star. If someone decides to look for him, they could find him instantly."

April popped the hood. I looked at the battery cables for a second and considered chopping through them with my Becker. Instead I used a Leatherman and unscrewed the bolts and popped the cables off of the terminals. I wasn't even sure if that disabled the tracking, but at least I felt better about it.

Joy was driving again as we continued on our way heading eastward.

"What he said about curfew... maybe we should wait until morning."

"I thought about that. I'd at least like to get out of this area in case people come looking for these FEMA guys."

We drove along the highway through the deep woods of Vermont and found another small path that went off through the trees. "That looks good." We followed the trail to a small clearing that was covered by the tops of trees. I looked at my watch, it was 2:30 AM. I felt tired enough, my eyes were heavy enough. "Let's make a fast camp here."

We pulled out the rolled pads and laid them out. Bed rolls, poncho liners, and ponchos. We didn't have sleeping bags. Too bulky and heavy. I stretched out, using my ruck as a pillow.

"It's creepy that we've not seen anyone but those FEMA guys... not a single zombie. It's strange." April was talking at the sky.

"It really is. Something is going on here." I said. "We'll find out what it is."

"Who's got first watch?" Jen asked.

"It's my turn." Joy said.

"Good. I can't keep my eyes open." Jen yawned. April rolled over on her pad and pulled her poncho liner up over her shoulder. A minute later, I could hear deep breathing.

I woke up still tired, with April's head on my shoulder and her arm over me. The morning had a slight chill in the air. I rolled out from under the arm and stood up. The sun was up higher in the sky than I'd have preferred. There was a stillness to the air that was unsettling. It felt as if I needed to be real quiet. I looked over to Jen who was awake and pulling on a sweater. The other girls were starting to stir, but evidently not wanting to open their eyes yet. I got dressed into some clean clothes. I was sitting in the open back of the car and was pulling on a fresh pair of socks when April stood up. She stumbled around looking for her clothes with a poncho liner held around her. She managing to step on Joy's hair.

"OUCH!" Joy was up now.

It really was quite funny and I had to laugh. Suddenly, I heard the call of a crow that was high up in a tree watching us. I stopped laughing. I didn't like that crow. I reached into the back of the Porsche and pulled out my ACR. The crow tilted its head as I fired a suppressed round into it. The round impacted center mass and the crow flapped for a second and was then still. After another call, it took wing and flew east.

"I think we need to be going."

After a couple more minutes, we were cruising again with Joy at the wheel and came into a small town. It had a small cafe type establishment that had a few people coming and going. I made note of their dress. No uniforms, no patches. Also, no firearms. As we passed slowly, the people refused to make eye contact. Some even turned their heads the other way as we passed.

"I think we need a new set of clothes or we'll stand out." April observed. I was thinking the same thing. Vermont-flage.

"Turn here." We rounded the corner. There was a clothing store that actually had an open sign in the window. "Park in the back."

We left our long arms in the back of the car, under our packs. The windows were tinted so it was very unlikely anyone would be able to see them. I wore my Glock 23 in my Adam's Sharkhide rig under my long sleeved Oakland Raiders t-shirt. The girls followed suit and went low profile as well. We walked around the store and quickly went inside.

"Hello." Called a voice from the back.

"Howdy." I said.

The shop owner looked up suddenly at the unfamiliar voice and was shocked at the unfamiliar faces. "Who are you?" The question sounded like a demand.

"Customers, if you don't mind. We've driven a long way and would like some fresh duds."

"Our credit card machine doesn't work and we don't take checks."

"Will cash do?" I pulled out my wallet and opened it, showing a thick wad of Benjamins.

"Yeah I guess." The man grumbled. The man was old, balding, wore wire-framed glasses and a sweater. His face looked like it had been kind and spent a life smiling, but he wasn't smiling anymore. The girls instantly went to work. They were buzzing about the store, holding up shirts and scarves and bags.

"I haven't seen these gals so happy since everything went to hell." I said to the old man.

The man looked up, looked at the girls, then back down at nothing. "They're just doing what women do naturally."

"The name is Greg, by the way. Pleased to meet you."

"Samuel... the same I guess." He shook my hand. "Haven't had a customer in weeks, so I guess I should be glad about it, I guess."

"So what's going on here, Samuel. I haven't seen a zombie since about New York. You guys have everything under control here."

"Yeah, I guess. Them FEMA guys have everything locked down pretty good."

"You don't sound like you like FEMA, but it looks like they're doing a good job."

"Piss on them. Bastards don't remember what the Constitution is. Buncha jack-booted thugs."

I noticed that he didn't say "I guess" to that, which had seemed his habit. I decided to go deeper with Samuel. "We came through Bristol on the way in..." I leaned in close and lowered my voice. "Saw a house there that looked all tore up... but not by the undead... had a lot of holes through it." Samuel looked up at me. "That would be FEMA's doing. They don't like certain people."

"Who would that be?"

"Anyone that could possibly resist them. When the zombies started walking the earth, those certain people are what stopped them. Those people left around here, we made it because of them guys with guns... ex police and military. Well about a week after everything, FEMA comes in. Establishes martial law. Next thing I knew, people started coming up missing. Just in the middle of the night – one day they are there, the next they are gone. Then them FEMA bastards started taking people during day light. Arresting them they said. You see, they put up signs. Turn in your guns. You have one day of amnesty. Well, people don't like giving up their guns. That's when the arrests started. No one has seen anyone that got arrested since."

"Samuel, you're telling me a horror story worse than zombies."

"I wish it was just a story."

The girls came up to me. They had a plaid button-down collar shirt with a canvas vest and khakis and penny loafers. "Is that what guys around here wear?"

I looked at Samuel. "I guess so." He said.

After changing clothes I looked at myself in the mirror. "I look like an LL Bean catalog".

"You look cute!"

"You look like a Professor."

"You look like my Grandpa."

I hung my head. The girls all looked very different from what I was used to. The hardness was gone, replaced by something feminine. They looked stunningly beautiful. I had to tear my eyes away from them.

"So how much do I owe you?" I handed Samuel the tags off all the clothes we wore. "Ah never mind that... here..." I held out ten one hundred dollar bills. "This should cover it... and, ah, we were never here. You never saw us. Okay?"

"I'm talking to myself." Samuel said.

"Me too." I agreed. "Tell me one last thing, Sam."

Sam looked up from the wad of cash in his hands. "If someone was arrested by FEMA. Where would they be taken?"

"I don't know for sure. Rumor has it, people get taken to jail, then taken to court the next day. The guilty get taken away."

"What about the innocent?"

"Everyone is guilty."

"Where are they taken?"

"No one knows for sure, but it's said to be the Ruggles Mine."

"Thanks, Sam. We best be getting on."

"Good luck."

We drove into Hanover and rolled past the court house. FEMA people were all over, dressed in black uniforms and driving black SUVs. They eyed us suspiciously as we went past. We stopped at a cafe, hungry for breakfast. We parked in the almost empty lot and went in.

Two large FEMA uniformed guys were hunched at the counter. We took a booth. Every so often the black uniformed guys would slowly look over their shoulders at us.

The waitress came over to us and asked what we wanted.

"Whatever you got... eggs, toast, grits, juice... I really don't care, we're all starving."

The waitress looked at us, but we just smiled. She walked away. One of the FEMA guys finished his coffee and went into the rest room. The other one turned around and looked at us blatantly. From across the room the man said "Who are you people?"

I looked at the girls. "Did you hear something?" I ignored the guy. I could see the guy out of the corner of my eye stand up and was about to come over to us when the other guy came out of the bathroom. Too fast to have bothered washing his hands... filthy bastard. He had just hung up his cell phone. "Come on, we gotta go... unit when missing. Mr. Bowdren wants us to help search." They walked out.

The waitress came back over. "That was really stupid."

"Why is that? He wasn't the police or anything."

She laughed a dire sort of laugh, "Take a look around you fools. You see a lot of police here?"

"No, come to mention it, not a one. Where are they?"

"That's what I'd like to know. Best customers were the police officers. They always tipped, which is strange for cops, but they did."

She walked back to the kitchen. After a while we were served fried eggs, grits, toast, and orange juice. "If you want I can make you some pancakes, but the milk is powdered."

"Powdered?"

"Zombie's got the cows."

"Speaking of zombies... How come we've not seen any around here?"

"Charles Bowdren. He shows up, the zombies disappeared. Creepy son of a bitch, but I can't complain none. He's the guy in charge of FEMA."

We ate our breakfast in silence until the waitress was out of ear shot. "Sounds like Bowdren is a Red Eye." I whispered. April nodded.

The waitress came back, "Hey, you guys have a lot of people in town... maybe the zombies didn't hit you guys so bad?"

A look of sadness washed over her. "They hit us. Probably only twenty people survived the zombie attack. Almost everyone you see about... they come from all around the state. Of those only twenty... that survived from here." A tear rolled down her cheek. "I'm the only one left."

She turned suddenly, "I'm sorry."

"No – please. I'm sorry for asking. It's not my place."

The small bell above the door chimed as someone walked in. I turned to look at who it was. The man was large, filled the doorway and his voice boomed out. "You still serving breakfast?"

My jaw hit the floor. The man looked at me and his eyes went wide. It was Harm, the Governor of Arizona.

"Hyrum!"

"Ogre?"

"Yeah man, come over here." I got up from the table. "What are you doing here?"

"I've got family here, I'm looking for them. Going to take them back to Arizona."

"Any luck?"

"None. House is there, but it's empty. Looks like it's been empty for some time. Can't find anyone with any answers. These FEMA assholes just laugh when I ask them anything."

"I think I know what happened." I started to fill Harm in. The more I told him, the more angry he got. I told him about the house I had found with the warrant on the door."

"Found the same kind of warrant on the house next door to my folks."

"Was there a veteran that lived there?"

"Yes, an old Nam veteran. Good guy."

"See, someone would have, could have stood up to FEMA." I whispered. "Everyone left here are just kittens. No one is left that's willing, or able to put up a fight."

I told him about the arrests and the possible connection to the mine. "I know where that is." Hyrum said.

"You have anyone with you?" I asked.

"CXB and a few other fellas. They are waiting around back with the car."

"Good, that's good."

"So what are you doing here exactly?"

I told him about the cluster bomb and the pilot. Hyrum whistled and shook his head. "Lucky".

"Well, I'm here to make sure that doesn't happen again. Evidently they think they had taken care of me. If they find out their little air strike didn't work, they'll send others."

"So what do you want me to do?"

I started putting a plan together.

Payback's a Bitch!

*A*fter leaving the little eatery, the Governor of Arizona went in one direction and we went in another. The plan was set and we had a time table. The girls parked the Porsche across from the courthouse. At the designated time, I walked from the cafe, across the street and along the sidewalk. I walked confidently, even if I didn't feel it, into the court house. The FEMA guys gave me a look over, but didn't stop me. No one would just walk in unless they were summoned. Right?

A woman at the desk near the entrance looked up at me over her glasses. "Mr Bowdren?" I asked.

She pointed down the hall and went back to reading her book. I walked down the hall. There was a door with a glass window in it. I saw Bowdren sitting at the desk talking to a man in sunglasses that was dressed in clothes that were a bit oversized for him. I looked at Charles and saw that his eyes were normal. He wasn't a Red Eye. What was going on here? I walked past the door down the hall. As soon as I was out of view from the window, the man in the glasses turned from Charles and looked at the window. He stared at the window.

I went into the bathroom at the end of the hallway. Partially, because I had to go... and also... I needed to psych myself up. Assassination was never my thing.

Just as I was zipping back up, I felt a wave of dread. I walked to the sink when the door opened. I didn't look up... I turned on the water. *Hey, I'm just a guy that took a piss... no threat,* I thought to myself.

I turned to the guy that came in. He stood there in front of the door, skin was pale and greyish. He wore sunglasses. He smiled a dry, joyless smile, his lips pulled back off chipped teeth. "I am sooo pleeaased to sssseee yooouuuu!"

"Who are you?"

He chuckled, which sounded like wind through dead leaves. "Don't you recognize me, George?"

"Should I?"

"Of course," The man pulled off his sunglasses. He was a Red Eye. I backed up a step. "I... am... your... death!"

Suddenly my skull filled with a scream and I realized that it was my own. I've lived off and on with migraines for twenty years. This, was as if a migraine had a migraine. My head felt like it was being squeezed. I gritted my teeth through the scream and resisted. I forced my mind to ignore the pain, because I knew somehow deep down, that it was false. I stood up straight and looked at the Red Eye.

"You'll have to do better than that." I said through clenched teeth.

"If you wissshhh." He raised his hand and cocked his middle finger, then flicked it. It felt like Mike Tyson punched me square in the face. I was knocked back and staggered. I touched my face and my hand came away with blood on it. Nothing false about that. The Red Eye chuckled as he raised both hands, palm up. An unseen force grabbed me and threw me bodily into the ceiling, then let me go. I crashed into the floor, knocking the wind out of me. I choked, trying to get my air back. The Red Eye stepped forward, pulling something from behind his back. "To think... My Master has been worried about you." It was a machete.

I scrambled backwards, putting my legs in front of me.

"Be cautious of him, he told me." The Red Eye raised the big knife up. "Why would I be cautious of you?" He laughed as he swung. I raised my knee and the machete came across in a slashing cut that ended in my upper shin with a THUNK sound. I screamed. The Red Eye pulled on the Machete, but it didn't come out of my leg. He looked surprised as I stood up. I was hurting, bad, and now I was pissed.

"How?" There was a look of confusion on the Red Eye's face.

"Because I'm the Bionic man, bitch!" Then I kicked him with a straight forward Shotokan kick with the machete still in my shin. The blow caught the Red Eye in the pelvis and took him off his feet and threw him back into the sinks. There was a crunching sound.

I screamed as I levered the blade out of my leg. Through the opened wound silver metal was visible. I've had steel and Titanium rods in my legs for decades. A left over from my days wearing the Crossed Rifles. I was almost blinded by the pain, but I held it together and charged the Red Eye with the machete. I was almost on top of him when he held up a hand and it felt like I ran straight into a brick wall. I dropped the big knife.

The Red Eye laughed as he crawled backwards up the wall with one arm, his body making cracking sounds as he moved. His other arm was still held straight out to me. He wasn't laughing anymore. He made a fist, then opened his fingers. A blast of force crashed into me and threw me back into the wall, almost knocking me out. I was held against the wall. Unseen fingers around my neck squeezed. My arms hung limp at my sides.

The Red Eye walked forward.

"Unexpected." It said as it pulled me off the wall and brought me face to face with it. I was off the ground, and it felt like I was held by my neck. "Perhaps I wont kill you... I'll just turn you... then you can serve the Master!" The Red Eye threw his head back and laughed. "Maybe I'll let you kill that idiot Bowdren. That's what you came here for wasn't it? The Master said you would come for Bowdren, and he said you would kill him."

I whispered something softly.

"What was that?" He turned his head a bit to better hear me. I pulled something from behind my belt buckle and stuck it in the Red Eye's ear. It was the North American Arms PUG .22 Mag April gave me. The Winchester SXT bullet had no problem crashing through the ear hole. As it went, the bullet expanded and was full diameter as it entered the brain, punching out of the skull above the other ear.

I fell to the ground, instantly released. "I said, after you."

My leg was on fire, the chop through the bone was stopped thanks to the titanium rod in the bone. But the pain was there in full force and my leg was reluctant to let me put weight on it. I hobbled out of the bathroom, into the hallway. The sound of the little gunshot must have carried because the woman at the far end of the hall dashed out of the front door. As I was limping and bleeding, Bowdren bolted through his office door into the hallway. He looked to the front of the building, then back at me. I was gimped up pretty good, but I kept going.

"Who the hell are you?" Bowdren demanded.

"I'm the Governor of Utah... the one you tried to kill" Bowdren's eyes went wide with shock and he reached back for his S&W model 640. I drew my Glock 23 from its concealment with the speed and surety of count-less repetitions. I punched the pistol out in a two-hand grip. The front dot covered my target's center mass and I fired. Eight rounds through the chest before he fell, dropping his little snub nosed revolver. I limped forward and looked down at the man. Charles Bowdren was still breathing. "An eye for an eye, Charles." I fired four more rounds into his head before I did a tactical reload, keeping the empty mag in my back pocket. I kept the Glock in a high compressed position as I moved as fast as I could to the front door.

Outside I could see several FEMA thugs running to the door, the woman at the front desk was shouting and pointing. I ducked behind the reception desk, more diving than ducking. The doors crashed open and the men ran into the hallway. Seeing Charles Bowdren on the floor, they rushed to him. Then they stopped and looked at the blood trail from my leg. They followed it with their eyes. When they looked at me, they only saw the flashes from my muzzle. Three thugs down.

Rounds tore through the desk, just above me. I rolled out and made a quick shot as I did, hitting the forth FEMA agent in the chest, momentarily staggering him. Another aimed shot caught him in the upper front teeth.

As I exited the building, doing another tactical reload, more FEMA guys came at me from either side. I continued my ungraceful run as I stowed a second mag in my back pocket. Shots tore through the shrubs across the street and into the FEMA agents, clearing my path.

When I crashed through the brush, April grabbed me and pulled me down. "HOW BAD ARE YOU HURT?" She checked me over for GSWs. "Just my leg... I caught a machete with it." She ripped open my pant leg and saw the gaping wound and the metal through the bone.

April instantly tore her new shirt, ripping the front of it open. She tied that around my wound, tight. "How's that?" She asked.

"Can I scream now?"

"Won't do any good." She reached over me into the car and pulled out my tactical vest and rifle. "Put this on!"

FEMA trucks screeched and slid to a stop on both ends of the street like a scene from *HEAT*.

Joy was on the radio calling for air support as Jen fired. April was back up and sighting with her SCAR. POP POP POP POP POP POP POP POP POP. Well-aimed shots made the guys in black either fall or stay behind cover. Jen and Joy fired in the other direction, fast enough to make a Daddy Mini-Gun proud, and accurate enough to make me proud. We were holding them... but more FEMA guys were coming. I knew the longer we stayed here, the more time they had to flank us.

Suddenly, were heard the sound of a high-pitched motorcycle, and I watched as one of the FEMA trucks was turned into confetti. Thump Thump Thump Thump. 40mm grenades began exploding on the other side of the trucks, some into the trucks.

"ROGER THAT," Joy said into the Radio. "THE DOOR IS OPEN!" I looked at my watch. More time. We need to give Harm more time. I grabbed the radio and ordered the Ospreys to cover Hyrum's operation at the Jail. Our door was open, we could go.

"LET'S GO!" I yelled.

April helped me into the back seat with one hand, and had her SCAR in the other. Jen laid down a full mag of fire as she backed up to the car. Joy jumped in the car just before Jen. As soon as Jen's door shut, Joy popped the clutch. We raced out of Hanover and crossed the bridge. April clicked my seatbelt on and got hers on too. I watched as Joy got hers on. Jen was firing out the window at a FEMA truck that had stopped on the sidewalk. "GOT THEM!" She shouted.

We raced over the bridge that crossed the river heading to Norwich. As soon as we crossed, we approached a figure on the shoulder of the road. As we went passed, the person swung both arms in a sweeping motion. All the windows in the Porsche were blown out instantly and the driver side of the car was crushed in. Everything happened in slow motion. Looking forward through the flying particles of safety glass I could see the horizon spinning like a fighter plane doing fast aileron rolls. The car came down on the roof and slid to a stop. I was dizzy, felt lost, completely disoriented. But I had enough wits about me to unbuckle and crawl out.

The Red Eye we passed was jogging this way, laughing. My rifle was laying inside the car, on the roof. I pulled it out and braced it on the back bumper of the Porsche. I fired until he fell with a head shot.

"April!" She was trying to crawl out. I helped her out of the vehicle. Joy was already standing up.

"Where's Jen?!" She asked in a panic.

"JEN!"

She wasn't in the car. "Oh Jesus!" I looked back along our flight path and off on the side of the road, I saw her. We ran.

"JEN!" Joy screamed as we got near her. She wasn't moving. There was blood coming from her nose and mouth.

"Oh no! Jen!" I checked for a pulse. It was faint. "I have a pulse! She's breathing!"

"Pick her up! Come on!" Joy was in a panic, pulling at me. April was screaming.

"Wait a second." I pulled off my tactical vest, then took off the LL Bean vest that Jen had said was cute. I rolled it up and made a neck brace which I secured with some duct tape April got from my pack.

I threw my tactical vest and rifle to Joy and picked Jen up in my arms like she was a child, holding her tight against me. "Hang on, Jenny." She was unresponsive. I was limping badly as blood flowed from my leg, but I carried my body guard to the LZ that was just in a clearing near the road.

As I approached the clearing a V-22 touched down with the ramp pointed at me. We ran in and I knelt down on the floor of the Osprey, still holding her. One of the Marines started checking her out, first for a pulse at the wrist, then reaching under the neck brace to find the carotid artery.

"There is no pulse, sir." He said.

The girls wailed and I just held Jen to me, rocking her as the V-22 picked up off the ground. A second Osprey touched down and Harm and crew ran aboard while the third Osprey provided cover.

After Jen's body was zipped up in the black bag I leaned back against the fuselage of the V-22 Osprey. Anger filled me. The Corpsman was bandaging my leg after he finished stitching the wound. The painkiller he injected into my leg worked well, but I still had the sensation of burning that rolled up and down my leg from my ankle to my hip. My two remaining girls, April and Joy were in my arms, they were still sobbing. Losing Jen hurt. But I used that hurt and turned the pain around.

"Where's Q?"

"He went out scouting and didn't make it back before you called."

"Where is he?"

"He's out of contact, so we are not exactly sure. But we have his last location."

"Then let's go there."

"Sir, we are heading back to CWS airspace."

"Bullshit! We're not leaving anyone behind. Turn this aircraft around. Now!"

A moment later the V-22's banked hard right and accelerated.

All Manner of Zombie Hell

Something was different. We flew low over the residential and saw zombies filling the streets. Humans running in panic, unarmed thanks to FEMA's tyranny. The zombies were coming out from under houses, from the crawl spaces, from tool sheds.

"What's going on? Where are they coming from?" The Marine manning the gun on the open ramp shouted.

"I think we killed the Red Eye that was keeping the zombies in check and now they are coming out. If the zombies are on the move, Q could be in big trouble. Hold on. Slow down."

The V-22's engines rotated up and the bird slowed. We began shooting the zombies that were closest to the living people, we tried to shoot first. But there were too many of them. We watched the zombies tackle and tear into them. The Marine started spraying all of them with no more need to watch for friendlies.

If there was any justice, it was the FEMA guys getting over run by the zombies. Even then, the whole situation was disgusting to me.

"We can't raise them on the radio. They are either dead or somehow out of contact." The Corpsman said.

"Then we find out. We don't leave anyone behind."

I rocked in a fresh magazine and chambered a round, then went back to the girls. I picked up Jen's rifle and slung it over my shoulder, then her Uzi and her spare magazines.

"You girls stay with Jen."

"Where are you going?"

"We've got lost men."

April set her jaw. "I'm coming."

"No, you're not. You're staying here. Watch them." I nodded to Joy and Jen's body.

Joy looked up, she was holding Jen's tactical vest. Her eye make-up was streaked. To her, Jen was more than just a best friend. She was her companion and lover. I felt a great deal of sympathy, because I cared for Jen as well. And her. But I didn't have the connection that they had. I whispered to April that she needed to stay with Joy. She understood. April could pull it together, but Joy needed an arm around her.

"Sir, the Governor of Arizona wants to know what's going on."

"Tell him we are on a search and rescue for the men that got left behind."

"Sir, we only have the air crew for the bird, and you just told your personal security to stay on board... And I suck in a fight. Who's going with you?"

"I'm going alone, to find our missing Marines. I want Hyrum to... Oh hell, get him on the radio for me."

The Corpsman took a minute, but then handed the radio to me. "Here he is, sir."

"Hyrum! Yeah... I know... V-22s kick ass." I shook my head, "No, I'm not taking back everything I said about them."

The Corpsman look puzzled.

"Do you see everything that's going on down there? The zombies are coming back, yeah.... That's right. FEMA took all their guns. They are defenseless. FEMA has to have taken all the guns someplace. Find the guns. Give them back to the Citizens. No, no idea where they would be. Grab a FEMA guy and shake him down for the information, and give his gun to the nearest citizen you find. I don't care. Arrest him. Put all the FEMA guys you round up into a jail. Let Vermont try them in an actual court of law. Yeah. Do that. Okay, I'm going hunting for our MIA Marines. Good luck, Vice President." I laughed, "You talk to your kids with that mouth? No man, you're it until you die or I find someone better."

Hyrum's V-22 banked and peeled out of the formation. The other V-22 stuck close by. I could see the Marine in the back manning his gun, the barrel tracking back and forth eager for a target. The V-22 started gaining altitude as we descended and slowed. I looked out a window and watched the engines pivot up into helicopter mode.

"This is it... this is where we last had contact with them."

"Where are we?"

"In New York, sir. Lake Placid."

Great. New York. Not a fan.

The bird was hovering over some trees. "Set her down over there." I pointed. The Osprey touched down and as I was about to jump out, a slender hand grabbed me. I turned and saw April's tear-stained face. "Be careful." I looked at her for a moment. "Keep an eye on Joy. She needs you."

I ran off the ramp into the tree line as the Osprey took to the air again. I looked up to see the Corpsman and the Marine on the gun looking down at me. The Marine gave me a thumbs up, the Corpsman was grinning, making the "Call Me" gesture. As I moved through the trees, I wondered if all Navy Corpsmen were that goofy.

The trees here were just starting to turn to the autumn colors, but the leaves had not started to fall. I found a trail that the Growler had run on. The Growler was like an overweight Side-by-Side ATV designed by a Marine for Marines. Which meant it was tough as hell, tore everything up that was in its path, and did so grinning the whole way. This made the Growler easy to follow. The trail went from the woods, out into a street and I could see the tracks making a wide arc across the street where it looked like it may have stopped in front of a building. I looked both ways before I crossed the street to follow, which was a good thing. Zombies were shambling around, about seven of them. A couple grown ups and the rest teenagers. A teenage boy wearing his pants below his buttocks was lurching his way in my direction. I whistled and waved at him. The zombie saw the movement and heard the sound and started running at me. His pants fell to his ankles and he went sprawling, landing on his face. I put a round through the top of his head. The other zombies were more interested in looking at their feet or gnawing on various severed appendages. I engaged and dropped the nearest ones. The M14 Sage EBR spoke with authority, but because of the SEI M14DC suppressor and 200-grain Lapua ammo, it did so with quiet authority. My shots didn't attract any more attention. Because of my leg, I couldn't run as fast as I liked, but I loped across as well as I could.

Up above, I saw two of the three V-22s circling. Occasionally the gunners would let a burst of fire rip. As I approached the building, I saw the smoke and fire through the blackened windows. Suddenly some of the windows blew out and flames shot out into the air. I ducked the flying glass shards. This was every bit as good as a neon sign saying "Marines were Here". It also meant that they would have moved on. I looked for more tracks. The Growler wasn't making any more now that it was on dry ground, but it had come from one direction, probably going in the other. I loped up the street. I soon came to bodies. Yup. They came this way. Olympic Village. There were bodies here wearing the same black FEMA uniforms as in Vermont. Charles had a long reach. One body wasn't in uniform. It lay on its back, but its arms were up, locked in place, one pointing, the other in a fist. Its eyes stared up into the sky. A bullet hole made a third eye in its nose. The eyes were red, completely blood shot. I followed a short trail of corpses like a sick Hansel and Gretel story until I came to a fence. Here the men cut the fence, and the tracks picked up again through the grass. Looking across the field, all I could see was a shed out there. But it wasn't on fire, no bullet holes, and no smoke pouring out of it. Yet the trail led there.

I was about to follow the tracks when I heard shouting. I turned and saw something quite strange. The shouting was from a man wearing black robes that flowed off his shoulders as he ran. At his collar was a clear indication of Catholic Priesthood. Behind him was a pack of zombies. The priest ran, shouting prayers like demands to the Almighty. Then he would turn and rebuke the zombies for their devil worship, call them to repentance and when they got close enough, he would turn and swing his large wood and gold cross, knocking the zombies flat. The priest would run again, and the zombies would rise up and give chase.

I leveled my M14 and took careful aim. The priest raised his cross. I fired. The zombie's head exploded. I fired again and again. It took a moment for the father to realize that it wasn't the Almighty that was smiting the undead, but a man with a rifle. He turned to me with a strange look on his round and red-nosed face. He looked at his cross, then at me as he ran to me.

"Mysterious ways, my son!"

"Come again?"

"The Good Lard does indeed work in mysterious ways, my son... mysterious ways to us that is. I have faith that He knows what He's doing, but it's a mystery to His humble servants such as myself."

"I don't think the Lord has anything to do with this." I said, meaning the zombies.

"Oh, of karss He does, lad, He's the creator." Then the priest stopped and looked at me with squinted eyes. "Or are you a shameful unbeliever in the Lard?"

"Yes, yes... I believe."

The priest looked relieved. "Aye, you looked like a good man. I can tell these things. The light of the Good Shepherd shines upon ye!" I fired a shot around the priest that knocked the top of a zombie's head off. The priest held out his hand, "and ye does the Lard's work. I am pleased to meet you. I am Father Shamus O'Donnovan."

"Pleased to meet you too, Father. George Hill. I'm... uh... I'm Mormon."

Father O'Donnovan was taken aback, shocked in fact, but recovered quickly. "Well, no one is perfect, my son." The father was breathing hard, but he was catching his wind. I noticed the Father's hand. There was blood on it, red and dripping. "Have you been bitten, Father?"

"Thankfully, no. But I did get a gash from broken glass. I had to make my escape through my gargious stained-glass window. Such a shame too. Such beauty is now destroyed because I had to save my own blooming arse. I'll be repenting for a month for that!"

"I'm sure the God of Heaven will forgive you for fleeing from the evil minions of the devil."

Father O'Donnovan stopped and looked at me, "Aye, you speak the truth, my son... even for an unfortunate heathen such as yourself, you speak the truth." He shook his head again, "Mysterious ways... He told me last night in a dream that I would find a monster and that I should follow him to safe havens... but all I've found was these blasted undead... who do no leading of any sort, just a lot of chasing and grabbing."

"We need to get the bleeding stopped on that hand, Father."

I keyed my radio, "Ogre to Marine One. Come in Marine One."

"Go ahead, Ogre, we read you."

"I have a survivor that needs some medical attention here. Requesting a dust off."

"Roger that, Ogre. Marine One is inbound. Did you find our Lost Boys?"

"Negative. Trail is cold. No sign of men or the ITV. Ogre Out."

Father O'Donnovan stood very still, "Ogre did you say? Ogre is it?"

"That's what my friends call me."

"Mysterious indeed. I am on the right path then." The Father pulled out a stainless flask and knocked it back in a nice, long snort. "Sometimes I think maybe I should have been Protestant." He looked at me sideways. "At least you are not one of those, my son."

The V-22 set down in the field, and I grabbed Father O'Donnovan's arm and ran him aboard. "Corpsman, this is Father Shamus O'Donnavan. He has a glass cut." He was on it.

I turned to look at April who was wiping her eyes, "You're not getting out of my sight again. I shouldn't have let you."

"You obeyed an order. That's what you should have done. That's what you did."

"That was an order from my boss." She said, as she reached her arm up around my head and pulled me down to her. "But I'm not just an employee." She held me tight. "I'm not letting you out of my sight again... not when you're away from the ranch."

A small group of zombies found the hole in the fence. The gunner in the V-22 shot them down before they could get into the field. He used short bursts, conserving ammo.

I crouched behind the pilot's seat. "Our missing brothers came here, but I didn't see where they went. I'm going to try again." The pilot nodded.

"Father, this is Joy... we lost someone close to us... closest to her." I indicated the black bag on the floor. "If you could be so kind as to watch over her while I'm gone? There are some sheep missing from my flock."

April and I went to the shed. It was concrete, grey and dull. Past the shed further out in the field, I noticed a huge concrete slab. Then it hit me and I knew what this place was. How did the Marines get in? Or did they? The tracks went passed the shed, but had come back to it. They had to have gone in.

The LED panel asked for a code. That was easy enough. I had the book. I put in my override code and could hear the sound of heavy bolts disengaging. I pushed the door open and found lights on inside and a Marine Growler parked there like an angry little Jeep. No one was here though. We walked past the ITV and found another door. It opened to a stairwell. We walked a couple steps down and I stopped and crouched on the stairs. "Is that Silly String?" April asked.

"Yeah, it is."

"Why?"

"They were looking for tripwires."

"What?"

"Tripwires... really thin. Hard to see. The silly string will lay on them, but not pull them. Let's you know where the trip wire is. Easier to see than the wire."

At the bottom of the stairs I could see a green glow. A chem-light. I walked quietly down the stairs and found that there was a short hallway with a heavy door at the other end. It was open. We went to it and found more stairs. The door was one of those vault-type doors, with a huge wheel on it and bolts the size of Coke cans sticking out of it. There was a plate on the wall inside the door. USAMRIID/CDC DARPA VIROLOGY BIO CONTAINMENT RESEARCH CENTER.

The stairs went down... deep. April was studying the map, I was listening. I couldn't hear anything.

"You know what this reminds me of?" She said.

"No, what?"

"Racoon City."

I shook my head, "I don't know what that is."

"Up top is Racoon City. This is going down in the Umbrella Corporation."

"Still lost here... taken individually, I know what the words you're saying means, but the way you string them together is like a different language."

"*Resident Evil.*"

"The game or movie?"

"Both." She said. "The Umbrella Corporation had a research facility under the city."

"I think I remember the movie."

"Not important, but that's what this is."

"What ever it is... this place is freaking huge! It's a maze. No wonder we can't get them on the radio. We either go down there and get lost hunting, or we can just wait."

"How long have they been down here?"

"Two, maybe two and a half hours."

"Let's give them a little more time?" April suggested.

While I didn't like it, it was probably the best course of action. "Okay. We wait." But I didn't want to startle the guys as they came back up. I tossed the chem-light down the stairs so they knew someone was up here, then we went back up to the first set of stairs.

After a few minutes, Joy came down the steps. "The good father was driving me nuts...wants me to repent of my evil ways." As surprised as I was to see her, I was glad she was here.

Her eyes had dried, but the make-up was still streaked. "I left him so he could give his sales pitch to Jen. She has more patience than I do. So, what are you guys doing sitting here?" She reached to me and I took her hand and squeezed it.

"Waiting."

"For what?"

From down the hall we could hear the sound of small arms fire. Lots of shots. Rapid fire and full auto. Suddenly all the lights went out. We turned on our weapon lights. "For them to come out."

We didn't have long to wait. Soon the light came back on. Then I heard a voice come up from down the stairs below us.

"Q, what color Chem-light did you use?" There was a pause. "Cause there's a green one on the landing here." A few moments later and I heard steps coming up. We kept our weapons pointed in safe directions. Soon there was the grinning face of Chris, one of the Marines that had gone with Q. He smiled. "It's Ogre and the Girls. Gee, I wish we had time to tidy up the place."

We entered the facility proper and Q explained what I had already known, but he was being a tour guide for the girls. He explained that this had been an old Atlas Missile silo during the cold war and had since been repurposed for medical research.

We rested here for a while before we readied ourselves for the trip home. In the mean time, the girls had cut their hair short and severe, longer in the front, it still framed their faces but gone was the look of softness they used to have.

Q made a request that I couldn't refuse. A side trip to Maine. His family homestead was in Maine. We were not that far away and I was in no hurry.

"Sure. Why not?"

"Something else. Gun shopping. You'll love it."

A Sidetrip to Maine

We made the hop to Maine the next morning. There was a reunion between Louis CQ and his family. "Walt, Barbara, I'd like you to meet George Hill, Former Governor of Utah, current President of the Confederated Western States, and acting President of the United States." Q made the presentation with a flourish and bowed low.

"Pleased to meet you." I shook hands with his family and leaned over to Q's Uncle. "He can be a smartass sometimes, can't he?" Walt nodded.

Walt was a man with some serious connections before the zombie uprising started. We went to a range they had set up on their property and waiting for us there was a small arsenal. Remington ACR's in 6.8SPC along with magazines and AAC Suppressors.

Q handed me a large SR-25 type rifle that looked just like a Crusader Broadsword. It was an LMT. The retail on the LMTs was about double the price of a Broadsword, but it was just as good. It was also a hell of a lot lighter than my Sage and that would make things a lot easier. Especially since my leg was hurting a lot. I didn't want to seem too excited. I broke the gun open and inspected it. It was flawless. I even liked the 1-6 scope on it.

"It's nice but I don't know if I'm ready to give up that Sage yet. But seeing as we're here." On the table was a bottle of Slipstream. Excellent.

I spent some time with it, getting it zeroed. It only needed two clicks of adjustment to bring it dead nuts on for me.

Q just grinned when I started dumping M-14 mags out of my pouches and replacing them with SR-25 mags. I left the Sage on the table and disconnected the single-point sling from it and clipped it to the LMT. "I thought you'd like that."

"Well, it's no Crusader, but it's good to go."

Q laughed.

We spent a couple days in Maine, shooting a few zombies and generally relaxing. When it was time to go, I honestly didn't want to. If I was Q, I probably wouldn't have. But duty called and we loaded back up into the Ospreys for the flight home.

TWELVE

The Crimson Guard

A **few days later** I was sitting at the table in Musket's Pub. I looked deep into my pint of Dr. Pepper and rubbed my temples. The reason for my headache was that I was trying to follow the logic of the argument between Musket and Father O'Donnovan.

Since coming to The Ranch (which was now a compound and airdrome for VTOL aircraft, and a Vehicle Maintenance Depot) Musket and The Father had argued continuously. Sometimes Musket would kick the Father out and he would be outside sitting on a stump by the wood pile considering his position. Other times, Musket would be out sitting on the stump. "Aye, he made a good argument."

Inside, the Pub had changed. A section had been added to the east of the building, two floors of rooms for people who have come to see me that had to wait until I came back from a mission, or for other dignitaries and officers. The other thing that had changed was the fire pit in the center of the Pub, and the large brass bell that hung down over it to collect smoke and take it up and out of the building. The fire pit had spits slowly rotating over the heat, upon which turned meats from various wild game. The pit was tended by the newest Bar Wench. She was pretty, with long red hair and very large breasts, but she was otherwise a very skinny girl. Musket never touched her, instead he would only ask where her fat sister was. This girl however made up for the lack of Musket attention by catching the occasional attention of other patrons.

Jen's funeral had really made me think. I analyzed what happened over and over. Just as the Red Eye moved and exerted its power, its eyes just for a flicker, glowed bright red, like there was flame behind the eyes. I talked to some of the others about this and they had witnessed the same things with other Red Eyes.

The funeral was small, just me, Joy and April, Father O'Donnovan, Musket, and some of the soldiers that had come to know her. It was short, with the Father saying the good words. Everyone else was off on missions. Not that they would have cared. Mrs Ogre was there too with flowers for the plain wooden casket. The little boys were home, Rosa was watching them. She had come back when her soldier had been killed in action by a Red Eye. I didn't know it at the time, but he was the guy that got bit by the first Red Eye we encountered in Central Utah. While Rosa was cooking at the Ranch House, and helping with the kids, she was back at making home-made tortillas and the best breakfast burritos I've ever had. She'd matured a lot. Gone was the Princess attitude. I felt sorry for her. She was spending a lot of time alone.

The Comms guys were doing a great job keeping track of messages. Those messages that could be taken care of by staff were taken care of. Those that needed my eyes were sent to my Acer Tablet. This was set up with a message system and it was tied into the Blue Force Tracker system. I had messages coming in, with report briefings. Each brief was summarized and if I wanted more information on it, I could click it and get the full report. I skimmed some briefings and read some reports. My job was becoming much more admin and a lot less hands on. I was bored.

One of the reports that I clicked on was the incursion of a CH-135 Helicopter from Canada into the Dakotas. It wouldn't have been much of a question however its flight profile was a real grass burner. It made its way to the Whiteshell Nuclear Research Facility. The facility was no longer active and all its nuclear materials had been removed, which was why no one was really worried at the moment.

I knew who this was. One of the people closest to him sent detailed reports of his actions to us every time he did something. When he shot his two lieutenants, those around him became very worried about his fall into madness. He was unstable and people around him were uncomfortable. I sent a message to the acting commander of the Minot Air Force Base in North Dakota, where the report came in from. "Response to Incursion: Activate STT. Observe from Distance. Track, Observe, Report. Do Not Engage." Minot AFB had a nice little group of Spec Ops guys, they called them Special Tactics Teams. They were really good at keeping an eye on things. This was a perfect task for them.

Moments later, the message came in, "STT has been tracking target since initial observation." I tasked some other troops to get ready to respond if anything happened and the STT reported overtly hostile action. The other reports were more ordinary as far as anything was ordinary anymore.

Winchester, Indiana was tightening their belts. They had a strong group of survivors. The only problem with them was they considered me to be a threat. Evidently they only hear rumor and urban legends in Winchester. Well, that was no problem. All I had to do was talk to them. I put that on the

313

things-to-do list.

Sitting beside me at the table was Joy. Since we got back from New England, the girls had taken a more severe turn. Their long hair was cut into a modern, bobbed style that was short in the back and long in the front. It framed their faces and looked cute, but it also made them look sharper, harder edged... a "Don't mess with me" look. On Joy's finger was Ruby, a ring I gave her as a symbol of the blood oath she gave me, like April did. They had taken to wearing only ruby jewelry. No gold or silver. Just red. "Crimson" as they called it.

"Are you going to talk to them?" Joy asked.

April was talking to a woman by the bar. She was short and thin, petite. She had long, jet black curly hair that almost looked like it had blue highlights in it, almond-shaped eyes and olive-colored skin. She was very pretty, but I didn't care about that. What I cared about was that she had come from Israel, and was a professional soldier there, with specialties in Intel. She was also a trained sharpshooter, and she wanted work on my security detail. Her name was Isabella.

The other lady waiting to see me was a police officer from Kentucky. She was pale-skinned, red-haired, button-nosed, blue-eyed, freckled, and just cute as a button as Joy said. She looked younger than she was. She was a champion on her department's pistol team and was the SWAT Armorer. Her name was Ruth.

The third girl was someone we had already met. Rebecca, the officer from Arizona who we dropped off in southern Utah. She had come up and wanted on with the security detail. I looked up at the women. I was told that I needed to expand my security team... all of them had the credentials and experience. Just being alive was experience enough to prove they were tough enough.

"Musket!" I barked. Uncle Musket looked up from his Guinness pouring, and gave me that Just a Sec nod. He and Father O'Donnovan, having exhausted the topics of The Good Word, were now arguing over the proper pour for serving Guinness. The Father having demonstrated, was standing with his arms folded ,watching Musket pour the dark liquid into a large glass. The Father's eyebrow was raised and he nodded approvingly. "Well I'm pleased you got something right after all. I can't disagree on the technique. That's a good glass."

Musket handed the Father the glass and walked over.

"See these girls here?" I asked.

"Aye, but they are all so skinny I can hardly stand to look at them. I've been tempted to force feed them more sandwiches. The poor things are half starved to death."

"They want to join my security team." I handed him the resumes and Musket sat down and looked them over carefully. "What do you think?"

"Well, I wouldn't take any of them to bed, if I were you. The frail little

314

things would break." He looked at Joy. "I'm surprised she's still alive at all let alone walking."

Joy blushed, the first time I had ever seen that. I shook my head, "No, Musket. I don't sleep with them. That wouldn't be in the cards for any of them."

"Uh huh... well what do you want from Uncle Musket?"

"Weed them out. Separate the wheat from the chaff."

"You mean drill them until one of them drops out."

"Yup."

Musket got up from the table, "Now listen here you aspiring guardians of his majesty the Ogre." He spoke loudly and clearly, commanding the attention of all three. "It's time for a little physical testing. If you lasses would be so kind as to follow me, please."

He led the applicants out the back door into the field. I just noticed the skinny wench at the fire pit was gone. I looked around and saw that she was coming out of the hallway with Outbreak following, grinning ear to ear and buttoning his trousers. I shook my head and went back to my reports.

It was two hours later that the girls came back, carrying Musket in by each arm and one at his feet. They swung him up into his hammock.

"Well? I asked from across the room.

"All three of them passed the tests." He said before he passed out.

April rubbed my shoulders. " We should take all three of them. We can use the extra help, especially since I'm not feeling well."

"She's right," Joy said. "Besides, I'm tired of lugging this damned thing around." Joy nodded to the silver brief case.

"I don't think we need to actually carry it around with us all the time here."

"Well, where else am I going to put it?"

I thought about it. "I've got a place."

"The applicants?" April said.

I looked at the girls then stood up. The girls stood tall, at attention. Well, Isabella stood as tall as she could. "You little girls want to be on my security detail? Really? You think you can handle the job? My last two teams of body guards are all dead. Right there," Pointing at Joy and April "Are the only two survivors left." I let that sink in. "You will be in harm's way, I will take you there. I will put you in danger."

None of them balked. "Joy, take them to the Valkyrie House to stow their gear, then take them to the armory. I want them geared up, armed, and ready to go."

Joy grinned, "Come on, ladies."

Over the next couple days, applicants came in. Many were turned away. Many were hired. Most would be used for more clandestine work. All that were accepted that were women who swore the blood oaths were given ruby earrings as a sign of their oaths. A few men that were accepted were given a ruby as well, but it was a collar pin. One girl who had multiple piercings also wore a ruby in her nose piercing. The Crimson Guard. My agents, my security team, my personal soldiers. I got to know each of them. One morning I took all of them and we went through weapons training with them to see who was the best. A handful of the agents were sent on different missions that I gave to them personally, with only myself, April and Joy knowing about. Better I send agents than I run around the country taking care of everything personally.

"What are you really up to, George?" April asked, trying to see the big picture.

"Pulling all the strings together."

The next day I was in Musket's Tavern eating a sandwich. Carl was trying to sell me something.

"The problem with the M-ATV is that the thing is too heavy and too slow." Carl said. Carl was an old friend of mine and a Ford Truck die-hard.

"Sure it is, but it's got us through a bunch of scraps and we came out just fine. It's a good rig."

"Okay, but say you could have all that but with some quick and fast thrown in?" Carl said with a sly grin. I know that grin.

"What do you have up your sleeves, Killer?" I said, using his old nickname.

"Well, I know you lost your Chevy, and I know you liked it for some dumbass reason. So, I thought this was a good time to upgrade you to something reasonable. Not every drive is a military operation." He jerked his head towards the door. I stood up and followed him outside as he picked up the radio, "Bring it in."

The sound of a roaring engine could be heard off in the distance, then suddenly a silver flash could be seen and quicker than I've ever seen, a truck raced up the highway from Shirley's and pulled up to a stop in front of Musket's Pub.

It was a big, silver truck with four doors, large tires, huge fenders in black that matched the monolithic black grill that simply said OGRE across the front. The windows were tinted black, keeping the theme of my old Chevy. The truck sat there idling angrily as the driver got out and high-fived Carl as he walked past. "It's too fast, Killer."

"What is it?" I asked as I walked around.

"It's a Ford Raptor... with some modifications."

I raised my eyebrow. Killer was the guy that started the whole Mad Max movement in Iraq with the Humvees. His modifications were legendary. He gave me the tour. "It's got a raised center seat in the back, turret ring up top accessed through a powered sunroof. Three Sixty degrees if you're careful where you put your feet. There are only a few of the four-door versions around, so it took a bit of hunting to find one. Weapon racks in the back window and vertical racks up front. Blue Force Tracker from one of the Humvees that's been taken off line due to a bad tranny. We've got dual batteries, an on-board air compressor... and back here, storage lockers for plenty of ammunition and a storage case for the Ma Deuce... Normal off road lights... a PA system, standard milspec coms, civilian CB radio, XM radio, Dolby five point one. The GPS came with the truck, redundant with the BFT, but the audible turn-by-turn is nice. We got you another Yeti in the back, a bigger one, for your longer trips this rig is going to be a lot nicer to ride in. IR strobe beacon up top as well."

"Okay, okay. I'm sold. I'm sold."

Carl gave me a fist bump and then I threw him a hug. "Thanks man."

"I'm just glad you'll be in a real truck now. Bow ties are for geeks."

Uncle Musket came out of the pub with a mutton leg in one hand. He looked around the truck and peered inside. He sniffed at it and shook his head in dismissal. "Too much infernal technology."

"Hey, let's take it for a test drive!"

I climbed in and Carl jumped in the passenger seat. Joy and April climbed in the back. The truck felt like it wasn't just alive, but that it wanted to run.

"Ford's SVT crew designed her for off-road racing made street legal.... nothing else like it." Carl continued his lecture. "You'll have to set the cruise control to stay in a convoy, because there is nothing gonna keep up with it. And that's the important part. Getting into trouble, you're good at. Getting out of it, that's what this is for. The windows are bullet resistant, we've got armor panels in the doors, and in the back. The whole crew compartment is armored against small arms. Oh, and the seats recline all the way back in case you need to catch a few zees."

In the back the girls stowed their 6.8mm ACR's in the racks. My SR-25 locked secure in the police-style rack, muzzle down. Everything was laid out well, and didn't feel cramped. The power and handling was amazing.

Back at the pub, Carl got out and said "Glad you like it. I'm tricking out a few more just like it for your executive protection, along with a couple Expeditions and Excursions. I never liked that the Commander and Chief had Yukon XL's and Suburbans. I'm going to fix that."

I looked at April who was smiling, "You think we should take this or the M-ATV on the trip east?"

"Don't even think about that old Army junker again."

"Ever" Joy said.

"Ouch." I said as I climbed out of the Raptor. Isabella, the newest and smallest of my Crimson Guard was standing by the Pub's entrance holding my Tablet. She looked agitated. "What's wrong, Bella?"

"We've got some problems, sir."

"Don't call me sir..."

"Okay... as long as you don't call me Bella."

"Okay, I can make that deal."

"My friends called me Izzy... before..." She looked down.

"I like Izzy. Now what's the problems?"

She held up the Tablet and I saw the list. "Shit." I took the little Acer and told Izzy to gather my security and get the Officer of the Watch from the Comms Tent. (Which was no longer actually a tent, but a small hanger like building that bristled with dishes and antennas.) Izzy ran off without a second's hesitation.

"What's up, boss?" The girls tried to read the screen.

"We're going to be heading east a lot sooner than I expected. Find Outbreak, pull him off that Skinny Wench, and tell him to get the C-130's ready to go."

A Very Special Plague

*T*he Vernal Airport, as small as it is, has enough room for a trio of C-130's sitting in stand by. As soon as the order came, flight crews started getting the planes ready to take off. Topping off fuel tanks, pre-flight checks, and getting the CAP overhead know that we were going to be taking off.

I drove the Raptor straight up the waiting cargo ramp into the Herc, following the Load Master's direction, and immediately the crew started locking it down for the flight.

"Nice truck, what happened to the M-ATV?" The Load Master, a man named Rankin, asked. Rankin was a Gear Head and loved the M-ATV.

"I was told I needed something faster, but it's coming too." I looked out and saw the M-ATV rolling into the airport and heading for the second Herc. Rebecca was driving it, and Ruth was riding shotgun. One of the new Crimson Guard girls was in the turret. I think her name is Caroline. She was a short, cute thing that kept to herself, quiet, but outshot every one of the new hires save for Izzy.

In the third rig, which was just now turning into the airport, was a Humvee. Different from normal military rigs. This one was a civilian Humvee, formerly owned by the previous Governor of California. The young man driving it had his elbow out the window, dark hair, sunglasses, huge grin around a fat cigar of some sort. His team, I didn't know them so much, but Paul Fitch vouched for them and I saw no reason, considering their mission that he couldn't bring his own guys on this one. FMJ was enthusiastic enough and wanted to come. I was surprised when he pulled up to Uncle Musket's Pub. I was even more surprised when he said something to April and she kicked him in the balls. She still won't tell me what he said.

"Are you sure that's a good idea, sir?" Izzy looked up at me, she was fully kitted out in tactical gear and armed with a 6.8 ACR like the rest of my girls.

"Nope, not sure at all, but it seemed like a good idea at the time. And THAT will be enough of a distraction to let us do our mission."

The bright red Humvee rolled up into the back of the 3rd Herc and within a few minutes we were taxiing to take off.

We kept in contact with the Air Force STT team. A distinct pattern had emerged. These guys would go into a town, and leave the next morning, and some of the folks in the town would get sick. Harrison, one of the STT leaders dropped his Swarovski EL binos and scratched his chin. The stubble had started growing into a full beard now and the itchiness was driving him nuts.

"Subject A is looking very pale and thinner than he was even yesterday. And look at his neck." He passed the binos over to Leroy. "Boils. The man is infected with something."

"And he's spreading it through the surviving communities."

"On purpose?"

"I don't know." Harrison said as he watched through the binos again. The subjects were talking to a tall, thin woman that looked like a long-haired Molly Ringwald. She wore a long-sleeved, tight shirt that looked like leather, and around her neck was like a Native American type necklace made of bones.

After some discussion, the men went about making camp. They were between towns and looked like they were going to stay here for the night. One of the men started swaying and fell down, spilling his mess kit full of canned stew. He tried to get back up, but seemed too weak to do so. His face was covered in boils and sores. The woman was laughing. Subject A stood up, walked over to the man and yelled something at him. Harrison watched as the guy pulled out a Glock pistol and fired a shot into the man's head. A couple seconds later, the STT team heard the shot. The dead man flopped to the ground and one of his legs kicked for a moment before it was still. Subject A went back and sat down and started eating again.

"That's cold, man. Stone cold." Leroy said.

"You notice something?" Harrison asked.

"What? That he's crazy?"

"No. He does everything with one hand."

"Huh?" Leroy took the binos and watched as subject A ate, then set the spoon down to pick up the bottle of water, then switched back to the spoon again. "Okay, so."

"Look... he's not even holding the tray."

"So?"

"He only has one hand. The other hand is a fake."

"Look at that!" Leroy handed the binos back to Harrison.

"Damn!" The woman had pulled out a long, thin knife, like a fillet knife, and carved a long section of bicep muscle off the dead man, and then cut out his tongue. As sick as that was... when she started eating the tongue, while still laughing, Harrison had to keep down the urge to gag. For some reason the sound of the woman's laughter carried. It was a cold, humorless laugh that made Harrison feel sick to his stomach. "Please tell me you are getting all this." Harrison said to another team member, Grant. Grant had a digital video camera set on a small tripod.

"Yeah, but I really wish I didn't, Chief."

"How long do we have to keep tracking these assholes? Why can't we just take them out?"

"We can't, because we were told specifically to not engage and to observe and report until further notice."

"Roger that." Leroy sighed and rolled over onto his back. The subjects have broken contact a couple of times, but their trail was easy enough for them to pick up again. They were trying very hard to not be followed, but they didn't seem to know that they were being actually followed. So they thought their efforts were working.

"Well, we only have to keep on target for a few more hours."

"Why's that?"

"The Ogre is coming."

"Bullshit.""He'll be here in a few hours to make the intercept. We support him, then we RTB for some down time."

"He's not going to nuke them is he?"

"Now why would you say some stupid shit like that?"

"Because that's what he does, isn't it?"

"He hasn't nuked anyone."

"Tell that to the Los Zetas."

"Those asshats had it coming. Besides," Harrison explained while look-ing through the binos. "The power plant was going super critical anyways, nothing to stop it, so he just led the Cartel to the place. He used what was going to happen regardless."

"What about Salt Lake?"

"It was one of our MOABs."

"People say it was nuke. It looked like a nuke."

"Because the damned MOAB makes a blast that looks like a nuclear mushroom cloud."

"So how do you know it wasn't?"

"Because I saw them load it onto the plane."

Leroy pulled out a power bar and started munching on it. Through his mouthful, "Could have been a different plane."

"Stow that talk! You are starting to irritate me more than my facial hair."

"Just sayin..."

Enter the Ogre

*T*he pilots were real good and landed the Hercs on a long, straight stretch of dirt road miles off from the highway. Once we got unloaded and under way, the C-130s took off and turned south west again before they headed to Cheyenne, Wyoming to wait for our call.

We drove east on the dirt road before we found the highway that took us north to our target. I turned onto the highway and found I had to really slow down to let the other rigs catch up.

"So how are we going to play this one out?" April asked. She was looking a little green from the flight. She hated flying, but had always kept it in check.

"I don't know just yet. I'm still working it out. Depends on the METT, I guess."

"Mission, Enemy, Terrain, and Time... Right?"

"Yeah. You know all that. Why are you asking?"

"Keeping my mind off things."

"Like?"

"Like not throwing up in our new truck. Oh... pull over."

I pulled over and April dove out the door, retching onto the pavement. She climbed back in, sweating, wiping her mouth off with a rag. I looked back at Joy, who just shrugged and handed me a water bottle.

"You going to be okay?" I asked as I gave April the bottle.

"I'll be fine. Just drive straight for once." She leaned back in the seat.

"If you're getting sick on us, you should have said something and you could have stayed at the ranch."

"No, I'm fine. I hate flying. You know that. Come on. We have evil people to kill. Let's get it done."

"You didn't get sick on the Ospreys."

"Marines are better pilots than Outbreak."

I looked at her sideways, but put the truck back in gear. Izzy pulled herself down from the turret. "Sir?"

"Damn it, Izzy."

"Sorry... uh. Why couldn't you just tell the Air Force STT guys to kill them?"

"If you sentence someone to die, and you can't do it yourself, maybe they shouldn't be killed."

"You've sent a lot of people to do fighting."

"This is an execution."

Izzy got quiet again and stood back up in the turret. I got the Raptor back up to speed and we continued, keeping the other rigs close behind us.

As we approached the location, it was still dark. I told Paul to hang back and wait here and I watched the red Humvee pull over off the highway before he clicked his mic twice in acknowledgment.

We drove further up the highway before pulling off and stopping ourselves. From here, we hoofed it, stopping only once more for April to empty her stomach again. As we approached the objective, I heard someone call out.

"Durango." It was the challenge phrase.

I called out the answer, "Ninety Five."

"You the Ogre?"

"Yeah."

"Bring any nukes?"

"Screw you! Where's Harrison?"

"This way." Leroy chuckled.

We snuck the rest of the way to the STT's location, and I belly crawled to where Harrison was laying, looking through some binos. I crawled up to his side and whispered, "Should I have brought a nuke?"

"Don't listen to Leroy. He's a dumbass. Pleased to meet you, Mister President."

"Just call me Ogre."

"Sorry, never even heard of a politician getting his hands dirty like this."

"I'm not a politician. I'm just an old grunt doing what he knows how to do."

Harrison grunted. "Everyone is just laying there, asleep... cept for that chick there. She's been eating on that dead guy for a while now."

I took the binos from Harrison and looked through them. "I'll be damned."

"What?"

"It's Shannon."

"Who's Shannon?" Harrison asked.

"My Sister."

I pulled back off the berm. Shannon. My sister. And she's a Red Eye. This doesn't surprise me at all. The sun was starting to come up, the eastern horizon was brightening. Let's hit them now. I picked up the radio. "Ogre to FMJ."

"FMJ here."

"Drive about a hundred yards past where we pulled off, you'll see a trail to the left. Take that trail. You have about five hundred yards before you come to the target camp."

"Roger that, Ogre."

"Shoot everything you can. Come in hard, Paul."

"On it."

I turned to the girls. "I think this is going to get ugly. So when we hit them, hit them hard. Get ready."

I turned to the STT guys. "I want you guys to make sure no one escapes. Flank left, get up on the higher ground there and cover that gully." The Air Force troops nodded and moved out.

I picked up my battle rifle, checked it, and moved forward. We stayed low, moving between cover, working our way closer. The men were laying there, asleep, but Shannon was acting like she wasn't aware of us. I had the feeling that she was. She was acting too casual. I could tell, because she was stiff and wooden, even more so than usual. Part of me wanted to take her out from a distance. That would probably be the smartest, but I didn't.

The sound of a racing engine could be heard, and I could see the glint of glossy red paint coming from the east. The men that had been laying like they were asleep, suddenly broke their act, and pulled out an M249 SAW that they had hidden. They fired a long burst of fire directly into the brush where the STT guys had been. Tracers lanced over our heads briefly before they turned the gun to the incoming Humvee.

I took a position and leveled my rifle. Through the ACOG I could see one of the guys with something small in his hand. I recognized it too late. A Clicker. I squeezed the trigger just as the guy squeezed the Clicker. There was an explosion just in front of the Humvee at the same time my bullet impacted the man's head. The SAW gunner opened up on the Humvee as it arched into the air. The girls opened up and shots from the suppressed 6.8's chewed up the guy on the big gun.

The remaining man looked over at me with wild eyes, his face a mask of hatred and rage. I pulled my gun over as he ducked and ran a few steps to disappear into a gully. Unsuppressed shots from the red Humvee rang out. Shannon fell backwards off the stump she had been sitting on. We picked up and rushed forward. I motioned to the right, "Ruth – go check on Paul's team!"

"Got it." Ruth said and took Caroline with her as she peeled off. We approached the small camp site and the sound of laughter rose up, the chill of it hit me like a bucket of cold water.

Shannon rose up from the ground like she was pulled by ropes. Her bloodshot eyes glared at me. Before I could pull the heavy gun up, she opened her hand and I was smashed by an unseen force. I was knocked backwards into April, my rifle disappeared out of my hands. The girls were bowled over.

I got back up onto my feet.

"This one has spirit... so persistent to die." Shannon hissed and cackled. I could taste blood in my mouth.

"Long time no see, Shannon." I said.

She stopped laughing and glared at me. "George!" Her eyes went wide with surprise, then narrowed at me. "Oh how delicious this is. I'm going to kill you so slowly."

"Yeah, love you too, sister. So how's the family? How's the kids?"

Shannon hissed. "They're here with us, brother." She gestured to the necklace. I recognized now that it was made of small bones, finger bones. "I always keep my children close to my heart."

The realization made my whole body recoil. "You couldn't."

"The sweetest meat I've ever tasted." She said as her eyes glowed bright red. I felt unseen hands around my throat that lifted me off the ground. "I think it was the mother-child bond that made it so... special." she hissed. But I've always hated you. You would probably taste worse than this idiot I was snacking on."

I tried to say something, but the grip around my throat was crushing and all I could think about was getting air.

"Let him go, you bitch!" Joy knelt with a pistol in her hand. She didn't wait for Shannon to comply, and fired a shot. Shannon reacted as the bullet hit her ear, blasting it mostly off of her head. Shannon made a slapping motion at Joy who squawked as she was knocked backwards like a bowling pin.

"She shot me! She's going to pay for that!" Shannon held her ear and then just laughed.

I was starting to black out.

"I believe she said to let him go." April stood up and walked out from behind me. ACR in hand.

Shannon threw her hand out and opened her palm. I felt the blast of energy and closed my eyes, fearing what I might see.

"That was the best you got?" April said. She had been untouched by the energy blast.

Shannon tried again, "Why can't I?" Then she just laughed. I opened my eyes and saw Shannon's face twist into a Joker Grin. "Oh! How DELIGHTFUL!"

April fired, a full 28-round burst. Her rounds tore through Shannon's torso and up through her throat. I was instantly released and fell to the ground as April reloaded. I stood up, gasping and stumbling over to April. I put a hand on her shoulder as I walked past.

I watched as Shannon grasped at her throat. She saw me and tried to exert her power, but it was just a weak push. Blackened blood pumped out of her like crude oil. I rubbed my own throat. "We should really clear the air between us, sister... You... you really hated me. I never knew why. Why was that?"

"You... had... joy." She wheezed and gurgled.

Then something happened. The red of the eyes started to fade out. As I watched, her eyes changed. They went from red to pink and soon I was looking into the same dead fish eyes I had seen so many times. Shannon moaned and reached up for me.

My Glock bucked in my hand once and she stopped moving altogether.

"You had Joy?" April looked at me with a raised eyebrow.

"Stop it."

"I got something for you, Ogre!" Harrison called out. I looked up and saw Harrison leading someone who was handcuffed behind his back. As he got closer I saw that the man's jacket was torn and bloodied, and the sleeves were actually tied back and not handcuffed.

"Who is it?" I asked.

"No ID.... GIRLS – Stay Back!" Harrison shouted. "He has Small Pox!" Harrison forced the man to his knees. The man didn't say anything. Just hung his head. He looked familiar. "Who are you?"

He said nothing. I walked over and grabbed his hair and pulled his face up. He spit at me, but it fell short of my face.

Harrison explained. "He has a missing arm... had to tie the arms of the jacket."

"One arm?" I looked at the face again. Gaunt, pale, boils, hair and beard unkempt. Recognition dawned on me. "Can't be... Sean?" Sean was a member of WeTheArmed.com back before all this started. He was a good man. Smart. But something had changed him.

The man shook with rage. Sean let out a blood-curdling scream. I pulled out my Becker Bowie to cut off the jacket.

"You killed my WIFE! My FAMILY!"

"I have no idea what you're talking about." I was thinking about where to take an infected prisoner.

"Liar! Who sent the Spectre Gunship?"

"What gunship?"

Sean screamed again and twisted inside his jacket. His one arm snaked out and grabbed the Glock pistol that Harrison had stuck in his belt. As he pulled it out, Sean started firing. Multiple rounds fired up into Harrison's chest and he started falling backwards.

As the gun swung towards me, I swung the Becker. There was a crunch of bone as the big knife chopped through the forearm, cutting it completely off. The hand with the Glock was still firing as it fell. Sean screamed and cursed. I swung the Becker again, and Sean's head landed 15 feet away.

I went over to Harrison. "That bastard!" He started to stand back up, painfully. I helped him up.

"You wearing armor?"

"Level two, a soft armor. I wear it all the time."

"Good for you. Saved your ass."

"Still hurts like hell though."

"Yeah, I know the feeling."

Leroy and the other STT guys gathered around their team leader.

"Sir," Leroy said, "I'd like to request some time off for R&R."

"Granted."

"Uh, can we get a lift back to base?"

"I think we can arrange that. You sure it's Small Pox, Harrison?"

"I've seen it before in Africa and South America. It's Small Pox."

"Everyone that came into contact with these guys – just strip off anything that could be contaminated." I said as I stripped out of my tactical vest. We put the clothes and gear into garbage bags. They would have to be decontaminated later.

Paul came up, limping and grinning with the guys from his team. All were accounted for. He looked at the SAW on the ground, "DIBBS!" I motioned for him to take it.

"Before you touch it, wash it down with hot soap and water with some bleach in it. The dudes that had it were sick with Small Pox."

Paul nodded then pulled out a pair of fitted leather gloves. "I'm going to take you back to California with me!" He said to the gun.

Isabella was holding up Joy, who had a bloody nose. I went over to her, "You okay?"

Joy nodded. "She can really throw a punch."

I gave her a hug, "I'm glad you're okay." Then I turned to April. She smiled at me. I pulled her into the hug and we had a laugh of relief. The other Crimson girls looked at each other and shrugged.

"Your sister was a real bitch." April finally said.

"You have no idea."

"What are we going to do with the bodies?" Harrison asked.

"Leave them for the coyotes."

A few minutes later I watched as the two remaining vehicles pulled up, the Raptor and the M-ATV. Not nearly enough room for everyone in comfortable seats, so the Air Force troops and Paul's team climbed into the bed of the Raptor. We drove north heading to the AFB. Paul was in the back seat sitting next to Isabella, he yawned and stretched and was about to put his arm around Izzy. "Don't even think about it, beach boy." She said.

Home at Long Last

The C-130's were flying in. I looked up and noticed a new logo painted on the nose as the aircraft flew overhead. I had seen some guys with this logo on other vehicles and aircraft. The symbol of the Confederated Western States. This gave me a mix of emotions. Pride in that we had held some form of society together, protected survivors, brought needed supplies and aid to those in dire need. We'd removed zombies by the bushel. We're getting through this. However, I remember my Oath of Service to my country. And right now, that country is still fragmented. The Western States have come together and have shown strength and independence, which I admired. The Eastern states, some have joined with us.

Florida, Georgia, Virginia, the Carolinas. What few survivors there were back east. The Mid West however, was the problem. They wanted to remain independent from everyone else. This would be a problem for us, and eventually a problem for them. Come spring, they will have a flood season with too few people to help deal with it. Then we'll need crops that they grow. We have to come together. We have to be united again. All of us. But what of Alaska? That's another problem. And Hawaii? We haven't heard anything from Hawaii since the uprising, since China's attack.

Much to think on.

I dispatched a full effort on fighting Small Pox, including inoculations for those that hadn't been exposed yet, to prevent further spread. Which was luckily a small number and they were reasonably isolated.

"Look what I have!" Joy shouted. I looked over and saw Joy walking across the tarmac towards us with paper bags with huge grease stains. Even from here – I could smell it. Burgers.

"Oh man – what do you have, Joy? Don't tease me!"

We dropped the tailgate on the Raptor and Joy opened the bags. Fries, thick-cut fries covered in salt and oil. Burgers, thick and juicy. Enough for the whole team. "They didn't have beef." Joy said. I stopped, frozen in horror, a fry almost to my mouth. *Please, for the love of all that is good in the world, Joy – DO NOT say SOY Burgers!* "They had buffalo." *There is a God in Heaven.* "And bacon." *And God loves us.*

I've not had a good burger in so long. I unwrapped the waxed paper and looked down at the Double Buffalo Bacon Burger. This was too good to be true. I looked over at April, who was already into her's. She had ketchup and mustard cheek to cheek. Isabella had opened hers up and picked at it suspiciously. I would have laughed at her, but I dug into mine. Amazing. We were eating burgers and fries and laughing. The Hercs taxied to the end of the runway. The cargo ramps lowered and some of the crew came out.

Outbreak walked up and looked at the grub. He took a fry. "I leave you guys for a little while..." He looked around. "What happened to the red one?" He looked over at Paul, who had a wrist brace and a hand full of burger.

"IED." He said through a full mouth.

Outbreak nodded and looked at a burger still in the wrapper. "Is that an extra one?"

"Nope." I said. "That's yours."

I didn't have to tell him twice. He dug in as he walked back up the ramp. "How come you get a burger and I don't?" The pilot asked him.

"Because I'm a friend of the President. It has its perks."

"I want a burger."

"We have some MREs."

"You are a bastard."

Outbreak just grinned. "Don't be jealous."

We finished up lunch and got the vehicles loaded. FMJ, having lost his Arnold Schwarzenegger's Humvee, settled for a spare military truck. A Chevy "Cut-V". Officially called a CUCV, but everyone called them Cut-V's. It was basically a Chevy Blazer converted to run on military 24-volt systems with a hardened radio and a camo paint job. The Air Force was going to drive it out to a bombing range, but they were just as fine giving it to FMJ.

Once we were loaded, one small detail. "Where are we going?" Outbreak asked.

"Home."

We got home late at night, the three Hercs came in one at a time, landed, unloaded and we were rolling back to the ranch. The girls went home to rest, and Paul, Izzy and I went to the Pub. The Pub had become the center of Camp Ogre.

Q and Sarge were there at a table. I noticed how Isabella slid up next to Q and lightly let her hand touch his. I smiled at that. Musket was in a close discussion with someone that I didn't recognize, but I caught him passing the man a small coin bag, because Musket never uses wallets or money clips. I knew what it was. The man stood and walked out the back.

"Gentlemen." I said as I sat down. A Serving Wench brought me a plate of grilled elk meat, cheese, and some crusty bread. She also set down a large pint of Guinness which I pushed away. "Diet Dr. Pepper, if you have it."

The conversation of the past events wound down and turned to what was next. "Guys, we have things coming together pretty well. The only big conflicts are outside of our borders now. Alaska-Canada being the number one. Do we know what's happening there?"

Sarge nodded, "Reports show the Republic of Alaska has swept through Canada's western provinces all the way from Vancouver B.C. to Calgary. Fighting has been relatively mild. Most of the survivors in Canada are just thankful for the help. ROA is being more beneficial than destructive."

"That's a relief." I leaned back and popped a chunk of elk into my mouth. "Now what about Indiana? I'll need a couple guys to go to Indiana. Bring them back to the table. In two weeks I want all the Governors here for an official vote. We're going to reestablish the United States of America and we have to do it as democratically as possible. So the first vote will be for the President, and the votes will be cast by the Governors... and Indiana is being the hold out. We can't do this without Indiana."

"What about Alaska?" Asked Neil.

"And the Republic of Texas?" Asked Q.

I dipped some elk in mustard as I thought about it. "We'll send Ambassadors and recognize and respect their Independence, if they reciprocate."

"And if they don't."

"They will." I said as I popped the chunk of elk in my mouth. "They want to be legitimate and they can't be until someone else says they are." I washed the meat down with some soda. "Canada and Mexico sure as hell aren't going to recognize them."

"Who's going to be the Ambassadors?"

"I'm looking at one of them. Neil, you are already an Ambassador. You could easily handle Texas too I'm guessing. Q, how do you like snow?"

He started shaking his head. "No."

I started to laugh. "I gotta have someone up there that I can trust and can read between the lines... and can posture our military strength to keep them from getting any ideas. Just at first. I'll send someone else up there once Palin comes off her menstrual cycle."

"What are you going to do?" Neil asked.

"I've got a man that's missing up north a little ways. He ran off and I need him back."

"Oh?"

"Norseman. I need someone to run the ATK factory so we can start making some new ammo. The Barnes factory is good to go, the Copper Mine is running again, we just need the powder factory going and someone to put it all together."

"You can send someone after him."

"I don't think anyone else could talk Ben back out of his mountains."

"Where is he?"

"I have no idea. It should be a snap."

"You could use the Ospreys."

"That would send him into stealth mode. I need to draw him out."

"How are you going to do that?"

"Carefully."

Hail to the Chief

The Governors were put up in the Weston Plaza hotel in Vernal. The venue for the meeting was in the Western Park Conference room. I shook hands with Governors from all over the country, gave a hug to some of them. The Governor of Arizona was resplendent in full Scottish regalia, including a long feather in his cap. In his belt was a Scottish Broadsword and Dirk. Carried across his back was an RFB duracoated in his Clan's Tartan with the Great Seal of Arizona on it. He wasn't the only Governor who was armed with a rifle. Each Governor had his personal security detail with him, making the large room crowded. The Crimson Guard provided physical security for the entire location.

The Lieutenant Governor of Arizona presided over the meeting. Jesse began with introductions. Then he told of the struggles of Arizona since the uprising and shared stories with the attendees.

Then the Governor of Washington stepped up, Maclean. He talked about the strife they faced, including the attacks of the Chinese. Other Governors took turns talking about the zombie problems and their solutions.

Then Jesse stood back up and took the pulpit. "Ladies and Gentlemen". He held up his hands, and the room got quiet. "We have seen the shattering of our nation, the fragmentation of the ties that bound our great union. And we have also seen those ties reformed, stronger than ever. Each state is still in the process of reforming state governments. Each state, still rebuilding. We have a long way to go. Right now, we have a Federal Government that has also been broken and rebuilt. The current acting President of the United States has pulled this country back together, but he recognizes the lack of a Constitutional affirmation. We want to make this condition official. We want to hold an election, each Governor representing your states and the will of surviving people. Governors, under your chairs is a piece of paper and a pencil... Mark your Ballots... You will find only names... No political parties... When this nation began, the first President admonished the avoidance of political parties. We will follow that advice now as we rebuild this nation."

The Governors marked their votes or wrote in the name of the person they wished to vote for. Each one approached the podium and placed his card in the box. The count was taken, out loud and openly. I had 30 out of 47 votes. Alaska, Hawaii, and Texas were absent. The remaining votes were one each for various eastern state's Governors. Always helpful when people write in their own names.

"Ladies and Gentlemen, Please rise. The President of the United States, George Hill."

There was applause.

I stood up. "Thank you for your support. Officially, I'd like to recognize the former Governor of Arizona, Hyrum Grissom as my Vice President."

I spoke for about ten minutes, laying out the importance of following the Constitution as written by the Founding Fathers. I also did away, officially with many federal agencies and programs, including the IRS and income tax. The majority of power would remain in the states. Congress would have to be rebuilt in time. I suggested in the spring as we all had much to worry about as we were looking at winter and the unique hardships that this first winter would bring.

We left the meeting with much handshaking, photos, and fanfare. I was taken out of the room first, and we exited the building through a side entrance into a waiting armored Expedition and we left the area. April and Joy were inside and my wife sat by my side, Neil was driving and Q was riding trunk monkey.

My brothers, Josh and Zack, drove in vehicles in front and behind me. The motorcade was small, but we made up for it with speed and taking roads less traveled. In the air however, was an OH-58 Kiowa and two AH/

MH-6J Little Birds, with Special Forces members riding on the fun seats, and a couple AH-64 Apaches for good measure. Less ground and more air meant better cover and security and less disruption and attention on the ground.

I was quiet. The meeting went as expected, right down to the votes. The weight of the responsibility fell on my shoulders with full force... a responsibility that I didn't want.

Epilogue:

I spent a couple of months doing administrative duties when Debbie came into the office, which was in effect the third floor of Uncle Musket's Pub. By her face, I could tell she was worried.

"George, we've not heard from Cathy in a while." Cathy was Debbie's sister, living in the UK.

"Oh? When was the last time you heard from her?"

"It's been two weeks."

"You guys normally talk a couple times a week, and it's been two solid weeks now?"

"I'm worried."

"Skype is down?"

"I tried calling her land line and it's always a busy signal. Today, it just says cannot complete the call."

"I'll look into it, Babe."

"Promise?"

"I'll do it right now." I promised, and picked up the phone.

Debbie sat down on the couch, next to April. She took April's hand and patted it. I spent a few minutes on the phone with the Comms guys. No contact with the UK. At that news, I tasked a satellite to get me multi-spectrum photos of London and other UK cities.

When the images came in, the Intel Officer pointed out what we were looking at. The cities had experienced a resurgence of zombies. Their heat signatures were hotter than the living, when they were active. If a zombie was inactive, the body cooled to a lower temperature, but they could flare and get active again. Most of the zombies in the bigger UK cities had all gone virtually dormant. But two weeks ago, the intel officer said, we saw a spike in temperature.

I looked at the photos. "They came outside". The zombies beforehand were all behind closed doors, in hotels, schools, apartments. Now, they were outside, in the streets.

"Looks like we're going to England."

April looked up at me. "When?"

"Now."

"Not without me you're not." Debbie said.

"How do you want to roll?" April asked.

"Not too heavy."

I made a call to Hill AFB, and they got some C-17's lined up and would be landing at the Ogre Ranch Airstrip as soon as possible.

"You have your gear ready?" I said, looking at Debbie.

"It will be."

The C-17's taxied to a stop in front of us. The Girl Squad rolled the Raptor and the M-ATV up into the first plane, and then an Excursion. In the other plane, three LAVs rolled up into the cavernous cargo bay. The third aircraft was filled with two Deuce and a Halfs, each with a cargo trailer attached.

"Hey, you should make room for my Centauro... looks like you'll need some added firepower."

I looked at Khorne and shook my head. "Not this trip, bro."

"What?"

"Don't know when we'll be back."

"You make it sound like I'm not coming."

I watched my boys run up the cargo ramp of the C-17, my littlest one with his mother, who had on her tactical vest, pack and Remington 870 HD Shotgun. I looked back a Zack. "You're not," he whispered.

"I'm taking my family... all my family," I said pointedly as April and Joy walked past. "to Scotland."

"You're taking them too?"

He looked shocked. "Like you have room for ethical lectures, Zack. When was the last time your nun went to Mass or Confession? You corrupted a freaking nun. I think we're both exempt from making moral judgments here." Zack's face got red.

"Look, brother – I'm not having an argument about this. We can put this aside... because no matter what – we are blood brothers." I looked up and saw Debbie and April smile at each other as they went deeper into the cargo hold.

"You can't just go... You're the..."

"When I get over there, I've instructed the pilots to return and to give the Presidency over to the Vice. Harm will then be given The Football. It's all taken care of."

Zack was quiet, he nodded. "But what about..."

"About what, bro? You don't even want to be here." I put my hands on his shoulders. "Go to Venice. Go to Rome. It's where you belong."

"And you belong in Scotland?"

"Did you know our family has a castle there?"

"Yeah... but... which one?"

"Inverness and Achnacarry. We'll probably take Inverness first."

"Ah... nice."

"And right now they are empty save for about a dozen zombies."

I gave my brother a hug and boarded the plane. Uncle Musket jogged up and threw his pack in. I gave him a hand up. "You're late, Musket."

"That's not possible. I arrived precisely when I meant to."

"You didn't bring any Tavern Wenches?"

"I'll get new ones.

"You're going too?" Zack looked stunned.

Musket just grinned. As the ramp started to close, "See you in the old world, brother!"

Moments later, we were wheels up and climbing.

About the Author

George Hill, a.k.a. "Ogre" a.k.a. "The Blogfather" a.k.a. "Dad", is obviously a man of many hats. As The Mad Ogre of MadOgre.com he says what he wants and says it like it is. He has been blogging about the gun industry, politics, and life since 1998 earning him the title "The Blogfather". George writes for *Concealed Carry Magazine* and is a frequent guest and occasional Co-Host on Armed American Radio. He is a Co-Owner and Chief Instructor for Crusader Weaponry. As the father of six boys he spends his free time shooting prairie dogs on Ogre Ranch, eating too much Tabasco sauce, drinking Gator-Bull and preparing for the Zombie Apocalypse.

Coming in 2012 !

Don't miss the continuation of
George Hill's exciting series in:

Uprising UK

Made in the USA
Lexington, KY
13 April 2012